# TEMPEST BLADES

## The Withered King

ISBN: 978-1-932926-74-3
LCCN: 2018967718
Copyright © 2019 by Ricardo Victoria

Cover Ilustration: Salvador Velázquez
Logo Design: Cecilia Manzanares & Salvador Velázquez
Cover Design: Alexz Uría, Ricardo Victoria & Salvador Velázquez
Map illustration: Marco Antonio García Albarrán.

Shadow Dragon Press
9 Mockingbird Hill Rd
Tijeras, New Mexico 87059
www.shadowdragonpress.com
info@shadowdragonpress.com

Follow Ricardo at: https://ricardovictoriau.com/

# TEMPEST BLADES
## THE WITHERED KING

by

## Ricardo Victoria

# Acknowledgments

To my wife Alexz. You are my whole world and the light of my existence, my Gift. Thank you for believing in and supporting me to share my stories with the world.

To my friends and family that encouraged me to get this book done.

And especially to Brent and Martha for being my sounding boards during the writing process and helping me to polish this story.

To Chris, Andrea, Matt, Nazario, and Stephen for graciously accepting their cameos.

To Marco for helping me give shape to my world in form of a super map.

To Salvador for bringing forth the vision that became the spectacular cover art for this book.

To the good people of Artemisia Publishing for believing in this project.

And to you reader for allowing me to share my worlds with you. I hope you enjoy reading about them as much as I enjoyed creating them.

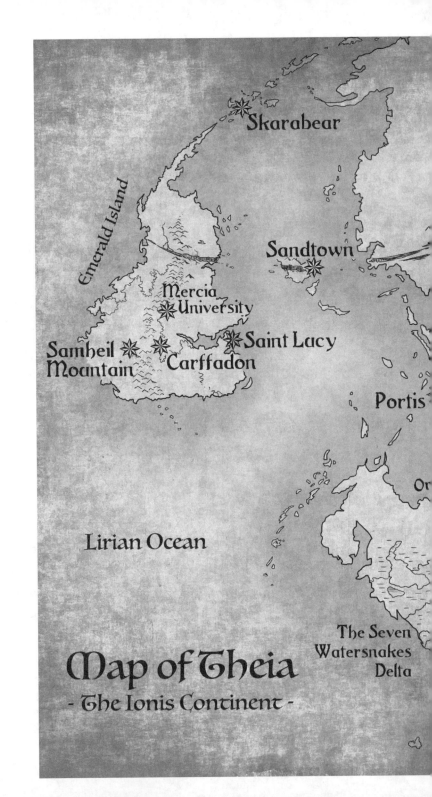

The Mistlands

The World's Scar

venstone

World's Scar

The Maze

The Grasslands

Manfeld

Belfrost

Jagged
Mountains

Lemast

ghorn
alley

y

Crescent Moon
Valley

Thander
Pass

The Courtain

# Chapter 1
## Sky Full of Light

The final minutes of the Battle of the Line.

Life is full of parallels.

*I hate this,* Fionn thought. He looked at the battlefield spread across Longhorn Valley and sighed. Two more of the enemy were running towards him, swords aloft. Black Fang, his own sword with its graceful and sharply curved blade, was gripped in his hand, the blade dripping blood from his last kill. Black Fang emitted an otherworldly green glow that contrasted with its silvery surface. Around him lay a dozen bodies, either unconscious or dead. These two approaching enemies were the last of that squad.

Dodging a sword blow aimed at his head, Fionn tackled the soldier, impacting with his left shoulder. He rolled his attacker over his back and threw him onto the ground, then kicked him in the head, while parrying a slicing cut by the second attacker with Black Fang. With his free hand, he punched the second man in the face, breaking his nose, before kicking him away.

The first man had recovered enough to try attacking from behind, but Fionn caught the movement, reversed his hold on the grip of his sword and stabbed back with Black Fang. Spinning to the side so the sword could gain momentum, he sliced the second man, stepping aside as entrails spilled onto the ground. No more of the enemy remained in range so he took a moment to catch his breath and relax his muscles, already tired from the long fight.

When it came to the reputed fighters of the decade long Great War, Fionn was not the kind of warrior that came to mind. Contrary to the archetype of a war hero –musclebound, charismatic, shinning smile, fancy signature moves and strength that can sunder a mountain – Fionn had both human and freefolk ancestry. This made him slender, taller than average and with a preference for speed and precision over brute strength. A white shirt covered a light chainmail beneath, the brown trousers and brown combat boots he wore matched his long brown hair. He was twenty-two, although he managed to look younger, even after six years of fighting. Only the lines around his big and expressive green-grey eyes, showed anybody familiar with him how haggard and tired he was of the war. Even with his reputation.

Reputation is such a weird thing to earn during a war. When it came to fighting in battle, Fionn avoided fancy moves. Experience had taught him that in all-out frays, the most efficient moves are the ones that were straight and clean. No sword twirling, not a free-for-all, and no spectacular flips or somersaults. Those would only get you killed. And he wasn't planning to die, at least not today. As a result, he had earned a reputation for being an efficient fighter, so efficient that the name of his freefolk clan had become his own nickname: The Greywolf, the famous warrior with the fabled sword that had helped the Free Alliance to stem the tide of the Blood Horde during the Great War.

At first, the Greywolf thing had been a badge of honor for him. The problem was it had led to the associated belief that he was a one-man army. He wasn't. He wasn't a weapon that Prince Byron, or any other lord or commander, could point and release at an enemy. Nor were any of the other Twelve Swords for that matter, not at Byron's whims in any case, even if the Prince was also his friend.

There was another problem with his reputation. It meant that he now had to face wave after wave of enemy warriors, all of them wanting to prove themselves against him. And he had to do it while evading the barrage of energy attacks from the Horde's giant source of power, currently sitting well protected within the main enemy camp: The Onyx Orb.

It was as if the thought had conjured the reality. Fionn saw the incoming green energy bolt at the last moment and jumped away.

*I really, really hate that thing.*

The force of the explosion threw Fionn flying and sent him tumbling into a crater left by an earlier attack. Winded, it took him a moment or two to recover. Then he began clawing his way out of the crater and pulled himself to his feet. He didn't see the sword blade descending until it was too late, but a white wood and crystal quarterstaff blocked the attack and swung back to cave in the skull of the enemy warrior.

"How many times do I have to save you?" Izia said, smiling at him. She leaned on her staff, her black hair framing her face. She held out a smooth, olive-skinned hand to help him up. She was no older than Fionn and had been fighting this war just as long. She was also his fiancée.

"Not as many as I have." Ywain said with a devilish grin. Electric currents jumped and ran across the teenager's arms at blinding speed. "Incoming, guys."

As he spoke, he turned to face a group of enemy soldiers advancing at a run. His sword moved in an arc, cutting easily through their blades. This was too much for the soldiers, brave warriors or not. When they saw what remained of their weapons, they threw them away and started running.

"Wise choice," said Ywain. The three of them retreated a few paces back down into the crater. Ywain was of short stature and quite slim. His messy, dirty brown hair and pale skin contrasted with the intense golden glow of his irises. His longsword, Yaha – with a handguard composed of six fully opened golden wings – glowed with the same faint color as his eyes. To most, he would look like a kid wearing a soldier's costume. But Fionn knew better. The whole Alliance knew better. Ywain was one of the few people in the whole army who had the Gift. If anybody in the Free Alliance was truly a one-man army it was Ywain.

"I think you scared them with your unique fighting style," Fionn said.

"You are the one that taught me how to fight."

"Yeah, but I was talking about the..." Fionn pointed at Ywain. Electrical currents jumped around Ywain's body, yet the younger man didn't seem to feel any discomfort. "Flashy effects."

"Oh, could you two stop praising each other?" Izia said impatiently. "We have a battle to win."

"Ok, ok. The battle is not going according to the plan," Fionn murmured to Izia and Ywain.

"Tell me again, when have they gone as planned?" Ywain asked, stifling a laugh.

"Never," Izia replied first.

"Exactly."

"We need to take down that thing now," Fionn said as he nodded towards where the Orb had just fired a second volley in the direction of the main forces of the Alliance. It was turning into a massacre.

"You know that no one will go after it to destroy it. Byron ordered us to capture it and his father didn't contradict him," Ywain reminded him.

"Byron is an idiot," Izia said. "I wish someone would shut him up. Sorry, I know he is your friend but..."

"I agree," Fionn said, painfully aware of the battle raging a few meters away from the cover of the crater. Gunfire, clashing metal, the crunch of bones as metallic golems crushed their victims, all mixed with the screams of the injured filled the air. Every few minutes the sounds of battle were interrupted by the explosions created by the Orb's energy bolts striking the battlefield. "But that thing needs to go. It's the source of their power. We are so close to ending this war."

"*You* are proposing to disobey direct orders," Ywain said in mock surprise.

"I can't ask you to come with me. The king will be disappointed," Fionn agreed, smiling, knowing the answer already.

"The king won't care." Ywain waved his hand. "And Byron can get stuffed for all I care."

"I'm going with you guys," Izia said.

"I would prefer if you stay," Fionn told her.

"I'm not having this conversation again," Izia replied, annoyed. "You don't need to keep me safe. I can help and you know that."

"I know," Fionn sighed. "This is not about me being overprotective. This is about the plan and a part of it only you can enact. You know better than anyone in the Alliance how destructive an energy explosion can be. And that thing will create a big one. If Ywain and I are successful, we will need protection to hide behind. And only you can set up things properly. Get to Sophia and Mykir; tell them what we are going to do, that their soldiers must raise a barrier with the titanfight shields and whatever else they have. Then, get the freefolk to cast a protection spell, you know which one, on the barrier to raise it even higher and longer to protect the rest of the army. You are the only one I trust for that. As you pointed out, you keep saving my ass; I need you to do that once more."

"I'm not happy with this idea," Izia bit her lips.

"I know," Fionn replied, gently holding her face and, pressing his forehead against hers, rubbing her nose with his. It was a freefolk sign of personal affection between husband and wife. For all intents and purposes, they were already married. "But while I know you can beat anyone in front of you, saving what's left of our army is a priority."

"Don't you dare die on me today, ok?" Izia said, fiercely.

"I promise. I'm not planning to die today. Besides, when this is done, you and I will travel around the world. Agree?"

"Always," Izia smiled and let him go. She turned to Ywain and gave him a brief hug.

"Make sure you bring him back in one piece," she said sternly, ruffling his messy hair.

"I have learned to never contradict you," Ywain told her. "I will, even if I have to drag him."

"Let's go," Fionn peeked over the edge of the crater. "We have a brief window to get there. Now!"

The three left the crater at a run, Izia heading back to their lines while Fionn and Ywain crossed the battlefield and ran toward a nearby grove of trees still intact despite the fighting. They did their best to avoid the fighting. Time was of the essence.

"What excuse will we give them?" Ywain asked Fionn, mid-run. "They will be pretty pissed off."

"We can always say that we tried to capture the Orb and blame it's destruction on a faulty safeguard. Happens all the time," Fionn said nonchalantly. He saw the two huge flying 'Orca Class' Air Dreadnoughts of the Alliance taking off in the distance to deploy more troops. Each of the large ship-like vessels would look more in place at sea, but they were propelled by giant engines fed by the power cores designed by Mykir to fly below the ionosphere, where their sensitive electronic components wouldn't be fried. They could carry five thousand living souls each, but the Alliance couldn't field that many soldiers in a good day. Things were getting desperate. Regardless, their deployment meant one thing: more casualties, from both sides.

Fionn increased his speed. His only concern was to end the war here and now.

††† 

The Onyx Orb loomed in front of them. It was a black sphere the size of an ancient dragon, or a building four stories high. It was rumored to be of ancient Akeleth origins – a long-dead civilization renowned for leaving their ruins full of dangerous things – and shown to possess excessive power. The Orb had been the key to the Horde's devastating campaign that had razed everything from the Grasslands, destroyed most of the Ionis continent, collapsed the old kingdoms and spilled across the Lirian Ocean, forcing even distant realms to take action. Only the remains of the Free Alliance stood against the Horde.

It was no wonder someone like Prince Byron wanted to capture it for the Alliance. "As a safeguard against rogue magick users in the future," he had declared in a speech. But Fionn thought that was bullshit. He had witnessed the full power of the Orb, fueling the dark magicks of the Horde, enslaving minds and casting a bolt large enough to take down a full-sized dragon. If the king had any hope of winning the war, that thing had to go, even if it meant disobeying direct orders from a friend and liege.

Fionn and Ywain had almost reached the Orb when they found themselves with a problem. They stood surrounded by a circle of dead bodies and injured soldiers. Nearby more soldiers, some even wearing the enhancing armor of Titanfight, stood waiting in a wide circle for their turn. All of them were shaking in their boots. Behind the soldiers stood two of the four leaders of the Horde: Argiol the Devil and Peremir the Warlock.

"I think this is a trap," Ywain pointed out, breaking the silence as the pair of them stood in front of the Orb.

"What clued you in?" Fionn asked, "The soldiers surrounding us? That Argiol and Peremir are watching, or that the Orb is sitting right there like obvious bait?"

"Y'know?" Fionn yelled at Argiol. "This is getting boring.

7

If you wanted to get us tired, this is a poor attempt. I thought you would have at least the balls for a one-on-one duel."

Argiol hissed loudly and made his way towards them, followed by Peremir. The circle of soldiers opened and retreated to give them space.

"Why do you always have to piss them off?" Ywain complained.

"Because..." Fionn replied, readying his sword. "They are walking clichés. Just look at their wardrobe."

"Since you started reading those design magazines, you have become really annoying," Ywain replied, drawing his sword, Yaha.

Argiol was taller than Fionn, musclebound and carrying an enchanted tetsubo. He was wearing chainmail, with metal plates covering the upper chest. His shoulders had carved dragonwolf metal skulls as protection. His legs were covered by pants made of leather with metal plates over them. And over the entire ensemble, Argiol wore a leather vest with metal studs and spikes. The vest had a red devil painted on it that had become his symbol. He was the most violent, ruthless general of the Horde, the bane and nightmare of many kingdoms. Peremir stood to his left. An older man with gray hair styled into a widow's peak and wearing long robes, he was a shame to the freefolk as he claimed to be a servant of the Masters of the Pits. The warlock had been the brains behind many of the monstrosities and spells that murdered countless innocents in the campaigns of the Horde.

"The Greywolf and the Freak," Peremir said, his tone gloating. "Nice of you to fall into my trap. It saves me so much time."

"Told you...wait a minute..." Ywain muttered and then paused. He asked Fionn, "Why am I the freak?"

"Because you can do that thingy where your eyes glow and do supernatural stuff?" Fionn shrugged his shoulders.

"Ah, right."

"Silence!" Peremir yelled at them. "Why are you still

talking? Who does that in the middle of a battle?"

"Us," Ywain replied. "We like it that way, helps to release tension, y'know. Gives us time to keep you distracted while we find a way to beat you, that kind of thing."

"Anyways, isn't it too risky of you to lure us into a trap with your biggest weapon?" Fionn mocked Argiol. "I mean, the trap could fail and we could destroy it."

"As if!" Argiol countered. "It was the fastest way to get rid of you. And with you two gone, the Alliance will lose their heart. Your old king won't last much longer, his armies will defect."

"Yeah, yeah right. I could say the same." Fionn waved at Argiol, dismissing his argument. He whispered to Ywain, who was staring at Peremir. "Who do you want to take?"

"Leave me the warlock. I have wanted to kill him since Arajuan and Larabe," Ywain replied through gritted teeth.

"Fine by me." Fionn pointed at Argiol with his sword. "You and me, let's go. Or are you two cowards that will avoid a direct duel?"

"Lead the way," Argiol spat. "Soldiers, stand and watch. See how the heroes of the Alliance fall before our might!"

Fionn and Argiol walked slowly, closing the gap between them, staring at each other. The Orb was behind Argiol. Killing the man was a secondary goal. The Orb was the priority. But Argiol glanced to the side and then grinned and pointed.

"The freak may have bitten off more than he can chew. We should see how that plays out before we fight."

Holding Black Fang ready, Fionn turned to see Ywain, who was facing off with Peremir. Regardless of how powerful Ywain was, Fionn worried about him. He was like his little brother.

Bad blood ran between Ywain and Peremir, as result from the battles at Arajuan and Larabe that had taken the lives of many innocent people, thanks to Peremir's cruel tactics. It weighed heavily on Ywain since he had been in charge of their defenses. Peremir was in for a serious beating, which would make one less problem for Fionn, no spellcaster to worry about.

Ywain called forth his Gift while Peremir cast a whole book's worth of spells in a rapid-fire sequence. The last one was a blue energy ball, known to be quite explosive. But Ywain contained it with his bare left hand. The irises of his eyes were glowing with intensity. Screaming, he threw the ball away. It landed several meters away in the Horde's camp and started a small inferno.

"Careful, Ywain!" Fionn yelled at his friend.

"You have a fight yourself," Ywain yelled at Fionn. "I can handle this!"

Fionn turned away and barely avoided a straight hit from the giant enchanted tetsubo, aimed at his chest. That weapon had proven capable of creating quakes and shockwaves when it hit things. Once during a battle, Argiol had collapsed a mountain over a rival army with one hit.

"I'm going to enjoy this," Argiol said, spinning on one foot with the tetsubo to gain more impetus as he struck his second blow, towards Fionn's head.

"They always say the same," Fionn stepped back bringing his sword up as he deftly parried the blow.

Both fighters clashed three times. With each, Fionn took a step back, blocking the attack. The strength behind each of Argiol's blows was tremendous. No wonder he had destroyed rival armies by himself, the man was a demon. Fionn riposted with a slash aimed at Argiol's left side that drew little blood but was enough to enrage the enemy's commander. Dodging a horizontal strike, Fionn kicked Argiol in the back of the knee, making him lose his balance. This gave Fionn time to catch his breath, but not for long as he found himself jumping to avoid an attack aimed to sweep his legs. If it had hit, the blow would have shattered his bones. While coming down from the jump, Fionn used the momentum to kick Argiol in the side of the head with all his strength. The impact knocked both opponents away. Fionn landed gracefully, but his ankle hurt.

*His head is as hard as a rock*, Fionn thought. Argiol wiped the blood from his lip; his eyes were bloodshot with anger. *Oops.*

Snarling, Argiol attacked in earnest and the two men entered a fast-paced duel sending shockwaves around the camp. Only the supernatural strength of Black Fang saved Fionn from becoming mush. A lesser blade in inexperienced hands would have been shattered by the first blow. But Black Fang was a Tempest Blade, forged with a living soul – the last of the Montoc Dragons. It had the force of the Tempest, the veil that separated the material from the spiritual realms. Ywain's Yaha sword was also a Tempest Blade, of older age and lost origin. Both men and their swords had become inseparable and part of the same legend.

Fionn's master had taught him that in life or death duels, there is an understated cadence on the attacks and parries. *Keep things on your own terms, not your enemy's,* she had told Fionn. *Wide swings use power rather than finesse, which means that your opponent leaves his guard open and the inertia keeps him from correcting once committed.* Finding your enemy's cadence and breaking it while keeping yours intact was paramount to surviving the fight. Every move had to count. None of them were flourishes, but a chain of causes and reactions. Every parry was calculated to minimize the damage received and maximize the amount delivered in return for the counterattack. Argiol's style was wastefully aggressive, relying on power, and had zero finesse. He swung his tetsubo with frantic energy, hitting anything in his path, obliterating any hapless Horde soldier that was unlucky enough to get in his way. It left cracks and dents in the ground wherever it landed. Fionn's muscles ached. His sword might be mystical, but he was still mortal and wouldn't last much longer. It was time to finish this fight. An idea came to Fionn's mind, and it made him smile. Fionn kept evading, countering with thrusts and slashes aimed to cut the tendons of his rival, hoping to tire him, luring him to the place he wanted.

Argiol swung the tetsubo in a horizontal arc. At the last second, Fionn dropped to the ground and rolled away. A soldier, who had been trying to hit Fionn with an axe, received the full brunt of the attack. The soldier's body exploded in a mist of blood.

"Stop interfering, idiots!" Argiol yelled at his men.

Fionn used that brief distraction to roll to his feet and run past Argiol to the Orb, unleashing a powerful strike against it. The strike impacted with the sound of a gong being hit and the booming reverberation echoed across the battlefield. But to Fionn's surprise, the blade of Black Fang bounced. The thing was tougher than he had thought. It was time for plan B. Always have a plan B.

"Really? Did you really think you can harm the Orb just like that? Don't make me laugh," Argiol ran towards Fionn, his tetsubo held aloft.

"It was a hard call, which large, fat, inanimate object to hit first." Fionn moved a few steps to one side, keeping Black Fang pointing towards the enemy commander. His body ached from having to evade the attacks. He was now in front of Argiol and had the Orb behind him. "So, I thought why not both at once? Regardless, it will end here."

"You are right, it ends here," Argiol raised his weapon and Fionn dodged the strike at the last possible second, rolling under it. Argiol hit the Orb with his tetsubo. The resonating boom rang out and Fionn could see the impact had left a dent with cracks around it. Argiol was now between him and the Orb.

"Seems that you made a mistake, Greywolf," Argiol sneered. "You won't pass me a second time."

"I don't have too. C'mon, hit me as hard as you can! Tell you what, you get a free shot, I'll not even parry." Fionn ran towards Argiol.

Argiol raised his tetsubo, but Fionn spun on his toes, in something akin to a dance step and wound up standing next to the enemy commander. With a reverse grip, Fionn impaled Argiol in the chest and drove his blade back, through Argiol into the crack on the Orb's surface. Changing stance he turned to face Argiol, as the tetsubo fell from his foe's lifeless fingers.

"Thank you for your help."

Fionn pushed harder. Black Fang's blade glowed with an intense green light, impaling Argiol and penetrating into the Orb. Fionn withdrew his blade, and Argiol slid to the ground, leaving a trail of gore down the side of the Orb as blood poured from the gaping wound. Underneath Argiol's body, a pond of blood slowly spread to cover the ground with crimson.

Such was the end of Argiol, one of the men that had scarred Theia. Fionn spat on him, then a scream brought him out of his fury. Turning, he saw electrical sparks flying around him. Ywain had just cut off Peremir's left arm. Blood was spouting from the wound like a fountain. The warlock was on the ground, crawling away. Ywain paused for a second and sighed.

He sheathed Yaha and walked towards Peremir and kicked him in the head.

"He will be dead soon anyway."

Sometimes, Ywain scared Fionn. His best friend was, most of the time, a sweet boy, joking around, helping others. But when he unleashed his Gift, especially against someone he had a grudge with, he changed. Like one of the infrequent colossal ionic thunderstorms erasing a town from the face of Theia, no mercy, no compassion, just plain fury with a single purpose. Not even Fionn's own fury could compare to that. It was frightening to contemplate what could happen if Ywain let loose, or worse, went bad. A Gifted gone wrong was the stuff of nightmares. It was terrifying just to think about how to stop one. And yet, Fionn sometimes wondered how it felt to have the Gift, what it was like trying to control it.

A second crack appeared on the Orb. Light began pouring from it and the ground started to shake. Fionn and Ywain barely managed to keep their footing.

"I think that's our cue to escape," Ywain said.

"You think?"

With the death of their two commanders, the Horde's lines were in disarray. Fionn and Ywain ran through without problem, cutting as many slaves free from their chains as they could. Wind gusts hit the place.

"Our plan has one glaring flaw," Fionn looked around.

"Lack of transportation for a getaway?"

"Yeah. We should have stolen a dreadnought."

"And you complain about me being flashy," Ywain said. Then he pointed to his left. "Why don't we take those?"

Parked next to a burning tent were two, battered black three-wheeled motorcycles. Their fronts resembled the face of a dragon, with a decent sized wheel beneath the menacing visage. Their long bodies ended in a massive bulge at the rear of the trike where the engine was housed. On each side of the bulge were two giant wheels. It could carry up to three riders or plenty of equipment with ease.

"Do we know how to ride a trike?" Fionn asked while getting on it. He started the engine.

"No, but we need to learn fast." Ywain tried to start the engine of his bike, but the engine choked. Frustrated, he punched the rear engine, covering it with electric sparkles. The engine trembled, but it finally started. He smiled at Fionn. "Handy ability to have."

"I can see."

Both trikes roared across the battlefield, which was now in complete turmoil. Rather than fighting, most members of the Horde were running away as word of Argiol's and Peremir's deaths spread through the ranks. Only the clockwork golems kept fighting, controlled by the reprogrammed fae inside them.

On the Alliance side, a barrier made of metal shields, two rows high and almost five hundred meters long, had been erected. On each end of the two rows there were metal poles with embedded crystals. The crystals glowed as the few freefolk spellcasters fighting with the Alliance cast spells into them. Two energy barriers formed from the poles and started to grow, running across the shield barrier.

"Seems that they listened to Izia!" Fionn yelled as their trikes ate up the ground still separating them from the barrier and their one hope of safety.

"Your future wife can be quite commanding when she wants!" Ywain shouted back.

They rode through a storm of explosions, having to weave around holes and craters which peppered the ground. The Orb was unleashing energy at random; lightning and stray bolts splattered the area landing on the fleeing Horde as much as over the rest of the battlefield. Glancing in his rear mirrors, Fionn saw the Orb start to glow. The cracks on its surface grew at an accelerated pace, like an egg cracking. It looked ready to explode from the energy contained inside.

Gritting his teeth, Fionn concentrated on getting every last ounce of speed from his trike. They were less than a hundred meters from the barrier when a stray bolt hit the ground right in front of Fionn. His trike bucked like a living thing and seemed to take flight. Kicking himself free, Fionn rolled onto the ground, dirt filling his mouth. Away to one side, his trike lay shattered, where it had landed on a rock. Spitting, Fionn got to his feet as he heard a familiar voice give a cry of frustration.

"Let me go, you stupid machine!"

Ywain was on the ground. His right leg trapped under the remains of the trike he had been riding. Fionn ran in aid to his friend. As he reached Ywain, he dropped to his knees and began trying to lift the trike.

"You always find a way to delay an escape," Fionn muttered under his breath.

"That time with the goat and the kid doesn't count." Ywain pointed at the Orb, glowing intensely. "You need to go. That thing will blow up soon."

"I know," Fionn agreed, getting to his feet and drawing Black Fang, "but we don't leave a man behind. Hold tight."

"Please tell me you won't do what I think you are planning to do," Ywain begged.

"It won't hurt, I promise."

Fionn swung his sword in an arc. Ywain closed his eyes. With a clean-cut, Fionn had sliced open the trike, freeing Ywain's leg.

"Try to move."

"For a second I thought you would cut my leg…"

"Crossed my mind."

Ywain managed to crawl free of the damaged trike, but Fionn could see his leg was badly mangled. Slipping an arm under his friend's shoulder, Fionn helped him up.

"I think my leg is broken."

"We will worry about that later, c'mon!"

Fionn supported Ywain as they crossed the last few meters to the barrier. It was becoming a battle to walk as the wind had picked up to hurricane strength and the ground trembled. A flash in the sky made Fionn glance back to see a column of light come out from the top of the Orb.

Then they were at the barrier and he could see Izia peeking through a small gap between the shields.

"Hurry up!" Izia yelled at Fionn. "You will need to jump over this. We can't open them or they will break the circuit and the protection will fail!"

Fionn looked at Ywain and his mangled leg.

"I'm sorry about this."

He picked up Ywain bodily and with all his strength tossed the younger man over the metal barrier, just as the energy shield was closing the gap. A loud thud came from the far side, followed by several expletives in three different languages.

*Now it is my turn.*

But as he prepared to jump, Fionn felt the world moving under him. It took him a few precious seconds to regain his footing. He could see the Orb was in its death throes. Its surface was completely cracked, with pieces falling away, uncovering a brilliantly shining interior. It was like staring at the sun. Then an unnatural scream echoed all over the valley. Fionn's left leg was trembling. He looked at the raised shields and took a few steps back, preparing a run up for the jump he needed to make.

A powerful gust of wind hit him as he started his run.

*C'mon! C'mon!*

His leg muscles burned with the effort. Despite the short distance, he needed enough momentum to clear the shield base. It would be like jumping over a well-fed war horse without any help. He had done it before, a couple of times. But those times he wasn't trying to outrun an incoming explosion with a hurricane strength headwind.

He cleared the distance and jumped, extending his body as much as he could. His goal was to dive over the barrier; he would deal with the pain of the fall later on. His arms were clearing the barrier. Time slowed down and that was never a good sign. In front of him, Izia yelled something, her face full of concern, but he couldn't make out the words. Beside her, Ywain jumped with his right arm extended, reaching for Fionn's extended left arm. Then it hit him, the full force of the energy wave from the explosion of light. The strength of the explosion's pressure wave buckled the shields. The shockwave sent his body flying into a spin, throwing him against the magick defensive wall.

Black Fang slipped from his grasp. He couldn't see. The flash had burned sight from his retinas and he could only hear a bass sound, as his eardrums exploded. His whole body was consumed with pain as each individual cell exploded and burned away. The adrenaline shock stopped his heart and his last breath. The only image running through his mind at that final moment was Izia's face. He had been unable to keep his promise to her. That hurt more than anything else.

Then there was something. A voice popped in his head.

*It will be alright. Have faith.*

The voice wasn't his own, or anybody he knew, and for a millisecond he believed it. Then his mind ceased to be as his body dissolved in fire.

# Chapter 2
## The Mysterious Vanishing

The Present Day.

"Yes, I'm here, Agent Culph. And what do you mean by missing?"

Harland Rickman was suffering from a migraine so intense, his head felt as if it was about to explode. His day couldn't have started worse. He'd been awakened by a call from The Foundation – the ground-breaking research center and technology innovator that Harland presided over – telling him that the police were trying to reach him. A missing researcher should not have been cause to awaken him so early; the Foundation had hundreds of researchers and those doing field work often failed to report on time. When Harland strode into the Foundation the staff was already at hand, working busily at their desks in the open office space. Harland commanded the place with a presence that defied his short stature, messy hair and beard, and casual clothes, including a hoodie that made him look like he was a vagrant.

As soon as Harland entered his spacious office, Amy, his personal assistant, handed him a cup of coffee. Before he could take a sip of the coffee, she handed him his datapad already loaded with the files on Professor Leonard Hunt's research. Harland sat behind his large desk and spread out the files. His eyes glanced over the only personal effect in the room – a framed photograph taken fifteen years ago. In it Harland stood with his best friend who was holding a little girl – named Samantha – in his arms on the day of her adoption. Everybody was smiling, but Harland's friend had an intense gaze that made his unnaturally green-grey eyes look intimidating.

"Ok, I'm opening the images you sent me right now." Harland took his seat, put his cell phone in speaker mode and turned on the holographic projector of his desk without letting go of his coffee.

"What should I be looking at?" Harland paused, retching, spilling his coffee. The images were very disturbing. "That's not good. Yes, I know, Agent Culph. I will be there soon with the files... are you sure you want him there? I know, it looks pretty grim and with signs of being caused by dark magick. Fine, I'll call him too. We will meet you there as soon as possible."

Harland turned off the holoprojector and pinched the bridge of his nose. Looking once more at the framed picture he thought, *I'm sorry for bringing you into this, my friend, but I really need your help.*

"How bad is it boss?" Amy said, breaking the silence.

"Bad enough," he said absently. His mind was running through what the Agent had told him while still looking at the files. He recalled reports of a town near the Jagged Mountains that had been destroyed under mysterious circumstances a month ago. It sounded familiar but he couldn't pinpoint why. "Why does Lemast ring a bell?"

"Excuse me?" Amy asked. Harland was so troubled that he had forgotten she was still there.

"Nothing," he replied. "Please get me a ride to Hunt's house."

Amy nodded and left. Harland was left alone with his thoughts and he looked at the photograph again. "Fionn, my friend, what sort of trouble are we getting pulled into?"

†††

Fionn drove at a reckless speed, his shoulder-length hair flowing behind him. The trike ate up the road with furious speed, roaring across the routes crossing the maple and red cedar forest known as White Creek. In its wake, the *Paidragh* lamps that protected the roads from spirits and fae trembled. The advantages of owning a stallion trike are that you could use less traveled roads and it was faster than public transport. And since most roads were empty he was making record time towards his destination.

He had opted for a civilian outfit rather than a more official one, white t-shirt with a black leather jacket, black jeans, and red sneakers, as it was more comfortable for riding and would help him to pass unnoticed. His hands were covered with dirty white bandages, the kind used for combat training. Only a pair of goggles protected his eyes from the dust of the road. It was the first time in months that he had left his house at Mount Shamheil. The 'haunted hill' gave Fionn much desired seclusion as lately he had good reasons to eschew human interaction. Namely, after a decade, people in the village near his home were starting to grow suspicious of the hermit living in the mountain who wasn't getting older. He wasn't in the mood to answer questions about this and it was becoming complicated to keep unwanted attention away from himself. His efforts to do so were becoming noticeable.

Black Fang was tucked neatly in the side compartment of the trike, with only half of the scabbard visible. From afar, the scabbard appeared to be carved as if it were a tree branch. Behind him, a duffel bag was secured on the seat. Harland's call had sounded tense enough to warrant bringing a few pieces of special equipment. His friend usually kept his cool, but this time he sounded worried. Fionn pressed the engine of the motorbike. Harland must have arrived at the house already and he wasn't a fan of waiting.

It was afternoon by the time he arrived at the professor's

house, which looked as Harland had described it. It was a closed gate affair, located on top of a small hill, no doubt to overlook the sowing fields below extending for kilometers. The style of the brownstone house was classical, from pre-war times, making it at least a century old. Professor Hunt clearly wasn't much into the renovation of the building, as the walls enclosing the place were dilapidated. Despite this, and the faint white paint now falling away from its walls, the actual house seemed to have been spared from most of the ravages of time. Not a mansion, but it seemed big enough to hold what Harland once had called 'the best-curated book collections on obscure topics.'

He took off his goggles and fixed Black Fang on his belt. Slinging the backpack over his shoulder he waved at Harland, who came out to greet him.

"Thank Heavens that you are here," Harland said, his intense gaze on Fionn. "You haven't changed at all, still looking the same."

"I know." Fionn gave a faint smile. "It has become an issue lately. Anyway, what do we have here?"

"Follow me," Harland replied, leading the way to the front entrance of the house. Fionn noticed the two police officers guarding the entrance. With them a man stood wearing a sharp suit. He was their superior officer. Fionn knew him very well as they had crossed paths on previous cases that the crown had considered sensitive because of the presence of dark magick. Culph was one of the few that was privy of Fionn's true identity.

"Agent Culph, nice to see you again." Fionn extended his hand. But Culph barely acknowledged the gesture.

"Leave the pleasantries for another day. This is bad."

Fionn's smile faded. He and Culph had a long-established friendly rivalry and he was used to trading barbs with the detective. Seeing Culph worried like this meant that what had happened inside was worse than Fionn thought.

"Can you give us more details?" Harland asked.

"Sure. So far we know that when the housekeeper left last night around eight, the professor seemed fine, absorbed in his work. She returned earlier this morning and found the place ransacked, the walls splattered with some black and oily liquid that smells like rotten eggs. It trailed out from the study, where we found it mixed with blood. I sent the investigators to the scene, but after a few minutes, they came running out, screaming. The only thing I could get them to say was something about 'walls bleeding black blood.' They were so unnerved I had to send them to the hospital. The housekeeper says nothing of value was taken. We are thinking, despite what rules tell us, that it was a dark magick ritual gone wrong."

Fionn and Harland looked at each other.

"This is odd," Fionn said.

"Told you," Harland muttered.

"There is one more thing: The woman," Culph said.

"Which woman?" Fionn asked.

"The housekeeper says that a young woman, by the name of Gabriella, kept trying to contact the professor through various means in the past weeks, to no avail. Then, the day before the professor went missing, she appeared here, yelling that he needed to hear her warning, as she apparently dreamt that something was going to happen. The professor chased her away from the house." Culph handed the case notes and data cards to Fionn. "I think this case is up your alley. And given your rank as Justicar, you can have it."

"And where is she now?" Fionn asked.

"I don't know," Culph said. By the expression on his face, he didn't like not knowing where she was.

"What do you mean by that?" Harland looked annoyed.

"She had returned early this morning to try to talk once more with the professor, but the housekeeper told her not to enter the house as 'something bad' had happened. She remained here with the housekeeper to keep her company until we arrived. We thought she was a suspect but her alibi checked, she was playing her guitar at her hotel's lobby bar and both the barman and the night manager can confirm that. We really didn't have grounds to book her. The only thing we could do was to take her personal details and ask her to keep in contact since she is considered a person of interest, before letting her go. Don't look at me that way. I'm not stupid, I sent an undercover officer to keep tabs on her, but he hasn't reported yet," Culph explained.

"We need to find her," Fionn said.

"Are you planning to take the case?" Culph asked with an uncharacteristic eagerness.

"Maybe," Fionn replied, clenching his left fist around the pommel of his fangsword. He turned to Harland. "Are you coming?"

The house emitted a black miasma. The whole environment was full of malevolence. Fionn could see a dark aura around the building. He had seen that aura before, on many places during the post-war days, when he travelled around with Izia. Everybody looked at Harland, who swallowed hard.

"Is it necessary?"

"Do you want to find out what happened or not?"

"Damn you," Harland replied.

They entered the house. Inside, the entrance hall seemed to be undisturbed. Besides a thin layer of dust, there was nothing out of place, not even a stain of humidity on the wallpaper, despite the cold, damp air circulating around. It was as if the house had been abandoned for years, which was at odds with the description that Culph had given to them. The remaining rays of light entering through the stained glass gave the place an eerie ambiance. It was no wonder that the police officers were reluctant to enter and search for clues when the whole place appeared to be trying so hard to keep you away on a subconscious level.

"Something is wrong," Fionn said, his breath condensing in the cold air.

"You think?" Harland rubbed his arms to keep them warm. "This place looks dusty but otherwise fine. Yet the pictures..."

"That's the point." Fionn handed the backpack he brought to Harland and from it took out a bullseye lamp, with engravings and sigils similar to those seen in older *Paidragh* lamps. "Brace yourself. Whatever you see from now on will probably be an illusion." Fionn closed the door behind them and lit the lamp.

"Probably?" Harland asked, his voice trembling.

"Eighty percent sure." Fionn smiled, trying to reassure his friend.

"What about the twenty percent left?"

"Let there be light," Fionn murmured while tightening the grip of his left hand on the handle of his sword.

The walls of the house started creaking in the places touched by the light of the lamp. Fionn removed the lamp's cover, the engravings on its body shining red-hot as if they'd been hit by dragon fire. The whole building rumbled, creaked and shook as if weighed down by the entire mass of Mount Shamheil. Dust danced in the air and the wooden floor tiles jumped out of their place. Harland closed his eyes, expecting the worst, such as some creature straight from the Infinity Pits, the realm of evil; but everything stopped and settled into an eerie calm.

An obnoxious odor filled the air, a combination of putrid fish and sulfur, coming from oily black ichor plastered all over the walls of the corridor that ended in the library of the house. It was the kind of smell that registered in the primal part of the brain, urging you to run away without stopping until you reached the next town, if not the next continent.

"What the Pits?" Harland was trying to cover his nose, looking around, disoriented.

"It was some kind of illusion. That gooey liquid is the reason people were feeling uneasy inside the house," Fionn said, covering the lamp and putting it back into the backpack.

He walked into the corridor, with a tight grip on the handle of his sword.

"How? What? You need to explain this," Harland asked, intrigued, but looking at the black gooey liquid with disgust on his face.

"Long story, you don't really want to know," Fionn kept walking across the hallway at a slower pace.

"Humor me," Harland insisted.

"Shortest version, this is not the first time I've seen something like this. The ichor is like the footprint left by gruesome events, which fades from sight with time but remains for ages. The lamp just brought it to the surface again."

"When did you learn that?" Harland asked, giving a good look at the lamp. He noticed that it was of freefolk origin and had Fionn's house sigil, a gray dragonwolf in mid-stride.

"A long time ago, with Izia and my grandfather," Fionn replied. His tone of voice left it clear that he was finished with the subject. "Let's go."

They reached the end of the corridor and came to an unlocked door. There were a few scratches on the inside of the door, but otherwise it looked perfectly fine. Beyond the door was a room filled with ancient tomes, maps, weird sculptures, and the occasional skull. The décor of the room didn't help to lessen the unsettling image of the house. This time Fionn stopped himself from using the lamp, to avoid destroying crucial pieces of evidence. The room was in total chaos, with papers, books, and broken statues all over the place. There were blood stains, recent ones, but not big enough for Fionn to think the professor was dead. It was clear that a struggle had taken place.

"Funny," Fionn murmured when he got close to the window behind a mahogany desk.

"What's funny?" Harland asked.

"The window is broken, but the glass fragments are on the outside, not inside. See the damage on the surface of the door? Those scratches are on the inside and yet, the lock is in good shape. Aside from the state of the room, the house is in perfect condition."

"You and I have very different definitions of perfect condition," Harland countered.

Fionn picked up some documents from the floor. Most of the papers were notes on the professor's current research. The handwriting was hard to read, tight and continuous, but Fionn noticed the mention of a cult, old temples, and caves under Belfrost, the city of spies at the edge of the Ionis continent. He decided to take the notes with him for further examination.

On closer inspection of the floor, Fionn noticed several wadded-up pages that looked like trash, but he could make out a symbol between the wrinkles. Fionn picked one up and flattened it out to reveal an omega symbol enclosed within a triangle, with three crossing lines on each side, like rays of light. Fionn's memory wasn't what it once had been, but he was well aware of where he had seen that symbol before. His worst fears were hitting him; he was grinding his teeth and his nostrils were flaring. It took him a few seconds to calm himself enough to clear his head.

Fionn folded the notes and put them into a pocket of his jacket then walked away, seeing pieces of candles and cheap trinkets on the side of the desk. It made sense now; the officers thought they were on the scene of a magick ritual gone wrong. Fionn rolled his eyes. Hunt might have been a bit over-enthusiastic in his studies in arcanotech and ancient traditions, but he certainly was smart enough not to try rituals that could go awry in the wrong hands. The trinkets were more likely protection wards, a reasonable precaution in a place full of old tomes of forgotten lore.

"There is good and bad news," Fionn took one of the seats and let out a deep breath.

"Tell me the good news, please," Harland said, letting out a sigh of relief.

"This is not the scene of a dark magick ritual gone wrong, nor a burglary."

"Good, and the bad news?"

"The bad news is that this was the scene of a kidnapping by a dark magick ritual gone *right*. Something from the Outer Side snatched Hunt and took him somewhere else," Fionn explained, his left hand opening wide to entrap his right hand, mimicking the way some plants entrapped their prey.

"And that's supposed to make me feel better?" Harland asked, waving dismissively.

"No. But it is funny to see your face." Fionn laughed while Harland flipped the finger at him.

"Can you guess who took him?" Harland asked, giving a look around at the ransacked room.

"Of that, I can't be certain yet. The blood on the walls is not human," Fionn said, offhandedly. "But I'm inclined to believe that whoever broke in here didn't find all they needed."

"How can you be so sure?" Harland inquired, leaning in.

"Those symbols and notes mention an ancient spell, but they seem incomplete. I will be sure when we give them a closer look. I wonder why the professor didn't heed the warning from that woman since he was clearly a believer. We need to find her too." Fionn's lips tightened. He knew he was going to regret this.

"Does that mean that you will take the case?" Harland asked, with hope in his voice.

"Sadly, yes. I can't say no to my best friend," Fionn replied while looking out the window and into the valley where dark clouds were amassing. Fionn clenched his hand and stood up to take a look through the open window. Outside, storm clouds reflected the inner turmoil inside him. He knew it was a secondary effect of the Gift. A sinking feeling in his stomach mixed with a speeding pulse sent his mind into a vortex of doubt. His mind was weighing the pros and cons of taking the case, trying to verbalize the source of a deep-seated anger and fear that were battling for dominance inside him. Memories long suppressed were coming to the front, racing to make sense of everything and making the sinking feeling even worse. This could be big. As big as the conflict he saw towards the end of the Great War.

*What that hell am I getting myself into this time?* Fionn thought, his gaze lost in thought, staring at a black and red raven flying outside the window.

# Chapter 3

## The Dreaming Woman

"I need to order more food," Fionn said.

"How can you eat so much food?" Harland asked, annoyed.

"I'm always hungry. A side effect of the Gift. Lucky for me that you are paying," Fionn shrugged, before downing a chicken wing.

"Lucky for you that we are in one of the few places where the whole menu is up to your tastes," Harland signaled a waitress.

A couple of hours after leaving the house, they were at The Harris, a local bar in the small city of Carffadon. Like many cities built in ancient times on the Emerald Island, it was crossed from side to side by the Breen, also known as the 'Dragon River' for its serpentine yet powerful current, connecting Carffadon to a trade route used by e-caravans in their boats. The river was a safer and cheaper option than the expensive warptrain or the spirit-ridden roads with rogue clockwork golems mindlessly walking the valleys.

Fionn had visited The Harris before and enjoyed the small bar, while he knew that Harland, with his bohemian proclivities, loved it. Carffadon was home to famous writers, artisans, and wealthy merchants. On the surface, the city was a cradle for creativity and snobbery, with its marble arches and thermal baths. It enjoyed a bustling nightlife with the coffee houses and pubs open for a good part of the night. E-caravan merchants lit their lamps to lure customers to overpriced wares.

Different pubs catered to different clientele, based on affluence or interest, sometimes both. From seedy dives to specialty pubs that catered to a more discerning customer base; people looking for mind-warping freefolk ales, strong samoharo spirit liquors, and delicacies from the far away Kuni Empire.

And then there was the odd pub, like The Harris, that on top of those rare beverages and private booths, offered its patrons a foray into the ancient and tortuous art of open mic singing. It was lucky for Fionn and Harland that the woman currently on the mic had a delightful voice, one that could easily go professional.

"Did you know that it is a franchise now?" Harland mentioned casually while eating some fries from Fionn's plate; the food was a mix of freefolk and human dishes. Fionn liked to taste the food from both his father's and his mother's species when he was in one of these places.

"The Harris?" Fionn replied before taking a bite of his burger and another from the dimwik roast, mixing the flavors. "Now that's good news. I hope they open one near my home."

"Trust me: No one will open anything like this near that cursed mountain. And how the hell can you mix dimwik and beef? And even more important, how can you fit all that food in your stomach?" Harland's hands were up, backing away with a shudder, much to Fionn's amusement. Dimwik was a small lizard endemic to the World Scar, which the freefolk roasted after bathing it in their trademark spicy sauce. The resulting flavor was similar to smoked salmon and chili and had a kickback that could mess with your brain temporarily if you were not used to it. And Fionn loved every second of it.

"I already told you, I need to keep my energy at decent levels for the Gift to work." Fionn smiled, the food making his cheeks round before he swallowed.

"That's a lame excuse." Harland laughed.

"I'm telling you the truth. I'm not good at excuses," Fionn countered. "Never been. Now can you explain to me those rumors you mentioned before?"

"There is not much to say, other than a few months ago the town near the Lemast cemetery at the Jagged Hills went POOF, along with the cemetery and all the people nearby."

"Whadaya mean by poof?" Fionn asked, curious, his freefolk accent slipping with the drinks.

"Just like that. Vanished, gone, erased. There is nothing there, not even a single rock, bone or rag. Just dead soil."

"Lemast is in the shadow of the Jagged Mountains. Not many people travel there, even less live near there on purpose. Only trappers and mercenaries go there to hunt beasts, and not many of them return. And the region is infamous for messing with radio communications. How do people know that the town and the cemetery are gone?"

"They found out weeks later when a government auditor never returned. Rumor has it that another party was sent there to document the situation and of the few who did come back had signs of mental trauma, claiming that the place is beyond haunted. They also mentioned a foul odor. Now that I think about it, not dissimilar from the one at Hunt's house." Harland stroked his beard. "The professor was looking up those rumors since, according to him, they were related to some of his findings."

"Which were?"

"Something about ancient Akeleth technomagick. You know, the holy grail of arcano-researchers. Lots of money to make there if it works," Harland said with a wave of his hand.

"You sound like you don't believe in that, despite what you just witnessed this time."

"I don't deny that there are things yet unexplained, but on this particular point I don't think that's necessarily true."

"You would be surprised at some of the things we saw

during the Great War." Fionn let out a sigh. The mention of Lemast brought forward sour memories that would need more than freefolk ale and dimwik to drown. Maybe the toxic mushroom pizza that made The Harris infamous would do the trick.

"The Great War was ages ago. You know that better than anyone," Harland said, sipping his pint. A few seconds later, he gasped, as he realized what he just said. "Sorry about that man, I forgot."

"It's ok." Fionn dismissed the subject with a wave of his hand and a smile. "Anyway, back to the case. The professor found something in Lemast. How did he go from looking into arcanotech to a vanishing cemetery? Which, by the way, is a concern in itself given what was sealed there."

"Why am I not surprised that you know what was sealed there?" Harland looked exasperated.

"Considering that I've been trying to get drunk since you mentioned Lemast, knowing full well that I physically can't, what do you think?" Fionn drank another pint in one go. It was annoying that he needed to drink gallons of the stuff to barely feel drunk, and he had to go to the bathroom every five minutes. Sometimes his Gift was a pain in the ass.

"What's the plan then?" Harland was being uncharacteristically impatient. Fionn wondered why.

"Look, finding the woman is our best bet to find out what is going on," Fionn explained, trying to quell Harland's turmoil. "It's not like we have more clues, beyond the crumpled papers and that ooze."

"I wish you could pull off one of your freefolk tricks to track the ooze to its source," Harland said dejectedly.

"I told you before. Magick doesn't work like that; I can't do magick and trust me, tracking the source of the ooze without knowing what we will face beforehand is a *really bad* course of action. Now, the woman is a better choice. It's clear she knew something was going to happen." Fionn relaxed against the back of the booth. His back hurt and it was then that he noticed all the tension he was trying to conceal from his friend, and even from himself.

"If that's the case, she might be a target. Or complicit in all of this. The problem is, where we do look? We only have her description from Culph's report and that her name is Gabriella. She told Culph she'd not leave the city but she is no longer staying at the hotel where she was registered. Doesn't sound like something a helpful person would do." He gave an exasperated sigh. "She said that she was an acquaintance of the professor through friends, but we don't know that."

"I will think of something." Fionn stood up, shuffling his feet. "Or something will appear. It usually does."

"The ale?" Harland asked while downing another pint.

"The ale." Fionn pointed to the restrooms, grabbing Black Fang as a matter of habit. "Back in a few. Try not to lose our money while I'm away."

† † †

Harland got tired of waiting after a few minutes and started to go over the documents Fionn had taken from the professor's house. The more he looked at them, the less sense it made. It left Harland with a sense of unease, like a hundred giant millipedes crawling over his back and arms. Just remembering the foul odor awoke some primal fear inside him.

Not even the spirits at the haunted hill where Fionn lived scared him. They were more of the playful, devious kind. But the odor betrayed a level of darkness that could spread evil across the planet. He envied Fionn's annoying calm in the face of the whole situation.

Harland was not getting anywhere with the professor's notes, so he decided to focus instead on the woman. It was odd that the police couldn't get anything more than her birth name and general description. While in principle he agreed with Fionn that finding her might cast light on the case – whether she was involved with the Professor's disappearance or trying to help – the truth was that finding her in a place like Carffadon would prove difficult and waste time they did not have. They would need a miracle to find her. Depressed, Harland downed more of his pint and looked around to see if Fionn was coming back any time soon. He looked at the stage and noticed that a new singer was taking her turn at the open mic. She was playing the guitar, chanting sweet lyrics about the meadows of the southern coasts and lost opportunities.

Harland was lost in her song for a moment, and then rubbed the drink from his eyes. *What had Culph said in his report?* 'Long, wavy, light brown hair, tall, and fit with a crooked smile.' That's how Culph had described the girl. The girl on stage was sitting on a stool, but she had long legs that would have made her as tall as Fionn. And she had wavy brown hair tied in a ponytail. He blinked again, because the woman on stage almost fit the description for Gabriella. *Miracles do happen,* Harland thought, *or I am way too drunk.* But if it was the girl then he thought that Culph's description didn't do her justice. While she was not a traditional beauty by current standards, it was undeniable that she was quite pretty, with a charming smile and the voice of a siren. She wore jeans, boots, a gray t-shirt with the image of a cybernetic angel from a popular animation, and a blue and black leather jacket. Mesmerized, he walked toward the stage to talk with her once she finished her song, without noticing the kind of crowd she was starting to gather in front of her. He bumped into another person, breaking his reverie.

"Sorry, mate."

"Watch it, dwarf!" the man yelled. He was a thin, bald man wearing jeans and a leather vest and he shoved Harland to the floor.

Usually, the word "dwarf" made Harland's blood curl. It had got him in serious trouble before. But this time, as he was sobering up fast, he was trying to remain focused on the singer. He knew somehow she was Gabriella, and so he did his best to ignore the man and just stood up to meet the woman. It could have been as simple as that if not for the big hunting knife the man pulled out and waved in front of him. "Don't even think about it, midget."

Harland looked on in growing horror at how the man's companions were slowly circling the stage, while the woman kept singing, apparently unaware of what was going on. *Crap. Where is Fionn?*

† † †

Fionn stepped outside the pub for fresh air to clear his mind. Lemast brought back painful memories. Not the actual place. He had been there only a couple of times. But what was buried there was another story and the sole memory of it was a beast, a shadow gnawing at his heart. He had promised himself to leave all that behind, that's what Izia would have wanted. Then again, he also promised Harland to help him with this. Harland was his closest friend, the one that had helped him to rejoin the world all these past years. He owed him. And as Izia said once: a promise is a promise and it shouldn't be broken.

*I should stop promising things*, Fionn thought.

Fionn had been looking at the Long Moon, shining far away from the Round Moon, one of the few days where that mysterious celestial body could be seen. He was musing about the oddity that was the Long Moon when he saw many of the patrons leaving the place in a hurry. Harland's voice echoing out from the pub convinced him that it was time to get back inside.

† † †

Fionn had to push through the patrons that were leaving at a quick pace. It was like swimming upstream.

When he finally managed to make his way into the pub, he saw a group of thugs surrounding the woman currently on the stage; she was so engrossed in her singing that it seemed as if she hadn't noticed them. Meanwhile, Harland was on the floor, trying to get up while facing down a big hunting knife. He was trying to talk his way out of this hassle.

*This scene is slightly familiar, Harland trying to weasel out of a sticky situation through talking. What in the Pits did he do this time to enrage them?*

"Listen, good man, why don't we calm down and share a few drinks," Harland said calmly, trying to defuse the situation.

"Share this, midget," The man poured a beer over Harland's head. That got Fionn's blood boiling to the point he could have been breathing fire. He clenched his fists till his knuckles became white.

"You know that is so clichéd, right?" Fionn walked among the group surrounding Harland and the woman, looking at all of the thugs in the eye. Fionn smiled, almost cheerfully, as a jolt of joy ran through his body. It had been quite some time since he'd had a proper fight. Then the tone of his voice dropped an octave. "Why don't you pick on someone your size? Or better yet, why don't you and your friends leave this place before I put that knife," he pointed at the weapon held by the thin, bald man. "In his ass." He pointed at a burly, bearded man. "And then I'll put your fist," Fionn grinned at the bearded brute, "into his mouth," he jerked his thumb back at the bald man. Fionn then slapped the bald guy's hand, making him drop a photograph to the floor. "And by the way, that's not the way to grip a knife, amateur."

A heavy silence fell over the place. The woman had stopped singing, but remained focused on her guitar, playing a few chords on it, bringing the tension up. The picture was streaked with bloody stains, but through them Fionn could see that it was a photo of the girl sitting on the stage playing the guitar. Only Culph had copies of that photo and with

37

certainty, he didn't give it away voluntarily. Regardless of what Culph might think about him, Fionn respected the man for his professionalism. Knowing these pieces of trash had injured him only added to the raging fire of anger he was trying to contain. But no more.

"You are here for her," Fionn muttered. His shoulders dropped and knees bent while clenching his fists and offering the widest smile possible. He was going to enjoy this. And then the woman sped up the guitar chords, which resembled a song famous for being used in fighting spectacles.

"Oh boy," Harland muttered while walking away and taking cover behind his table, picking up the papers. He was a thinker, a politician, not a fighter unless he was drunk enough. But there were pub fights and there were Pub Fights. He had seen Fionn in a few of those and right now his friend had that smile that Harland used to call the 'smile that a wolf shows you while it is considering which dressing would make you taste better during tonight's dinner.'

The bald man tried to slash Fionn in the face, but he just dodged it, placing his left foot back. Then he used the heel of his right hand to hit the handle of the knife, making it fly upwards. The bearded man threw a punch aimed at the right side of Fionn's head, but Fionn countered by grabbing the man's wrist with his left hand. Then he spun on his toes and used the inertia of the punch to move the bearded man and slam his fist into the bald man's mouth. He proceeded to bring the bearded man down with a knee in the solar plexus, taking out all the air from his lungs. The bald man, bleeding from the mouth and slightly dazed, was an easy target for Fionn now, who grabbed him by the ears and brought down his head to be kneed. Just then the knife finally came down and cut deep into the bald man's ass, leaving him knocked out and in pain.

"Anyone else?" Fionn asked with a smile, cracking his knuckles. The members of the gang that had surrounded Fionn and witnessed the quick fight took a step backward.

They had the look of men wondering if the severe beating that could fall upon them was worth the hassle of whatever they came to do. Harland, on the other hand, was rolling his eyes.

"Stop showboating. The woman, Fionn, help her!"

"I got this," she replied calmly. She closed her eyes while putting the guitar inside its case. The three men surrounding her tried to grab her, but by the time they reached the stool, she wasn't there. With the grace of a panther stalking its prey, she withdrew two sheathed, short swords from the guitar case. She used them as batons to beat the three men in a flurry of hits. The first one was hit in the nose, breaking it. The second was caught on the ribs, from which a crunch was heard. And the third one would not leave any progeny after him. The hit was so hard that it made everybody wince in pain, Fionn included. The woman then opened her eyes and smiled, crooking her lips up, and only said, "Shall we dance?"

Then, she jumped from the stage and fell upon the rest of the gang, who stood with narrowed eyes and fists clinched around weapons and mouths open in shock at the beating their three companions had just taken.

Fionn could only admire the fluidity, the grace, and skill that the woman showed. Swift, practical movements, linked together in a rhythmic sequence, like a dance. There was a mix of southern Mizu-do kicks, pirouettes, parries and deflections, locks and precise punches at nerve points with the swords working as batons, all in a combination designed to help a faster yet slender fighter against men weighing the same as an ox. It wasn't a style Fionn was entirely familiar with, but it matched the descriptions of the martial arts used by the Sisters of Mercy. He nodded to Harland. "It doesn't seem that she needs much help."

"And what? Are you going to stand there watching her have all the fun? We need her."

Fionn sighed and then made his way to her by punching a few obstacles out of the way and dodging the woman's attacks as well. After a few seconds, he ended up back to back with her, facing the whole gang, which by now was battered and bloodied. The gang decided that there was safety in numbers and started attacking at the same time. Fionn and the woman smiled, nodded at each other and fought back.

"Nice form of yours. Your Mizu-do is quite fluid. Although I barely recognize the rest." Fionn connected a strong left uppercut on the jaw of a guy who could have used more training and less food.

"Thank you. You are not bad yourself. I haven't seen that form of yours except in books of ancient styles." She parried several punches coming from different sides at a speed that made her look as if she knew they were going to be there.

"I'm a fighting purist when it is possible." Fionn hunched and used his sheathed sword to bring down one guy by hitting him in the back of the knees.

"Ah! But I've never seen somebody using the Mendicant Monk Staff form with a sheathed sword before."

"I admit it is not a pure form, but it works when there is no need to hurt them more than needed. Do you know why they are after you?"

"Maybe they didn't like my music," she said while spinning on her right foot and connected a roundhouse kick on the head of a guy sporting a mohawk. "More likely for the same reason as you are."

"About that…" Fionn dodged an attack and replied in kind with a backhanded punch.

"We need to talk, but not here. Somewhere less crowded," she proposed after applying a counter block to the mohawk guy that ended in a painful snap and crack, breaking his arm in three places.

"Let's wrap this up then." Fionn unleashed a flurry of kicks and punches that the woman not only dodged with ease but synchronized with as well. Regardless of how well trained she was, the fact that she seemed to know exactly where each punch and kick would come from seemed strange. Following a hunch, he took a moment to look at her in the eyes and noticed a faint unnatural blue glow in her irises. The glow was all too familiar to him. She had the Gift. They managed to knock everybody out, but the pub was all trashed and the alarm was blaring.

"Time to leave, pick up your stuff," Fionn yelled at Harland and the woman.

"I already did," Harland replied in a huff, running as fast as he could towards the back door and into the alley. Fionn held the door open for his friend and the woman carrying her guitar case and her twin blades. The three of them left the pub through the back alley. Fionn, Harland and the woman ran through alleys and small streets, until they reached a bridge that crossed the river. The three of them tried to catch their breath, the cold night air hitting their lungs without mercy. The place was empty, not a single soul in sight.

"Now that was a pub brawl. How exciting." Harland smiled. "We kicked them hard."

"We? You did nothing." Fionn laughed.

"We are a team, remember? Besides, I'm a diplomat, not a fighter. That's what I have you for."

"Fighting is diplomacy by other means, or so they say," the woman interjected. "I think you were looking for me." She smiled.

"I'm guessing you are Gabriella, but how did you know we were looking for you?" Harland asked.

"Yes, I'm Gabriella Galfano, although you can call me Gaby. No need for formality. And as for your question, I dreamt about you." Gaby flashed her quirky, yet endearing, crooked smile.

Fionn looked at her. She would be the first Gifted person he had met in ages, and a non-crazed one to boot. It made him smile, even if he didn't want to admit it.

"Wait a minute, Galfano as in the powerful and very ancient merchant Galfano family?" Harland asked, surprised.

"The one that not only survived the war, but helped to

rebuild the continent," Fionn added. "I thought you liked your privacy and were very reclusive. I never expected to meet a member."

"Says the man who lives at a haunted mountain," Harland quipped.

"Yeah, but that's not important here. Can we talk in another place, please?" Gaby pleaded, rubbing her arms from the cold.

A thick fog was falling upon the city, the temperature dropping as fast as a stone in free fall. Fionn looked around because something felt odd. Goosebumps covered his back.

"Are you ok?" Harland asked.

"Yeah, it's just the cold," Fionn replied, not entirely sure that his answer was the whole truth. His instinct was telling him something.

He remembered that once, when he was a kid, his master had told him that Evil is cold.

# Chapter 4
## Nightmares

"So your name is Fionn and yours is Harland," Gaby said. "As in Harland Rickman, the Foundation president?"

"Yes," Harland replied, examining her. Fionn could only let out a chuckle. He couldn't blame Harland for being paranoid, after what had happened to the professor. But if this woman wanted them dead by now, she would have done it already. After all, she trained with the Sisters of Mercy: courtiers, diplomats, spies and lethal assassins masquerading as students in an all-female private boarding school for the fine arts, culture, and manners.

The three of them walked down the well-lit streets, while a thick fog was starting to cover the city, giving it an eerie, almost malevolent feel. Harland treated them to hot chocolate, for which Fionn was thankful. He studied Gaby and the faint aura around her. When Fionn saw others like him through the Gift, they always looked like beings made of light surrounded by fog. It gave them an unearthly look. But in Gaby's case, she looked warm, happy, and downright angelic, with only a hint of shadow, a sign of inner turmoil. Fionn had never expected to meet someone with the Gift again.

He gave her a closer look. Gaby's aura flickered, fluctuating in power. If Fionn had to guess, she had obtained the Gift not long ago, perhaps no more than a decade and a half ago, as it took time to be fully integrated with the recipient. It wasn't a rule of thumb of course, as age sooner or later became moot when you had it. The way Fionn had received his forced the integration faster than usual, and yet it took him years to get the Gift under control. Then a heavy feeling in the bottom of the stomach hit him as it dawned on him. Culph's notes stated that she was twenty-five, which meant that she had been barely a teenager when she received the Gift.

Fionn shuddered. Considering that you had to die to obtain the Gift, he wondered what she had gone through to get it, especially during peacetime, and at such a young age.

"Why you are looking at me that way?" Gaby asked, examining Fionn's features with a crooked smile on her lips, blushing. "You look so green."

"Green?" Harland said, confused.

"So you can see my aura, too. I expected that. I was wondering: You were trained by the Sisters of Mercy. Was it then that you got the Gift?" Fionn was curious. Controlling the Gift required training as it enhanced the senses and the way the body reacted and connected to the world, thus affecting how you perceive it and even your fighting style. That's why it took years to fully mesh with a recipient and more often than not, it caused mental trauma, even madness as he had seen once before, a long time ago. But Gaby acted calm and in control.

"Halfway through my training, it was painful. Then I ran away," Gaby replied, looking down as if recalling a hurtful memory. "And you?"

"Let's say that it was some time ago. It wasn't pretty either."

"You two are freaking me out," Harland interjected, tapping a foot.

"Relax, she has the Gift, just like me," Fionn said, waving his hands up and down, trying to reassure his friend that everything was fine.

"My friend here might be at ease, but I need answers. A man's life depends on this. What's your story, kid?" Harland asked after taking a big gulp of his chocolate.

"I don't know how to explain it. Sometimes I get these vivid dreams that kind of tell me what is going to happen. But they are not accurate, they only offer hints. I saw images that you would be looking for me at a bar with an open mic. I assumed that it was because of what happened at the professor's house."

"And you dreamt that something was going to happen to Professor Hunt?" Fionn asked.

"Yes, that's why I've been trying to contact him for days, to warn him. But he didn't believe me. Until it was too late."

"Do you know if he is alive? Why didn't you tell that to the law officers?" Harland asked with eagerness.

"In my dreams he is. And seriously, do you think they would have believed me? They are so slow at understanding these things that I fell asleep at their headquarters."

"That's a very convenient ability to have," Harland said. Fionn noticed the skepticism in his voice. In a way, Harland was right. It was too easy, too convenient. There are no such things as luck or coincidence.

"It is... when it works. Most of the time I don't have control over it. It comes randomly," Gaby rubbed her arms to warm them. "Listen I would love to explain more, but could it be in a better place? My hotel is nearby and the weather is starting to chill too much for me, even with the hot chocolate."

"Lead the way." Fionn pointed to the road.

Fionn and Harland followed Gaby down the street that led to her hotel. The chills in his spine and the way his breath condensed when speaking told him how cold the air was getting.

"I can barely see anything with this fog," Harland complained. And he was right. Fionn was having trouble making out the silhouette of his friend, and he was right next to him.

The three of them reached a square, where Fionn noticed a shadow approaching.

The shadow was misshapen and seemed out of proportion to anything Fionn could think of. Only creatures from the realm of nightmares could look like that. It had to be a trick of the fog or a hallucination.

Once it was in full view, Fionn wished it was just a hallucination. It was a man with a deformed face, its mouth wide open and his tongue replaced by black tendrils. It walked on its arms and legs, like a spider, but with its back towards the ground, its neck twisted in an inhuman way. It moved fast but with stilted, almost mechanical movements. Soon, several similar creatures followed, infesting the square.

"What the hell?" Harland exclaimed while the man-spider moved faster into the fog. "Was it me or did it seem to be running away?"

"I would hate to find what they were running away from," Gaby said.

Then another shadow appeared from the fog. It was the same bearded man from the fight at the pub. His eyes were bleeding profusely; his jaw was slack and he was stumbling more than walking. He held what remained of his left arm, a bloody stump, with his right hand. He reached Fionn and cried for help, before his skin melted away like a wax figure, followed by his muscles and what was left of his bones, leaving a puddle of human remains in front of them.

"Wasn't he one of the guys from the pub fight?" Harland asked with a tremor in his voice. He started retching.

"Yes," Fionn replied.

"I think I'm gonna be sick, excuse me," Harland said before turning to his left and vomiting.

Fionn felt a new wave of goosebumps rising from his lower back to his neck. It was the way his body alerted him to danger. He saw Gaby pinching the bridge of her nose, and guessed it was the way her body was alerting her.

A chilling, wailing sound pierced the air. It was the

kind of scream that no human throat or any animal from this realm should be able to produce. For a second, Fionn thought that it sounded like a soul does when it is being torn asunder, and even he wondered how he knew that.

In the middle of the square, there was a man with the weirdest visage, wearing a mishmash of clothes, similar to those worn by the gang members they had fought at the pub. He had a circlet around his neck, glowing with a turquoise light. The man was babbling incoherently, grabbing his head and pulling his hair, scratching his skin with desperation, to the point that he was bleeding in several places. Under his skin it was possible to see wailing faces trying to escape, tiny heads and hands begging for help. All of his body was covered in a substance which smelled similar to the ooze found at the professor's house.

"*Gig aug ngg ma nil.*" The man said in what Fionn recalled were words of an ancient language. The kind of language one can find in books that should not be read. "It's coming, it's coming and my mind is only the door, only death and oblivion will cure my affliction. It's coming, it's coming and it has no skin in this realm, it will wear me like clothes, my souls are feeding him," the man screamed.

"That doesn't sound good." Fionn had heard similar words before and although he couldn't make total sense of them, he knew what they meant: big problems.

"I wish I hadn't understood that." Gaby retched, barely holding herself against a wall, dropping her guitar case onto the ground with a loud thud. Harland came to her aid.

"Breathe, deep breaths," Harland rubbed Gaby's back. She managed to get her bearings back. "Doing that helped me."

"Those faces… they are his companions, the guys that attacked us. He absorbed them. We need to help them."

"We can't," Fionn said with a somber tone. "Those poor buggers are goners. They are being used as a door for a creature from the Infinity Pits."

"Hell," Gaby said with a hint of fear in her voice. "What's happening?"

"I assume that whoever hired those guys didn't want to leave any witnesses alive, including you. And somehow he or she tricked them into being used as a door for a possession from a creature from the Infinity Pits," Fionn replied. The muscles on his shoulder blades tensed. He had seen this before. Humans were prone to dig their own graves if they allowed themselves to be convinced. That's how the Great War started and that's how it ended. The real end.

"Door?" Harland asked with fear in his voice.

"Door, host, it doesn't matter. Something is using them to bridge an incursion. We can't save them," Fionn explained, his lips tightening up, his hands reaching instinctively for his fangsword.

"Fionn, we haven't had an incursion anywhere in Theia for centuries," Harland said.

"Not that you know of," Gaby said with a somber tone.

"If it were an incursion, the magick alarms would blare by now," Harland said candidly. "It has to be something else."

A booming sound exploded through the air as the circlet shone bright and finalized the transformation. The man's head grew to a point where it exploded in a big gory mess of innards and foul smells. The final scream was even worse, coming from a beheaded neck. It was a primal exclamation of fear, pain, and hate, which reverberated against the walls, shaking the city to its foundations. The headless body started to grow, ripping the skin away, while its muscles bulged and changed color to an oily black.

A foul, viscous liquid covered its new 'skin.' Its muscle-bound arms ended in four fingers with sharp claws, and its legs with inverted knees ended in talons not unlike birds of prey. Scales formed over its skin and on its bloodied neck. Above the metallic circlet, and where the head had its place before, a deformed skull now grew. It was a grotesque caricature that mixed the muzzle of a wolf with the upper part of a goat and the eyes of a human. The creature finished ripping apart the remaining human skin. It kept increasing in size, becoming taller than a three-story building.

The creature roared and started its rampage, demolishing the obelisk in the center of the square and crushing the stalls of late night food vendors around it. Its massive claws slashed through concrete and hit a gas pipeline, causing an explosion and a fire that soon spread over other buildings. Smoke, mist, and screams blended in a cacophony only interrupted by one thing: the alarms, at last, going off.

"Told you, Harland." Fionn forced a smile.

Harland facepalmed himself. "Now what?"

"Now I do my thing. Look at it this way. You always wanted to see me in a real fight, full power and all, like in the books." Fionn cracked his neck to the left, relaxing his shoulders. He started to walk towards the creature, saying, "You should take cover. This will get ugly."

"What are you planning to do?" Gaby asked.

"First, I will deal with the big guy there. Then I will clean up the mess of the smaller ones."

"Let the guards deal with it," Harland said.

"They don't stand a chance against that. I do," Fionn smiled. A part of him was glad to finally have a fight of this level, he missed the adrenaline.

"You will reveal your secret."

"What secret?" Gaby asked, confused.

"You will see soon." Fionn winked at Gaby and walked away from her and Harland. Fionn walked slowly towards the creature. His left hand crossed in front of him and reached the pommel of his sheathed sword. The wind howled like a dragonwolf and a green glow started to come from the sword. Fionn unsheathed his blade and the wind picked up. The fangsword's silvery blade was covered by the green glow, the engravings on it shining with words from an ancient tongue. Fionn's irises went from regular green to an intense, almost surreal shade of bright green with golden specks. He smiled, feeling his muscles and bones welcome the surge of energy dormant for so long. He reached inside him, to the source, his Gift. It felt familiar even after so many years of not summoning it, like an old friend that had always been there. Its warmth energized him. He continued walking until the creature took notice of him.

"The engravings, the form of the blade. I remember reading about it. It's the Black Fang! One of the Tempest Blades..." Gaby's eyes opened wide in sudden realization. "Wait a minute. That means..." Gaby said to Harland, as they both took cover behind the columns of the arcade.

"Yes, you are right."

"He is the legendary Greywolf! How? He must be..."

"Over one hundred and thirty-three years old? I had the same reaction when I found out. Apparently, the Gift slows aging."

The sky was raging in fury, lightning slashing across the dark skies, the wind blowing away the mist. The square was being emptied, the townspeople trying to get as far away as possible from the giant creature, whose red eyes were locked on the man standing in front of him in defiance. Any other mortal would cower before the behemoth, but this one was smiling. The creature started a conversation, its deep, booming voice echoing all over the place.

"Why don't you run like the other mortals?"

"Not really my thing."

"I will crush you."

"You can try."

The creature roared with anger, stomping its way across the plaza. Fionn didn't waste time and jumped into the fray, slashing it with Black Fang. The creature replied in kind, raising its massive right claw and trying to shred Fionn like paper. He parried the attack with the sword, but the strength behind it almost broke his arm. He got ready to parry the second one, biting his lips to tolerate the pain, when an attack by Gaby on the creature's back interrupted the exchange between them.

Gaby's twin blades were out of their sheaths and each shone with a clear, bright light, one glowing blue and the other red.

"Are those Tempest Blades too?" Fionn asked with an incredulous stare.

"Yes," Gaby replied with her crooked smile. "Their names are Heartguard and Soulkeeper."

"How did you..."

"You are not the only one with secrets, Greywolf," Gaby said. "But that will have to wait, there is work to do."

Both Fionn and Gaby jumped, attacked, dodged and parried the blows coming from the creature. But after every attack that the creature suffered at the hands of Fionn and Gaby, it regenerated immediately. It was growing angrier by the moment, picking up trash cans and throwing them, breaking walls and destroying the windows of the shops and pubs. The creature kept throwing things at them, forcing them to take cover behind a semi-crumbled wall. Behind the cover, they saw the men-spiders returning, attacking the scared patrons who were trying to get away from the creature.

"Those civilians need help. Would it be too much to ask you to help them?"

"As much as I would hate to leave you with all the fun, you are right. They need me more than you do." Gaby winked at Fionn. "Be careful."

"I'm always careful."

Fionn could only smile at her with admiration in his eyes. Gaby ran towards the running people, not losing a second in attacking the men-spiders. Her blades were streaks of red and blue light in the dark. Parts of the spider-like creatures started to fly off. She was efficient, Fionn thought, too efficient even for a Sister of Mercy. There were so many things he wanted to ask her. But that would have to wait. A girl, running away from the conflict, broke a heel and fell in front of the path of destruction of the larger creature. Its collection of sharpened teeth was in full sight in a mockery of a smile. Seeing that, Fionn ran towards the girl, covering her with his body as the claw descended upon her.

"Oh shit," Fionn managed to say before the creature hit him fully in the back with all its strength, sending him flying away with the girl in his arms. He managed to twist his body mid-air to absorb the blunt force of the imminent impact when they hit the ground. His jacket and the skin of his back were torn to shreds and he was bleeding profusely. His head was spinning. Fionn looked at the girl who was scared and crying, but safe. He shook his head to clear it and smiled at her.

"I will distract him while you escape. Can you run?"

The girl only replied with a nod and Fionn let her go. She ran away into the streets. It was then that Fionn noticed a faint cut on his right cheek, a cut that started to heal amidst tiny green sparkles of energy.

*This is gonna hurt tomorrow.*

The open, bleeding wounds were mending and closing at an unnatural pace. Weeks of the healing process compressed into seconds. For Fionn, the sensation was akin to a faint tickling. Catching his breath, Fionn ran again towards the creature, picking up his sword along the way.

With a powerful leap, Fionn landed his knee on the creature's face, making it bleed black ichor as if it were a fountain. The creature responded by throwing a slashing hand towards Fionn, who dodged it by jumping into the air with a back flip and then descending, cutting off the arm of the creature. At first, it remained quiet, in shock, while the open wound sprayed black ichor over the white tiles of the ground. Fionn smiled, satisfied, but soon his smile turned into tight lips. The creature stood tall while laughing. The circlet on its neck glowed brightly for a second. Its arm grew back from where the stump was.

"That's new," Fionn exclaimed. The creature then spat, which landed near Fionn's feet. It bubbled and sizzled on the tile. "And that's gross," he added, running away from the incoming acid barrage. He ran towards an alley and turned the corner, finding himself next to Harland.

"Nice view, isn't it?"

"Your definition of nice is skewed," Harland retorted. "While you were dancing around with that thing, Gaby has been taking care of the smaller creatures. She can fight, I give you that."

"I didn't expect any less from her."

"I expect more from you. That thing can regenerate like you. That circlet on its neck may be the reason."

"I noticed that too. I need to destroy it before cutting off its head and piercing its heart."

"Why?"

"It's the only way to really kill it. Don't look at me; those are the points where the powers of those creatures reside."

"Aren't you scared?"

"Why should I be? It's part of the job. I'm used to it," Fionn said to Harland, confidence in his eyes. "Enjoy the show."

Fionn ran out from the cover towards the creature once more. Its roars only made him chuckle as he stopped a few steps from the beast, trying to keep it focused on him.

"I admit that the acid spit was a nice trick. But you need more than that to scare me," Fionn yelled at it, while the wind picked up once more. The creature spat the acid once more, combining it with slashes at blinding speed. Fionn kneeled slightly as if building impulse. Taking a deep breath, he let himself feel the world in a way no one without the Gift could. The energy inside him filled him with warmth.

The wind, the specks of dust, the ample square, even Harland and Gaby felt different, surreal, but with more substance. He felt in the air all the connections between things, between beings, and for a brief second, his body moved faster than the wind itself, light and free. Fionn analyzed the attack patterns of the creature. He dodged each of the attacks and slashed at its feet, damaging its balance and making it fall to one knee. He then jumped onto the knee and the right arm, evading a slap.

Fionn jumped onto its shoulder and rode the creature, raising Black Fang. With a swift move, he cut off the creature's head, a flash of green light trailing. Another cut sliced the circlet in two as the head started to regenerate. Those moves were followed by a single circular movement that cleaved the creature's heart with force. The creature's body collapsed on its side, and once it hit the ground, it started to melt away, leaving ashes and black blood behind. Fionn looked at the corpse while it dissolved, leaving only the damaged circlet behind.

Gaby walked towards him, while Fionn picked up the pieces of the circlet. Harland soon reached both and gave Fionn a few pats on the back, which sent prickles of pain up his spine. Although his injuries had healed, his back was still sensitive. He had to develop a high tolerance for pain to compensate for that.

"I have to admit, that was pretty impressive," Harland exclaimed. He had a wide grin and if Fionn knew him he probably would have filmed everything on his cell phone.

"I'm a bit rusty," Fionn replied while rotating his right shoulder to warm up the muscle.

"How did you do that?" Gaby asked.

"Killing it?"

"No, evading its attacks that way."

"When you have the Gift, your senses are more attuned to the world, but it takes practice to get used to it, to let the energy flow through your body. You need to clear your mind and focus. Once your body and mind are in sync, then your body can move as fast as your mind."

"Sounds eerily familiar," Gaby replied in low voice.

"To what?" Harland asked.

"An old training technique from the Sisters of Mercy," Gaby replied, evading Harland's gaze. Fionn saw that and choose to change the topic.

"We need to find out what this thing is and how this works, and more important, who gave this to those men." Fionn pointed to some engravings on the broad side of the circlet. "These symbols are the same as those I found scribbled on the papers at Hunt's manor. This thing is tied to his disappearance."

"This doesn't look like a magick item," Harland said while examining the circlet. "More like advanced technology."

"I might know of someone who can help us then," Gaby offered.

"Who?" Fionn asked.

"My best friend. He is a former student of the professor and is well acquainted with new technology. He lives not far from here." Gaby smiled again while walking towards the hotel as if nothing had happened. Fionn was curious about her and he hated to admit it, but he was starting to like her. Harland looked at his friend and smiled.

"Careful or you will end up with a new student. Or maybe even... a date!"

"Very funny," Fionn walked away.

# Chapter 5

## The Inventor

"Now, in the fourth hour of Mr. Funkatastic's marathon of oldies but goodies, this song is a classic anthem by the legendary group Que..."

The sun filtered through the dirt-stained window into the small room. Specks of dust floated everywhere. It gave the place an ambiance of sadness, reflecting the mood of its current occupant. Alex was laying on the bed, on top of the covers, still dressed in jeans, a black t-shirt with the logo of a cartoon, and white sneakers. The room was sparsely furnished, with just a small bed, a desk with a chair and some upper shelves, a sink and a closet. The shelves had some books, comics and a pair of action figures, nothing remarkable. The only thing out of place in the small student's room was a sheathed long sword, a family relic with a unique handguard, designed to resemble six wings fully opened.

Alex looked at the sword and then at his right hand. He raised his hand, fingers extended, in front of his face, examining how the light illuminated it. His left arm was resting on his forehead, keeping strands of his messy, brown hair from his face. He was stuck in a rut, his postgrad research going nowhere, and his personal life wasn't doing any better. The nightmares continued to plague his sleep. The only good thing going for him at the moment was the side project he was developing with a few friends. With any luck, it would work any day now. But meanwhile, his mind had trouble remaining focused. He needed something to get over his funk.

*A road trip might not be a bad idea*, Alex thought. He looked at the sword again. He felt that the sword called to him from time to time, bringing about a natural instinct to wield it. But, much to his chagrin, he admitted that he wasn't good with it. He preferred the bow. He was brought out of his reverie by the ringing of his cell phone.

"What's up?" Alex asked in his thick accent, typical of those from the Straits, not moving from his spot on the bed.

"Youneedtocometothelabrightnow! Wedidit!" The excited voice on the other side yelled without stopping to breathe. It belonged to Birm, one of his friends at the university. "You were right, we did it!"

"Calm down. I can barely understand you." Alex rose up, trying to make sense of what he was hearing, but to no avail.

"Just get yourself here now!" Birm yelled at Alex through the phone, and then hung up.

It took Alex a few seconds to process everything, but once it dawned on him, his eyes opened wide. He grabbed his backpack and stormed out of the room, leaving his cell phone behind, unattended, which rang once more.

Mercia University, located in the Midlands of the Emerald Island, was considered one of the most innovative schools in the whole Free Alliance territory. It excelled at sports, design, and engineering, and was making inroads into the latest generation of arcanotechnology. The new cell phone system, which overcame the heavy ionized charges of Theia's atmosphere that limited the range of communication technology, and new possibilities for air travel, had been developed here. The university had cutting-edge laboratories filled with the latest (and most expensive) equipment as befitted the leading university on Theia. The equipment was like catnip for a creative student with attention deficit disorder and special abilities. And those required an outlet.

In the lab, four sets of eyes were admiring the black goo – composed of carbon nanotubes and metaling nanoparticles with memory – twisting and floating inside a transparent case, stimulated by electrical currents. The monitor showed computer-assisted graphic designs of a recurve bow with variable shapes. It looked as if it could collapse onto itself and become portable. Alex sported a wide grin, filled with childlike glee as he and his three companions – Birm, Andrea, and Quentin – admired their work. The three were his best friends at the university and each of them knew about his secret abilities and how he had acquired them a decade ago.

"So your material works," Alex stated, trying to contain his excitement. He was smiling.

"Of course it works!" Birm replied with a wide grin. "Did you ever have any doubts?"

"Well... after twenty-nine failures, I learned to keep my expectations in check."

"Yeah right," Andrea said. "Weren't you the one planning on creating a whole range of products with this material, to make us very rich, just two weeks ago? You were even planning paid vacations for all of us to Korbey World."

"I might have been getting a tad excited, yes. But it was just because we made progress. Besides, without my input on the electrical current, it wouldn't have worked," Alex gloated.

"You mean your twenty-three 'try an error' experiments?" Andrea replied, deadpan. "Yes, they were really helpful."

"Yup. You were right about the electrical current," Birm said, ignoring both. He couldn't stop staring at the material. "The input you calculated was exactly what it needs to regain the preprogrammed forms and shapes between them. You can actually make a collapsible bow!"

"What he means," Andrea added. "Is that a bow made of this material should be able to collapse and expand to its full form with the right electric input. And then, you just need to practice the inputs."

"Won't the material become fluid after a while?" Alex asked.

"No," Andrea said. "The alloy catalyst I used this time will make sure the nanoparticles stay in place forever, once the chemical reaction from the printing process cools down. They can only change shape to their predetermined forms with the right input. Otherwise, it would be as solid as a regular bow."

"And while the bow will work with normal arrows, the best part is that the same principle extends to these cartridges," Birm continued, handing a small black case to Alex. He was bursting with pride. "You insert this into the bow and you have here preprogrammed material to form arrows with heads of any shape you need. And if you can recover them, you can reuse them. Even charge them electrically! You don't need a quiver anymore!"

"Full, lightweight body armor able to withstand the impact of a titanfighter attack or even magick spells is within reach," Andrea said.

"As they say," Quentin said. He stood with his perpetual cup of coffee in his hand. "The sky is the limit."

"I just want a bow," Alex said.

"Way ahead of you," Birm replied. "After the success with the arrows, I fed the goo to the 3D printer and put it to work. The bow should be ready in a few minutes. Take a look!"

Alex eyed the material 3D printer that was finishing his bow design. He looked like a child in a toy store, eyes wide, a goofy grin and tapping his feet, while ruffling his own hair. The 3D printer finished working on the bow, or at least the riser of a bow. It was black, shiny and with smooth edges. Alex opened the door of the printer and took the riser with his left hand. It felt lightweight but balanced. He placed his left thumb on the red dot painted on the side of the riser and concentrated. The irises of his eyes took a subtle golden glow. He concentrated and felt a jolt of energy running from the core of his body into the length of his arm and released through his thumb into the riser. The electrical current ran through the black material of the riser, from which two limbs grew, one at each end. A string formed between them and the whole object took the form of a full-length recurve bow.

Alex tensed the string without releasing it; an arrow was starting to form on the string. His design felt perfect in his hands and his grin grew wide. It was the kind of grin a child would have if he had free reign in a candy story.

"We need to take this for a ride!"

††††

The night was falling on the university campus when Alex, Birm, and Quentin returned from the archery range. Andrea had stayed at the lab to work on her degree project while she made a backup of all the data on her and Birm's material and Alex's bow design. As the project was something they were doing off the books, the data couldn't be saved on the university's servers. Only the basic theory, enough to grant them a patent and their degrees within three years, remained on those servers.

"You are improving, Alex," Birm patted Alex's back.

"You still beat me by a hundred points at the range," Alex admitted ruefully. "And yours is a traditional bow."

"No matter how fancy your equipment is, there is no replacement for talent and practice," Quentin said.

"Thanks, man," Alex rolled his eyes. You really know how to cheer someone up. You should really lay off the coffee; this is your eighth cup today."

"The extra security makes me tense," Quentin pointed at all the security guards inspecting the campus.

"Yeah, what's that about?"

"Well, there have been reports in the news," Birm explained. "That research laboratories and universities all over the Free Alliance had been robbed in the past months. There were even a couple of deaths. I assume the Dean is not taking any chances."

"Anything in particular?" Alex's curiosity was piqued.

"Some high-energy power sources, alloys, catalysts, superconductors..."

The pieces clicked in Alex's mind. He opened his eyes wide in realization.

"You mean like the very stuff that Andrea is using for her Ph.D. project?" Alex asked. There was an edge to his voice.

"Yeah, why?" Birm asked. "Oh no."

The three of them sped up. Alex's body tensed while they ran towards the building where their lab was located. As they arrived he saw three shadows slipping into the building.

"Did you see that?"

"Those weird shadows moving into the building?" Quentin said. "Yes. Shouldn't we call security?"

"Andrea!" Birm exclaimed. Concern for the safety of his fiancée was showing on his face.

"Not a bad idea. But while they get here, you two stay outside. I will go inside and get Andrea," Alex said. The tone of his voice had gone from friendly to stern. Tension built up in his muscles as a buzzing in his inner ear increased. It was the way his body alerted him to danger, to something unnatural. The last time he had heard it was ten years ago and he hated what it meant.

"Like hell you are going inside alone, she is my fiancée," Birm cracked his knuckles and punching the security code to open the door, without success. Quentin just pushed the door, opening it. Birm ran inside without waiting for anyone.

"They probably deactivated the security system beforehand, otherwise we would have seen several guards running this way," Quentin explained.

"Always the smart-ass. Call security and stay here and let us know if more of those guys enter the place," Alex said, entering the building, following Birm.

"Don't worry, I will," Quentin said, sipping from his paper cup.

The building was pitch black, except for some of the open labs with independent generators, which still worked on automated projects. Alex and Birm moved as silently as possible. Once they reached the stairs, they ran up to the third floor where the lab was located. They opened the door slowly and noticed four more assailants in the hall, packing their loot from the other labs.

"I wonder if those are all of the robbers or if there are more in other labs." Alex said in low voice.

"Any ideas?" Birm asked.

"Keep them busy here while you reach Andrea through the side doors," Alex said. "Remember, just because you have military training, it doesn't mean it will be easy. Take care, please! Don't be a hero; just get her out of harm's way."

"Remind me, who won our last practice fight?"

"I know," Alex replied, "But that was a practice and you can't do this." He expanded the bow with a small electric crackle breaking the air and filling it with the sweet, pungent zing of ozone.

"Show off," Birm muttered.

Without waiting, Alex shot a couple of arrows at the assailants, distracting them long enough that they failed to notice Birm entering the labs through the side doors. Without a pause, Alex moved, hitting and punching the guy in the hallway. It wasn't a clean fight for either side, as they landed some punches on Alex's ribs and mouth, but he used his knowledge about the labs to beat them. He used metal canisters to crack their ribs and snap their legs, crashing them through the windows and slamming their heads into crates and metal tables. Alex wasn't trying to kill them, just leave them unconscious. But a part of him deep inside was enjoying this. It wasn't pretty, it wasn't swift and it certainly wasn't done with elegance, but it was effective and surprisingly relaxing. By the time he finished, the floor was littered with the bodies of four would-be robbers lying unconscious.

"I feel for the janitor tomorrow. Cleaning this will be tough."

Alex approached the lab where Andrea had been working. Inside, he saw a tall, muscle-bound guy, wearing dreadlocks and a gas mask. He was slamming Birm into a metal table as if he were a rag doll. Then he lifted him by the neck. Next to the brute, there was a smaller guy wearing the same outfit but with messy red hair, holding Andrea back. His high-pitched laugh encouraging the big guy to kill Birm by crushing his neck. Alex was enraged.

*No one hurts my friends, you giant piece of crap.*

He took aim and shot two arrows in quick succession. The first one broke the glass window, while the second, trailing behind, hit the arm holding Birm. The tip of the arrow cut the arm tendons, forcing the giant robber to drop Birm. He hit the floor gasping for air.

"Try that again and I will turn you into a pincushion," Alex aimed a third arrow, this time at the neck of the assailant. The brute ignored Alex, catching him off guard, as he ran toward him, moving faster than a person that size had the right to move. Alex discharged the full cartridge of arrows into him, not even slowing him down.

"Aww crap," Alex muttered, getting ready to dodge the incoming tackle when the redhead yelled.

"Let's go, big brother, we have what we came for. There will be plenty of time for mayhem later."

"Next time chubby, next time," the big assailant grumbled, pointing at Alex. The redhead shoved Andrea to the floor, then mumbled words that Alex could not understand, some sort of spell that transformed his body and that of his giant companion into shadows that flew through the window. With that, the lights returned and the alarm started to blare. Alex ran towards Andrea and Birm, who were getting up.

"I'm fine, I'm fine," Birm said groggily.

"I don't think so, we need to take you to the medical services," Alex replied.

"There is something more urgent right now. Alex, take the things and get out."

Andrea nodded and grabbed a case full of data crystals, all the arrow cartridges, and a small metal box labeled *Wanderer*, tucking them into her duffel bag. She gave it to Alex. Birm got up and with Andrea, pushed Alex towards the open window.

"What the Pits?" Alex asked, surprised.

"Alex, you need to get out of here with all our unregistered projects. Now," Andrea yelled.

"But why?" Alex was confused as Andrea reacted fast and started to pile up more things into the duffel bag.

"Once the alarm goes off, the security protocols close all access and then it gets restrained for months until it is cleared off, and they will take our research," Andrea explained.

"But the window?" Alex yelled as they pushed him through it.

"All the ground floor doors are locked by now, this is the only exit and you are the only one that can make the jump," Birm said.

"What about you?" Alex asked, peering behind him at the three-story fall.

"Birm looks like a textbook assault victim who may never recover his previous face. We have our cover," Andrea replied nonchalantly. By now they had Alex sitting pretty much on the edge of the window, his hands holding the bag.

"Did you forget that I hate heights?" Alex said with a faint voice.

"It's just three stories. You will be fine. Now go!" Andrea ordered while Birm pushed Alex out of the window.

"Awww craaaaap!" Alex yelled while falling out of the window. Bracing for the impact, Alex extended his arms forward and his body was covered by faint electric arcs. Alex felt as if he was surrounded by something invisible, pushing him up, lessening the fall. He had tried this before, to generate a magnetic field not unlike that of a levitating warptrain to soften a fall. He had never succeeded. The landing hurt like hell, but luckily his body withstood the fall with nothing but some pain in his legs. Alex got up slowly, while Quentin admired the landing from his position by the wall.

"I will give it a nine for effort but a four on technique," Quentin said, still sipping coffee from his cup. "But you could lose some weight as well."

"Ha, ha. Let's go," Alex mumbled, not amused, dragging Quentin with him while they ran away from the building. They avoided the security guards now arriving at the lab. Alex wondered what the assailants would want with Andrea's research. After all, she was still a student. Her research had to do with batteries coupled with miniature superconductors – like the one embedded inside his bow. It was more efficient than a regular battery, and she'd told him previously about some of the other possible uses. Something to do with cell phones and high-powered signals. He couldn't remember, but something in his mind was racing to connect the dots. Alex was sure that when that happened, he wouldn't like the answer.

† † †

The next morning Mercia University was full of rumor and speculation about what had happened in the labs. This was the first case to leave survivors and a few of the perpetrators had been arrested, although none of the suspects were talking since they had all suffered serious injuries. Guards were everywhere, scanning students and lecturers alike, looking for clues to give to the law officers. What had been a quiet, friendly campus was now a highly impregnable fortress.

Alex reached the fair, which was taking place in one of

the open sports fields and outside the main gym. His legs still hurt from the fall, but he was used to sharp pain. His body had developed a degree of endurance that he couldn't explain. Only Birm, Andrea, and Quentin were onto that secret, although he knew there were rumors about the weird things that happened around him, like electronics turning on or off without human input. His hope was that the buzz of the fair would distract people from asking him things he didn't want to explain.

The fair was the place where clubs sought to recruit new members, like the fencing club or the board game club to which Alex and his friends belonged. More members meant more funding and higher social status within the social micro-cosmos that was the campus. There were religious and political clubs as well, but they weren't gathering much attention lately. Talking religion outside family settings was considered rude, at least in the Free Alliance, where faith was meant to be something personal. And the political environment was already charged due to the actions of the New Leadership Party. The NLP had recently formed to proclaim inflammatory ideas, bordering on demagogic and racist, against the freefolk due to their ability to use magick. Political speech had been restricted at Mercia, as well as at most university campuses, to keep at ease the few freefolk students that attended them. While most freefolk kept to themselves and attended their own schools, Mercia University had plans to open joint projects with some freefolk schools, thanks to the efforts of Professor Leonard Hunt. Now that he thought about it, Alex hadn't heard much from his old mentor since the professor had changed jobs to a freefolk school last year. Alex thought about calling him after the fair was over.

The stand of the board game club seemed small, thanks to the massive number of props, replicas and test games, both commercial and home-built by its members. At the moment it was being looked after by Quentin, while Andrea looked after Birm's wounds. Alex walked towards them, carrying the compressed bow in a duffel bag and the sword on his back. This was one of the few days he could carry the sword without raising many questions. The odd handle made it look like a prop for the stand.

"Are you expecting problems?" Andrea asked as soon as he approached. She was pointing at the sword.

"I can't shake the buzz in my ear, so yes," Alex said. "I'm surprised they haven't canceled the fair."

"Paranoid much?" Quentin replied.

"Luckily for you, you weren't there," Birm interjected. "Not last night, nor ten years ago. That sword is a good safety measure. And if Alex can still hear the buzz, any extra precaution is welcome. As for your question, the Dean is trying to get re-elected. Thus an image of stability plays in her favor. The fair is meant to showcase that everything is fine. Even if the tension is palpable on every corner."

"You seem rattled. Did something else happen?" Alex asked Birm, who exchanged glances with Andrea.

"A guy from that NLP club came by. He threatened us with reprisals if we don't move our stall. According to him, this was his spot," Andrea explained with a tight voice. "We even showed him the floor plans and one of the representatives came to settle the issue, but he didn't back off. He said he would return later to teach us a lesson. Asshole."

"They seem to attract the worst of the worst," Birm shrugged his shoulders. "He was really weird, with a smile that gave you the creeps."

"I will deal with him if he returns," Alex started to say, but the buzzing in his inner ear became stronger. Time slowed for him and the world acquired a different texture. He could see the energy flowing around him. Alex turned around and saw the red-haired thief from the lab last night, swinging a large metal goal post towards them, a chunk of concrete still adhering to one of its ends.

Alex felt his muscles tense, an all too familiar feeling

after what had happened ten years ago, when he'd gotten his special gift and cursed his luck. He turned to push Andrea and Birm out of the way with his right arm while extending his left arm to catch the post. He could feel an electromagnetic field extending around him, providing him with extra strength.

Alex caught the post and time resumed its regular flow, as if a river has been finally freed from its constraints.

"I think that post belonged to one of the sports clubs," Alex said. The redheaded man pushed harder, forcing Alex to increase the energy output and push even harder in response. He looked over his shoulder at his friends. "Guys, I think you better leave. Call Gaby or Sid!"

Alex and the redhead were intertwined in a contest of strength. With his free hand, Alex reached for his sword. As he unsheathed it, the blade glowed with a faint golden light, similar to the glow now present in Alex's eyes. As he pushed the post forward, he used the gained centimeters to swing the sword. With a swift movement, the blade sliced through the post. Both Alex and the redhead looked at each other and at the post with surprise a couple of times until the redhead decided to use what was left as a club.

The redhead was being oddly quiet. Alex didn't like that.

"What? Is this not funny anymore? Why so serious? You were all laughs and talk last night," Alex teased him. "You don't like it when someone stands up to you?"

Alex dodged the attacks. He was sensing the electrical currents of his opponent's nerves, seeing them as orange lines of energy, and that gave him precious few seconds to guess where the attack would land. He dodged one attack, rolling to the side. Kneeling, he gripped his sword with both hands and started to parry the attacks. Alex put all his strength into his parries and counterattacks, cutting off pieces of the post until nothing was left.

Annoyed, the redhead backed off. Alex took a few seconds to regain his breath. He glanced at Andrea talking to someone on her cell phone, and Birm yelled at him to move. Alex sidestepped to his right, just in time to avoid a trash can hitting the spot where he had stood. When he turned around, the redheaded man was extending his arms and several objects, including parked cars, started to shake and launch towards Alex. He ran, dodging the rain of objects.

*I need to learn that trick*, Alex thought. Unfortunately, a crate full of cookbooks from the hosting club hit him in the hand, making him drop his sword. The redhead stopped the assault, smiled, and threw a car towards Alex.

"Aww crap," Alex muttered. The sword was far from his reach, but he still had the duffel bag with him. He rolled away, dodging the car, which hit the ground with a heavy, loud impact. Alex took the bow from the bag, expanded it, and shot at the man, but the arrow was deflected before reaching the target. Alex aimed again, this time focusing his abilities. It was then that he noticed a larger aura surrounding the guy. It was shaped like the silhouette of a scorpion. Its tail was picking up the cars and throwing them towards Alex. The pincers were deflecting the arrows he had shot. Alex hesitated, swallowing hard. He'd seen this same aura before, ten years ago at the Straits. It was the incident that had given him his abilities. A deep, sinking feeling formed in the bottom of his stomach.

*Aww crap. How the Pits am I going to defeat that thing?*

And then, a voice broke him out of his fear.

"Aim for his heart, I will take care of the rest," Alex heard from behind him. He saw a young long-haired man, not much older than himself, charging towards the redheaded guy. The man was followed by Gaby, both of them with swords in hand. Gaby's blades shone blue and red, while her companion's sword was bright green. Seeing this, the redhead intoned a few words and he started to mutate into the form of a scorpion with biomechanical implants protruding from his skin.

"Now, Alex!" Gaby yelled.

Alex took aim at what he guessed was a heart, following the orange energy threads that his eyes were able to see. Putting all the energy he had left into the arrow, he let loose, the arrow flying true to its target.

The arrow hit at the same time that the long-haired guy's sword cut off the creature's head. It unleashed all the energy of the incomplete transformation into an explosion that sent Alex tumbling backward.

Alex's head rang. Dizzy, he tried to stand up as his stomach churned. His shoulder hurt badly, but at least he was alive. Someone touched his shoulder, and he turned around. Gaby was standing next to him, smiling and handing him his sword. He noticed that the long-haired guy stared at the handle with an expression of shock and recognition.

"You seriously need to answer your calls, Alex," Gaby slapped him in the arm.

"I ran out of batteries," Alex replied sheepishly.

"You, especially you, running out of batteries has to be the lamest of all possible lame excuses," Gaby countered. She nodded to her companion. "Anyhow, Fionn meet Alex, Alex meet Fionn."

"Fionn? Why is that name familiar?" Alex asked while still trying to get to his feet.

"Think it through, see the fangsword," Gaby said with her crooked smile showing on her face. Then it dawned on Alex and his eyes opened wide as saucers.

"No freaking way! The Greywolf?" Alex exclaimed. The man seemed to be no older than his mid-thirties, not more than a decade older than Gaby or himself, who were just in their mid-twenties. It didn't make sense. The Greywolf had lived during the Great War and that had been a century or so ago. Then again, the Queen had lived so long and had been ruling since...

"Yup." Gaby flashed a wide smile, while Fionn extended his hand to Alex, who shook it a bit overenthusiastically. He was, after all, meeting his childhood hero.

"We have to talk," Fionn said, while Harland brought the rental car to pick them up. "C'mon."

# Chapter 6

# Back of the Napkin Explanations

The sun shone through the windows of the coffee shop. The place was almost empty; most people had gone home for the day after the attack in the fair. Fionn saw the waitress approaching their booth. The four of them were the only customers. The waitress left a bag of ice and refilled their cups of coffee.

"Your food will be ready soon," she said and left them.

Fionn examined Gaby's friend, focusing on the sword he had left resting on the side of the seat. Harland seemed to be distracted, looking for something in his datapad, streaming something from the aethernet.

"You are being a crybaby, Alex," Gaby said to her friend, who was sitting next to her on the left side of the booth.

"No, I'm not. It hurts like I was hit by a freight train," Alex was, holding the bag of ice on his shoulder.

"First, you don't know how a freight train hits," Gaby sipped her coffee and fell silent for moment before continuing. "Besides, this is hardly the strangest thing you will see today."

"What do you mean?" Alex had a confused look.

"I will let them explain that to you," Gaby's concern showed on her face. "They have something to ask you…" She never finished because Alex interrupted her.

"I can't believe I'm sitting in front of you," Alex startled

Fionn. This certainly wasn't the kind of reaction he was accustomed to when someone found out who he was. "You are my childhood hero. I have devoured every book that has been written about the war, the Twelve Swords, and you. Of course, I assume that half of them are wrong. Most mentioned you died under mysterious circumstances and yet here you are. Wait a minute, wouldn't that make you around a hundred and thirty-three years old?" Alex said in one go, without breathing.

"Forgive him, he tends to be a motormouth when he is excited," Gaby excused Alex, rolling her eyes.

"It's ok. And I prefer to say that I'm only thirty-three, I don't count the missing century," Fionn replied, trying to keep his composure with a polite nod. Fionn shuffled in his seat, as the thought of having a fan made him wary and uncomfortable. But he was starting to trust Gaby, and she trusted Alex. Maybe a leap of faith was in order.

"I have so many questions I want to ask," Alex continued. "About your sword and about the Light Explosion that came from the destruction of the Onyx Orb. Is it true that you beat a succubus and a raiding gang before you were sixteen, all by yourself?"

"Yeah, it's true. Listen, I'm sorry, but we are tight on time here. Once we finish this I will answer any question you have," Fionn interrupted him. "You might have heard of Professor Hunt's recent disappearance and..."

"Can we trust him?" Harland interjected, looking up from the datapad. Judging by his expression, something was perturbing him. He addressed Alex. "You are a curious person with an interesting file. Studying an advanced degree in a field not many can understand. You come from a family of scholars from the Straits. You have a couple of medals in archery. Otherwise a model citizen... and yet you have a rap sheet, with several arrests due to unruly behavior and countless fights. This says that you even beat a police officer once."

"In my defense, he hit a homeless man with his baton, just for standing in his way. And I know who you are: Harland Rickman from the Foundation," Alex replied, staring at Harland. For a brief second, Fionn saw tiny sparks coming from Alex's fingertips that hit the metal on the cutlery, rattling it. "I know your work. I even agree with some of your ideas. But you need to do your homework. Those records you mentioned? They are wrong. And I don't like the tone of your voice."

"Guys, we are getting sidetracked." Gaby put a conciliatory hand over Alex's. "And he is right."

"Look, Harland. Not many people jump in front of others to save them from a monster, Gifted or not Gifted," Fionn added with a raised eyebrow. "Besides, he is carrying Yaha, and that sword has a mind of its own. I know. He is on our side."

Alex looked at Gaby confused and murmured, "Gifted? Yaha?"

"That's what he calls our abilities. The Gift. Yaha must be the sword," Gaby replied.

"Look, as I said, I will answer your questions later. First, do you know what this is?" Fionn asked, taking the damaged circlet out of his jacket, the one they took from the creature they had faced at Carffadon. He tossed it to Alex, who examined the item in detail for three minutes until his eyes opened wide and then closed. He rubbed his forehead.

"Aww crap. I can't believe that someone is doing these in miniature," Alex left the circlet on the table. "Although that would explain the attacks on the universities and labs all over the country."

"What is it?" Harland asked.

"Long version short, it's a puncher that can open a portal for an incursion. I saw one like this in action ten years ago," Alex replied, sure of his answer. "Although it was bigger, about the size of a horse. Not as polished as this one. More like a test prototype. This one looks mass-produced."

"How can you say that? There hasn't been an incursion since the war," Harland countered.

"Not reported, but trust me, there was one. Gaby was there and I have the scars to prove it," Alex lifted his shirt and showed his bare chest covered with long scars on his right side over the liver. The scars were as long as an adult man's hand. "My liver got chopped by a creature that I'm sure wasn't from here."

"He's right," Fionn added. "I saw those scars multiple times on felp orcs that had tried to escape from the Blood Horde. The creature that makes them can render itself invisible. And it is really hard to kill."

"We had to kill what? Twelve? Twenty?" Alex asked Gaby, covering his scars.

"Something like that."

"All by yourself?" Fionn asked. During the war, he had hunted one of those creatures and it had been a difficult task. And he had training. Gaby could have fended off the creature as she had training, but Alex didn't seem the kind of person that had combat training. "I take it that's when your Gift woke up."

"If you mean my abilities, yes. And we had help, from a hunter that was around there at the time. He taught us how to kill the monsters ourselves," Alex explained. Fionn waved his hand, signaling him to continue. "It was a sports tournament for schools around Theia. Gaby had just transferred to mine. Some crazy cultist arrived with that machine at the nearby rainforest and the shit hit the fan. The rest is history, I guess. It wasn't pleasant. I survived, but I lost friends there. That's why I developed the bow and started to train. I don't want others to go through that kind of ordeal all over again. The nightmares are already hard to deal with."

Gaby hugged her friend, while Fionn felt Harland's gaze upon him. The downside of having the Gift is that nightmares, already bad enough for those that had suffered traumatic events, were more vivid and harder to forget. It made Fionn wonder what he had missed when he decided to retire. Gaby and Alex had seen and survived things that many brave men during the war hadn't. He respected that, even admired the fact that both had managed to find a way to keep the nightmares at bay. Izia would have been proud of them.

"Why didn't you tell us before?" Fionn asked Gaby.

"It wasn't my secret to tell. And I thought you wouldn't believe me about the incursion. Almost no one does. However, Alex has proof of that. One of his friends, who passed away last year, had it all recorded. And Alex has been harassed because of it." Gaby evaded Fionn's gaze as she wasn't keen to dwell further on that topic.

"When the government finally arrived, they tried to force us to lie or risk prison to cover their asses. They knew about the cult and did nothing. So when I didn't comply first, they faked my rap sheet, or most of it," Alex said sheepishly. "If it weren't for Gaby's family, or the hunter, or Professor Hunt, who vouched for me to enter Mercia, I wouldn't be here."

"I owe you an apology then," Harland replied, looking embarrassed.

"It's ok, I get that a lot." Alex smiled.

The waitress arrived with their food, burgers and sodas, milkshakes and fries.

"Do you want anything else?" She asked.

"We are fine, thanks," Fionn said with a polite smile. The waitress left.

"Back to the circlet, what else can you tell us?" Harland smiled back at Alex.

"As I said, it's basically a puncher," Alex replied, wolfing down a burger and drinking his soda.

"Alex, for a moment remember that not everybody has the knowledge you have on advanced physics, cosmology, and high energy engineering. Keep it simple, please," Gaby interjected.

"Fine," Alex replied, annoyed, taking a few napkins from their holder. "Ok, let's assume that this napkin is our reality, the universe we exist in. Then you add another napkin and so on and so forth, all neatly nested and folded into a tight package that we call our dimension." He showed the folded napkins to the group and continued.

"Then you have other dimensions, above and below, whose energy states vary. They are in theory inhabited by beings that can't interact directly, but do so through others. Y'know, possessions, voices in your head, that kind of thing. That's because of our dimension's fundamental physical make-up. Sound familiar? Metaphysics and philosophers call them the Last Heaven and the Infinity Pits. Heaven and Hell," Alex said matter-of-factly. Although Fionn wasn't dumb, he was having trouble following Alex's train of thought, between his thick accent and Fionn's lack of knowledge about advanced physics.

"Now let's say you want to cross from one dimension to another as a shortcut to somewhere else, you need to punch a hole..." Alex punched a hole through the napkins using a pen. "...through reality, which takes a considerable amount of energy and time, besides the need to transform whatever you want to transport through the hole into a stable form of matter for that dimension. Size matters here, as massive objects can only pass in sections that can be translated to the rules of our reality."

"And how does that link to that circlet or Hunt's disappearance?" Fionn asked.

"Well, as you know, he is a proponent of archanotechnology, the fusing of science and magick that gave us the warptrains. Part of his research project dabbled in the premise that the Akeleth weren't mythical beings, but a precursor race that had something similar to the ability to travel faster than light, even planetary teleportation technology. As far as I know, a teleportation spell is really useless because of its technological appropriation, so he tried to circumvent those limitations."

"I saw the report," Harland added. "He believed that he had found something in the ruins below Belfrost a year ago."

"He and others call that Stringspeed, basically traveling between the folds of the napkins and breaking the lightspeed limit. And the description he gave to that legendary technology is slightly similar to what we have here. The incursion we witnessed ten years ago seemed to confirm his initial guess, and that's why he searched around for that, tracking thaums and dark matter. You know, the residuals from a spell or an incursion," Alex continued. "The thaums are related to gravitons somehow, not so harmful to humans, I think. That's because they are too weak to interact if not funneled properly through a conductor. That's why he left Mercia to join that private school. Ravenstone, I think. They are the only ones I know of that have the knowledge and equipment to track it. Last time I heard he had found a massive amount of thaums generated in modern times, bigger than anything else seen, in several places."

"Where?" Fionn asked, already suspecting the answer. He just needed the confirmation. A part of him wished he was wrong. There were times when being right was not always a good thing.

"Lemast was one. The Long Horn Valley was another. According to Hunt, the Light Explosion punched a hole through dimensions, and for a few seconds, the passage between them was open. I shudder to think what crossed. And I still wonder how that happened," Alex finished, taking another sip of his soda. The table remained silent for a while.

"We blew it," Fionn broke the silence, stealing the plate full of fries from Alex.

"What? Who?" Alex asked, surprised.

"Me and the previous owner of that sword of yours. My best friend, Ywain. During the battle of Long Horn Valley, we found the power source for much of the Blood Horde's magick and technology. I guess they got confident because they brought that massive black Onyx Orb, the size of a mature dragon, to their camp. We infiltrated their camp during the battle and hit the Orb hard with the Tempest Blades to break it. The problem was that we didn't know that it had so much energy stored or what was inside," Fionn explained. "It exploded and took half the armies with it. It was a stupid thing to do."

"And how did you survive that? Records describe it as akin to a thermonuclear explosion," Alex said with his eyes wide open. "It leveled the whole place."

"I have no idea. I just woke up a few days later, my body healing the burns at an accelerated pace. Part of the Gift's awakening process, I guess. But let's go back to what you were saying." Fionn cut off that line of conversation, unsure of going further. Even now his memory of the event was blurry, not because of the years that had past since then, but because he truly couldn't recall the memory clearly beyond the waves of pain from his burned nerves while they healed.

"I'm inclined to believe that Hunt thought he wasn't the only one pursuing such clues. He became paranoid and his research was sidetracked," Harland added. "His notes were missing from the file."

"That's when I had the dream and went looking for him," Gaby interjected, stealing Alex's soda and drinking it, much to the chagrin of her friend.

"His assistant might have more information about it. But I don't know her," Alex said. "And I have no way to contact her."

"So how does that circlet thing work?" Fionn asked, changing the subject. "I remember that the person wearing this muttered some strange words before it fully activated."

"He was wearing it around his neck," Gaby added, shuddering at the memory.

"Oh, that's just… Look, from what I can deduce, it is some type of miniature portal. It uses these runes to cast a spell, these crystals to harness the thaums, the superconductors to carry resulting energy in a closed circuit, and then uses a body as a tether to merge with the being and be able to exist," Alex explained while pointing with the pen to the runes and the circuitry of the circlet.

"I still don't see why he went through so much trouble developing that thing when there are stories of demons able to exist in our reality before this was invented. You have fought them before," Harland added, turning to Fionn, remembering the stories his friend had told him.

"Maybe the aim is to make the process more stable, unlike a regular spell, or to create some kind of hybrid soldiers that combine the creatures' powers with something resembling a human mind that can follow orders. Or even to bring larger things," Alex said. "Those are the only explanations I can think of. And all of them are scary."

"As I see it, the fact that someone wants to develop a more powerful version of this is concern enough to solve this case fast," Fionn replied and then sighed. He could feel the gnawing fangs of a migraine starting to chew his head. He just hoped, no, prayed to the Heavens that no one had thought of bringing *him* back. The last time *he* roamed the world, Fionn ended up losing most of the people he loved, including Izia.

"Do you mind if I order another burger? The downside of this ability is that I burn blood sugar as if was it was, well, candy, and the migraines hit me like a mule," Alex broke the silence this time.

"You haven't been hit by a mule either," Gaby replied.

The four of them signaled the waitress and ordered another round of burgers. Fionn noticed how Alex had to eat a considerable amount of food just to stave off a migraine, even more so than Fionn usually did. Alex's Gift seemed to require so much energy just to work. *So that's how it looks to others*, he thought. No wonder Harland often looked surprised at the amount of food Fionn could eat. Even Gaby had to eat more than usual. However, unlike Alex, she did it with proper manners and elegance. Sometimes the Gift came with downsides. In Fionn's case, and while it wasn't apparent, the healing factor that helped him to overcome lethal injuries didn't come painlessly. Once he broke his arm and could feel and hear the bones resetting and melding together during the night, and no painkiller had an effect on him. He couldn't but wonder what drawback Gaby's Gift had. Fionn then turned his gaze to Alex and his sword, Yaha.

There was a certain familiar air around Alex, the way he laughed at Gaby's comments and the glee he took in eating. But the most telling sign was that sword: the hilt, with the six golden open wings and the pommel covered in brown leather with the two straps at the end hanging down, ending in two golden clasps. He had once held that sword in his hands, while he was teaching his best friend Ywain during the war how to fight with a sword. It had been lost along with its owner after of the war, under mysterious circumstances.

"Can I ask you a personal question, Alex?" Fionn asked.

"Sure, I mean, you are the Greywolf," Alex replied, putting down his second burger. "You can ask whatever you want."

"Where did you get that sword?" Fionn asked bluntly.

"This?" Alex lifted the sword and handed it to Fionn. It felt heavy, but Alex handled it with ease. "It's a family heirloom. It belonged to my great-grandfather. I got it along with his journals in a box after my granddad passed away."

"Did you ever meet the man? What was his name?" Fionn continued as his heart beat like a racehorse. After Ywain had disappeared, he and Izia spent every resource at hand to find him, but to no avail. He was like their little brother and one of the bravest members of the Twelve Swords. Not even Yaha had been found to mark his grave. During the years after Fionn woke up from his 'slumber,' he secretly retained the hope that Ywain had survived and might have found some semblance of peace somewhere else. But tracking that had proved futile, as before.

Yaha, if the legends were true, was the first Tempest Blade to have been forged. It wasn't easy to handle because it seemed to have a mind of its own. Ywain used to talk about it before the battle, and it had never let him down. Having it there was a fortunate coincidence. And yet Fionn didn't believe in those. *I wonder if this was your doing, Izia*, he thought, while briefly looking up as if he could see her in the Last Heaven.

"My great-grandfather, Ywain? No, I never met him. He died before I was born. What I know is he was a reclusive man with health problems and a lousy memory, who couldn't recall much of his early life beyond his name. But he was a kind man," Alex explained with a smile. "Now my yaya, Zyanya, his wife. She was another matter. My grandparents said that she was a tough lady even at her advanced age. She was the one that taught archery to the family. And she loved Ywain with all her heart."

"Are you thinking what I think you are thinking?" Harland murmured. "He might have got a happy ending after all, halfway across an ocean and in another continent."

"I can hope," Fionn rubbed his eyes. "Back to business. Do you know where Hunt could have hidden his notes?"

"If they weren't at his manor," Alex replied, looking at Fionn as if examining him. "He might have stored a copy in his office at Ravenstone. As I said, his assistant might know more. But I don't have access to that place. I don't know anyone that does."

"Don't worry, we know of someone," Harland laughed.

"That's no good, in more ways than one," Fionn exclaimed. The migraine, which had subsided somewhat, was back in full force. This was going to be a really uncomfortable conversation.

"Why?" Gaby asked him quizzically.

"Let's say it is complicated." Fionn smiled ruefully.

"The only issue is that it will take us a while to get there and we are already pressed for time," Harland interjected.

"Sorry to interrupt, but we might know a way to get you there fast, but only if we tag along," Alex added, finishing his burger and turning to Gaby. "Do you think he will agree?"

"Maybe if we can pay him. It won't be cheap though," Gaby told him, making calculations in her head.

"Money is not the objection," Fionn replied, turning to Harland, taking him by surprise.

"Wait, what?"

"If you are sure..." Alex began. He lifted his hand and called the waitress, who arrived with her notepad in hand. "Ok. Please bring me six shell-headed burgers with everything for takeaway." Alex then turned to Fionn and Harland. "Part of the payment."

# Chapter 7
## The Figaro

"Your guy lives here?" Harland asked, looking at the abandoned industrial warehouse sitting in the middle of nowhere. The place was on the outskirts of Lafabra, the town where Mercia University was located. The nearest sign of civilization was a couple of farms more than five kilometers away. And the warehouse looked dilapidated. Whoever lived there wasn't interested in keeping the place in good shape. It made Fionn wonder what kind of transportation Alex could hire here.

They left the car and the trike parked outside the main door of the warehouse, under a group of macabow trees. Several of the trees peppered the terrain, covering the building behind their limbs and foliage. Fionn wasn't surprised to see that a few of the trees were growing through the roof. The warehouse was four or five times longer than most buildings he had seen before, with the exception of the Royal Hangars during the war. Airships weren't common in Theia. The atmospheric characteristics of the planet, including a thick ionosphere that generated severe electric storms, made it difficult for flying ships without the right shielding. Most airships were dirigibles, private enterprises and the few dreadnoughts used during the war. That had been the reason behind the development of the warptrains that crisscrossed the planet. They were a more practical means of transportation than dirigibles, for example.

But the warehouse's appearance didn't give Fionn the feeling that it belonged to a rich dilettante and, certainly, it was not a military installation.

"Sometimes the best way to hide something of value is to make it look like there is nothing of value, and in plain sight," Alex punched a code into a small door's datapad. He waved at a camera barely hidden by a brass bell. The door opened and Alex let them in.

The inside of the warehouse was divided by a wall that separated the living quarters from the larger space behind it. Metallic debris littered the floor, making it look more like a junkyard than living quarters. There was a small loft, held up by wooden posts of dubious structural integrity. Fionn could see a small bed and a fridge in the loft. How it hadn't collapsed was a wonder. The walls were covered with bookshelves and tools of every description and use. But what piqued Fionn's curiosity were the aerial photographs, star and pressure charts, atmospheric ionization measurements, navigation maps and high-altitude topographic maps. None of these could have been taken from a dirigible. And access to the feed of the few satellites was limited. But these were taken and printed recently and bore no mark of who had done it. Only a few countries were rumored to have access to such technology.

Alex guided them through the door that took them to the rest of the warehouse. It had ample room and was filled with more tools, machinery, and right in the center, resting on a couple of metal rails, was a bulky object covered by a massive canvas. It was thirty meters long, almost twenty meters wide and twelve meters high. Fionn was sure that if he stood on top he'd be able to touch the warehouse's roof. It was considerably smaller than a dreadnought but looked heavier than a dirigible.

The four of them were staring at the bulky object, the sunlight entering through the dirty windows, when a shadow moved fast around them, taking Fionn by surprise.

Harland was startled and the sudden movement made him jump backwards. But Alex walked with ease and confidence around the covered object patting it from time to time, releasing a metallic thud. And Gaby was relaxing, taking a seat on a dilapidated sofa, the only piece of furniture in that area. Alex reached one of the ends of the massive object and, from his duffel bag, took out a hamburger he had brought from the diner.

"If you don't get your hard-ass here soon I will eat your burgers," Alex yelled, holding the burger aloft. Soon a blur swung from the loft, hanging from a rope and ending up on top of the bulky object. The burger was gone from Alex's hands, which left Gaby muffling a laugh.

"He always does that," Gaby explained to Fionn and Harland. "Don't worry, he is friendly... in a way."

"More like an acquired taste," Alex added.

"I could say the same about you," a voice behind them said. It had a weird quality but it was not guttural. And it had an uncommon accent, thicker than Alex's. "And you forgot the ketchup, again."

Harland and Fionn turned around to face their host, who promptly struck Harland's face, leaving it dripping red.

"I'm injured!" Harland exclaimed at seeing the red drops falling onto the floor.

"It's ketchup. Geez hoomans," the voice said. "At least your burgers are a delight to die for. I'm Sid, by the way," the small green creature left the ketchup bottle on the floor and offered his open hand to Harland.

"A samoharo?" Fionn muttered. Samoharos rarely left their homeland, with the exception of a few merchants. Their home was the Hegemony, located on the southeastern continent of Ouslis.

Ouslis was located across the Lirian Ocean, separated from the Auris continent by the Slender Sea and the Straits, Alex's homeland. It was said that only samoharo lived there because everything else had evolved to be as lethal as possible to humans and freefolk alike.

It all started to make sense for Fionn. Alex was from the Straits and its inhabitants were on good terms with the samoharo, even adopting some of their customs and beliefs while working as a bridge between the Kuni Empire in Auris and the Hegemony is Ouslis. Fionn then remembered that Alex had mentioned a hunter that had helped them during the incursion. Samoharo hunters were known for being willing to hunt dangerous game. They might be one of the few cultures on the planet that would see an incursion as a challenge or a job rather than a crisis.

He had seen a samoharo once, during the Great War. His name was Sir Lionel the Cursed. He had fought alongside Fionn as a member of the Twelve Swords, the special operations unit that Fionn had led. Sir Lionel had been a *Meemech* samoharo, large and bulky, especially in full armor, close to two meters tall. His reptilian features resembled a humanoid iguana or a gecko with long hair, long fangs, and slit pupils. His tails had been strong enough to smash a tree. However, Sid, slightly taller than Harland but not by much, looked like a mix between an iguana and a turtle. He had a shell-like structure on his back. He also had hair on his head, styled in a mohawk. His humanlike eyes moved fast. His appearance was completed with worn sneakers, short cargo pants and a ragged t-shirt with the logo of a rock band. It was a poor attempt to cover the extensive tribal tattoos covering his shoulders, chest, and back. He was an *Áak* samoharo.

And it clicked for Fionn: This guy had some kind of specially-designed airship hidden under the canvas. But what nagged him was the fact that Sid was resting here, in the middle of the Emerald Island and not half a planet away. The samoharo were secretive with their technology. They had joined the war effort a century ago, when the war escalated, and had helped the Free Alliance. That had helped to even the odds against the Horde. The few samoharos that could be seen from time to time in ports around the world boasted that they were the best navigators in existence. Their legends said that they even navigated the stars eons ago, thanks to their special form of magick known as *wayfinding*. And unlike other reptiles on the planet, samoharo were warm-blooded and knew how to hold a grudge.

Alex and Gaby were acting friendly with Sid, hugging him and laughing at a few jokes. Then Sid got all serious. He was staring at Fionn, examining him. Fionn wasn't bothered by people staring him, but this time it made him feel uneasy. He had seen that kind of look before when someone measures you while planning to kill you. And the description of 'hunter' that Alex gave him took on a new meaning. Whoever Sid was now, he had been an assassin before.

"I have seen Shorty there on the aethernet," Sid pointed at Harland, who was clearly not amused. "But I haven't seen you before. Who are you?"

"My name is Fionn Estel," Fionn replied, not amused either but extending his hand nonetheless.

Sid gave him a good look once more and his eyes opened wide in realization. "Estel? The Greywolf from the war? I thought he was dead. Sir Lionel told us as much. Also that he was shorter," Sid said to Alex with a snigger. "Oh man, Alex, you must be giggling from meeting your childhood hero."

That wasn't the kind of reaction that Fionn had expected either. But he had to admit that it made a nice change; instead of people being wary or scared, Alex, Gaby, and Sid had taken it all in stride. Well, Alex not so much.

"Sorta," Alex replied with anger. He smacked Sid on the head, which started a slap fight between them. It was more comical than serious. Fionn pulled Gaby away, followed by Harland.

"Are they always like this?" Harland asked Gaby.

"Unfortunately, yes. They are like siblings. The same sense of humor, zero mouth filters. I apologize on their behalf."

"Don't worry, I'm used to the dwarf jokes," Harland told her, waving the apology away.

"How do you know him? Seeing a samoharo outside the Hegemony is not common," Fionn said.

"He is the *hunter*," Gaby emphasized that word. "Who helped us during the incursion. It was thanks to him that we made it out alive. From there he became best friends with Alex and taught him how to fight. When Alex moved here he followed, with this whole thing. He is a good person. I trust him with my life."

"What is he doing here? I mean in Ionis, besides building whatever he is building," Harland interjected.

"We don't know the exact details, but apparently he was expelled for disobeying orders. However, he seems to have retained enough clout and money to be left in peace. Apparently, he has a cousin that vouches for him in his homeland."

"Who's that cousin who has such power?" Fionn asked, intrigued.

"Have you heard of Yokoyawa?"

"The current titanfighting champion and a member of the Royal clan?" Harland exclaimed in surprise. Yokoyawa was considered one of the finest warriors the samoharo had, and had been adjunct ambassador to the Free Alliance.

"That one," Gaby stated, looking at Sid, who was still slapping Alex. "I know. Hard to believe."

"Now it all makes sense," Fionn added. Only a former royal clan member would have enough money to finance such a project. "That explains most of the tattoos. Except for the one on the back of his neck."

Fionn pointed at the design on Sid's neck. It looked more like a burn than a tattoo. Gaby paused for a moment, looking at Sid with sadness.

"He doesn't talk much about it. Samoharos have weird rules. It's the mark of his banishment. It covers the mark of his clan. I guess he refused to hunt someone. Sometimes you are forced to do things that you don't want to do, and refusing has consequences," Gaby explained with a tight voice.

"You shouldn't look all gloomy," Fionn replied. "Take it from someone who has been there: Your training doesn't define who you are, it's what you do with it that does. And yesterday you helped a lot of people."

"Thanks," Gaby replied, grabbing his arm and smiling at him. She then left to break up the fight between Sid and Alex.

"Spoken like a true master to his apprentice," Harland murmured to Fionn, standing next to him.

"Stop pushing it, Harland. It's not happening. I won't take a student again," Fionn replied, not amused.

"Bullshit. You helped train the current Dragonking a few years ago. And then there is Sam."

"That's different. I was one of many teachers for the Dragonking. And Sam is family. We are talking about people with the Gift, and you know how it truly ended last time."

"A waste of knowledge, and you know it," Harland replied with anger in his voice. "It's about damn time you get out of your head. These kids are not pampered princes. They can fight, you already saw that. They might be rough around the edges, but with the right guidance they could help. Especially if you are planning to drag them into this."

"I'm not planning to drag them into anything." Fionn trembled in anger. "As soon as we get to Ravenstone and find what we need, I will search for the professor and close the case. Alone. You can take them back home."

"Sometimes I wish I could smack some sense into that thick head of yours," Harland murmured. "For someone who has lived so long, you still have plenty to learn about life."

Fionn glared at Harland. He wasn't in the mood to have that conversation right now.

"Hey, wanna explain why all of you are here?" Sid interrupted them, approaching Fionn. "Because the kiddo is cursing me in my mother tongue, and I suspect this is not a social visit."

"I was going to explain that to you before you tried to be funny," Alex replied.

"Enough from both of you," Gaby exclaimed. Alex and Sid were going to say something but she shushed them.

Sid and Alex remained silent, shuffling their feet, embarrassed like scolded children.

"We need to go to a remote location, fast. As in needing to be there before the nightfall," Fionn explained while Sid looked at Gaby with an eyebrow raised.

"You can trust them as I do. You can show them," Gaby finished, appeasing Sid.

"Wello," Sid said. "You have come to the right place. This is the Figaro." He pulled a rope that lifted the canvas from the bulky object, revealing it to be a ship. "I have been rebuilding it from the carcass of an old mining ship, with the finest of samoharo and hooman technology and a bit of freefolk stuff. They do know their power couplings." Sid was beaming with pride at his work.

The Figaro was unlike any other flying ship Fionn had seen before. It did not have a gas bag like a regular dirigible, but instead had three pairs of wings attached on the right side and three on left side of the fuselage, making it look like a bird... or a dragon. They were currently closed, but judging by the mechanisms, they could fully open once in flight. Behind each wing, on their back edge, were propulsors. On the sides, where the wings joined the fuselage, there were two horizontal exhausts, two meters wide. They opened to reveal several ion turbines in the back end, similar to those used in a warptrain. Both exhausts were large enough that they protruded from the back. Between them, there was a hatch that led to the cargo bay. Smaller thrusters were placed on the rear, belly, and front of the ship.

On the belly, there was an armored cockpit with protruding twin cannons. Similar cannons were placed on the top, in the front, and on the sides of the cockpit. Three massive domes of semi-transparent material could be seen on the top of the ship, two on the rear side and one in the front, near the upper cannon. The front of the ship, where the cockpit was placed, looked eerily similar to the head of a dragon, with a short square snout and glass panels instead of eyes. Below the glass panels, an open mouth was painted with baring teeth. The entire ship had a green and red paint scheme, completing the impression of a dragon.

"This baby runs on a classical samoharo three core engine configuration," Sid started to explain. "Providing it with enough power to reach the upper atmosphere. With the right improvements, it could even reach the Round Moon!"

"It's also capable of vertical lift and has inertial dampeners for those with sensitive stomachs," Alex added.

"Like you," Sid interrupted. "And the cannons have enough power to cut through thick rock and even military grade shielding."

"Mining ship? What kind of mining operation do they have on the Hegemony?" Harland asked, amazed at the sheer magnitude of the ship. "This thing is like a Montoc Dragon. How did you manage to get it built without no one noticing?"

"Who said it was for mining on the planet? And regarding your other question, that's a secret," Sid replied with a grin, or the closest thing a samoharo face allowed, which was him baring his teeth that looked more like the teeth rows of a shark. "So where do you want to go in such a hurry? Warptrains are not fast enough for you?"

"We need to reach Ravenstone as soon as possible. It's an emergency," Fionn explained.

"That place is in the Maze, right? What kind of emergency would make you go there in a hurry?" Sid asked, leaning against his ship.

Fionn showed Sid the damaged circlet. At first, the samoharo examined it in confusion, but then his eyes opened with realization, and he stared at Alex.

"This thing looks like..." Sid started to say.

"The portal we saw ten years ago," Alex finished.

"Someone is planning to do something worse than that and they need the notes from Leo Hunt's research, who, by the way, is missing."

"We don't expect you to help us for free. We can pay you. And by we, I meant the Foundation and by payment, I meant more than just burgers. Upfront, if needed," Fionn added.

"Ahem," Harland cleared his throat and dragged Fionn away. "I need a word with you."

Fionn had to bend forward to be able to listen to the whispers of his friend.

"You can't offer that." Harland was angry.

"Why not? This is to help find one of the researchers you are sponsoring," Fionn replied, confused.

"Because the Foundation is broke," Harland explained, raising his voice. "We were hoping that Hunt's research turned up something that would help us cover the recent losses before he went insane and got kidnapped."

"Why didn't you tell me that? I could have helped. Please tell me you didn't gamble the Foundation away," Fionn replied.

"Of course not, you moron. I haven't gambled since you helped me go clean," Harland replied, smacking Fionn in the head. "It was a couple of rough years, that's all. Let me handle the negotiations, alright? Before you promise to give away my house, too."

Harland walked towards Sid with decisive steps, whistling a tune, confident of being able to deal with a samoharo. Fionn shrugged his shoulders at Alex and Gaby.

"Mister Sid, can I call you that? Do the samoharo have last names? Anyways, the payment will have to wait," Harland explained, embarrassed, while Sid looked at the man. "But I'm sure we can arrange some sort of payment later."

"I'm not sure I wanna risk my ship for promises," Sid replied.

"Think of it, not as a risk, but a test drive. Do it as a favor for me," Gaby walked towards Sid, embracing him, while he had his arms crossed, looking away. She kissed him on the cheek.

"I hate it when you do that, kiddo," Sid told Gaby, freeing himself from the embrace. "Navigating the Maze is a challenge but it is possible, since you are looking at the best pilot in all of Theia. I just need to install something on the ship."

"That's why I love you. What are you going to install?" Gaby asked.

"A prototype of a semi-empathic Artificial Intelligence that a friend of Alex's developed. I'll need it to calculate the different vectors once we enter the Maze."

"AI? I thought no one had developed a trusty AI," Harland said. "They either go insane or can only do specific actions. The Foundation almost went broke funding a research project on AI that ended badly."

Fionn could hear the bitterness in Harland's voice. That a kid in a garage somewhere in the world managed to do what Harland's researchers haven't been able to do didn't sit well with the man.

"Wello, this one here is a semi-empathic, quantum neural pathway, baby!" Sid exclaimed in a way that sounded like it was the most logical thing. "Which means that it reacts similarly to a human mind but is able to handle massive amounts of data in real time without burning out, provided that you allow it to rest from time to time. That said, it is not entirely sentient nor independent, which is why it can't run amok. We still don't know how he created it, but it works."

"Why do you need its help? Didn't you just claim to be the best pilot on Theia?" Harland asked, lifting an eyebrow.

"Being the best pilot doesn't mean being a reckless yahoo. I like to play it safe. The Maze is full of space-time oddities that confuse senses and sensors alike," Sid explained, simulating with his hands the flight of a ship crashing into a wall and then falling in flames. "Why do you think the freefolk built their school there? Because it's the only place where they can practice their arts without blowing up the planet! The AI might improve our chances of getting there on time."

"I will help you," Alex offered. The two of them entered through the cargo bay into the ship.

"At least he didn't nick that AI from a lab." Gaby sighed.

† † †

A few minutes later Alex and Sid came out of the ship, looking miffed.

"I don't know what's going on with that thing," Alex said to Sid while descending from the cargo bay ramp. "Who would have thought that AI had egos?"

"Duh, it's a semi-empathic, quantum neural pathway brain emulator designed by hoomans. Of course, it has an ego," Sid replied, annoyed.

"Problems, gentlemen?" Gaby asked, suppressing a laugh. It was like watching a stand-up comedy routine.

"Nothing that can't be fixed later or prevent us from our trip. Now if you are ready to board, follow me," Sid declared, doing a curtsey.

Gaby led the way, followed by Fionn and Harland. The cargo bay was packed with dozens of crates all tied down with straps and security nets, designed to safely hold fragile cargo. Several large coils of super strength tensile cables, similar to those used by harpoons, were also stored in the bay. Despite the cargo, there was enough space for them to walk around. Coming off the cargo bay was a padded corridor, looking more like a cave tunnel than a straight hallway. Along the corridor, different signs could be seen, both in core language and samoharo, pointing to places such as 'kitchen,' 'living quarters,' 'gunnery station,' 'wayfinding,' and 'lab.' Above a small stair, Sid opened a door, allowing entrance to the cockpit. The thickness of the door surprised Fionn, as it was more akin to that of a military grade shield.

The cockpit was spacious, located in the front of the

ship to allow for a clear view.

"Looks impressive doesn't it?" Sid said.

"How safe is it to have such a wide glass?" Harland asked.

"Quite. It's actually reinforced glassteel screen view mirror, with sliding metal planes to offer an extra layer of protection in case there is a breach. Similar to those of a warptrain, or one of those ancient dreadnoughts. Except that it can work as a display, too. Technology marches on," Sid replied, beaming with pride and a grin that showcased his sharp teeth.

The cockpit had two main chairs, for the captain and the copilot, with four additional chairs lined up behind. One of the second row chairs sat in front of a computer station, a hand written sign above it read "COMM." The chair on the other end of the row sat in front of a similar station, but the sign above it was faded and Fionn couldn't read it. Sid jumped into the captain's chair, the one on the center left from the point of view of the door.

"Strap yourselves in, this will get bumpy," Sid announced with a wide grin, while everybody in the cockpit fastened their seatbelts. Alex, Gaby, and Fionn took the back seats, behind Sid, while Harland had to take the copilot's seat. The Figaro's engines roared, and after a gentle push of the yoke, it started to fly towards the end of the large industrial warehouse. However, the warehouse doors remained closed. The Figaro was approaching them at increasing speed with no sign of slowing down.

"The door is not open. The door is not open!" Harland started to yell, panicking.

"I would be more worried if this thing falls," Fionn said. He was actually enjoying the ride. He wondered if this was how it would have felt to be a Silver Rider during the apogee of the Montoc Dragons and the heroes of yore.

"Relax," Sid said with a dismissive gesture. He pushed a button on the control console and the warehouse doors opened slowly. The Figaro reached the end and crossed the threshold, barely missing the doors by centimeters. Outside, the Figaro followed a metal track that spanned five hundred meters and ended in a curved ramp pointing upwards. The ship used that ramp to clear the surrounding trees and shoot into the sky, the acceleration pushing everybody against their seats. While the rest were feeling a bit dizzy from the push and the speed, Sid acted as if nothing was happening. Fionn wondered if samoharo bodies had evolved to withstand these kinds of exertion. The wings opened fully, expanding. The ion thrusters roared, unleashing their fury to increase the speed.

"Woohoo!" Sid yelled while the Figaro reached cruising altitude. Once there, Sid stabilized the ship and the trip became more comfortable for all the occupants, except for Alex, who was breathing into a paper bag. "Alex, please don't throw up again."

"I don't feel well," Alex mumbled.

While the ship flew at cruising speed, through the screen window Fionn could see tiny houses, roads and warptrain tracks with their light trails. Clouds above them created a maze of light with the sun rays coming through.

"This... this is amazing. The closest thing there is to flying on a dragon," Harland exclaimed, looking through the windows as well.

"Flying is one of the most exciting experiences in life. Hoomans should do it more, if only they wanted to invest in better technology for their ships' shielding instead of those crappy warptrains. Reaching the stars again is a dream," Sid declared proudly, almost wistfully.

"What are you talking about?" Harland asked the samoharo.

"My people came from the stars and have forgotten that, but not me. I didn't build the Figaro to merely fly below the ionosphere," Sid said, proudly. "I plan to make it the first ship on Theia to reach outer space. Then the Moons, both of them, then the stars." Sid explained, pointing to the skies.

"Lofty dreams. Expensive dreams, based on belief," Harland scoffed.

"Sometimes belief is all you need," Gaby replied.

"I have a long lifespan," Sid countered with a dreamy look in his eyes. "I have nothing but time to prove legends right. And if this flight helps me to test some of the new systems, then I will be a step closer." He was still admiring the sky.

"Are you expecting enemy fire?" Fionn asked jokingly, pointing to the button labeled 'Countermeasures.'

"It's Theia. I have learned to expect everything, and you better than anyone should know that," Sid replied teasingly. "Anyhow, we will be at the Maze in a couple of hours. Now if you don't mind, I like to listen to the news while I fly."

Sid turned on the radio, catching the middle of the transmission, the voice of a female newscaster with a posh accent.

"Breaking news, a seventh freefolk settlement, north of Manfeld, has been hit by tragedy. Hundreds are dead after the massive explosion. No groups have taken responsibility for the blast, but anonymous sources within the government have stated this is the work of the New Leadership Party. The NLP has been under increasing pressure from the continental congress for its racist rhetoric. A spokesperson for the NLP has said that, 'all these deadly incidents are the direct result of unsupervised use of magick by the freefolk freaks as they did during the Great War...'"

"That's a lie." Fionn punched a panel in anger, leaving a dent in it. While he had a mixed history with the freefolk, at least from his point of view, they were still part of his heritage. His father had been human, his mother freefolk. Although he had never felt at home with either side, he still cared deeply for both, even if most people thought of him as only human. "Sorry. It's a sensitive topic. I hate that the freefolk get blamed unjustly. The same thing happened during the Great War when they were being used as slaves and weapons against their will. And people often forget that I have freefolk blood too!"

The radio broadcast continued, breaking the uncomfortable silence that Fionn's unexpected outburst had created.

"The NLP leadership headed by Lord Adhemar and Madam Park, contested the accusations of racism by saying that rounding up the freefolk in special camps to be supervised was just a sensible measure to protect humans from potentially dangerous experiments. Both the Royal House and the Kuni Empire ambassador have declined to make any declaration...."

"I think I better put on some music before he punches up all my ship. Suggestions?" Sid asked nervously.

"I have some tracks on my datapad," Harland offered, quickly plugging it into the control console.

# Chapter 8

## Ravenstone

"This is your captain speaking: We have arrived at the Maze. The weather is warm, and a beautiful sunset welcomes us. Please adjust your seatbelts as the ride will get bumpy," Sid said through the audio system of the Figaro.

Fionn took a look through the window, seeing the enormous canyon that formed part of the World's Scar. Unlike most of those with freefolk ancestry or blood, he had barely been in the Maze, one of their sacred places. It wasn't a place he had frequented as much as he should have, even though his mother and grandfather had insisted. The Maze was a holy place for the freefolk, where the different tribes went on pilgrimages with the hope of communing with the Trickster Goddess, the Red and Black Raven. She was one of the Twelve Ancient Gods of Theia, mother of two of the Mortal Gods of Theia and one of the few with actual proof of her existence. She was revered as the patron god of mothers, heroes, magi, and freefolk. And she was known for her peculiar humor, which informed how she taught lessons and helped people in a way they didn't expect.

The Maze was just a small part of the World's Scar, a trench that ran across the lands – and perhaps under the oceans – of the Northern hemisphere, extending from the Yumenomori lands of the western corners of Auris to the eastern limits of the Grasslands beyond Ionis. The legends said that the World's Scar was created when the Trickster Goddess decided to intervene and stop a war, using her full power, almost cracking the planet. The Maze, located in the northeast section of the World's Scar, was where she entered the mortal realm from Last Heaven and where her fabled library, the Ravenhall, might appear to the worthy.

As such, the Maze was one of the weirdest places in Theia. The region around it was surrounded by tightly packed, dense forests and limestone formations, reminiscent of ancient temples built by someone whose sense of dimensions differed from the standard geometrical canons. These structures stood as sentinels, watching over the travelers that crossed it. Whispering Fireflies were a common feature of the forests, their rhythmic chirping conferring on the place an eerily peaceful ambiance to the densely packed red cedar and pine forests surrounding it.

But the most significant characteristic of this ancestral place was the odd way time acted inside it. Some travelers said that crossing the Maze took them several days, while others declared that they were gone for only a few minutes. An unlucky few never got out. Most people from the nearby towns avoided crossing it unless it was needed, forcing most of the trade and travel warptrain routes into longer detours to Portis or Mainfeld and then traveling to the settlements near the Maze on paved roads to find a guide to take them to the northern side, towards the freefolk populated Mistlands. Only some freefolk tribes and powerful wizards dared to live within it.

These anomalies made the Maze the perfect location for a place like Ravenstone. A private school for magi, the practitioners of the magickal crafts. As Sid had pointed out, the space-time oddities of the Maze created the perfect place to practice spells in a safe environment. People knew about the school, but getting there without a natural affinity for magick or a guide was almost impossible.

But with one of the few flying ships in the world, and

a guide that kind of recalled how to get there, reaching the school should be easier, provided that you could navigate the time-space oddities that the Maze threw at your vessel.

"I think I will fly over the Maze and then go down once we reach the school," Sid said.

"To reach Ravenstone you need to go into the Maze. Otherwise you won't find the place," Fionn replied.

"Why? That's bonkers!" Sid exclaimed.

"Consider this: you have young students there, future generations of freefolk, which as a group, have been on the nasty end of aggressions for centuries. It's logical that the school was built to be safe and unapproachable by conventional means or a guide. The spells that protect it keep it hidden from view. Bear in mind that when it was built, people rode dragons. Aerial attacks weren't unheard off."

"I'm not sure that makes one hundred percent sense," Alex interjected.

"I hope you called beforehand to let them know we are on our way," Sid muttered. "I would hate to be shot down by a trigger happy spellcaster."

"They know..." Fionn replied. *I just forgot to tell them how I will be reaching the place.*

"I'd better turn on the AI," Sid said warily, eyeing the canyon while flipping up a few switches before pushing the yoke and steering the Figaro down to enter the Maze.

A small shadow flew out of the corner of Fionn's eye. He turned around to see if anyone else had seen it, but most were busy talking about the limestone peppering the cliffs. Except for Gaby. Her gaze was lost in the horizon and she stood up, walking towards Sid's chair.

"Did you see that black and red raven? Flying alongside us," Gaby asked with a faint voice.

"What raven?" Harland asked.

"That one," Fionn said. He could see it as well, a red and black raven, larger than usual for its species.

"I don't see anything," Sid replied.

Gaby pointed at a spot to the left and in front of the ship.

"I just see a shadow," Alex added.

"Focus your mind, Alex," Fionn advised him. He was seeing the raven through the Gift.

Gaby kept staring at it, her body relaxing. Her eyes were glazed as if entranced by a mysterious force.

"Are you okay, Gaby?" Alex asked her, carefully poking her shoulder, to no avail. The ship started to rock, as if struck by waves from an invisible ocean.

"We are within sight of Ravenstone, but the gravimetric readings are off the chart," Sid said. "I can't seem to find a safe passage and the AI is still processing the data, saying how the hell we are gonna land in there. The forest is too thickly packed for the Figaro."

"The place has a landing platform below the edge, deep into the chasm," Fionn added, pointing to a rendered image of the college appearing in the holographic HUD at the controls. Fionn was nervous, his left leg trembling without pause.

"And how do you know that?" Sid inquired.

"If I recall my history right, the place was already built by the time of the Silver Raiders and the Montoc Dragons, which means that it had landing platforms for them. One of them should be strong enough to bear the weight of the Figaro," Harland said.

"I hope you are right," Sid said with resignation. "Fasten your seatbelts, the ride might prove jumpy if the AI calculations are right."

The Figaro started its descent into the deeper levels of the Maze, soon flying inside the chasm. Sid had to apply himself by dodging the rocks that appeared from nowhere, floating in front of their path. While the AI managed to keep track of the rocks, it also signaled that they were flying upside down and on a collision course with the ground.

"That can't be right, I haven't done a barrel," Sid

exclaimed, starting to push the yoke.

"Wait!" Gaby stopped him, staring at the raven. "It's an illusion."

"Are you sure?" Harland asked nervously.

"Sure," Gaby replied faintly, her mind apparently lost in the flow of time and space. "Let's just follow the raven."

"Not again," Alex mumbled.

"What's going on, Alex?" Fionn asked with growing concern.

"You know about her dreams and visions, right?" Alex said. "Well, she is having one. Sometimes they can get..." Alex grabbed Gaby's hand and paused for a second, looking upward, trying to think of the appropriate word. "Intense. Holding her hand helps her to be at ease."

"This is getting intense, too. The AI can't cope with all the space-time oddities," Sid growled while dodging the rocks. The AI beeped its danger alarm. "If dragons were supposed to fly through this place, I'm not surprised they went extinct."

"Let me," Gaby said quietly, taking her free hand and grabbing Sid's hands. His knuckles were a lighter shade of green because of his tight grip on the yoke. When she put her hands over his, Sid relaxed his grip and allowed Gaby to guide him, requiring less dodging and easing the flight.

"I think she is following the raven vision," Alex explained. "I still can't see anything beyond a shadow, but I can feel it as well."

"How's that possible?" Harland asked, confusion showing on his face.

"The Gift," Fionn shrugged. "Like most oddities in life, you can explain them with the Gift, magick, nanobots or a combination of them."

"Thank Heavens no one has managed to invent time travel," Harland said.

"Actually, under our current understanding of physics, time travel is not possible, not even with magick. See, the issue lies..." Alex started to explain.

"Not now, Alex," Sid cut him off.

Sid let Gaby guide him, following the raven's apparition.

"This place is full of non-Euclidian structures. How do those arcs and angles...? How do those rocks manage to stand or simply float in midair?" Alex pointed out. "The architect had a..."

"Strange sense of perception?" Fionn continued with a chuckle. "That may be the handiwork of the Trickster Goddess. You will enjoy Ravenstone then. Look."

Ravenstone, or better said, the rock it was built upon, appeared in their sight floating in the middle of the canyon.

"How is that possible?" Alex asked, amazed, pressing his face against the window.

"As I said before, it isn't a traditional school," Fionn started to explain. "It was originally built as a seat of government during the times of Queen Khary, back when the freefolk were the most powerful nation on Theia. It's meant to be hard to find. They don't like prying eyes."

"And if I were an arcanotech researcher, this would be a good place to take my projects farther away from unwanted attention," Alex continued, not taking his eyes from the sight.

The school building, more reminiscent of a closed temple or a ziggurat, appeared to be carved into a floating rock, suspended above the chasm of the darkest section of the Maze, crowned by a giant statue of a raven carved from solid stone.

"And the school is not actually floating," Fionn continued. "It is an optical illusion. See below? There is an ancient base of the rock, barely noticeable thanks to a mirage spell. The platform I told you about is located there."

A sound from the comms indicated an incoming transmission.

"*Allushc wydellygh was bork?*" The transmission filled the cockpit with a language that Alex had trouble recognizing.

"Sorry, we don't speak freefolk," Sid replied. The landing

platform was now in sight but the Figaro didn't seem to get closer.

"Allow me," Fionn took the microphone. "*I bork Fionn, Clan Estel, mac cuin Fraog, mac kind Samantha Ambers.*"

"*Llywellyn.* You can land," the voice replied in core tongue.

"Was it so difficult for them to speak Core?" Sid complained while taking back the control of the yoke and starting the landing procedures.

"Like samoharo is easier," Alex replied.

"It's not my fault you have a lousy ear for languages."

Gaby broke out of her reverie, shaking her head. Her eyes returned to their normal state. "Was I too long in a trance?"

"Just enough to help us get here in one piece," Harland replied, placing his hand on her shoulder in a reassuring gesture. "It seems we have a welcome committee waiting for us." He pointed at the landing platform where a group stood waiting, headed by a redheaded woman.

"Who's she?" Alex asked. "Do you know her? She is really pretty."

Fionn felt a knot in his stomach. He wondered if it was due to the woman's presence or Alex's comments about her beauty. Neither of those options sat well with him.

† † †

Alex's eyes didn't depart from the sight of the people gathering around the ship. He focused on the young woman. If he had to guess, she was only a couple of years younger than he and Gaby. She was wearing blue jeans with ripped knees and a flowing violet blouse under a leather jacket, similar to Fionn's. She looked more like a rock musician than a magus. That look made her stand out from the rest of the welcome committee, who wore more traditional magi robes and armor.

There was something familiar about her, about the way she was standing there, her arms crossed, her mouth tightly closed and her eyes full of steely determination. It was a familiar look, but he couldn't place where he had seen it. A lousy memory was a family trait.

"You can disembark through the back, through the cargo bay hatch," Sid unfastened his belt and took something out of a box.

"Aren't you coming?" Alex asked his friend, remaining behind while the rest started to leave the cockpit.

"Nah, I want to work on the AI parameters. They are good, but they will need some improvement for when we leave this place," Sid replied, keying a few strokes into a touchscreen. "But take this." Sid handed Alex a pair of glasses with small earbuds attached to the frame.

"I don't need to wear them. My sight is fine," Alex replied, studying the handmade object.

"Your sight is not fine and you know it. But this is a two-way portable screen. I can send you images along with sound, and what's more important, you can send me images back."

"So you want to see how this place looks on the inside. Where did you get these?" Alex asked, examining the glasses.

"Trade secret. And yes, who wouldn't?" Sid replied, with a smug smile on his face.

"You are not staying for the AI, are you?" Alex looked at his friend quizzically.

"I want to keep the Figaro ready in case things get ugly," Sid explained, resting on the back of his chair.

"You are properly paranoid," Alex told him, shaking his head.

"I prefer the term 'properly prepared,'" Sid countered while attending the console and turning on the sensors of the ship one more time.

Alex left the cockpit and joined the rest in the cargo bay. The hatch slowly descended, allowing artificial light from the platform to fill the space. From there, he could see the young woman standing, barely moving. At her left side was a man, middle-aged but with apparent youthful energy, dressed in long green robes with a golden brocade that barely concealed armor covering his body in small plates, not unlike how a dragon skin should have looked. Around them, were four robed magi, one human holding a grimoire, a freefolk lady with green hair styled in a wild pompadour and pixie ears, a tall, dark-skinned man with a stare that could freeze a lake, and an elderly man whose fingertips sparked.

"This welcoming committee looks not-at-all welcoming," Alex scratched the back of his neck.

The young woman had her arms at her side as if she were ready to quickly draw a pair of guns. She walked towards them. Fionn's left leg was now trembling in a noticeable way, which made Alex nervous. *Who was this person that could rattle the Greywolf so much, the 'one-man' army?*

She ignored Alex and Gaby and hugged Harland, who greeted her with warmth in his voice. Then she stared at Fionn, holding his gaze. He was sweating. Whoever this woman was, Fionn was clearly scared of her.

"Hi, Dad, what do you want here?" She asked in a serious tone, while the man in the green robes could barely contain a laugh.

*Dad? Well, I guess that makes sense.* Alex thought. He wondered if he was allowed to laugh as well. Right now, he could use a restroom.

† † †

"Hi, munchkin," Fionn awkwardly hugged the woman in front of him. His daughter was nearly as tall as he was. Her skin was a lighter shade of olive, peppered with freckles. But her most noticeable feature was the pair of big, expressive green eyes above the freckled cheeks that gave her a playful look. Her accent was thick and emphatic, without many of the verbal ticks Fionn had.

At Fionn's initial touch the woman had been stiff, reluctant to acknowledge the contact. But slowly, as Fionn continued to hold onto her, the woman melted into the arms of her father.

"I hate it when you use that nickname," she told him, pulling back, her face still sporting a serious expression. Alex could now see that around her neck, she wore a thin silver chain from which hung a pendant made of a purple, quartz-like crystal held by a three-fingered dragon's claw made of silver.

"Ok, ok, sorry. How are you, Sam? Or do you prefer Samantha now?" Fionn asked, messing the hair on the back of his head, trying to regain his composure and failing miserably. Alex shared a look with Gaby and saw her smiling.

"Fine, but right now it seems that's the last of your concerns," Sam replied with a serious voice. It was then that the man in the green robes closed the gap and reached Fionn and Sam, extending a hand towards the former.

"That's the Dragonking, the highest-ranking member of the freefolk hierarchy when it comes to studying magick," Harland explained, whispering to Alex and Gaby. "And the headmaster of the school. The rest must be the school council. Something must be happening for all of them to be here ready to blast us. Don't say anything unless you are asked. Let us do the talking."

Harland walked away, towards where Fionn, Sam, and the Dragonking were standing.

"Good thing Sid stayed on the ship then," Alex whispered to Gaby, who suppressed a laugh.

"Welcome, Greywolf. I didn't expect to see you in this fashion or in such a strange ship." The Dragonking embraced Fionn, as if they were old friends, and then pointed to Gaby and Alex. "Who are your companions that carry weapons into my school?"

Alex felt sweat beads rolling down his back. The last

thing we wanted was to be the target of unfriendly magi. He had heard nasty comments regarding a 'disintegration spell.' They had given him nightmares.

"I wish it were under better circumstances, old friend. I assume you know why am here?" Fionn replied.

"Aye," the Dragonking nodded.

Fionn then pointed to where Alex, Gaby, and Harland were standing. "They are Gabriella Galfano and Alex León. They are helping me with the matter at hand. Let's just say they are deputized Justicars, hence the weapons. And I assume you remember Harland."

"Of course." The Dragonking bent forward slightly, to offer a handshake to Harland, in deference to his physical stature. "I apologize for the reception. But as you must have heard, freefolk all over the continent have been attacked. We have young kids here, hence the extra precaution."

"We understand, m'lord. The Foundation vouches for them and the pilot of our transportation," Harland replied with a smile.

"That's the highest recommendation. We accept it; I just request you don't draw your weapons inside these halls for our *and* your safety. The security measures of the building might not be so aware of your intentions." The Dragonking pointed to the several wooden totems that decorated the building while leading them inside.

He signaled to the council members and they relaxed. However, none of them moved from their spots. Instead, they pointed at the Figaro and talked in hushed whispers in the freefolk tongue. The Dragonking led Fionn and the others inside the premises. Once inside, the Dragonking continued. "Now, regarding pressing matters. We are as worried as you are about Professor Hunt's whereabouts. You are welcome to look around his office if that helps to find him."

"It's my office too," Sam mumbled.

"That's accommodating," Alex murmured to Gaby. He had failed to notice that Sam was walking next to him. She gave him a quizzical look, to which he responded with a nervous smile. She looked at Alex the same way Fionn had when they were at the coffee shop. As if she was examining him. But whereas Fionn was intimidating, she was unnerving.

"Dad's a Justicar and is well-known by the Dragonking and the freefolk," Sam explained. "So I know why he's here. But why are you here? I think I remember hearing your name before. The professor spoke highly of you, but I don't see why."

"Wait a minute," Alex said. He had just realized something. "*You* are his assistant? You hung up on me once!"

"I'm not his 'assistant,'" Sam replied, making air quotes. "I'm a junior research partner and doctoral student. And if I hung up on you it was because we were busy."

"That's not an apology."

"Who said it was?" Sam left Alex in silence. She had a smug smile on her face while leaving them behind. Sam moved to the front of the line, alongside her dad and Harland.

"Seems that you have finally met your match." Gaby laughed.

"She is really pretty," Alex replied, smiling too. Now he understood the meaning of 'feeling butterflies in the belly.'

† † †

The walk towards the professor's office was a long journey, requiring climbing up several flights of stairs. The school seemed bigger inside than outside. Once they arrived at the main floor, they saw a massive hall spread out in front of them. In the middle of the hall there was a large, circular promenade surrounded by a pond full of fish that connected to the other hallways by bridges. The edges of the promenade, as well as its walls, were decorated with bushes and flowers of colors not commonly seen in nature, at least not in regions lacking magick energies. In the middle of the circle, there was a shiny, metal sphere, the size of a small vehicle, floating on top of a fountain. Its silvery surface reflected everything, including the light filtered by the tempered glass that entered through a tunnel that descended from the roof.

The fountain was surrounded by carvings on the floor, which glowed with a faint yellow light. Above the sphere floated a pair of concentric circles crossed by four beams of the same yellowish light. More runes floated inside the circles. Everything put together had the appearance of a sigil or a seal. The halls were decorated with wooden totems of different mythical creatures: the dragonwolf, the Montoc Dragons, the Feathered Serpent of the samoharo, the hawkdove, the wingedlion, the silverfox, and the raven, amongst others. All of them were sculpted from the same silvery metal of the sphere but had their features enhanced with golden decals. They gazed at the visitors with stern looks on their faces.

*I bet those totems are the security measures that the Dragonking mentioned*, Alex thought, admiring their craftsmanship as they walked past the massive totems and out of the hall. There were no signs that they had been carved with tools of any kind. *Maybe the freefolk made them through magick?*

It was the first time that Alex had been so close to the freefolk culture. Back at his natal land, the freefolk presence was minimal, instead replaced by the samoharo culture, which had mixed with his own after centuries, or the culture from the Kuni Empire.

While the walls of the building were made of stone, the wide rooms they walked through featured wooden poles, beams and walls covered with lush vines. Tribal paintings done in leather canvas, depicting the different freefolk clans and their story, decorated the free spaces between vines and walls. The air smelled of red oak, maple syrup and incense. Light was provided either by cleverly hidden skylights or luminous quartz orbs. It was a relaxing environment.

The entrances to the offices of the teaching staff were

located after the research labs. They were accessed by going up a broad staircase. The entrance door to the offices section opened to the sides, like an elevator door. In front of it, a marquee with luminous letters provided general messages to the students, staff, and teachers. The hallway for the offices was narrower than the wide-open spaces of before, full of doors whose design and material seemed more linked to the user's personality than a concerted design effort. Departing from the traditional wood, one door seemed to be made of living, sentient ivy and another was of marble with engravings of spirits dancing on the surface.

They finally reached the last office of the corridor. An oak door barred access to it. On the door were two metal plates indicating who worked there: Prof. Leonard Hunt, arcano-researcher, and Samantha Ambers-Estel, junior researcher, teacher and postgrad student. Alex paused a bit. Maybe he could ask some of the nagging questions he had when it came to magick. But he needed to get her somewhere else. He doubted she would be so accommodating with the Dragonking or her dad around. Fionn hadn't let him out of his sight, and he looked uncomfortable. It was the kind of look Alex had known before: an overprotective father.

"Well, I'll leave you to it," the Dragonking said. "Let me know if you need any extra help. Heavens knows that the professor is not the most organized man in the world."

"I tried to reign in his worse habits," Sam said defensively, but the Dragonking was leaving already.

Sam opened the door. The smell of paper and humidity invaded their noses. There was a faint smell of incense, probably an influence from Sam. To Alex, the space seemed quite similar to the office Hunt had at Mercia University, full of leather-bound books and ship diagrams, including one of a dreadnought from the Great War. His desk was littered with data crystals.

On a bookshelf, there were the familiar statues and a few trophies from sagewar tournaments. Alex smiled with fondness at them. It was at one of those tournaments where he had first met his former mentor. Alex still kept in his bookcase the figure Hunt had given him after trouncing Alex's 'army' during a game. The figure was meant to remind him to learn from his mistakes and enjoy the games. It had been a token of friendship as well. Alex could only hope that the professor was still alive.

"I'm hungry," Alex said out of the blue.

"You always are." Gaby rolled her eyes.

"It's not my fault that my body needs the calorie intake," Alex complained with a pout. Gaby only shook her head in disappointment.

"Let's go, I will show you the cafeteria," Sam said to Alex, grabbing his arm. Then she stopped and said to her dad, "Unless you need me for this, Dad. This is my office, too."

"I think I have it covered," Fionn replied with a smile, but Samantha's dour expression didn't change. She walked away, pulling Alex's arm with strength.

"I'll go with them. I need a drink and you need better parenting skills," Harland added, following Sam and Alex.

††††

Sam, Alex, and Harland sat at a table in the cafeteria. The place was large, designed more like a food court from a shopping mall than a school cafeteria. It had, however, large drawings of many of the cities from across Ionis, and a few from the Kuni Empire and the Straits. They piqued Alex's curiosity because they were top views of the cities. They weren't traditional urban blueprints, but sketches focused on the roads inside the cities. Alex wondered how those drawings were made. At first, he considered that they were the works of dragon riders. However, there were drawings of modern cities such as Saint Lucy, the capital of the Emerald Island, whose current configuration had been built more recently, centuries after the dragon time.

"The cafeteria is empty right now because most of the students are on holiday, and the few remaining ones are in elective courses. What's with the glasses? You look like a total dork." Sam pointed at Alex, eliciting a laugh from Harland. Samantha, unlike Fionn, was direct and didn't mince words.

"It's just temporary," Alex replied, somewhat offended. "Can I ask you a question, Sam? An honest question?"

"Yeah?" Sam replied doubtfully.

"Why is your hair glowing and changing color?" Alex pointed at her head,

"What?" Sam replied in a higher pitch. She grabbed a strand of her hair and saw her previously lustrous red hair was changing in swirling waves to a bright lilac and back to red. Embarrassed, she took a knitted cap out from the inner pocket of her jacket and put it on, tucking her hair inside to hide it. Alex saw that she was clearly embarrassed, as her cheeks were turning red. "You shouldn't have seen this."

"Sam, I think you can tell him," Harland told her with a reassuring tone. "He won't mock you. I'm sure."

"Do you promise not to laugh?" Sam asked coyly to Alex, looking intimidated for the first time.

"I promise. Cross my heart," Alex replied with a smile, making a cross in front of his chest with his right index finger. "Is it a magick spell?"

"No. It is... how can I explain it? It is like an allergic reaction," Sam started to reply, trying to think of an appropriate answer, while Harland watched, amused by the exchange.

"To what? Peanuts?" Alex asked, confused.

"No, silly. To magick energy," Sam replied, laughing. Her shoulders relaxed.

"You will need to elaborate because you lost me there." Alex made a gesture with his hands, asking for more explanations. The waiter brought them a pizza topped with applelime and pepperoni slices. Alex helped himself to the largest slice.

"Regular mortal bodies are not exactly designed to handle magick energies well, although freefolk have a natural endurance to withstand them longer than humans, because at the beginning, during the Dawn Age, we were shapeshifters. Now, once those energies run through your body, they start altering it, even at a genetic level. At times, it is something minor, like eye or hair color, and the changes don't last long. But for people that live in a magickal nexus or cast massive spells, the changes are permanent and even inherited. Like the pointed ears or peculiar hair color that many freefolk have," Sam explained. "The same can happen to humans with time, and if they survive long enough. After all, freefolk and humans are now similar in all but one aspect: natural attunement to magick."

"There are worse effects than what she has mentioned. Severe cases when they end up transformed into metallic statues or animals permanently," Harland added.

"So anyone using magick can get those features?" Alex asked.

"It is not that simple. Not everybody can handle magick energies. Most freefolk can, but not all. There are few humans with a natural inclination to magick, but others have been studying for decades how to cast a few mirages and most can barely harness or feel the energies. To compensate for that, most learned wizards use staffs, grimoires, pendants, stuff to channel the energy. Magi like me, or many of the freefolk, have a genetic trait that allows us to eschew that and use our own bodies. And even then we use some crystal or staff to regulate the energy," Sam added to her explanation while pointing at the crystal hanging from her neck. "That's dangerous too. Crystals like my pendant tend to resonate with them as if they were entangled with each other. Too much magick and everything will blow up in a chain reaction. Then again, the crystals are useful for other things such as power couplings, fuses, and tracking devices. We have plenty here. The whole Maze is full of them."

"It sounds as if magick acted similarly to radiation or the warp energies... Wait a minute, can you ride a warptrain?" Alex asked.

"Yes, but I hate those things because I get all sick and my hair changes. And if I'm not careful, other things happen. I tend to stay in the cabin, bored out of my mind..."

"What else can happen?" Alex bent forward in a conspiring attitude, giving Sam more privacy.

Sam was embarrassed, her cheeks turning as red as the pizza sauce.

"My ears transform into silver fox ears," she said while looking at the floor.

"I bet you look cute with them," Alex replied, reassuring her. He was keeping his promise of not making fun of her. Besides, he did find the image of her wearing fox ears cute.

"Thanks," Sam said, her cheeks flushing with blood. Harland stifled a laugh.

"So back to the topic, warptrains run with magick energies?" Alex asked.

"That's the common agreement, yes. Hence the development of something as stupid as arcanotech. Using ancient knowledge to develop trains. You can thank Mykir for that. That's why freefolk stay away from civilization as much as possible." Sam shook her head in disappointment.

"I can't argue with that." Alex rubbed his chin. "And I studied that subject in college. Anyway, so if magick acts like a radiation field, it should follow the same rules of energy conservation... But how would that explain a disintegration spell, for example?"

"Look. Magick, for all its potency, has to follow simple universal rules. Like the energy conservation law you mentioned. You can't create nor destroy energy or matter, just change it," Sam explained plainly.

"So, following that, there is no such thing as a disintegration spell?" Alex asked.

"No, instead, it's actually just a teleportation spell used

in a creative way." Sam smiled.

"You don't teleport the whole subject at the same time to the same place... That must hurt." Alex grimaced at the thought of having his limbs ending up half a planet away from his torso, or worse.

"It is also the number-one cause of death of many rookies working magick," Sam added, stealing a bite from Alex's pizza.

"Your craft sounds more complicated than I thought. It is as if a magick user is warping reality using high energies while their brain is calculating thousands of quantum states," Alex reasoned, after a while.

"That's why I believe that arcanotech is to magick what engineering is to quantum physics. Not even in the same league of understanding," Sam replied with smug satisfaction.

"What about spells?" Alex asked her. "How they do work? They must have rules too. I have seen your spell books. They look complicated."

"Well, it works in rules of three. Three types of magick, three levels and three types of characteristics," Sam said.

"Go on," Alex said.

"There is divine magick, the one that the priests use by asking boons from the Great Spirit, the Old Gods or even the few Mortal ones that can do it. There is natural magick, the one that draws from the magick field of the planet using spells or raw power. And demonic, that one is self-explanatory. Then you have spells of the first level that require massive preparations and rituals, a second level that uses incantations and gestures, and the third level, the toughest one to achieve: It is when you simply think and then reality warps." Sam paused to catch her breath. "It is said among the freefolk that you get only one true third level spell and that reflects your inner nature."

"Makes sense. And the characteristics?" Alex prodded further.

"Easy: range, duration, and intensity. You usually can focus on one, maybe two of them. Only dragons and mythic people like the Akeleth or Queen Khary could use spells of great range and power that lasted more than a day. A regular spell at most lasts a few hours, and has a range of no more than thirty meters, and the more intense it is, the more explosive the backlash is. Reality doesn't like being played with."

"I have to admit that I find it really fascinating," Alex said, his face sporting a look of happiness. He was enjoying this explanation. "Usually, no one back at the university elaborated beyond the basic tenets of magick, even when dealing with arcano-research: Magick doesn't make sense and it's explosive."

"Thanks," Sam said out of the blue.

"For what?" Alex looked at her confused.

"For actually listening and for not making fun of my condition," Sam replied, smiling at Alex.

"Hey, trust me, I know a thing or two about being mocked," Alex replied. After a brief pause, he continued, "I was wondering, and sorry if this is too intrusive, but I couldn't help noticing. Why the cold shoulder with your dad? Was he a bad dad? Actually, how come he is your dad? You don't look older than me. How old are you?"

"Oh boy," Harland exclaimed. Until then he had remained silent, just watching and listening.

"Did I ask something I shouldn't have?"

"Nah, it's ok. Unlike my dad, I do talk about these things," Sam said. "I'm twenty-two. I'm his great-granddaughter. He and his wife Izia had a daughter before disappearing. After his return to the land of the unfrozen, he adopted me. I was a child then... And before you ask, he is a great dad, the best I could ask for. Just that in recent years he has been retreating from the world."

"That's true," Harland added. "I have tried to force him out of that funk. I'm still surprised he took this case."

"I don't know," Sam continued. "Maybe I remind him a lot of Izia. Maybe the memories are hard to cope with. Maybe it is hard to explain why he doesn't look a day older than thirty-three. But in any case, it hurts when someone you care for rejects you."

"I know the feeling. Dysfunctional families are the rage now," Alex replied, looking dejected.

"That's why you moved to Mercia?" Sam asked.

"How do you know that?" Alex asked, surprised.

"The professor told me about it."

"Do you believe it?"

"My paternal figure is a man with regeneration powers that was born a century and a half ago. I work in a school full of arcane secrets. And you arrived on a flying ship with a samoharo in the cockpit. What do you think? An incursion wouldn't be out of the question," Sam replied.

"Thanks for believing me," Alex said.

"You are welcome, geek," Sam teased him.

"I think it is time to get back," Harland stood up. The three of them walked back to the professor's office. When they walked past the map of Saint Lucy, Alex stopped there. The layout of the roads, as drawn on the map, reminded him of the magick sigils that decorated the walls of the school.

"Funny map," Alex pointed to the map. "Saint Lucy seen from above, as in that map, looks like the sigils decorating this place. With the three crystal obelisks in the middle. Like an antenna..." Alex stopped as his eyes opened wide as a saucer. It suddenly dawned on him. The diagram followed the same circuit principles of the circlet. It was a summoning sigil. But the batteries stolen from the labs wouldn't be enough to empower that. They needed more than that, and someone who could guide the energies. And the Maze was the perfect place to find both.

"What are you thinking?" Harland asked, concerned. Just then, the school's floor shook, as if a minor earthquake had happened. This was followed by another, and the sound of explosions on the outside could be heard thanks to the echo of the halls.

"That you haven't been following clues, but were lured here..." Alex explained as he tilted his head to the right as if trying to hear something. "Yeah, I'm hearing you."

"With whom are you talking?" Sam asked, intrigued.

"My friend, the ship's pilot. He is sending me images through the lenses," Alex explained, pointing to them.

"You've been spying on the school! Never mind, I need to know what is going on." Sam said, biting her lips. Dust fell from the ceiling and the whole place shook with a loud boom echoing through the halls.

"Aww crap. I can't believe it!" Alex exclaimed. "He says that it's a dreadnought!"

"How in the Pits did a massive thing like a dreadnought manage to enter the Maze? We had troubles and the Figaro is way smaller," Harland said, surprised.

"I have no idea. Some kind of magickal protection perhaps. Good construction quality... who cares? The problem is that it's attacking the school!"

"If that were true, the alarms would have gone off by now," Sam stated, sure of herself, but the constant biting of her lips betrayed her concern. It was then that the alarms of the school blared at full volume.

"Don't you hate it when that happens?" Harland told Sam, clearly not amused.

† † †

Fionn and Gaby had gone over Hunt's office several times, without any luck. The clutter taking up most of the space was a stark contrast to Sam's desk, which was an example of order and discipline.

"Seems that Sam is very strict and disciplined," Gaby said, looking through Hunt's bookcase, while Fionn examined the desk with the pile of papers on it.

"Only at work. Trust me, she can be a handful outside of here. I don't know where she got her rebellious streak," Fionn replied, distracted.

"It might run in the family if half of what the books say about you is true. How old is she, by the way?" Gaby asked while reaching for a leather-bound book with the title of 'Sunny Days at Belfrost' on its cover.

"Twenty-two. She is technically my great-granddaughter, but I adopted her when her parents died," Fionn replied, while he admired the detailed map Hunt had drawn of the Ionis continent, marking the places where the major battles of the Great War had taken place. "But she reminds me so much of my baby girl. My actual daughter, her grandmother. It breaks my heart that I wasn't able to watch my daughter grow up..."

Fionn let out a long sigh.

"And I take it that's why you haven't visited her much lately." Gaby handed the book to Fionn. "Check the title. Belfrost is high in the mountains; there are no sunny days there. This is something else."

"It gets painful at times. I missed so much while trapped in that freezing spell for years, until Harland's dad found me," Fionn turned the pages of the book. The writing was not clear and the latter pages seemed to have been done in a hurry.

"I'm so sorry about that," Gaby told him, feeling compassion for him. "Was Izia with you when it happened?"

"Yes and no, she was the one casting the spell after she barely managed to seal off an incredibly powerful monster. The place was collapsing and we were being buried alive in snow. She used her last spell to save me, while I was healing a wound that went from here," Fionn pointed at his belly button, then he crossed his whole torso until stopping at his chin. "To here. If it weren't for that I would have died too. The injury was so bad that I couldn't move. She not only saved me but the whole world. And I couldn't save her. That's my biggest regret. At the most crucial moment, I failed her. Sam reminds me so much of her that it hurts too much."

Fionn let his body fall on the couch, the only piece of furniture not covered by documents. Gaby sat next to him and hugged him. She couldn't even imagine the guilt and pain he had suffered.

"I love Sam to bits. Being her father allowed me to recover a part of myself I thought I had lost forever. And she really helped me adapt to this new age. She is a bright kid. But I admit, between being depressed and the adjustment, I wasn't the happiest dad to be around and she deserves much more. That's why she came here." Fionn looked around, dejected.

"Talking to someone who has had a toxic relationship with her father, I don't think she thinks the same as you. She does seem to love you as well. But I bet she resents that you haven't kept in touch with her more," Gaby held one of his arms. "You need to fix that before it is too late. Trust me, I know about dysfunctional father-daughter relationships and yours can still be fixed."

"Thanks." Fionn smiled at Gaby. "I take it that you were enrolled at the Sisters of Mercy by said father?"

"It is more complicated than that. But I will tell you my story once this whole thing is solved and we have found the professor."

The floor trembled.

"That was odd," Gaby murmured.

"About that..." Fionn started to say, but Gaby placed her index finger on his lips and got closer to him. Then she took the book in her hands once more.

"I have an idea of what this is." Gaby pointed to a drawing on one of its pages. "I think the professor hid his journal inside this fake cover."

"These scribbles are similar to the one found on the floor at his manor," Fionn compared it with the ripped page he had taken with him from the manor.

"He might have made copies."

"He wrote all by hand. That is a lot of work to create copies. It's safer that way, I guess, but his penmanship leaves a lot to be desired," Fionn said ruefully.

"It's not lousy penmanship, it's a code. I can read it." Gaby smiled, putting the book on the desk. She turned on a lamp to have better illumination to examine it.

"Can you?" Fionn asked, surprised.

"The Sisters of Mercy force you to learn how to read coded manuscripts in poor handwriting. Part of the trade of being a spy," Gaby replied. "Hunt is clever but he is also absent-minded. He'd have to use a simple code to keep track."

Gaby looked around and saw the Great War map that Fionn had been admiring. And then she realized. The map was placed just in front of Hunt's desk, across the room. It was the perfect place to look at the map discreetly and at a distance. She got closer to the map. On it, there were scribbles that seemed to make no sense but were placed in front of the map's coordinate grid points.

"See? He hid the code in this map. Not that hard if you know where to look. Wanna talk about lousy handwriting, you should see Alex's. He writes like a six-year-old with a broken left hand."

"Somehow I'm not surprised," Fionn said. "You are quite the detective. What does it say?"

"He talks about his travels in recent years. Whatever he found during them unnerved him, as his notes become more hurried. There are lines about a group working for some nefarious end. He then mentions a creature named the 'Bestial of Ulmo.' Does that ring a bell?" Gaby asked, confused.

"It's an old freefolk legend," Fionn explained. "Ulmo was the first kingdom of the freefolk. It was also the last one, after the times of the Silver Riders. It got into a conflict with the Asurians, which soon escalated into a full transcontinental war. The Great War paled in comparison to what the legend says. Anyways, it got so bad that both sides used more extreme tactics, forcing the last of the Montoc Dragons to intervene. However, the Asurians summoned one of the strange deities, the Bestial. They didn't realize that summoning a creature of destruction was a bad idea. It destroyed them first, then killed most of the dragons and then went after Ulmo, totaling the place. The last of them, the one named Black Fang, fought the Bestial until it managed to send the creature into some other dimension, or maybe even outer space, nobody is sure where, before dying. But by then Ulmo was gone, like its rivals. It marked the end of the freefolk domination on Ionis at least."

"Wait a minute, Black Fang? As in your sword?" The floor trembled once more. "Did you feel that?" Gaby asked.

"Yes," Fionn replied, he looked around, but nothing was moving, concern grew in his face. "Anyways, yes, the dragon's giant fang was forged into it after his death," Fionn touched his sword as he talked about it. "And then the Trickster Goddess dropped it into a lake near Skarabear, where Izia and I grew up, for safekeeping till the time it accepted an owner."

"This is too much of a coincidence then," Gaby said. "Because Hunt wrote that someone is planning to summon the Bestial again and use it as a key to open the door." Gaby pointed at something on the page.

"A door to where?"

"It doesn't say. It does say, however, that the key needs a will, a master to rule it and that the group will ensure one is created in the Bestial and its rider. He also mentions the need for a freefolk caster to empower the spell. He then wrote down the name of the group: The Fraternity of Gadol?" Gaby looked at Fionn.

"I haven't heard that name in ages," Fionn replied, standing up. He looked tense, walking around the office as if he was a caged animal. "If I recall correctly, it was an old, mystery cult, originated in the Empire of Asuria, where Meteora stands now. The cult resurfaced during the war. It was the sacred mission of the Masters of the Infinity Pits to fight against the children of the Akeleth, their enemies. We believed that they were the true power behind the Blood Horde but never found proof. They disappeared after the real end of the war."

"Real end?"

"It's a long story. Why I didn't think of it before?" Fionn pinched the bridge of his nose. "It's too obvious."

"Maybe because you have been trying to repress those memories. Sometimes the obvious escape our minds when we are too emotionally close to it." Gaby rested her hand on Fionn's shoulder. "Besides, you were disconnected from everything."

Both remained quiet for a few minutes. Gaby was trying to wrap her mind around Fionn's whole story. How much of the world's fast progress had he missed? How many places had he never visited? How much of his family's lives had he missed? Gaby's heart filled with sadness and concern for him. She had seen what depression and mental trauma could do to a person, every day, with her and with Alex. How Fionn hadn't gone insane was either credit to the spell Izia cast out of love, or to Fionn's willpower. Now she understood why Fionn acted the way he did and why he had insisted they remain on the Figaro. Why he was so protective of Sam and Harland. He had lost everything and everyone in his life once before.

The floor trembled a third time, breaking them out of their reverie.

"I felt that," Fionn broke the silence. "We should hurry. Is there something else in his notes?"

"Just that the NPL might be a front for that cult. He wrote: 'NPL a front for Fraternity of Gadol?? Need to learn more about NPL leaders! Doctor (?), did he perform surgery on his own children? How did he die? Did he actually die? Something escaped Carpadocci three generations ago. His first experiment? Was that related to the Fraternity? Madam

Park is key.'" Gaby showed Fionn the photo of a lady dressed in the typical gala Kuni robes at a fundraiser. "He added a photo of her. And he also mentions the word Tovainar. I don't know that word," Gaby continued

"If I recall correctly, it's a word from an ancient tongue, meaning 'Harbinger,'" Fionn said. "As in harbinger of the Masters."

Gaby continued, "Hunt wrote the following entry, dated three months before his disappearance that there will be five of them. 'One seems to have been awakened decades ago, but I can't find evidence of activity. Maybe it failed or went into torpor? There is a second one, of which they recently found its location. They plan to awaken it in the coming weeks. It is trapped in a place named Lemast. Why does that name sounds familiar? Need to ask Sam about that urban legend related to her family.'" Gaby paused. "The last entry here is just a few coordinates, and the words 'Withered King' next to a drawing that looks like a..." Gaby said before Fionn interrupted her.

"An ox with red eyes as a symbol?"

"Yes, how do you know that?"

"That's the monster Izia sealed away. And it's free again. We need to warn everybody," Fionn told Gaby, grabbing her by the arm and running towards the door. A bigger tremor shook the office, making them both falter in their step. Fionn helped Gaby to remain steady. The office door opened and both Gaby and Fionn reacted by getting into combat stances, drawing their swords. Both relaxed when they saw Alex, Sam, and Harland, out of breath, entering the office.

"We might have a problem. A big one," Harland said.

"Not as big as the one we will have later," Fionn said.

# Chapter 9

## Can't Catch a Breath

"I hate it when this happens," Sid complained through the comms. He pushed the yoke wildly from left to right and left again, all while the ship's alarm blared. The Figaro jumped, jolted from an impact that shook the cockpit.

"Sorry about that, Miss," Sid said to his companion. In the seat next to him, the female magus with the green hair lay unconscious. She remained in place thanks to the belts holding her tightly against the seat. Her emerald hair and clothes were burnt at the edges, and beneath the damaged threads, burns peppered her skin. "I can't catch a breath here!"

"What's going on?" Alex's voice could be heard, breathing heavily. Sid suspected that he had been running.

"I'm under attack, genius," Sid replied, pulling the yoke to evade falling debris. It hit one of the drones, which went up in flames in a tiny explosion.

"Someone is invading the school, I guess both of us are under attack. What happened there?"

"Ha, ha, very funny. I was relaxing, enjoying your feed when the proximity sensors went off. The energy readings were off the chart for most human vessels that I know of. I had a bad feeling about that, so I called through the speakers to the magi that were guarding the platform, to show them the readings. The lady with green hair saw them and was on her way out to alert the other magus when a barrage obliterated the platform, killing most of them. I managed to pick up the lady before the platform collapsed, but she is badly injured and unconscious. We barely escaped the second round of fire. So now I'm flying for my life, dodging what I assume are drones shooting at me." Lights on the console flickered when the Figaro got hit by another shot. Behind it, there were still five drones, heavily armed, trailing the ship like hounds to their prey.

"Drones?"

"Yes, drones! Now tell me what the hell is going on!" Sid yelled at the comms, barreling down to pass under a limestone arch. The whole place didn't make any geometrical sense for him, so he was flying the Figaro more by instinct than by following a particular plan of action. Even the AI had conceded defeat and was just focusing on helping dodge the floating debris.

"Harland says that it's an old flying fortress built during the Great War. They were decommissioned and buried in a secret place in the Grasslands. Only the royal family knew the exact location..." Alex started to explain.

"Tell him to spare me the history class," Sid cut him short while pushing the throttle forward; the Figaro needed more speed to have any hope of getting out of the Maze. And yet it seemed that the edge of the canyon was out of reach. This was proving to be quite a test of his abilities as a pilot.

"Long story short. The evil guys that kidnapped Hunt are attacking this place and shooting everything in sight. We need to escape. It might have been a trap."

"Really? I thought you were gonna do the idiot thing of fighting them," Sid said nonchalantly. He knew that his friend had the proclivity of doing stupid things when facing a fight.

"Well it's that or inviting them for tea," Alex replied, amused.

"That's amusing. Almost as much as trying to shake

these drones from my tail," Sid replied. The AI was having problems locking on the targets for the rear blasters. If he managed to get the Figaro out in one piece from this, he would work on that AI to teach it to deal with spatial distortions.

"The Maze is full of random gravimetric waves, use them to your favor," Alex replied.

"The drones are more maneuverable," Sid explained, annoyed. "No one likes backseat driving!"

"Hey, I'm just trying to help. Besides, the Figaro has more power and is sturdier. You can compensate. Think of this as a test run."

"Again with that! If I manage to get out alive from this I will give you a test run! Find me a place to pick you up," Sid said. Then he muttered. "B'ax"

"Sam says that there is a second service platform a few levels below. We will meet you there. Try to stay in the air a bit longer."

"What the frig you think I'm trying to do! Get to that platform before I decide to leave you behind, smartass!" Sid barked at Alex.

"I'm working on that," Alex replied before cutting the communication line.

"I'm working on that," Sid said, mocking Alex's words. "This is what I get for helping people I don't even know. When am I gonna learn?"

The sensors blared once more, alerting Sid of an incoming gravimetric wave. In front of him, floating, there was a cluster of limestone debris from what he assumed had been a garrison perched on a wall of the canyon. He considering evading it, but then, against his better judgment, he pushed forward, reluctantly following Alex's advice. The Figaro rocked, the unconscious magus jolted in the seat, the belt barely holding her in place. Sid felt the pounding that his vertebrae were enduring. It was then that he thanked the Prophet that his species was able to withstand the pummeling associated with traveling in a flying ship. The wave hit the Figaro, but thanks to its power, it managed to stay afloat, dodging the debris around it. The drones weren't so lucky; three were destroyed by the sheer might of the wave, while the other two were damaged by the debris. Soon the Figaro cleared the wave and the alarms stopped blaring.

"Huh? It actually worked," Sid said aloud, to his own surprise.

† † †

"Wait, so they are planning to bring back some moldy freefolk god and start tearing up the planet?" Alex asked while the five of them were running. Gaby and Fionn had been updating Sam, Harland, and Alex on the way to the promenade.

"Asurian, not freefolk" Fionn replied.

"Yeah, big difference," quipped Harland.

Fionn's breath was accelerating, shifting, sounding uncomfortable. "And it's not a god, it's a creature from the Pits revered as a god. And they might even have something worse here already."

"Worse than that?" Harland asked, breathing heavily. It was hard for him to keep the pace.

"The Withered King," Fionn mumbled under his breath.

"Crap... Wait...who the heck is the Withered King?"

"I will explain later," Fionn said. "We need to find a safe route to escape first."

"There's a secret passage hidden in the kitchen, near the walk-in fridge, we can use that one," Sam replied.

"If it is secret, how come you know about it?" Alex said.

"Duh, I have been studying here since high school," Sam replied once more, rolling her eyes. "What do you think I do in my free time? Those passages are good for playing pranks. Follow me."

Sam and Alex took the vanguard, while Gaby and Fionn took the rear, to offer Harland some protection. The group turned around a corner, reaching the cafeteria once more. But they came face to face with troopers dressed in black, their faces covered with darkened goggles and helmets, holding rifles. When they reached the cafeteria they shot at the kids. The hail of bullets took Alex by surprise, not allowing him to react to them. But there was no need as they hit an invisible wall of energy that flickered with a purple and blue light where they hit it. Next to him, he saw Sam making swift gestures with her hands. Not wasting a second, Alex expanded his bow and let loose a rain of arrows that hit most of the troopers. Sam then proceeded to send them flying away against the walls with a hand gesture, a wave of purplish energy hitting them square in their chests.

"A bow *and* a sword?" Sam asked. "Isn't that overkill?"

"The bow is good for larger spaces, the sword for close quarters. I like being prepared."

Alex collapsed the bow and drew his sword.

"Except that you barely know how to use it," Gaby quipped, drawing her own swords.

"Details, details."

"Sorry to interrupt what I'm sure is a longstanding debate," Harland interrupted. "But who are they?"

"Odds are that they are the mooks of the owners of the dreadnought. Their outfits look similar to the guys that broke into my university," Alex noted.

"If I have to guess, their bosses call themselves the Fraternity of Gadol," Gaby explained.

"I take it they are not nice people," Harland replied.

"Understatement of the century," Fionn added.

Through the school's sound system, a feminine voice could be heard. Not amicable and certainly not warm.

"Deliver us Professor Hunt's research and you will be left in peace," the voice said.

"That didn't sound nice," Harland said.

"They are lying about leaving this place in peace. We need to go." Fionn hurried them.

"We can't let them have the professor's research," Sam said.

"We have his notebook with us," Gaby replied.

"No offense, but with that mess, I'm sure you left behind more than that. I should know," Sam complained.

"I don't think they are here only for that information," Fionn replied. "They also need casters for the spell. And here in Ravenstone are the best casters, all in one place."

"Pretty convenient," Harland added. "I suspect the random attacks on freefolk tribes weren't as random as everybody thinks. They may be looking for certain types of casters."

"We need to get everybody out of here, Dad," Sam said with concern in her voice.

"Don't forget the crystals," Alex left the other three confused.

"Sorry?" Gaby asked.

"To punch a hole big enough to bring back a moldy god, they need massive power, remember?" Alex explained. "Sam just told me that crystals serve as conduits for magick. What better source of power than the huge collection of crystals they have stored here, or those at a city that was designed to be a circle of power with three massive crystal antennas, like Saint Lucy?"

"Listen, I will go and warn the Dragonking. We will destroy the passage to the crystal vaults and defend Ravenstone until everyone has evacuated. I want you to go to the platform and get out of here," Fionn ordered.

"But, Dad!" Sam said, concerned.

"I will find a way to get out of here and reach you later. Right now, *my* main concern is to know that you are safe. This is not your fight. It's mine."

"Well, it is ours now," Alex said.

"We can help," Gaby added. "You are trying to do too much alone. Let us help."

"They are right, you know?" Harland looked at Fionn.

"This place has enough guards and security measures," Fionn said.

"I know that better than you, but more help can only be a good thing, Dad."

"Listen, this is not a democracy. I'm not subjecting this to a vote," Fionn said with a tone of voice that left no room for discussion. "And despite what you have been through, you are not used to the kind of fight we are facing. So I'm asking *you* to help me by getting *my* daughter out of here. That way I can focus on what I have to do. I'm trusting you with the most valuable thing in my life. That's all the help I need for now."

Alex tried to reply, but Gaby put a hand over his mouth.

"Count on us," Gaby said with a tone of voice that left no doubt on who was taking charge of the escape. "Let's go guys."

Fionn found that attractive, if he was being honest with himself. But that train of thought would have to wait at the station. Then Gaby surprised him, and everyone else, by kissing his cheek.

"I need to play the hero more frequently," Alex muttered to Harland.

"With any luck, you won't have to," Harland replied somberly.

BOOM!

A blast shook the room, taking down several walls. Clouds of dust covered the place. Debris peppered the floor. Sam stood in front of them, her hands extended. The protection spell she had hastily cast had protected them from the worse of the explosion.

The explosion had opened a new corridor to the other end of the school, where the promenade used to be. There were now chasms between the rooms, as several of the bridges connecting them had crumbled. On the far end the group saw broken totems and corpses of teachers, security staff and a few older students who had been killed. Only three intruders stood in the remains of the promenade. The first was a lady in metallic armor and long silk sleeves, by her looks, someone from the Kuni Empire. Next to her, there was a big man with a beard and sporting shades, wearing the same gear as the troopers and carrying a war cannon. Behind them stood a creature that looked like a man, taller than the bearded guy by a head and half, built like a mountain and wearing a full set of armor, with a helmet covering his face and a sword that looked eerily familiar to Fionn.

"That's the lady from Hunt's report. Madam Park," Gaby pointed out.

"And that is the guy that broke into the lab and beat up my friend. You can't beat them all by yourself," Alex sheathed his sword, expanded the bow and got ready to let loose an arrow. Fionn stopped him.

"I have faced worse odds. Stick to the plan." Fionn told them, his voice betraying concern. Alex noticed that even Harland's demeanor had changed. Both he and Fionn were nervous about something. "Now go!"

"Be safe, Dad." Sam hugged him.

Fionn pushed them into the kitchen and then ran in the other direction towards one of the bridges connecting the promenade to the cafeteria.

As they entered the kitchen, Alex pushed a button on his glasses.

"I sent the signal to Sid, he will be tracking us now. But I couldn't help notice, why is Fionn so worried?"

"He got that way once I mentioned the Withered King and Lemast," Gaby replied. A trooper appeared from one of the doors. Gaby kicked him towards the stairwell.

"Lemast is where an old mausoleum stood, on the far reaches of Ionis," Harland explained. "It had a royal detachment to keep it secured." He ducked as Gaby kicked another trooper and Alex shot at a third one standing a few steps below. Both fell into the stairwell with a loud thud.

"For a mausoleum that no one has heard of before?

Why?" Alex asked, letting loose another arrow, allowing a student to escape a trooper's grasp.

"Because a monster from the war was trapped there by Izia, Fionn's wife. It's a long story," Harland said, reaching the mezzanine that would lead them to the platform. "If we make it out alive from this I will tell you the rest."

# Chapter 10

## Escape From the Ravenstone

"Are you sure he will pick us up?" Sam asked.

"I only got static and what I assume was a lot of expletives in samoharo, which I take as a yes," Alex replied.

"Shush!" Gaby interrupted them. "I heard something. Wait here."

"Are you sure she should go alone?" Sam asked.

"When it comes to sneaking around, she is one of the best," Alex replied.

Gaby tracked through the labyrinthine design of Ravenstone's corridors, following the echoes of the footsteps. She found a heavy oak door ajar. Through the slight opening, Gaby saw a full platoon in the next room, the one they needed to cross to reach the pick-up point. She heard footsteps behind her.

"I thought I told you to wait for me," Gaby whispered, without turning to see who was behind her.

"We got worried that you would get lost through the corridors," Sam replied in low voice.

"And it was boring," Alex added.

"Well, you will have plenty of action in a few seconds. There is a full platoon of armed troopers in front of us."

"Is there any other route to the platform?" Harland asked.

"Yes, but it is too long of a detour and I doubt we have that kind of time," Sam replied.

"I will open the way, you follow me once I deal with them."

"All by yourself?"

"Please tell me you are not planning to do what I think you are planning to do," Alex pleaded to Gaby.

"Fionn was right, you are not used to fighting multiple opponents," Gaby replied, her voice full of coldness.

"I did at the incursion."

"That doesn't count. You were out of your mind, literally. And those creatures were more beasts than thinking opponents."

"What are you two talking about?" Sam interjected.

"The proof that Fionn is not the only 'one-man-army' around," Alex replied, shaking his head. "I'm gonna regret this."

"Get those arrows ready just in case," Gaby ordered. Her grip on her blades tightened. Goosebumps ran across her arms. She wasn't a fan of what she was about to do, mainly because it was addictive. But sometimes the best way to untie a knot, was to cut it.

A few seconds later, the door exploded in a rain of splinters and debris, knocking down a few of the troopers. Where the door used to be, there was now a slender woman, with long braided golden hair and piercing blue eyes, staring coldly and unflinchingly. The troopers looked at each other and then at the woman. In her hands, there were twin blades that glowed red and blue. The wind started to pick up. Extending her left arm in front of her and holding aloft the right one, she challenged them.

"It's just a dance," Gaby said.

The troopers ran at her, their weapons ready to strike her down.

"Get ready for the show," Alex murmured to Harland and Sam, looking at the scene from a vantage point on a balcony a few meters away, just within earshot of Gaby. "It will get messy and fast-paced."

"What do you mean? Why are you not helping her?" Harland asked him.

"She doesn't need my help. I would get in the way. When she enters that thing she calls the Ice State, it's better to let her be. She hates it when I interrupt before she's given me the signal."

"What is the Ice State?" Samantha asked.

"I'm not entirely sure how it works, because Gaby has never wanted to explain it properly to me. As far as I know, it is a trance-like state she was taught by the Sisters of Mercy that makes her fight like a dervish at blinding speed. Opponents can barely hit her. It's amazing to watch, in a way," Alex explained with a pained look.

"Which, added to the Gift, makes her a one-woman army," Harland added.

Gaby slowly approached the incoming troopers, selecting her targets. The first one got a kick in the head so hard that it smashed the mask that concealed his face. The noise of a cracking skull echoed on the walls as he hit the floor. With a spin, Gaby delivered a roundhouse kick to the plexus of a second trooper, breaking his sternum and sending him flying backward.

"That must hurt." Harland grimaced.

A third trooper grabbed Gaby from behind, but she stomped on his left foot with such strength that the trooper released the hold. Then she used her heel to kick him in the nuts, which resulted in a squishy sound. The trooper let her go and she followed by thrusting one of her blades back and stabbing him. The trooper fell to the ground like a rag doll.

"Not as much as that," Alex replied, wincing. He knew how hard Gaby could kick. Those family jewels were now marmalade.

Gaby now faced a larger trooper. He tried to cut her head off with an axe, but she deftly dodged the axe. The trooper pressed the attack, this time aiming at her torso, but she parried each blow with her twin swords, the clash of metal filling the air. The trooper looked at his axe, which fell to the ground, cut in pieces. Gaby then kicked him in the face, hitting his chin and sending him flying backwards as well. The crunching noise of a broken neck followed. Two troopers ran towards Gaby, but she received them with a jumping split kick, making them fall. She then dropped on them, her blades pointing down, and stabbed them so hard that the floor cracked. But blood didn't come from their wounds, just black ichor. Without effort she pulled the blades out and looked towards the remaining troopers, who had discarded their close range weapons and now were shooting at her with their firearms without any concern for hitting each other. Gaby continued walking towards them, dodging their attacks with precise movements. When she reached the troopers, she sliced through their firearms. Then she kicked the troopers and cut off their limbs with ease.

"She is getting more ruthless," Alex observed. He was worried. He wanted to make her break the trance before she went too deep, but getting closer without her allowing it would be a bad idea.

When one trooper got close to her, Gaby ran up a column and with a pirouette landed behind him and slashed his legs above the knees, cutting the tendons and nicking the femoral arteries. Bullets crossed the air, aimed at Gaby, but she deftly dodged them by somersaulting and jumping around until she got closer to the shooter. With a swift move, she sliced the rifle and his hands, before kicking him away. The leader of the squadron called for reinforcements while he ran towards Gaby, who received him with a punch in the face and a slash on the throat.

"Seems pretty handy," Sam added, impressed. "Why do you say it like it is a bad thing?"

"A mystic trance called 'Ice State'? The more she uses it, the more she loses touch with her humanity."

"The perfect assassin," Harland added.

"Exactly," Alex said. "Look, those guys probably deserve a stomping. But Gaby certainly doesn't deserve to have their blood on her hands, nor the regrets. Even less, to lose her humanity. I think it's time to call it off."

He approached the edge of the balcony. A sinking feeling formed at the bottom of his stomach. His heart was thumping so hard that it was the only noise he could hear.

"I hate doing this. I hate heights and the landings are hard on my knees," Alex said, before jumping from the balcony, landing on three troopers and smashing their heads. He then yelled at Gaby at the top of his lungs.

"Gaby! Time for a break!"

But Gaby was so into the fight that she jumped, twirling in the air and landed on her feet, with her right arm extended. A few brown hairs fell to the floor. Heartguard's blade stopped a few centimeters from Alex's neck. Gaby blinked several times until her eyes returned to normal. When she realized what she was close to doing, she dropped her twin blades to the ground and hugged Alex.

"I'm so sorry," Gaby said tearfully.

"It's ok. I'm fine. Let's go." Alex smiled at her.

"These two are insane," Sam followed them down the stairs.

"Not as much as your old man," Harland said. "Trust me."

††† 

Fionn reached the section of the promenade where a defensive force was barricading, under the directions of the Dragonking.

"I came here to get you out." Fionn looked around. Everybody looked tired, injured or downright scared. A few guards were whispering about the towering man who was impervious to spells, and whose sword had shattered the best of their weapons as if they had been made of glass. A stout guard arrived, dripping sweat.

"Wait, my friend. What news do you have?" the Dragonking asked the arriving guard.

"My Lord, they have killed Master Ali and Master Kellback," the guard said. "Master Bayara is injured, but he managed to escape with all the rest of the students with the help of Master Gillian, while Master Samantha and her friends have made their way to the lower levels. However, the attackers have captured three students and two professors, Ortiga and Vertiz, and have taken them to their ship. The worst thing is that the creature is coming this way and there are a few older students still behind us, trying to evacuate. That thing is unstoppable."

"That thing is called the Tovainar," Fionn said with a serious tone. "And it is nullifying any energy attack or powers around it. That's why none of your wizards could stop it. You need to escape. All of you, now."

"How do you know that?"

"I have encountered something like that before, during the War. We need to leave. Now!"

"I won't leave," the Dragonking replied. "Not while there are students captured by these monsters. Watts, take the remaining students and lead them to the lower levels and into the caves. We will hold the line to give you time."

"Yes, my Lord," the guard replied with a salute. He then ran, followed by a few guards and older students, into a passage that opened on the side of a wall.

"Can I count on your help, my friend?" the Dragonking asked Fionn.

Fionn knew in his gut that he was going to regret it. "You know damn well that you can, Tharvol. I don't run from a fight," Fionn replied, using the Dragonking's first name. "But we need to escape as soon as everybody is out. Your students, the freefolk need you alive more than dead."

"I'm not planning to die today, my friend." The

Dragonking smiled at Fionn, extending his arm to embrace him. As Fionn took the other man's arm, they were rocked by a shockwave hitting the hall.

Another wall crumbled and through the dust a towering creature walked slowly, emitting a noise through its helmet that resembled a laugh, an unnerving, blood-curdling, familiar laugh. Some guards tried to stop it but their blades shattered, the life from their bodies leaving as the creature's sword pierced their chests. Others cast spells, but the creature was protected by an invisible barrier that caused their spells to dissipate into thin air. Just as Fionn had predicted.

*I hate being right.*

A guard next to Fionn threw up at the sight of the creature, and a faint whiff of it permeated the air. Clearly, everybody was scared beyond belief, everybody but two people, the Dragonking and Fionn, the legendary Greywolf, the hero of the war.

Or at least it seemed that way but inside, Fionn felt a heavy pain in his chest. His breathing became difficult as he gulped down breaths to muster the courage. He didn't run from a fight. But this occasion was bringing back a flood of bad memories. On the other hand, the Dragonking stood defiantly, like his predecessors stood before against overwhelming odds, and he walked towards the creature and its minions. Fionn couldn't help but admire him. *Ignorance is bliss*, he thought, and he followed the cue by unsheathing Black Fang, whose steel blade glowed with green light. People depended on him.

Both started to fight the approaching troopers. The Dragonking was more than just a title or a sobriquet; it represented a tradition stretching back since the Dawn Age of Asherah the first magi, to the Golden Age, from Queen Khary of the first freefolk kingdom to Tharvol today. The Dragonking or Dragonqueen was the most powerful, most well-versed and usually wisest magick user of all the freefolk, even of all people on the whole planet. To reach the title at a relatively young age, as Tharvol had done, with his black curly hair not yet marred by the gray hairs of advanced age, was nothing short of prodigious. Fionn had grown fond of the man who had proved to be a true friend. As much as he was worried about Sam, he knew that by keeping the Tovainar distracted, he was giving her time to escape. And he wouldn't let a friend fight alone against something that even Fionn had to admit was frightening.

While Fionn cut through the weapons of the troopers, knocking them down with kicks so hard that they could break stone, he noticed two things. The first was that neither Madam Park nor the bearded man were anywhere to be seen. They were either ransacking Hunt's office or going after the students. The second thing he noticed was the hilarious sight of the troopers running towards the Dragonking, expecting to hit a squishy wizard and facing instead an accomplished hand-to-hand fighter. Tharvol was not only a magick user but a titanfighter, trained to focus immense power through his armor in order to battle creatures beyond mortal ken.

Tharvol and Fionn, working in concert, had moved swiftly, and eloquently against the squads of troopers to clear the hallway of enemies. By the end of their advance, it was just the Tovainar and a few remaining guards against them. Fionn thought for a second they might have a chance, that maybe an easy fight was just that: an easy fight.

The Tovainar opened its arms, inviting attack, mocking Fionn and Tharvol with its unnerving laugh. He pointed his sword at the corpses of the dead guards. They were animated by a blue energy that raised them like puppets, with their relaxed arms barely holding their weapons, and a black ichor spilling from their pierced guts. They stood in order despite their broken bones. It was then that Fionn noticed that the troopers had circlets around their necks, similar to the one on the creature he fought before.

"Damn," Fionn muttered. He said to the Dragonking,

"Listen to me, Tharvol, it's time to leave. It will get ugly. You have to trust me on this."

"I won't see Ravenstone fall into the hands of a heathen," The Dragonking said, not pausing for a second. "Let's see if that thing can nullify this." He then made circular movements with his hands, generating a blue sphere of condensed energy that grew with every moment.

*Why do you have to be so stubborn?* Fionn shook his head, he knew all too well the spell Tharvol was about to cast. "I wouldn't do that, you are going to bring the whole place down." But the warning came too late.

The Tovainar just laughed and opened its arms once more, mocking them. The Dragonking was furious, grinding his teeth. He continued his hand motions, as the blue sphere grew in size and started rotating. When it picked up enough speed in its turns, the Dragonking threw it towards the Tovainar, who didn't move. The sphere kept growing along the way, drawing energy from the hallowed halls of Ravenstone. But the Tovainar just walked towards the sphere with unnerving calm. Using its sword, he hit the sphere like a ball, sending it towards the Dragonking. Fionn ran towards Tharvol to get him out of the way, while the magus tried to cast a protection spell.

"It can't be!" Tharvol yelled.

The last thing Fionn saw was a blue flash of energy exploding against Tharvol's spell. The walls crumbled around him and a shockwave hit his chest.

The blue flash engulfed the whole place.

† † †

"We are almost there."

Sam was leading Alex, Gaby, and Harland through dark corridors. Alex and Gaby, well mostly Gaby, cleared the path of enemies. Alex liked to think that he could hold his own in a fight, though not at Gaby's level. But right now he was more occupied with keeping Gaby from slipping into the Ice State again. And he did it the only way he knew: telling the group lame jokes.

"So I asked this guy at the board game club, you know the guy, the one that looks like a hobo and doesn't wear shoes: Did you take a shower today? And he replied: Why? Is there one missing?"

The joke got a collective groan, but Alex noticed how Gaby's lips crooked into her trademark smile. He sighed in relief and let himself get distracted. He didn't notice the massive fist flying towards his face. It hit him square in the jaw and almost knocked him out.

A brute with long, greasy hair, wearing a vest over his bare blueish chest and wearing a circlet, was blocking the way like a wall made of muscle. Alex could see a blurry form. Harland was in front him, trying to keep the creature distracted. He looked around but Gaby and Sam were nowhere to be seen.

"Excuse me, but you are in my way. Could you please let us through?" Harland asked politely.

"Urgh?" That was the only reply.

"Wonderful." Harland pinched the bridge of his nose. "And if I offer you a sizeable amount of money? You know, to buy alcohol or whatever you want?"

The brute reacted the only way that his brain allowed and picked up Harland, crushing him with his arms. Alex got up to help Harland. He picked up his bow and let loose an electrified arrow which hit the man in the thigh. The shock wasn't enough to knock the brute out, but was enough to make him drop to one knee and release Harland.

Gasping for air, Harland grabbed a nearby plank from a broken door and used it to hit the brute as hard as he could in the back of the head. The plank broke in two. The brute fell unconscious to the floor with a loud thud and blood trickled from his head.

"Nice hit," Alex teased him, extending his fist for a fist

bump, which Harland barely acknowledged.

The brutish man started to stir and tried to get up once more.

"Aww crap," Alex muttered. But then he saw Gaby jump on the man and cleave her twin swords into his head and chest. This time the body didn't move; instead, black ichor started to flow from beneath it.

"Are you two ok?" Gaby asked, followed by Sam who had returned to them.

"I have had better days, to be honest," Harland replied with a raspy voice, rubbing his neck. The air was slowly returning to his lungs.

"Why did you stop?" Sam asked them.

"Someone sent its pet after us." Alex pointed to the dead body.

"A ghoul," Sam examined the body. "I guess they brought them here in case they found more opposition than expected."

"That explains what we saw in the way towards the landing deck," Gaby added, pointing towards the corridor.

A few moments later, peeking through one of the shattered doors, Alex and Harland noticed the increasing number of ghouls barring them from reaching the landing deck where Sid was supposed to pick them up.

"Now that is a lot of ghouls," Alex said to Gaby and Sam.

"I can go into the Ice State again," Gaby offered.

"Hell no! I wouldn't risk it. I know I'm not the best fighter around and that's why you chose to deal with the troopers. But I can take on the ghouls. I can properly test the bow."

"Fine. But if they bite you, don't come crying to me," Gaby exclaimed.

"C'mon, this will be fun!" Alex said with a wide grin.

"I hardly see how dealing with ghouls will be fun," Harland said.

"It's like a video game. I don't have to worry about killing them," Alex explained with a grin. "Seeing as they are dead already."

"You need to lay off the bad jokes, seriously," Sam crossed her arms in front of her, with a scowl in her face. "This is not funny at all."

"Follow me." Alex kicked the door and shot a ghoul right in the middle of the eyes, taking him down. Alex shot down more and more ghouls, which moved faster than he expected for being dead bodies. Although he was smiling, his eyes were focused on taking down any incoming ghouls, whether from the sides, the balconies or from the front.

"He loves shooting galleries and haunted houses. This is a theme park ride for him," Gaby explained to Sam and Harland. The three of them followed Alex. "But just in case, Sam, what do you think if we take down any strays that he missed?"

"Fine by me." Sam cracked her knuckles. "Part of the job."

Gaby pierced their hearts or cut off their heads with her twin swords, and she could feel the temperature increasing thanks to the heated plasma fireballs that Sam was casting at her side. They made a good team.

"Are you always like this?" Sam asked Alex, after blasting the face of one of the ghouls.

"Best way to keep my stress levels down," Alex explained while shooting two ghouls in the head with one arrow.

"Trust me, the alternative is worse," Gaby kicked the head she just cut off like a ball.

"What? More lame jokes?" Harland asked.

"Worse! Constant nagging and complaining," Gaby replied with a sigh.

"I'm not that bad!" Alex complained while releasing three arrows in succession, taking down three ghouls to his left.

They reached the landing pad, but the Figaro was nowhere to be seen. However, the hordes of ghouls keep coming in waves. Alex kept shooting at a steady pace, but he could feel the soreness in his shoulder blades. By his account, there were more ghouls than he had arrows in his cartridges. *I should have asked Andrea for larger cartridges.*

"There are too many," Gaby rested her arms on her knees, with a heavy breath.

"Not for long," Sam replied, casting a different fireball. Instead of the usual red-orange one, this was a blue sphere. Sam let it go and it moved slowly, drawing power from the walls of the school until it was right in the middle of the hall that led to the landing pad. The sphere stood there, floating over the heads of the ghouls who stopped to stare at it.

A roaring of engines was heard then. The Figaro approached the pad slowly, opening its cargo bay. Gaby helped Harland get inside, while Alex gave cover with the last of his arrows.

"I'm ready if you are," Alex told Sam.

"Jump now!" Sam yelled as they both jumped into the open cargo bay.

Once inside, Sam snapped her fingers. The blue fireball exploded in a flash of light, the heatwave incinerating any creature still standing, and with them, half of the landing pad. Gaby looked at Sam, surprised.

"Wasn't that overkill? And won't you get into trouble for damaging the pad?" Gaby asked.

"It saves time. And we can always pin it on the ghouls and a gas line," Sam replied, shrugging her shoulders. "It's a school for magick practitioners. These things happen more often than you think."

"I'm glad I wasn't landing just then," Sid said through the comms.

"Your horrible voice is a relief for tired arms," Alex replied.

"Yeah, yeah, you can kiss me later. We need to go or we will be goners," Sid said, and the Figaro rocked, throwing Alex, Gaby, and Sam to the floor.

"Damn it, damn it, damn it!" Sid yelled frantically while maneuvering the Figaro to dodge the aerial fire that the dreadnought was shooting at the smaller ship. Alex, Sam, Gaby, and Harland reached the cockpit. Alex saw Sid sweating; moisture covered his brow and scalp. "Who told hoomans to build that thing with railguns? Your whole species is crazy!"

"We need to go back for my dad," Sam pointed out. She was biting her lips and Alex hugged her, startling her.

"We need to get out of here, honey," Sid replied.

"She's right," Alex insisted.

"You are crazy," Sid pulled the yoke to his left. "We are in an enclosed space and dealing with a ship that has more firepower than us."

"Sam is right," Gaby insisted. "Fionn needs our help."

"Not you too," Sid replied, annoyed. "I expect that from him and his hero complex, but not from you, sweetie. I barely made it out the first time."

"Fionn is trying to keep the attackers busy while the students, many of them children, are escaping. Do you remember doing the same ten years ago? The least we could do is help him escape as well. We don't leave behind one of our own, you taught us that," Gaby muttered into Sid's ear. Alex mouthed 'low blow' to her.

"I really hate it when you do that," Sid replied, turning the Figaro around.

The front screen window flooded with a blue light as the shockwaves of an explosion shook both ships. By the time their vision recovered and the screen filtered the excess of light, the sight of what had happened filled them with dread. Half of Ravenstone had been blown up; most of the walls were crumbling, leaving open a whole side of the ancient building, while its superior spires fell into the canyon below. The totems that guarded the place were blasted to pieces. Fires peppered all levels, but especially in the gardens. Smaller, colorful explosions went off every other second, as the dangerous liquids of the alchemy labs mixed. On the floor, charred corpses of troopers and guards were moving like puppets following the Tovainar, which stood in the middle of the mayhem as if nothing had happened. Next to a burning door, Fionn was trying to get up but seemed dazed by the explosion.

"Get up. Get up. Please get up," Sam said, while Alex extended his bow once more and walked towards the rear of the ship.

"Where are you going?" Harland asked him.

"To the cargo bay. Open the hatch, we need to get him out of there."

† † †

Fionn had been blown through the doors of the burning school onto the cold, hard floor. A metallic taste invaded his mouth. He could feel his nose was broken and pouring blood. He clutched his chest. He felt a couple of broken ribs and suspected that his breastbone had fractured as well. Crashing through the thick door, even if it was made of wood, left him with more bruises and cuts that he cared to count. Then he realized how bad things were: His ability to heal wasn't working at all.

Fionn felt a cold shiver run down his spine

The last time something similar took place, it required the combined efforts of what was left of the Twelve Swords, the magick powers of his wife, and considerable luck just to stop the same monster facing him now. And it had barely worked.

Fionn's head was ringing, which left him unable to focus properly.

His worst nightmare was being replayed all over again: those he held dear betrayed and killed by an unstoppable monster.

Fionn felt a knot in the bottom of his stomach. His instinct screamed at him that his initial fears were true, that he might be back. And yet, he hopped that his instincts were wrong. No matter what, he needed to get everybody out of there fast.

All around him was a cacophony of noises and screams, blurred images of people fighting for their lives and dying all around him. He didn't know where the rest were, but at the moment his main concern was to stand up and find Black Fang. Fionn kept falling, still disoriented, when he noticed the silence around him. That could only mean that the Tovainar was right behind him. The knot in the bottom of his stomach grew; his heart raced so fast that it made his broken ribs and sternum hurt more. His skin crawled with goosebumps. He wanted to be somewhere else.

The Tovainar didn't waste time. It started to attack, trying to impale Fionn on its sword. Fionn could only roll and dodge the attacks, barely avoiding being hit. Fionn kicked the Tovainar in the knee, making it lose its footing and earning a few precious seconds to get away. The tenuous dust cloud around the battlefield made it difficult to pinpoint Black Fang's location. He tried to focus, using the Gift's sight to find his sword. He saw a familiar green glow to his left. The sword was 'talking' to him. He got up, still dazed and ran towards Black Fang.

The green glow was there, Black Fang was within his grasp. Fionn grabbed Black Fang just in time. The Tovainar's sword hit the ground hard where Fionn had been lying, its sword firmly stuck into the ground. Fionn jumped to his left side. He used the few precious seconds that the Tovainar took to unstick his sword to catch his breath. Once the sword was out, the creature spun on its heels to hit Fionn in the chest, a hit that if landed, would crush his chest and heart at once. Fionn raised his sword to parry the blow.

Both blades hit in an explosion of green light. Black Fang took the impact perfectly, whereas other weapons had disintegrated from a mere touch of the Tovainar's sword. As Black Fang glowed a bright green light, Fionn pushed the other sword away. The Tovainar attempted a couple of quick slashes with the edge of its blade, but Fionn expertly parried them, gaining some confidence. Fionn swung his sword to cut off the Tovainar's head. Then a brief silence surrounded him as if time had stopped. A sense of dread ran down his spine. And then the laugh came again.

In his daze, he had failed to notice that the Tovainar had blocked the hit. The laughter brought him back to reality. The screams of the moribund, the body of the Dragonking a few yards to his left, now charred remains. Feeling more anger now than fear, Fionn moved deliberately, trying to go for the killing blow. But the laugh kept unnerving him.

"Hello, old friend. Or should I call you *master*? I prefer mongrel. It fits you," the Tovainar said, derision dripping from each word. He lifted the faceplate of his helmet. Behind it was the scarred but otherwise beautiful face of a man in his mid-thirties, with a carefully trimmed beard and eyes with irises as blue as polar ice, surrounded by a sea of red where the white of the eyes would otherwise be. In another time, those eyes had offered a sense of comradery and friendship, but now they were a mockery of the man he had been.

"Byron," Fionn uttered, sweating cold.

"This reunion is worth a picture. Or your head on a pike," Byron pushed Fionn again with enough strength to break a wall.

Fionn tried to gather his bearings, but so many memories, feelings, and thoughts rushed through his head. The only thing that brought him out of his reverie was Gaby yelling at him. He glanced to his left and saw her waving at him, yelling at him to come to the Figaro. Byron raised his sword to strike Fionn in the head, but an arrow hit his hand, piercing it.

Alex stood next to Gaby, readying the second arrow.

"Wait here for a second, Fionn, I need to get rid of the vermin first," Byron started to slowly walk towards Alex and Gaby, followed by a couple of his ghouls. The ghouls soon fell to the ground, their heads pierced by a pair of arrows.

Alex let loose a fourth arrow towards Byron, which hit him in the neck. But Byron simply ripped it out without losing pace. Instead of blood, black ichor and white worms came out from the wound, which closed almost immediately.

"We need to go now!" Alex kept yelling at Fionn while drawing his sword. Gaby did the same.

Byron just laughed. And it enraged Fionn so much that the 'wolf' inside him overtook his better judgment. Quietly, he cleaned the blood from his mouth and face, using his shirt. Disregarding the pain in his chest and nose, he moved as fast as his battered body allowed and cut down the remaining troopers, putting himself between Byron and the Figaro.

"Leave now!" Fionn yelled at Alex.

"How cute," Byron readied his sword. "Always dragging along those unfit or foolish enough to die for you. Don't worry, I will see that they meet their predecessors in a swift manner. I can't promise it won't be painful, though."

"We won't leave without you!" Gaby yelled. Fionn knew the look on her face. He had seen the same look on his wife Izia before the whole world came crashing down on them. But this time Fionn wasn't going to allow history to repeat itself. He had failed Izia, Ywain and many more by being afraid. This time he knew what he had to do. He just hoped Gaby and Sam would understand.

"Please," Fionn mouthed to Gaby and then ran towards Byron, who counterattacked his blow. Byron and Fionn traded blows faster than the naked eye could see, but it was to no avail. Byron was toying with him and Fionn felt the weariness of the duel taking over his battered body. There was no way he would get out of this alive, not without his healing ability. But as long as Gaby, Sam and Alex were alive, maybe there was still hope.

"A century passes and you haven't learned a thing, Fionn."

"I have learned to have a better fashion sense than you at least," Fionn replied, smiling through the pain, backing up slowly, Black Fang barely up. Fionn found himself between the bottomless Maze and Byron. Fionn went for broke, launching a final strike that Byron deflected with ease before impaling Fionn in the gut with his sword.

"Your technique has improved... but your left guard is still open," Fionn said, bleeding profusely.

"Always the master, trying to teach me," Byron said. "The thing is, you were never my master. You were just a means to an end. A tool to be used and discarded, like the rest."

"You won't win." Fionn's voice was almost gone.

"Foolish hope. That's your main defect. But be glad you won't be around to see how utterly you have failed. Say hello to your wife from me."

Byron then pulled out his sword, a sudden movement that made Fionn release his grip on Black Fang, which fell into the chasm, its green light getting lost in the darkness.

"Déjà vu," Byron paused. "I have seen this before. This is how I killed Ywain. I know how the story will go from now on: your daughter will attempt to attack me with a spell, she will fail and then she will die, just like Izia. And then you will be next. History does repeat itself when it comes to losers like you. How does it feel to fail your friends and family again?"

Fionn's eyes opened wide at the mention of Samantha. "Yes, I know you have a daughter. Hunt finally broke down. Any last words?"

"Bite me," Fionn replied, spitting a blood clot towards Byron's beard, which elicited only a laugh.

Byron kicked Fionn into the same chasm and waved good-bye. The last things that Fionn saw while falling into the dark pit of the Maze were the Figaro in flames, starting a descent into the depths, while the shadow of a raven flew towards Fionn.

# Chapter 11

## Realizations

The Figaro's alarms were blaring as the hatch gate closed. Gaby felt Alex dragging her to the cockpit, followed by Harland, who was tightly holding onto Sam to keep her from jumping out of the ship to avenge her father. Alex led them into the med bay and closed the door to keep them safe. The ship rocked under the heavy fire of the dreadnought. Alex and Gaby reached the cockpit and strapped themselves into their seats just as Sid pushed the thrusters to get the Figaro out of there, away from the platform and into the Maze.

Gaby's heart ached as if it had been skewered by a thousand needles. The image of Fionn being impaled, his healing ability not working, and then falling into the void, seemingly dead, was stuck in her brain. Fionn was a hero. The Hero. The one she and Alex had grown up worshipping, reading about his exploits and how he always found a way to come victorious. He couldn't be dead.

But the reality was a different thing. And then she thought of Sam who had witnessed what happened to her dad and to her students. They needed to go back to help but Gaby only wanted to cry. She shook her head. This was not the time to get lost in her thoughts. She took a deep breath and turned towards Sid and Alex.

"How can I help?" Gaby asked.

Alex was frantically pushing buttons and trying to help Sid with the additional systems, while the samoharo flew the ship around the Maze, trying to evade the barrage of fire from the dreadnought. To his credit, the samoharo had maintained his cool after witnessing what had happened to Fionn, and had taken them out of the place before that creature closed the gap. It had been a narrow escape. But they weren't out of the fire just yet.

"Can you shut up that damned alarm?" Sid yelled. Gaby punched the dashboard and the alarm stopped.

"Better?" Gaby said with a calm voice. Alex and Sid freaking out was already enough. Someone had to keep the calm.

"Thanks. What's our status?" Sid asked.

"Seems that we are going down in flames," Gaby replied dryly.

"Care to be more specific? I can't check the readouts and keep us from crashing at the same time."

"The radar is offline, structural damage in the outer hull, the AI has called it a day, and for some reason the cores are being drained out," Alex replied, looking at the instrumentation readouts.

"Drained out? By what?" Sid said, confused.

"I can't say. But the closer we get to the dreadnought, the faster they drain. It doesn't make any sense," Alex tried to explain. Gaby saw his brow covered in sweat. "At this pace, we won't have the power to be airborne."

"And we will fall like a rock." Sid cursed under his breath. "Damn it. Alex I need you to go and check the cores, and see if you can keep them working."

"How?" Alex replied, clearly frustrated.

"I don't know! You're the energy expert. Plug them directly into the emergency batteries if you must. I need power to get us out of here!" Sid almost screamed. He was busy guiding the ship to avoid the fire from the dreadnought's cannons and the new batch of drones tailing them.

"If I do what you say, they will crack. And you can't pilot this thing without a co-pilot with half the systems shutting down," Alex countered.

"It seems that this is the end of the line then," Sid mumbled.

As Sid and Alex argued and more alarms blared in the cockpit, it dawned on Gaby that this was the moment. Right now. It was the first clear realization of the day for Gaby that, if they were going to make it out alive, she would have to step up and take the lead.

She would have to be the one turning this up. She stood up from her seat.

"Kiddo, I suggest you return to your seat," Sid said, without looking at her. He was focused on what was in front of him, making the Figaro dance in the air, dodging blindly the enemy attacks. "This will be a rough trip to the ground."

"Alex, go and do whatever you can to keep us afloat. Now!" Gaby ordered. Alex stared at her for a second and without saying a word, unfastened his harness and ran towards the engine room.

"Keep the comms open!" Alex exclaimed before disappearing inside the ship.

Gaby took his place, fastened the harness and looked at the console in front of her. Many of the switches and buttons had been labeled by Alex, with his horrible handwriting. Others labeled by Sid, with his cuneiform handwriting.

"What are you doing, kiddo?" Sid asked her.

"Helping you to fly the Figaro. What else?" Gaby said matter-of-factly.

"No offense, but you don't have the required training."

"What training do I need to crash a ship? It's not like you have other options," Gaby winked at Sid.

"Can't argue with that. Just don't enter into a trance, like before."

"Don't worry. I know what I'm doing, trust me," Gaby replied, as the irises of her eyes started to glow with their icy blue intensity. She just hoped she could use her heightened senses to predict the attacks. "You have a bogey at your eight."

Gaby focused her Gift and her innate ability to predict things to help Sid dodge the attacks. She had never done something like this before, reaching through the ship to feel the surroundings. And she got a few calls wrong. But Sid's skills at flying compensated for the mistakes. Even then, he was starting to get tired, as the drones kept chasing them. He was taking the Figaro far from Ravenstone. And that was the last thing Gaby wanted, as Fionn remained present in her head. In her heart, she knew he was there, somewhere at the bottom of the canyon and he needed their help.

"We need to descend into the depths of the Maze," Gaby said, keeping an eye on the malfunctioning radar.

"That's the opposite direction to where we need to go. If we don't get out of the Maze now, we won't have enough power to take off later," Sid pointed out.

"Assuming we reach the top of the Maze, we won't have enough power to get far, that thing will shoot us down anyways. Going deep down will give us a better chance to hide and will save energy by riding the gravitational waves to the bottom."

"That... that makes sense," Sid conceded. "But they could send drones after us once we get out of reach."

"Not if we create a diversion. We could use those mining explosives as a decoy, make them think we crashed against a wall, timing it with one of those gravitational waves," Gaby offered. "Alex, can you find a way to use the explosives crate as a decoy?"

"Already working on them...bzzz... I put a timer... on one," Alex said through the comm. "I was listening ...sounds like a good plan. Actually sounds like one of my plans!"

"Great, now there are two of you with the hare-brained plans," Sid said, rolling his eyes. "I hope this works."

"Have faith," Gaby replied. Deep inside her chest, she

knew this would work. It had to. Fionn's life depended on it. Then she added, trying to stifle a laugh. "Besides, I know how much you enjoy surfing."

Unlike the stereotypical samoharo, Sid hated surfing.

††† 

Gaby stared at the gravimetric sensor and concentrated her senses on feeling the surroundings of the ship once more, while Sid kept dodging the drones and their fire. His green skin was covered in what passed as sweat for a samoharo. The veins in his neck were bulging under the strain. They had to find a wave that suited their plans and they needed to do it soon. Using the Gift in this way was draining Gaby's energies. Her head was heavy and her stomach was grumbling for food. Then the sensor blinked.

"There is an incoming wave in twenty seconds. Get ready," Gaby said through the comm.

"This better work," Sid mumbled.

"Now!" Gaby yelled through the comm, as Sid pulled the yoke of the ship to the right. Gaby felt the gravity pull changing. Her stomach churned.

Sid opened the hatch bay and the crate with the explosives flew out of it. The crate floated in the air for a few seconds, a small gravitational wave keeping it afloat, before the timer activated, creating a decent sized explosion and generating a cloud of dust and debris. The Figaro started its descent with a certain grace, hiding in the debris cloud. Rock fragments impacted the hull, altering its trajectory.

"Now comes the tricky part," Sid murmured

"Which is?" Gaby asked him.

"Not crashing. Everybody brace yourselves!"

Sid guided the Figaro, dodging most of the stalagmites protruding from the ground. The belly of the ship hit a few, making it jump and almost roll over. But Sid managed to keep it steady through a clever use of flaps and the smaller directional thrusters.

Gaby and Sid braced themselves for the rough landing. To its credit, the Figaro managed to land as softly as was possible for a ship that size with failing power. It slid for several meters, until it finally stopped, leaving a groove as a trail. Sid turned off all the systems and tried to contain his breathing as much as he could.

Then, with bated breath, they waited. And waited. Until the canyon known as the Scar fell into the silence of a graveyard. Until no enemy was in sight.

"I'd better start checking the ship if we are going to get out of here before they consider returning to check our 'remains,'" Sid said.

"And I will check on Sam, Harland, and Alex," Gaby replied, unbuckling her harness.

"For the record, you did well," Sid said to her.

"Thanks," Gaby said softly. Coming from the gruff samoharo, it sure felt like the best compliment she had ever received.

† † †

"Wello, we are screwed!" Sid yelled, throwing a wrench to the floor.

Gaby watched as Sid went into a longwinded rant. If the situation wasn't as dire as it was, it would have made for an amusing scene.

The samoharo was angry. His cheeks were changing colors, the way his species showed discomfort. "The AI refuses to work, the electric system needs severe reroutings to work at least at partial capacity, the hull has considerable damage, and I won't even mention that the landing gear is shot. More important, the cores are almost drained, so we have no power for the time being."

"In summary?" Gaby asked him, trying to smile. Her smile calmed the samoharo just enough to stop him from ranting the whole day. Or at least make him pause and breathe.

"In summary, kiddo, I might be able to repair most of the damage, but we need a miracle just to find a way to recharge the cores. We. Are. Stuck. In the biggest crack on the planet," Sid said with anger, finally catching his breath. He had been surveying the state of the Figaro's systems alongside Alex, trying to find what to fix so they could at least reach the top of the canyon. Climbing was out of the question as its walls didn't provide enough hand holds.

Gaby knew Sid well enough to know that part of his anger was frustration for having his beloved ship damaged. It was his life's work. But the other part was because at heart, Sid was still a warrior and hated losing, even more, when it meant that his charges –and there was no doubt in Gaby's mind that Sid looked at her and Alex in that way – were stuck in a dangerous place and he couldn't do a thing about it. She walked towards him and gave him a hug, startling him. Then she broke the embrace.

"Look, I'm sure you will find a way to fix the ship. Then we will find a way to recharge the cores or replace them. The Scar, and especially the Maze, is famous for possessing crystals of all kinds. I'm sure Alex will figure out which ones could help us to recharge the ship."

Sid looked at Alex, who shook his head.

"It's not that easy, Gaby," the samoharo said.

"What do you mean?"

"If we were at the Thunder Pass, I would just put a lightning rod on top of the ship and catch some energy from the constant lightning and ion storms, even if it meant frying half the circuits. But here? I can't see how we can recharge the cores, not without a lot of patchworks to avoid systems buckling under the stress of the process," Sid explained, waving his arms to make his points. "Yes, the crystals of the Scar pack a punch, energy-wise, but they are unstable in their raw shape. Without the proper fixes, we could end up exploding. If we had a self-sustaining core or a regenerating battery to recharge, it would be easier. It's not like I can plug Alex into the system and ask him to power the thing up."

Alex looked up as if he had just started to make the calculations in his head.

"Don't even think about it!" Sid exclaimed, pointing to Alex. "That's stupid. We don't know if that's possible or won't kill you. I prefer to take my chances with the crystals lying around here."

"I'm sure you and Alex and Harland will figure out something," Gaby winked at Sid, trying to calm him down. He tried to smile, but it was clear his mind was already making the calculations of their real probabilities. "Meanwhile, you better start patching up the Figaro. Alex, you are the only other person here that can work the relays of the electric system to implement the recharging process using the crystals at hand. Harland, can you lend a hand to Sid with the repairs? Maybe the AI and the computer systems? They seem to hate him but maybe you could reach an agreement with them."

"Sure. What are you going to do?" Harland asked her.

"I will find Fionn."

"I hate to be the one saying it, but he was not healing during the fight. His Gift failed." Alex interjected in a whispering voice. Sam wasn't paying attention, as she was sitting on a crate by herself, seemingly lost in her thoughts. "The odds of him being alive are not good."

"He is alive," Gaby replied with a determination that not even she knew where it came from.

"How can you be so sure?" Harland said.

"I just simply know." Gaby walked towards Sam. She had been silent since the crash-landing. Gaby put a hand on her left shoulder and broke her out of her reverie. "Sam, are you coming with me to search for Fionn? You know this place better than me."

"Ah, yes, of course," Sam said, looking up. "Let me just

gather some water and medical supplies. We will need them," Sam replied.

Gaby had to give credit to Sam. Despite being still in shock after what happened to her father, Sam had the presence of mind to think of the needs for a rescue mission. In her experience, people in shock became muddle-headed at best, and unresponsive at worst. Fionn had taught her well to remain collected. Gaby appreciated that as it would make things slightly easier.

"Of course. We will leave when you are ready. Sid, can you help her, please?" Gaby said, with a tone of voice that made it clear she was not asking for a favor, but was giving orders. Sid just nodded and went inside the Figaro with Sam. Gaby's expression must have hardened for the samoharo to comply without one of his usual complains. Then she called Alex to come closer.

"I need you to lend me your hoodie."

"Yeah, sure," Alex took it off and handed it to her. "What for?"

"I just need it, it's getting colder, I guess," Gaby hated lying to her friend, mainly because he rarely fell for it.

"Yeah, right," Alex replied, crossing his arms in front of his chest. "I know when you are lying, Galfano. You are expecting to use that thing you do and the hoodie would be a tether of sorts to bring you back."

Alex only used her last name when he was really serious or mad at her. They had been friends for a decade, maybe a bit more, and they had developed their own way to communicate.

"I hope it doesn't come to that. But if it does, then we will be thankful for you lending me this."

"C'mon, you know as well as I do that it could not work. We've been there before. And back at Ravenstone, it took too much time to get you out of that trance. The more you use it, the more it takes to bring you back. That technique is cursed."

"I know the risks. And you say that as if it were something from a fairy tale."

Alex raised his voice, startling Harland, who started to approach them.

"Well, maybe it is. Like that child's tale about the maiden turned into a statue that was brought to life by the kiss of her true love."

"Aren't we a bit old to believe in fairy tales?" Gaby muffled a laugh.

"We have survived incursions, we have weird powers, legendary weapons and have been traveling the past days in the company of a former soldier that puts the 'living' into 'living legend' and kinda lives up to it. Plus we have a magus and a flying ship. A fairy tale wouldn't be out of place."

"You make a good point," she conceded. "Regardless. I will be fine."

"Are you sure you don't want me to go with you, chasing your hunch?"

"It's not a hunch, I'm certain," Gaby said, her tone of voice leaving no room for argument. "And no, you need to stay here. Harland is not much of a fighter, we still have an injured magus in the med bay and apart from Sid, you are the only one who knows the Figaro inside out. He can't fix it without your help, and we need the ship ready as soon as possible."

"Yes, ma'am. Who died and made you a leader?" Alex said and by his expression, and the way Gaby winced, realized he had put his foot on his mouth, again. "Too soon? I'm sorry. You know I'm not good at social skills."

"Just be glad Sam didn't hear you. Learn to read the room, León." Gaby gave Alex a weak slap in the head. "And take care, I need you to be alert to keep alive those two and the patient in the med bay."

"Aye aye, captain!" Alex replied, embracing his friend.

Gaby and Alex did a fist bump and Gaby turned her back, walking to the edge of their improvised camp, but keeping

Alex still within earshot, while Harland approached him.

"Is she going to be alright?" Harland whispered to Alex.

"I hope so."

Gaby heard Alex's reply and the concern behind it. But at that moment, she was more worried about finding Fionn. To make sure he was still alive. The second realization of her day was that her heart ached when she thought of Fionn. But why? They'd only just met each other a few days ago, and most of the things she knew of the guy were from the books Alex had lent her years ago. From the outside, he was a legendary figure, a hero. But there was something else that she hadn't told anyone, not even her best friend. It was even difficult for her to admit.

When she had the dreams that led her to Professor Hunt's house, she wasn't dreaming about what happened to the poor guy. She had been having dreams about Fionn for months, for reasons she couldn't understand. Some were of things mentioned in the history books, others of things that hadn't been recorded. All were blurry memories and they had come out of the blue. But after several weeks, they made him feel familiar to her. So when they finally met in person, she had felt a connection to him, one that she had never felt before. He had been close guarded, but he had accepted her in their adventure without questions, welcoming her as an equal. And they needed him to stop what was going on. But they would need to find him first and help him. With any luck, his Gift would be working now and maybe he would be healing. She had to hope that was the truth.

Gaby pulled up the zipper of the hoodie and secured her blades in the holsters tied to her back. She put her hand inside the pockets of the hoodie. It was starting to feel cold, like that night at Carffadon. It was a bad omen. They needed to hurry.

Sam came out of the ship, with a backpack full of supplies. She was smiling. Gaby assumed that Sid had cheered her up with his peculiar sense of humor. Probably making fun of Alex, based on the way Sam eyed him. Sam reached Gaby.

"Now where?"

"Based on Fionn's trajectory when he fell, probably near the base of the rock where Ravenstone was. Can you lead the way, Sam?"

"I think so."

"Then let's go."

# Chapter 12

# On the Trail of Asherah

Sam was dragging her feet. She was trying to orient herself. Gaby felt that they had been walking in circles for hours and yet they had been walking straight. The Maze had its name well earned. It was confusing even for the freefolk that had walked in the place for generations since the Dawn Age.

"Are you ok, Sam?"

"Yes. Just... just trying to feel the flow of the magick energies that are attracted to the crystals located at the base of the school. It's the only way to get a sense of direction here. If I try to navigate through conventional means we will get lost for who knows how long. Maybe till we are elderly ladies."

"That would be bad."

"Yup. But don't worry. I might be rusty, but I do remember how to use the freefolk techniques to move around the place. It's part of our culture after all," Sam replied. Gaby could sense the nervousness hidden in her voice. She had been taught to notice things like that. Sam was worried about her dad, but that was to be expected, even shared.

Gaby looked around. The walls of the canyon seemed to be growing. It was hard to see the sky, just a blue line at the top of the grey stone. Dimwik lizards scurried away when they got close. The corridors were peppered with moss and limestone ruins. Gaby wondered if they were remains of the ancient freefolk kingdoms that ruled here ages ago, before their fall. But their design didn't look similar to the one used for Ravenstone.

"Are these freefolk ruins?" Gaby asked Sam, pointing at a half arch close to a dying tree.

"No. They are Akeleth in origin. But we used them at first until we started building our own. We left them here as they are part of the place. "

"So, why is this place so important to the freefolk? I mean, aside from being a safe location to learn magick. It doesn't seem to have much in terms of food or resources."

"It is the birthplace of our people," Sam explained.

"Birthplace?" Gaby asked, confused.

"Not in a biological sense. More in a cultural or spiritual way," Sam explained, with a wave of her hand.

"That sounds interesting. Can you tell me more?"

"Are you trying to keep me distracted while we search for my dad?" Sam smiled.

"Would it be wrong to do so?" Gaby smiled back. Sam was clever. She had to be to have gotten an advanced degree in a difficult field of study at such a young age. It intimidated Gaby a bit, since she was a college dropout. But the chat was as much for her sake as for Sam's. It helped Gaby to keep her anxiety at bay. Maybe Alex's bad habits had been rubbing off on her again. "I mean, you are worried and probably in shock. I get it. I feel the same. But I can't do this without you so I think a bit of talk will help us to release some tension."

"Sounds like a psych major. Did you study that?"

"In a way. The Sisters of Mercy did teach us psychology, you know, to better understand and manipulate people. And I tried to continue at college but never finished."

"Sounds like a delightful place to be," Sam replied with a hint of sarcasm in her voice. "The Sisters of Mercy, I mean. I have heard tons of rumors about them."

"You have no idea nor heard half of it. Anyways, you said the Maze is important for freefolk culture as your birthplace."

"Way to deflect." Sam laughed. "But it's ok, I like sharing my culture. It's not just the Maze but the whole World's Scar. Legend says that after the Battle of the Life Tree, at the Dawn Age, the three species: human, samoharo and freefolk had to leave the Tree and travel across the Frozen Lands to colonize Theia. Humans took most of the planet soon enough and the samoharo, well, they are who they are and with their metallic birds conquered the whole continent of Ouslis, leaving no place for us. Back then the freefolk were outcasts, splintered in several small tribes, despite having been allies of the human and the samoharo during the battle."

"Why?"

"Because we are different," Sam replied, this time, her voice had a tinge of sorrow. "Now we are feared because we are the ones that can use magick with ease, as a second nature. Back then, the freefolk were shapeshifters. We had no gender, no discernable features beyond our eyes and a humanoid form. That scared the humans. They are still scared of us. The Great War showed us that. Most people blamed us for the power of the Horde but in reality, we were the first victims of it. Most of our people hid inside here for the duration of the war. Several fought with the Alliance, like my dad or Mykir, the inventor. The rest were tucked in internment camps or used as slaves by the Horde. But one of us, Peremir, really screwed us over. He fought for the Horde, he enslaved his own people and that gave us – and any magick user – a bad rep. Just one devious freefolk made the rest of the world be afraid of us. That's why my dad takes very seriously the attacks on freefolk, despite him not being the most tradition-observant person. For him, having freefolk ancestry is a matter of pride. That's why he took it upon himself to clear our name by fighting in the war."

"The more things change, the more they remain the same," Gaby replied with a soft voice, shaking her head.

Sometimes humans could be as bad as the monsters they fought. "And now his attitudes makes much more sense. It's a heavy burden. But explain this to me, if you started as shapeshifters, how come now you look human?"

"Let me finish the story," Sam interrupted. "The legend says that one day, the Trickster Goddess appeared in front of Asherah, a young freefolk, the first ever magick user. The goddess told her to lead our people across the World's Scar until they reached a promised land, signaled by a red and black raven resting in a stone. And so she did, helped by a small Montoc Dragon. The trek across the canyon took them through the Maze and forced them to fight creatures that feed on magick, parasites called Lurkers. The trip took a toll on freefolk as well, starting with Asherah. The more she used magick, the more she was locked into the form of a human girl. To save her tribe from those creatures, she sacrificed all she had been. She invoked, no, she created the first combat spells and that sealed her fate. By the time they reached the Promised Land, a good part of the tribe had followed her example and were now human-like. Over time, the rest of the tribes made the trek and transformed into what we are now."

"That must have been quite a shock," Gaby said, musing on the story. She wondered if she would have the same strength if the time came to it.

"Can't say for sure," Sam continued with increasing passion in her storytelling. "I mean, that should have taken place thousands of years ago. Asherah is a legend, the supposed first Dragonqueen. But no one is really sure she even existed. There are so few records. We tend to favor oral traditions so details get lost or changed. In any case, that event marked the birth of our nation. That's the origin of our Pilgrimage, one of our most sacred traditions. It is said that every freefolk should connect with the spirits of our ancestors at least once in their lives, to recall why we are a strong people and our origins. We do that through the Pilgrimage. I mean, we can't shapeshift now, but you can see the signs of that ability in heavy magick users; weird hair colors, animal features and so on. The radiation still changes us but that's why we can survive using it for spells. Humans just get fried from inside out without something to channel the energies. We might have intermingled with humans long enough to be as one global civilization, but deep down we are still outcasts looking for a home. The Pilgrimage reminds us of that and makes us stronger for it."

"Did you or Fionn take it?"

"Me? Not yet, but it's in my plans," Sam explained. "Dad... as far as I know, he never did. After the war, he traveled with Izia, my great-grandmother, around the continent. I think he was still trying to clear the name of the freefolk by becoming a wandering hero, as silly as that sounds. He only settled after they became parents and returned to Skarabear. They never left the place till...."

Sam paused, clearly finding it difficult to continue.

"Till what?"

"Dad never talks much about it," Sam continued, her voice acquiring a somber, almost sorrowful tone. "I know Harland knows the exact details, he always does. Something happened a few months after the birth of my grandmother that made Fionn and Izia take on a last mission, leaving their daughter behind in the care of Fionn's mother. But they never returned. I know that Izia died, and my dad disappeared for a long time, until he returned to civilization when Harland's father found him. And by then he had changed. Harland says that he only returned to his cheerful personality when he adopted me.

"It was lucky that your ancestor adopted you," Gaby said with a smile.

"Kinda, he was looking for his family –his descendants– and tracked my parents. But by the time he arrived, I was already orphaned."

"I'm sorry," Sam shrugged her shoulders.

"Don't be. I love my parents of course. But I also love my

Dad. The fact that we are blood-related is just one of many things that connect us. He is the best dad I could ask for," Sam smiled when she said that.

"So why did you grow apart, if you don't mind my asking?"

"If you are asking that, it means he already told you part of it. Which is odd because he likes to bottle up things. He must really trust you."

"I guess we just connected." It was Gaby's turn to shrug her shoulders. But she could feel the blood rushing to her cheeks.

Sam laughed, confusing Gaby. That was not the reaction she was expecting if any.

"Anyways. I think that as I grew up, I reminded him more of Izia, at least physically. Everybody says that we look alike, aside from the hair color. I guess it came to a point where he fell into a depression due to the memories. It was roughly around the time I asked to be sent to Ravenstone to start learning magick in earnest. I wasn't an easy teenager to deal with. I almost gave him a heart attack when I got my first tattoo! So a lot of things combined. It took me some time to understand everything."

"I know what you mean. You were angry. Sometimes when we are younger we have so much anger bottled up and take it out on people we love. I did it with my grandparents after I left the Sisters of Mercy. It took me time to let go all that anger and understand that my grandparents loved me. That they were nothing like my father, who had been the one to enroll me there."

"Angry? No," Sam shook her head. "I was hurt. I still am. But he is still my dad and he's been taking care of me. Heavens, I wish I could fix things with him." She stared at the distance, concentrated. It was as if she had picked up some sort of track.

"I'm sure you will get your chance," Gaby offered, trying to reassure Sam. She sure hoped so.

††† 

They started climbing over a pile of rocks. A rockslide had taken place recently. Gaby examined it and then the walls around them. Something was off. There weren't visible marks of cannon fire that had hit these rocks, but in a couple of them, there were some discernible scratches. The rock in this part of the Maze seemed to be hard as nails, so no regular animal could have left them. The sense of unease she'd had since they left the Figaro was growing. Gaby was about to say something to Sam when the other woman interrupted her.

"Why are you so sure that he is still alive? I mean, I hope so too but it was a long fall, his Gift didn't seem to be working and that thing impaled him. How come you are so damn certain?"

"Something is telling me that he is."

"The Gift?"

"In part, well, no, just something inside here," Gaby pointed to her heart. "I don't know if it makes sense."

"In part? Do you hear voices? Dad said he did during the days after he got the Gift. How does it feel?"

"It is weird, I confess," Gaby tried to put her thoughts in order. It had never been easy to explain what had happened to her, what others called the Gift, to someone who didn't have it. It was such an alien experience, the way it made your skin crawl when something felt off, the way your stomach felt empty no matter how much you ate. The constant influx of sensorial inputs. It messed with your head in ways not many could understand. You felt elated one moment and then depressed the next.

It was as if her brain had been disassembled and then put together in a different way. And she had gotten away with it easy, in part thanks to her training. Alex had gotten it worse, suffering from anxiety attacks and bouts of depression for years after he'd gotten his Gift. The occasional inhuman voices the Gift made you hear didn't help. That was in part why she tried to take psychology at college, to help her friend. That's why she took to playing the guitar and singing, to help herself cope with it. Gaby wondered how Fionn would have felt after he got his Gift. Had his friends and family understood it? Helped him to cope?

Gaby took a deep breath as they descended the other side of the rockslide.

"When the Gift is on," Gaby started. "You get a heightened perception of the world. Every one of the six senses gets enhanced. And you keep hearing a voice that is not yours, telling you things that can or can't be useful. And then, of course, there are the increased physical attributes and special abilities. It is as if you have a brand new body that's alien to you, like when you get new shoes and have to wear them a while to feel more comfortable. And then you have to learn how to turn the Gift off to cope with the day to day."

"You can turn it on and off?" Sam sounded surprised.

"More or less. You learn to block it most of the time. If you have it 'on,' you get tired and hungry faster, all the time, you can barely sleep. And the sensory input is so high that you get dazzled. I tend to block it. Alex for sure blocks it most of the time, otherwise he wouldn't be able to live a regular life."

"What do you mean?"

"His Gift manifests as electromagnetic pulses. If he is not careful, he can fry anything electronic around him. It gets worse when he has a cold or the voices get too strong for him."

"Dad never had those issues."

"I guess Fionn has had several years to learn to deal with it." Gaby paused suddenly. She closed her eyes and focused on her hearing. Taking several deep breaths, she opened herself to the world, using the Gift. She blocked the sounds of the insects and the dimwik lizards climbing the walls. It was a faint noise, with a specific cadence.

"Did you hear that?"

"No," Sam replied, confused. "What did you hear? Voices?"

"Heavy breathing. Moans. Coming from that direction," Gaby pointed to the right of a side passage, it seemed to end in a crevice about a hundred meters further away. Sam looked that way and walked a few meters. She knelt and touched something with her index and middle fingers. She smelled it.

"It's a blood trail. Human or freefolk, judging by the color and the smell," Sam explained.

"I think we are getting close. We need to hurry. I have a bad feeling about this."

They started to run towards the side passage. There was little light inside, so Sam took out a flashlight from the backpack. Gaby found it odd that she didn't cast a spell in a place where that would be easier. Sam seemed to be tense. Maybe she saw something that put her in that state. Gaby was about to ask her what was going on when they turned a corner.

Gaby felt nauseated at what she was seeing. Blood and entrails all over the place.

"Oh, Heavens."

She bit her tongue and walked towards the mangled, badly battered, bloodied body in front of her. It was difficult to tell if it was human or freefolk, or even alive. But the faint speckles of light emanating from the body told Gaby that it was Fionn. And it meant that his Gift was back and was trying to heal him. But given the current state of his body, it wasn't working properly.

"His healing won't work if we don't put that back inside him," Sam managed to say. "He once cut off his hand and had to hold it to his arm with his other hand for a day until it healed."

Gaby knelt near the damaged body. Her hands were quickly covered in blood as she started to put Fionn's entrails inside his belly. Fionn's injuries weren't just from being impaled. There was torn flesh as if something had taken a bite. As she worked, she silently thanked the training she'd received at the Sisters of Mercy. It had made her many things, but being squeamish at the sight of blood and gore had not been one of them. She put herself into the task, helped by Samantha, collecting what had to be collected. It was a matter of determination as much as of love.

Then she felt them. Before she could react they made enough noise to startle Sam as well. Gaby and Sam turned around. Crawling down from the walls of the canyon two strange, insect-like creatures. Most of their body was black, so black that they seemed to eat whatever light ray dared to touch the surface of their carapaces. The only source of color were the brilliant neon stripes and shapes that peppered their bodies, in stark contrast to the black. Gaby couldn't make a clear shape and got distracted by the stripes and shapes. They were so pretty, so relaxing that she couldn't stop looking at them.

"Don't stare at them," Sam told her, grabbing her by the shoulder, waking her up from her daze. "They use those lights to hypnotize their prey."

"What are they?"

"The creatures Asherah fought in the legend: Lurkers. They are not animals. They are sentient predators that come from the Infinity Pits. They eat freefolk, especially those that use magick. They feed on it," Sam said, her voice trembling, betraying a sense of fear. Gaby couldn't blame her. It seemed that for her people, they were the boogeyman. That would explain why Sam used a flashlight instead of a spell. It made sense now.

"So they are incursions," Gaby replied, biting her lip a bit. She tried to remain in front of them, blocking the creatures from Sam and Fionn. "That explains the drop in temperature."

"Natural occurring ones," Sam added. "They never leave this place though."

Gaby took another look at the Lurkers, being careful to not stare at their hypnotic patterns. Without the distraction of the hypnosis, Gaby thought they resembled the mud scarabs from the Watersnakes, mixed with the deep water crabs found at Orca Bay and blended with the furry limbs of a tarantula. They spoke, their voices taking on the resonance of nails scratching a blackboard, and Gaby was surprised she could understand them.

"They would make for a nice meal," one of them hissed.

"I tasted a bit of the human bleeding there. It was delightful," the second one replied.

"The younger one is teeming with magick. Her flesh will be a treat."

The fact that they had preyed on Fionn enraged Gaby, breaking any leftover of their hypnotic effect on her. She felt her blood boiling. She clenched her teeth. They would pay for it.

"Sam, can you help your dad? I need to carry out some pest control," Gaby said, standing up and unsheathing her twin short blades.

"Just hold them off long enough until I pick him up. With any luck, we will manage to evade them."

"How much time do you think you will need?"

"Just a few minutes," Sam said with short breaths.

Gaby stared at the two Lurkers surrounding them. To know their true size was impossible, as they were camouflaging part of their bodies within the canyon's shadows. She just needed to keep them at bay long enough for Sam to work her magick in Fionn's body to help him heal. But her magick and Fionn's aura turned them into a tasty snack for the creatures. The only option Gaby had was to give them a meal they couldn't ignore and even less, pass up. Her grip on her twin swords tightened. Their blades glowed blue and red. Her irises started to glow icy blue.

Gaby faced the Lurkers, keeping Sam and Fionn behind her. Twirling her blades, she stood at a ready stance.

Heartguard, her left blade in horizontal position, the arm holding it extended to its full length. Soulkeeper, the right one, with the blade in vertical position, retracted. It was a hand-to-hand combat stance adapted to the shorter blades. She waited for the first attack, a horizontal strike from one of the first Lurker's claws, and parried it. The second one, the smaller one, attacked her from the flank. They were trying to surround her. Their claws packed a punch, as each parry made her bones ache, even as she deflected the attack. Taking the hits in earnest would have surely ended with her limbs being pulverized. More than a combat, it became a game to keep the Lurkers busy long enough to help Sam escape with Fionn and maybe, just maybe, get a lucky hit to scare them off.

For a second, Gaby felt that time slowed enough for her to see the fast attacks of the Lurkers' claws, but her body couldn't react with enough speed to counter them. Even if the Gift gave her heightened senses, the truth was she had neglected to practice with it. Having prophetic dreams wouldn't help her now.

The Lurkers increased their speed and Gaby found herself blocking rather than evading until one strike landed on her right side and sent her flying into the wall of the canyon. Dazed, she struggled to get on her feet.

The creatures closed in on Sam and Fionn. Sam was occupied trying to keep Fionn's body together long enough for it to start healing and her defensive spells were unfocused and weak. Gaby tasted her own blood, her lip had been split and she was having trouble breathing. The creatures were stronger than she had surmised at first, even with the Gift activated.

Going by what Sam had told her about the Lurkers, they were parasites that fed on the magick energies emanated by the Maze. They would only get stronger with time. Gaby needed to take them down with all her might. And that meant entering the addictive and dangerous Ice State without Alex nearby to bring her back. It would unleash a dark side she still had trouble keeping in check, even after more than a decade of trying. Letting it free would mean sacrificing her own mind. But she looked to where Sam was, and to where Fionn lay. He had sacrificed himself to cover their escape. It was her turn to return the favor. And then it came to her. Her third realization was that if she wanted her loved ones to be safe, she would have to do it herself. And that meant confronting her inner nightmares and use the teachings from the Sisters of Mercy to do so. It was like the legend of Asherah that Sam just told her. Fionn would need a miracle to heal himself this time. And that miracle would have to be her.

*Sorry, Alex, but I just need to do it once more if we are going to make it out of this place.*

"It's just a dance," Gaby murmured and just like that, her heart slowed, freezing, her eyes glazed and glowed with more intensity. She had entered into the 'Ice State' of the Merciful Assassins. Her mind was now locked in a single objective: to kill the enemy in front of her in order to protect Fionn and Samantha.

She ran towards the Lurkers and slid beneath one to reach the other side, putting herself once more between them and Sam and Fionn. Then, putting all her strength behind it, kicked one of the creatures on the side of the 'head' and sent it crashing the other.

"You want them? You will have to pass through me!" Gaby yelled at the creatures.

The first Lurker launched an attack, aiming to crush Gaby flat against the ground, but she somersaulted backwards. Spinning in the air, she extended her legs and landed on top of a rock. The second Lurker dashed forward, and pulverized the rock with its claw.

Gaby leaped forward, striking the head of the second Lurker with Soulkeeper, her right blade. It cut deep, taking out one of the creature's eyes, spilling blood that glowed blue against the shadows. She landed on the ground and launched herself forward, evading another slashing attack by the first Lurker. Rolling away, she ran towards the wall of the canyon and jumped on it, thrusting herself forward toward the second creature, still disoriented from its injury.

With combined slashes from Heartguard and Soulkeeper, Gaby cut what she assumed was its head. Or at least one of them. With another jump using a rock as a step, she descended upon the first Lurker, hitting it on the back with her two blades.

Gaby kept slashing the Lurkers until only a pulp was left. But she couldn't stop. She didn't want to stop. A part of her mind was asking her to stop, but she couldn't. It was as if she was trapped inside her own body, watching it from afar acting on its own volition. In previous occasions she had been able to break free, either through the help of a loved one or through a memento, like the hoodie she had borrowed from Alex. But this time, in her anger, she had gone too deep. Her heart remained frozen. Such was the curse behind the 'Ice State.'

She could hear Sam yelling at her, begging her to stop. But for Gaby, it was just a distant sound. Once she unleashed her dark side, it was hard for her to stop. Maybe Alex was right, maybe only true love could break the spell.

Then she heard another voice. Not the usual one she had acquired after the awakening of the Gift. It was his voice.

"Gaby, please stop. Come back. Please."

She turned around. Sam was cradling Fionn's severely injured body within what seemed to be a bubble. He was unconscious. And yet Gaby could hear his voice calling her to break the self-inflicted spell. Her heart thawed and a tear rolled down her cheek. A sensation of warmth grew inside her chest.

For a brief second, she saw a vision of Fionn, floating away in a strange space, extending his hand to her. "Please, stop. You can break it."

Gaby extended her hand and the vision disappeared.

"Gaby! Gaby! Are you ok?" Sam asked, breaking Gaby from her vision. Her eyes were red and it was clear she was trying to contain tears. "My dad is not responding. It's like he is not there, his body is empty. I need your help. Please."

She blinked a few times. Gaby's eyes returned to normal and the grip on her blades loosened. Her heartbeat slowed and she could feel herself breathing normally once more.

Something had changed in her but she had no idea what it was. Correction, two things had changed. On the first, regarding her Gift, she now had an inkling of a new way to use it.

But that would have to wait. On the second, at least she had a better idea what it was. Fionn was breathing with difficulties, but his healing ability was starting to kick in. As long as they could keep him in one piece, his body would recover. And his mind would return soon. As long as she was there with him, he would come back. And her heart bounced inside her chest. Gaby was having trouble admitting it but she was starting to care for Fionn more than expected. Otherwise, his voice wouldn't have been able to break the trance. Only those she cared for were able to do that.

"Let's get him back," Gaby said.

She smiled her trademark crooked smile, sheathed her blades and went to help Sam carry Fionn's body back to the Figaro. Once there, she would help him return from wherever his soul was traveling. And then she would never leave his side. Not in the coming battle. Not ever again.

# Chapter 13

## Rock Bottom

*This doesn't feel that bad. Not this time.*

Fionn was floating in space. Or what he thought was space. It wasn't warm, but certainly it wasn't cold. It was like when he was half asleep in a comfy bed. Or like when he floated in the lake near Skarabear during a summer day, long before he dived into it to get Black Fang. He was tempted to keep his eyes closed, but curiosity got the best of him and he opened them. He tried to make sense of the surroundings. Here, in this 'dimension,' there were drifting derelict ships, massive planets, and asteroids.

*Last time it really felt awful. I wonder why?*

The first time he died, when the Light Explosion hit him, disintegrating his body, the pain shockwave kept hitting at him for a while. He had been disconcerted, confused. It felt like an eternity, although according to Ywain, his badly burned body hit the ground just a few seconds after being hit by the explosion.

Below him, he saw the same labyrinth he had seen the first time he 'died.' Just gazing at that place filled his core with dread and horror. As if he had been there once. As if he had to escape after months trapped in a twisted landscape.

*Had that been real too?*

That labyrinth was the infamous entrance to the Infinity

Pits. Above him, a verdant planet full of light called him. He felt his body... was it his body or his soul? He couldn't tell. He felt his body being dragged by a black and red raven, grabbing him by the belt, towards the planet.

*I must be dead, again, because this doesn't make any sense.*

He landed in a grass field in front of a woman with long black hair and Kuni features, clad in demon hunter armor with large shoulder fins and spaudlers. She was sitting on a big limestone rock.

"You are not dead yet. But if you keep leaving your guard open like that, not even your Gift will save you. You had way too many thoughts in your head," the woman smacked Fionn in the head with a bamboo stick. "Now sit, my student!"

Fionn obeyed, sitting with crossed legs.

"Master?" Fionn exclaimed. The woman in front of him looked like Hikaru, his teacher. She had been a former demon hunter from the Kuni Empire and friends with his parents. Hikaru, along with his mother, had taken on the responsibilities of his training when his father passed away. She trained Izia as well. But one day, Hikaru simply left without saying a word and never returned. It was months after her disappearance that Fionn claimed Black Fang from the depths of the lake, and wielded it to defend his town from Horde raiders. That fight motivated him and Izia to join King Castlemartell's army.

But there was something off with the woman sitting on the rock. It was the way she kept smiling at him. Hikaru might have been a dear person to him, like a second mother, but she rarely, if ever, smiled.

"Wait," Fionn said, tilting his head to the left, examining the person in front of him. "You might look like her, but you are not Hikaru. Who are you?"

"Does that matter?" The woman's smile grew wider. For a second she looked menacing.

"Yes, I don't like being tricked," Fionn replied, standing

up. He wasn't in the mood to be intimidated by some spirit.

"Interesting choice of words," the woman said, laughing. She stood up and changed into what Fionn assumed, was her real shape. It was a tall woman, taller than Fionn, with red and black hair held back by a tiara. Her eyes were big and of an emerald green color. Her skin color changed with the light. She wore silvery plate armor with feather-like engravings worked into its surface. Over that, she wore a cape made of red and black raven feathers. Her ethereal beauty complimented the aura of ancient wisdom that she emitted. Fionn could see a certain resemblance to the freefolk. The colors, the raven motifs... all of it fit with the legend. Now he was actually scared. Because if he was right, he was in the presence of the patron deity of his people.

"Are you... are you the Trickster Goddess?" Fionn asked. Goosebumps ran across his back and a knot formed in the bottom of his stomach. A spirit, a demon, he could deal with. Coming face-to-face with the most revered goddess of his people made him nervous.

*I guess this is how Asherah must have felt,* he thought.

"Asherah was more curious and less of a dunderhead," the Trickster Goddess looked curiously. Fionn felt as if her gaze was piercing his true self. It was unnerving. "Yes, I hear your thoughts. This is a place for the mind and the spirit after all. I admit that Hikaru is right, you are not that dumb. Maybe just too stubborn for your own good. Now, take a seat before I hit you again in the head."

"Sorry, it's not every day that you meet one of your deities." Fionn sat down once more in the grass. "So you know my master. Do you know where she is?"

"Curious that you are more concerned about her than about yourself. But yes, she is fine, let's say that she has been taking care of family business for the past century." The Trickster sat down again on her rock. "She gave me two messages for you: one, if by some chance you manage to get out of this alive, go and look for her."

"And two?"

"That you need to take the final step so you can truly complete your training." The Trickster smacked Fionn again in the head.

"Oww!" Fionn rubbed his head. If he was dead, why did the pain feel so real? "Can you stop that?" It wasn't helpful when Hikaru did it and certainly was not helpful now.

"I would, if your skull wasn't so thick as to stop you from actually getting my advice inside it. Now, as I was saying, you need to take a final step to finish your training."

"Which is?" Fionn asked, half confused, half frustrated.

"Become a master," the Trickster replied with a face that pretty much said *I thought it was obvious, you dunderhead.*

"No," Fionn said, meeting the gaze of the Trickster with defiance.

"What do you mean by no?" The Trickster was taken aback. Fionn guessed that not many mortals defied her. But when it came to this topic, he wasn't in the mood to change of opinion.

"No. I won't do it. Not anymore. Not again."

The goddess just stared at him. Her head tilted to the right, as if she was examining, judging him and waiting for a more elaborated answer. The unnatural eyes of the goddess made the whole thing feel a tad unnerving.

Fionn sighed.

"For starters, I'm lousy at teaching. Also, being a teacher is a bad job in this business of helping people. Odds are that you will get killed by distracting the bad guy so the rookies can escape. You know how many legends go that way?"

The Trickster laughed at that last comment.

"I find it amusing that you say that, given your current predicament. I mean, you did exactly that. For being a warrior famous for being smart, you are disappointing me with your lack of self-awareness. As for those legends, they are just that, legends, not an actual account of reality. And you of all people don't have much excuse about the dying thing."

"My point is that me being here proves that I can die. So there is not much point in asking me to teach someone if I'm already dead. Unless you want me to come back to haunt them as a ghost."

"The thing is, smartass, that you are not dead. Yet. Let's say that this is a teleconference I set up given that you left your innards all over the floor of my Maze. Now, you will be dead if you don't teach those kids and insist on doing things alone. You can't win a war alone."

"It has worked fine for me so far," Fionn crossed his arms.

"Tell that to your belly," the Trickster pointed her stick towards his stomach. "Or the Dragonking."

"That's a low blow."

"I'm not here to sugarcoat things," the Trickster explained. "I'm here to do my job, which funnily enough is the same job you should be doing: teaching."

"Last time I tried, it blew up spectacularly and I ended up creating a monster."

"Technically, your last time was when you taught Sam how to defend herself. And while she is a capable fighter, she could have been better. She can be better. The Dragonking saw that and taught her what you should have."

"I was trying to keep her safe."

"She'd have been safer if you'd done your job and trained her properly!"

"You don't mince words, do you?"

"No."

An uncomfortable silence set between them. Fionn averted his gaze, instead focusing on a very interesting blade of grass.

"Ahem," the Trickster said, breaking the silence.

"Look, I don't want to do it." Fionn looked at her. His heart was beating hard inside his chest. He would have preferred to be anywhere but there. His bones ached. If he didn't know better, he would say he was suffering a panic attack. He wasn't prone to having panic attacks; he had faced monsters, great fighters and strange beings. Then again, this was not a common situation. "Byron is my fault. I made him the monster he was, and is. I was too trusting, too green, and too blind to see that I was not ready to teach forms of combat that combined too well with the Gift. Doing that does nothing but make you a monster."

"Hikaru taught you the same forms when you were a kid and you didn't have the Gift. What's the difference?"

"I don't know. What do you want me to say? That she believed that I was a good person?" Fionn felt his eyes welling up. It was hard for him to admit this, but he had been contemplating the issue for years now. "Well she failed. I'm a bad person, a lousy one. I have hurt many people because of her failure. I have killed many. I made countless mistakes and paid a high cost for them."

"Being a fallible person doesn't make you lousy. And it certainly doesn't make you a bad person. You are mortal. And let me tell you, even gods make mistakes. That's why Life is full of parallels, to give you a second chance. Those kids waiting for you? They are your second chance.

"Why are you dragging your feet?" The Trickster looked at him, tilting her head to the side. It was hard to decipher what she was thinking. "I know you are stubborn, that's why you can heal your injuries quickly, because your body refuses to accept them. But this is ridiculous. Be honest with yourself. Why?"

"Because... because I'm afraid of failing again!" Fionn yelled at the top of his lungs. "Or worse, succeeding and creating another Byron. I don't want to lose anyone. To lose them. Because they remind me of them..."

"Of Izia and Ywain?" the Trickster said, with a soothing tone.

"Yes. I trained Byron because I considered him a friend and that cost me Izia and my family."

"Last time I checked you had Sam."

"I trained Ywain and it ended badly for him," Fionn said, not hearing her comment.

"He actually had a decent life, you even met his great grandson."

"I can't do that to him again. To them."

"Do what?"

"To fill their heads with ideas of becoming heroes. It will ruin their lives."

"Like when you were a kid?"

"Yes. Being a hero."

"Doing the right thing is never easy," the Trickster said sagely.

"It will ruin their lives."

"You don't know that. And it is their choice in the end."

"Well, I'm taking that choice off the table."

"You can try, but it won't work. They will do what they believe is right. With or without you. Look."

A mist wall formed between them. Images appeared in the mist, like a movie. Fionn saw Gaby jumping on a rock and hitting a Lurker with her blades. She kept slashing at the Lurker in an emotionless frenzy. Fionn heard Sam asking her to stop, but Gaby didn't seem to be listening.

"What's that? That look in her eyes. I have never seen it."

"It's called the Ice State, a very powerful, very addictive trance-like state taught by the Sisters of Mercy. The more Gaby uses it, the more she will get trapped in it, till she becomes cold as ice, emotionless."

"If that is so risky, why is she doing it?"

"She is fighting to save Sam and to save *you* from the Lurkers. Why? Because she is a good person. Because it's the right thing to do. Because maybe she has feelings for you? She is doing exactly what Asherah did to save the freefolk: risking everything for those she cares about. For *you*. So don't dare to cheapen her choices."

"Please, stop. You can break it." Fionn extended his

hands towards the vision and for a second, Gaby turned her head towards him. It was as if she could see him. Her eyes returned to normality. Fionn couldn't hear what she was saying, but saw her smile. The vision disappeared, leaving him and the Trickster.

"It's clear that you need to go back now. As you saw, they need you and your guidance. You really need to think about what we discussed here."

The raven came back, this time picking him up by the collar of his t-shirt. It lifted him from the ground and took him back into the weird space.

"I will think about it, but I don't make any promises."

The raven flew away with Fionn at an incredible speed for a bird that size. Fionn passed out once more. He could now clearly hear a familiar voice calling to him.

"Why do I have the feeling that you are gonna forget this whole discussion? I need to knock more sense in you." the Trickster told him as he was being pulled away.

"You can try," Fionn yelled at the distance.

† † †

Fionn opened his eyes again, but this time, instead of seeing the ghostly vision of his master yelling at him, he saw Gaby's face with blurry eyes. She was saying to him words that he couldn't make sense of and was smiling and waving at someone outside his field of vision. Then a ringing noise came to his head and he felt dizzy, almost ready to throw up. His vision cleared, a prelude to an intense wave of pain that flowed through his body. The pain was followed by a feeling of extreme heat. Faint specks of light floated around him. His healing abilities were back and working overtime. He could feel the broken bones in his sternum, legs and arms placing themselves in their right places and fusing together. When that happened to his shattered skull and chopped ribs, he felt as if his head was going to explode, and he gasped for air.

He righted himself and tried to stand up, but Gaby and someone else held him back. His hand was reaching instinctively to the place where Byron had stabbed him. It hurt as Pits, a burning sensation waved through his belly. He could feel his enhanced healing working. He might heal fast, but the pain lingered.

"I don't feel well," Fionn mumbled, his throat coarse and rough.

"That's what happens when someone has to shove your innards back inside you to save you," a voice to his left said. It was a sweet voice. The same voice that called him back from that strange place. It was Gaby.

"Keep him down or the stitches will open again and the healing won't work," a voice to his right said. It took him a few seconds but he recognized it as coming from Sam, and he smiled.

*She is fine. I'm glad,* Fionn thought. Once the ringing in his head subsided, he could make out what Gaby was saying, while Alex kept him seated and Harland examined the stitches.

"You need to rest, Fionn. You are pretty banged up and you are healing slowly," Gaby indicated. "Well, slow for you at least."

She was smiling, but her eyes looked red. Had she been crying? Fionn wondered. Fionn noticed she had bruises on her arms and a slight cut on the left side of her neck. A close call with a blade without a doubt.

"Your guts are still bleeding and not healed totally, Dad," Sam appeared in his sight. She had a split lip and a bruise on her forehead. Out of everyone, she seemed to have the least amount of injuries. "Oh, this?" She pointed to the bruise on her forehead. "A little encounter with the Lurkers."

"Lurkers?" Fionn asked. "Those things are dangerous. We need to move."

"You need to rest," Sam said, pushing him back. "Don't worry, Gaby got rid of them."

"She is right about your guts, though. We don't want to pick them up. Again," Gaby said with a deadpan expression. Fionn wasn't sure if she was being honest or just pulling his leg, but judging from the burning on the lower side of his abdomen, the truth may be somewhere in the middle. He turned around and saw Alex, who sported bruises and cuts on his left arm. He was breathing slowly, which meant injured ribs.

"Your injuries. Were you also saving me?" Fionn asked Alex.

"Nah, we got these when we crash landed. I miscalculated something with some explosives and... look, it's a long story. And not the important one here."

"You got me worried man," Harland added, offering him a bottle of water. Fionn saw Harland's bruises on his face and a bandage closing a cut on his left eyebrow.

Fionn tried to remember what had happened. His mind made a blurry recollection of the destruction of Ravestone, the death of the Dragonking and his fight with Byron. Then everything went blank. A shiver went down his spine because of the memory. He also remembered parts of his out-of-body experience, if he could call it that.

"How long was I gone? And how far was the fall?" Fionn asked in a raspy voice. The water was clearing his throat.

"Long enough for them to find you," Sid replied, his voice sounding far away. "You know time is tricky to measure here. About the second, I can tell you it was almost two kilometers. It's lucky that you started to heal during the fall or you would be a pizza now."

Gaby and Sam glared at Sid with disapproving looks.

"What?" he asked. Sid shrugged. He was cleaning his hands with a greasy rag. "Look hooman, I'm glad you are ok and I'm sorry for being a humbug, but we need to fix the Figaro if we will ever have hopes of getting out of here."

"He is right," Alex admitted. "While you heal, there is nothing else we can do but fix the ship."

If what Fionn remembered was right, the last time he saw the Figaro, it had been hit on what he assumed were the engines and was descending at a worrying speed. The fact that all of them were alive and apparently in one piece made him feel slightly better.

"I can help with the ship and you know it," Gaby mentioned, a tad annoyed.

"I know and I really could use your help because Alex keeps frying the fuses when he touches them, but none of us have a damn clue about first aid or how to keep someone alive, besides you," Sid replied a bit sheepishly.

"We need to keep him awake," Sam added. "Hits in the head heal slower and he could suffer memory loss."

"Ladies, don't worry, I'm feeling better and this time my liver will stay in its place. I can sit a while and keep talking to you while you work on the Figaro, so you don't have to worry about my head. I promise," Fionn moved into a reclined position, using a rock as a rest for his back. "Besides, it is not the first time I've been impaled."

"Not funny, Dad," Sam said, clearly not amused.

Gaby and Sam joined the rest who were trying to repair the ship, whose hull was riddled with holes. Fionn tried to rest. Usually, the effectiveness and speed of his healing ability depended on the level of damage suffered and how much energy he had left. This time, it had been pushed to the limit and he felt spent.

Fast healing or not, it hurt. He wasn't a pain addict, and thus had never tested his abilities to this extent. He knew he had survived the Light Explosion and Longhorn Valley and it hadn't been a pleasant experience. While his skin healed the burns, the pain had lasted for weeks. But that had been his 'first death' and the process always worked differently for everybody. Of those he had known with the Gift, only he and his friend Sophia had kept the initial healing abilities.

"This is the second time you got impaled? Is that a kind of record?" Alex asked, trying to keep Fionn awake. Gaby rolled her eyes at the comment. But even Fionn had to admit that the question made him chuckle, which hurt a bit. "I hope it wasn't the same guy," Alex replied, now joking. "I mean that would be really bad luck."

"Well..." Fionn started.

"No way!" Alex turned his head from the welding gun. "Who's that guy anyway? Not a fan of yours apparently."

Fionn exchanged looks with Harland, who nodded at him.

"It's a long story," Fionn said, weary and tired.

"Trust me, we are not going anywhere soon," Sid yelled from inside the gaping hole in the hull. "Alex, be careful! You are going to burn my face with that! *B'ax!*"

"Sorry. Go on, Fionn," Gaby said, apologizing on their behalf.

"He used to be a friend, ages ago before he turned into that... that thing. His name was, sorry, is Byron Castlemartell," Fionn said.

At the sound of that last name, Sid came out from the hole and Alex stopped welding. Fionn now had all their attention.

"My world history is a bit rusty, but wasn't he the elder son of old King Castlemartell? The one you fought alongside during the Great War?" Alex asked.

"Heir apparent to boot," Harland added.

"Judging by the way he beat you up, there is a lot of bad blood there," Alex said. "What happened? Didn't he die in a tragic accident while visiting the Northern Provinces?"

"Ughh," Fionn complained while getting comfortable. By now most of the fractures were healed and the internal bleeding was diminishing. The ringing in his ears kept coming and going, as his brain healed from the concussion. The talk was helping him keep focused and alert.

"Byron was the heir apparent to the throne," Fionn started. "And at the time, a good friend and a great leader of men, even if he had certain, let's say, uncomfortable views on magick users. We won many battles thanks to him. But while he was a good man on the surface, he had a dark side, a bloodlust for power and conflict that the war kept sated. The problems started once the war came to an end and the King fell ill. Most people expected Byron to inherit the crown and with it, the power to lead the Alliance. But I guess the King knew his son better than the rest of us, and stalled the matter until he found a way to change the rules and pass the leadership to another of his surviving children."

"I bet Byron didn't like that," Sid interjected.

"Not at all, especially since he suspected that his father would choose someone else, like Princess Sophia, the youngest of the heirs. Despite her age, she was a member of the Twelve Swords and a fearless warrior. Of all the heirs, she was the one who took more after her father. And she had the support of several people, including Ywain, my best friend and previous owner of Yaha." Fionn stopped for a second, noticing how the mention of that name briefly caught Alex's full attention. "Yes, Alex, I think we are talking about the same person."

Alex stopped what he was doing and walked towards Fionn.

"Ywain was by far the most powerful of us, having the Gift with him almost since birth. He was kind and certainly didn't like Byron. After the war he planned to move to a secluded place and start a new life, maybe a family," Fionn continued. "The King was fond of him. Ywain had started as the King's squire and later became one of his personal guards. The first Solarian Knight so to speak. And he later became Sophia's personal guard. I thought they would end up marrying, which would have pleased the King. That's why Byron went for him first. He was the only one of us who could bypass Byron's nullifying ability that canceled magick and Gifts alike. Ywain was the one who could challenge him on even ground. That was our first mistake. Half of the Twelve Swords got the Gift roughly around the same time, so we assumed Byron got it the same way, through the Light Explosion like me, or during an earlier event, like his sister. But we were wrong. What we didn't know was that he got his abilities much earlier, in another way, one far more sinister as he belonged to a cult that worshiped the Outsiders. That frigging bastard played us for years!"

"Was he part of the Fraternity of Gadol?" Gaby interjected.

"Yes. The same guys that I suspect started the incursion when you two met. They have been trying to bring forth the Masters of the Pits for who knows how long," Fionn explained. "Byron was that good at concealing that fact. We never had reason to suspect him. Not at least until he started to quell rebellions of remote outposts towards the end of the war in a bloody fashion. The King asked Ywain to look into that and as far as we knew, Ywain suffered an accident during the taking of a city, falling into a chasm. Later we found that Byron had fought him and apparently had killed him."

"But you suspect that somehow Ywain made it out alive after all?" Alex asked, confused.

"The fact that you have Yaha, and that you kinda look like him, but slightly more chubby — no offense — makes me think so. Or at least I hope so." Fionn smiled.

"See? I told you to lay off the pizza," Sid whispered to Alex.

"Shut up."

"Anyways, Ywain's disappearance and the following attacks on freefolk villages clued us into what was going on. Byron might have been a great military leader, but he was sloppy when anger got the best of him. A lot of times we were blamed for his extreme measures during the war. That's how the Greywolf name earned the 'colorful' reputation it holds now," Fionn concluded ruefully.

"Like the damn incident that destroyed a whole town?" Gaby inquired.

"No, that was totally mine." Fionn laughed. "But in my

defense, I had everything covered until Byron messed up and Ywain had to go back for that girl and her goat."

Fionn felt fully healed but still weak. All of them were tired and hungry.

They took a break to start a fire and cook the food stored in the Figaro's pantries. To no one's surprise, it consisted almost entirely of hamburgers.

"Care to finish your loooooooong story?" Alex said, making the 'o' sound long enough to leave him breathless.

"I never said it was short. I'm summarizing a decade of events in one go. When we found out about Byron's betrayal, we faced him and he killed, or left for dead, most of us before we were able to trap his soul on the Outerside and his body in a mausoleum. We were desperate after seeing how much power he had amassed, how indestructible he seemed, and couldn't think of another approach at the time, not one that had more of a chance at succeeding. That's when he impaled me the first time..." Fionn paused and let out a sigh. "...and Izia died to seal him away."

He felt Gaby's gaze upon him. She was blushing and smiling faintly at him. He didn't know what to make of it. Except that the way she looked at him reminded him of how his wife used to look at him when he was feeling under the weather. It felt... familiar.

"At least he is consistent," Harland chimed in. "You have to admire that." Fionn only cast him a sidelong glance that could freeze a bottle of water.

"My wife died there, most of my friends too, because I was arrogant and cocky and eager to fight in the war. In order to get accepted into the Twelve Swords, I taught him all I knew for combating monsters. And when he became one and betrayed us, I was so sure that I could take him on, while the rest tried to seal his power. I mean, it was my duty to protect them... and I failed." Fionn punched the ground with anger and stopped. It was painful thinking of Izia's body freezing to death while the spell took action and kept him safe and the seal closed. The last image he had of his wife was looking at her sweet face, her eyes closing with tears in them, while Fionn, unable to move to help her, was stuck in place. The memories turned into nightmares that never ceased and even to this day, falling asleep took a monumental effort for him. But not as big as waking up. Dreams were the only place where he could truly be at peace and see her.

"Will whatever you did back then to stop him work this time?" Gaby asked.

"I don't think so," Fionn shook his head and then lowered his chin onto his chest. "Only Izia knew the spell. It was an ancient shamanic incantation that she found who knows where. There were also some special components that can't be found nowadays, you can thank extinction and progress for that. And even if we managed to duplicate the whole plan, Byron's followers would find a way to break the seals again. I'm not going to risk anybody else's lives just for a half desperate measure. He has to be killed. For good. I already have lost so much because of him. People have suffered enough."

Out of the blue, Gaby walked over to Fionn and hugged him. She let go after a minute.

"Ok..." Fionn was surprised by the gesture. Sam and Harland shared a look and smiled.

"Well, if we approach this from a different angle, the best course of action is the simplest one: do to him what you did to the monster at my university," Alex stated, looking at the ground, doodling in the dirt. He was either too focused on the problem or was ignoring the hug. Now that he thought about it, Fionn never asked what kind of relationship Gaby and Alex had. But there would be time for that later, hopefully.

"I assume Ywain tried that and it didn't work. He knew the basics of monster killing. It works for monsters because usually they are too prideful or dumb enough to let you get that close. And you need to be really fast. But Byron is a whole different thing. He knows how to deal with that kind of attack. And now he has more power than back then. Getting close enough won't be easy." Fionn got up.

"You now have the advantage of a century of technology over the man. And you have us." Alex got up as well and smiled at Fionn.

"You don't know enough of your abilities to take this on." Fionn was starting to get exasperated. He wasn't going to risk someone else's life to finish something he couldn't do the first time.

"Then teach us." Alex defiantly got in Fionn's face. The sight from the Gift allowed Fionn to see the storm inside Alex brewing, trying to be unleashed. Ywain had been the same. And Byron too, for that matter. But the last time he had seen this mix of darkness and light in someone, Ywain ended up dead and Byron betrayed him.

"Last time I did, it ended poorly for everybody. Including me," Fionn countered. Deep down, he was afraid that training either of these two would end with disastrous consequences. Gaby was still concealing too much pain under her compassion. Alex, on the other hand, was a bomb of anger waiting to explode.

"Boohoo. I get it, you trusted someone and were betrayed. That's life. But right now you are stuck with us. And you got beaten in Round Two. It's time to win in Round Three. Don't be a coward." Alex was still challenging him and not backing down. Fionn knew as well as Alex that a fight between them would end poorly for the younger man. But Alex stood his ground. Just like Ywain used to do. "You want us to survive this? Fine, show us how, damn it!"

"Sam, you have been quiet, what do you think?" Gaby asked her.

"I want to fight Byron as badly as you," Sam replied. "But I don't know if we will be enough."

The tension was high and the atmosphere was turning unpleasant. It was as charged as the Thunderplains.

"Alex is right," Harland broke the silence. "I can't see

another way, considering our precarious situation. We need all the help available."

"Even if he is, we don't have enough time," Fionn conceded. "Besides, I can't beat him without Black Fang. Given what I saw during the combat, only my sword withstood a clash against his."

Sid, who had remained quiet for the last part of the talk, stopped what he was doing and walked towards them. He was listening to the sounds of the wind in the canyon.

"Silly hoomans with your size measuring contest. Shut up and listen, we have company," Sid pointed to the lights coming their way. He had his battle axes already out and Alex picked up his bow. Sam and Gaby stuck together, examining the visitors.

Two giant dragonwolves almost five meters in height, glared at them while silently padding out from the shadows. One was white as the snow, while the other had beige fur. Both dragonwolves were carrying large nets containing several trinkets and flasks that glowed with different colored lights. Two riders sat bareback upon the wolves, casually guiding them with minute flicks of their reins.

One of the riders was a stocky man, about Alex's height. Blond and dark brown strands of hair mixed on his head. Beneath his clothes, several markings and tattoos in black and blue ink could be seen, which determined his tribe of origin and rank. He was from the Fire Tribe of the freefolk, one of the oldest. The other rider was a little girl. She was wearing an old green poncho with raven feathers knit into it. Her hair was a wild combination of black and red strands. Her face had some tattooed marks under the eyes, and on top of the wild mess of hair, two rabbit ears could be seen. She had bright, large eyes whose color changed from blue to purple, to golden, depending on the angle. But the brightest feature was her wide smile.

"Who are you?" Harland asked, keeping Fionn on his left.

"This is my assistant Stealth Drakglass and I'm Mekiri the Wise!" The little girl replied, increasing the volume of her voice to add a dramatic effect. Fionn could have sworn that he heard thunder but figured it was part of the concussion he was still nursing. Mekiri then grabbed a long, black stick from one of her bags and lifted it above her head. "And I think this is yours," she tossed the stick to Fionn, who caught it. A question formed on his face as he looked upon the blade of Black Fang.

# Chapter 14

## Mekiri the Great... Librarian

"What? Haven't you heard of me?" Mekiri asked, looking at the confused faces staring at her. "I am greatly offended, especially by you, Greywolf. How quickly you have forgotten your roots!"

"Oh, I have heard of you," Fionn replied with a chuckle. "It's that I thought Mekiri, the greatest magus of the freefolk, would look different... you know... older? I mean, you were a legend even in the times of my grandfather. And he was quite old."

"I knew your grandfather. Crazy old man. Good alchemist. And like you are one to talk." Mekiri frowned, climbing down from her dragonwolf and walking towards Fionn. She was even shorter than Harland and looked young, really young. Like a six-year-old kid. It made for a stark contrast when she stood in front of Fionn, who out of respect knelt in front of her. She then smacked Fionn on the head with her cane. "Besides, why would I choose to look aged if I have enough magick to choose my looks? I could look like a dragon or a giant raven with six wings if I so wished. Human minds are so constrained by your assumptions of how the world should look. A shame indeed, your kind has much potential and imagination. At least the freefolk tried. Failed, but tried."

Mekiri shook her head. There was a tinge of sadness

and regret in her voice.

"Who is she?" Alex asked.

"Mekiri is a legendary magus amongst the freefolk," Sam replied. "The greatest of them all. She is the one chosen by the Trickster Goddess to keep watch over the Ravenhall."

"The what?"

"Ravenhall, the largest repository of knowledge from all corners, from all times in Theia." Mekiri said to Alex. "Created during the Dawn Age, it appears inside the Maze to the weary traveler who honestly searches for knowledge."

"Ah, that makes sense... not," Alex replied, still looking confused.

"Forgive him, Great Mekiri. He is new at this," Sam said, apologizing with a curtsey.

"Ah, at least one of you knows the proper forms." Mekiri smiled at Sam. "You must be a student at Ravenstone. I have seen you from afar, little one."

"Actually, I'm a junior researcher," Sam said. Then she added somberly, "Not that it matters now with what has happened."

"Everything matters. Everything. Right, Greywolf? Or should I address you as Fionn?"

"I'm surprised you know about me," Fionn replied.

"You too are a legend for our people," Stealth finally spoke. "The child of two species who fought to protect them regardless of the cost. The monster hunter, the last of the Greywolf clan, the Wind Tribe. We have kept an eye on you," Stealth explained, without elaborating further. Fionn was going to ask more about that but was rudely interrupted by Sid.

"Leave that alone, you hairball!" Sid yelled at Mekiri's dragonwolf, which was chewing one of the wings of the Figaro, to the amusement of Mekiri. The little magus approached her dragonwolf and petted it.

"Now, now, that's not a toy, Cookie. Let it go. You too, Moka," Mekiri said to both dragonwolves. They stopped chewing the Figaro's wing and lay in front of their owner. Then she turned again to Fionn. "I know a lot of things. Knowledge is power."

"If you are so powerful, why don't you help us?" Harland asked.

"Because I'm needed here to stop Ravenstone from crumbling." Mekiri pointed at the damaged school. "And to protect the rest of the freefolk. That's my job. Yours is to stop those who have been attacking us all over the world. Your world."

"Makes sense. A whole nation of magick users could be the only thing to stop Byron and whatever he is planning to summon," Harland said, stroking his beard. "Either way he has enough summoners now to move to the next step of his plan."

"Besides, Fionn, what do you need me for? You have here all you need to fight back," Mekiri added, pointing at Gaby and Alex, then to Sam, Harland, and Sid. "You have your Twelve Swords back... well half of them. You only need to look closely."

"They are not trained," Fionn replied. "Not in what they need to be."

"Teach them," Mekiri stated with a sly smile. "Do you think that you were already a proficient student in what you needed to be when your old master took you under her wing? Don't be presumptuous."

"That's a different thing; she trained me since I was old enough to hold a wooden sword. And she was an accomplished warrior and teacher before that. I... I'm a failure at that. History proves it."

"I don't see them being less able than you at the same age. They can do this. And more important, you can do this. Whatever happened before, leave it in the past. Look forward. You are only responsible for what you can do. And right now, if you want to defeat your enemy, you need to teach your friends what they need to know in order to help you. This is a battle that you don't have to fight alone," Mekiri said. Then she smacked Fionn on his head once more with her cane. "Dunderhead."

Fionn looked at Mekiri, with suspicion, rubbing his head. It all felt too familiar.

"We already told him that, but he doesn't want to accept our help," Alex interrupted.

"And I already told you, I can't," Fionn countered. "And even if I agreed, we don't have the time."

"Tsk, tsk, Fionn, you are letting your past drag you back," Mekiri hit Fionn in the leg, eliciting a grunt from him. She smiled at him. Fionn had seen that smile before but couldn't remember where. "And about the time, don't worry. The Maze and Ravenhall will provide answers to all your questions."

"Yeah, yeah, all that is fine, but we can't get away from here anyway. The Figaro's core is damaged, among other systems," Sid interjected.

"We can help," Stealth offered with a smile.

"No offense, but you don't strike me as knowing how to fix a sophisticated aeronautical masterpiece like the Figaro," Sid said. Alex facepalmed himself while Gaby shook her head and Harland rolled his eyes.

"I'm surprised that a samoharo has such a narrow mind," Mekiri replied. "Especially one that desires to visit the stars."

"I hold a few advanced degrees in engineering and physics," Stealth replied dryly.

"Plus I have this here," Mekiri said while jumping back on her dragonwolf. She rummaged through the bags hanging at the sides of the animal. A myriad of objects fell to the ground, mostly junk belonging to a hoarder's cave, including a sink. "Bingo!"

Mekiri rose and held aloft a pulsating orb that was bigger than her. It was a sphere, whose polished surface showed swirling streaks of green and red energy. It glowed with intensity. Sid's eyes opened wide, his mouth agape.

"I can't believe it!"

"Excuse me, but what's that?" Gaby asked politely to Mekiri, but Sid cut her off.

"It's a freaking dragoncore!" Sid took it from Mekiri's hands. "I thought they disappeared alongside the Montoc Dragons!"

"I surmise that it could help fix your ship," Stealth climbed down from his dragonwolf and removed some tools out of a bag.

"How long will it take to fix the Figaro?" Sam asked. "I'm worried. Byron and his followers have students with them, as well as Professor Hunt. We don't know how long they will keep them alive."

"Four, five hours providing we work nonstop," Sid explained. "Even then we don't know where they are heading."

"That can be solved," Alex replied, grinning. "They must have stolen a considerable amount of crystals for their spell. If we synchronize the Figaro's sensors with Sam's own crystal and the spare ones littering this place, the resonance will help us track them."

Sam cast a look of surprise towards Alex.

"What? I do pay attention," Alex shrugged his shoulders.

"The Maze won't let you go just yet, though," Stealth said out of the blue. "You need to pass a test first to receive the help you need from Ravenhall."

"Test? What are you talking about?" Fionn asked, confused.

"It's a shame you haven't kept in touch with your roots, Greywolf," Mekiri explained. "Ravenhall can answer your questions, provide you with help. But only if you undertake a test of character, a lesson from the Trickster Goddess, so to speak."

"That would explain why so many get lost here. But how do you know we have a test to pass?" Harland asked.

"Because that door with a stone frame wasn't there five minutes ago." Mekiri pointed towards a stone threshold, crowned by a raven statue. "That's the entrance to Ravenhall. The test has begun, your prayer for knowledge has been answered."

"This place is getting weirder with each minute," Harland murmured.

"What do I need to do?" Fionn asked, his grip on Black Fang tightening to the point of whitening his knuckles.

"Just enter, the test will reveal itself," Stealth said.

Fionn tried to open the door, but it didn't budge.

"The door is locked. Can we go now?" Fionn asked, annoyed.

"It won't open until you accept your test," Mekiri said, clearly exasperated. "Why do you have to be so stubborn? Hikaru was right in trying to knock some sense into you."

"How do you know about that?" Fionn was surprised. It had been a vision, not an actual event. Unless Mekiri was...

"Just take those two with you," Mekiri pointed to Alex and Gaby. She raised her voice. "And get the frigging test started. Kids these days! So damn stubborn!"

Mekiri hit Fionn once more in the knee.

"Ok, ok. We are running out of time. We'd better start with this," Fionn mumbled. He wasn't happy with his hand being forced while Byron was on the loose.

Gaby and Alex walked towards the entrance, followed by Sam.

"You can't go there, little one," Mekiri stopped Sam with her cane.

"Why?" Samantha looked confused.

"Because you haven't witnessed the Path of the Dead yet," the wizard added with a somber voice. Her expression turned sad. "Don't be in a hurry to follow it just yet. If it's in your personal fate, you will face it when the time is right."

"Forgive me wise one, but what do you mean by that?"

"Having a near-death experience is what awakens the

Gift. And it works only for a few lucky ones," Mekiri replied with a shadow of pain covering her face.

"You mean all of you have died or have been close to it?" Sam asked, opening her eyes wide in realization. "How? Not you Dad, I know that story. You got caught in the Light Explosion and ended up like a burned steak."

Gaby and Alex looked at each other and then at Sam. Alex lifted his t-shirt, showing his back and chest full of scars.

"Stabbed multiple times, left to bleed out," Alex replied. "Not funny at all and I got it easy." Alex pointed at Gaby with his head.

Gaby sighed.

"When you refuse to take the Last Rite with the Sisters of Mercy, they throw you into a labyrinth carved inside the mountain. If you solve it, then you are free. But the place is so dangerous, dark and devoid of anything edible that you end up dead from starvation, dehydration, or broken bones. In my case all three of them," Gaby replied, looking not at Sam, but at Fionn.

Fionn fought the urge to hug her and soothe away the pain of the memory. Now he understood Gaby better. His reluctance to teach them grew. It would be cruel and unfair to put them in further pain for a problem that was solely his.

Sam was speechless, barely mumbling an 'I'm sorry' that garnered smiles from Gaby and Alex. Fionn looked at his daughter with a mix of sorrow and love in his eyes. That was the reason he had tried to keep her away from any danger. He couldn't bear the thought of losing her. She was the only family he had left. He knew that training Gaby and Alex was a bad idea. They should be able to walk away from all of this and have normal lives. He was responsible for Byron, not them. Dealing with what Byron had become was his responsibility. Instead, they were being exposed to the horrors and dangers that being awakened brought. Having the Gift wasn't life insurance, not even for him. Long-lived, higher stamina or endurance didn't mean being eternal or indestructible. And with Byron's ability to nullify the Gift in others, the risk was even greater.

"The Gift comes with a hefty price. It gives you great power, but comes with a great..." Mekiri started.

"A much more likely chance of dying horribly or going insane," Fionn interrupted.

"Not if you train them. Not if you pass the test," Mekiri said.

"We'd better start the training and test then, shouldn't we?" Fionn said sarcastically. "Will you be ok, Sam?"

"I will, Dad. Please go easy on them."

"I will take care of her," Harland offered.

"Yeah, while you help me to install this beauty. A freaking dragoncore!" Sid said with clear excitment.

Alex and Gaby started to walk towards the entrance of Ravenhall. Fionn tried to open the door, and this time it worked.

"A few words before you start your test, Greywolf," Mekiri said. "Remember, the past is a lesson, not an anchor. The present is a gift, not a test. The future is an opportunity, not something to fear. All of us will arrive at our destination sooner or later. The difference lies in the path we take and with whom we choose to walk it."

Fionn remained silent as Mekiri let him go after Gaby and Alex. This was going to suck.

# Chapter 15

## Teachings

Fionn walked to the threshold and inhaled deeply. He entered the darkened tunnel; its shadows soon engulfed him like warm water. He struggled to move, as if the dark had the consistency of mud, heavy and warm. Yet he could breathe perfectly.

After a few steps, the tunnel became dimly illuminated by a few half-lit torches. On the walls, engravings and bas-reliefs with faded colors portrayed several stories. The images showcased the story of the three major species and how they had arrived at Theia. Curiously enough, none of them depicted the species being created by the gods or the spirits; instead, they were transported to Theia from somewhere else. The freefolk, guided by the so-called Last Hero, came out from the woods of Yumenomori, their spirits escaping from oblivion, originated from a book in a world whose main god had passed away.

The humans appeared by arriving through a ringed portal, led by their leaders, a group known as the Forefathers, in floating arks. They were escaping a destroyed world surrounded by unknown constellations: one that looked like a casserole and another like a man with a belt composed of three stars.

Led by their Prophet, the samoharo descended from

the stars in arks similar to the human ones, escaping from an exploding star surrounded by ships that resembled eldritch squids. All the races were guided by winged beings, the Akeleth.

No one, to this day, could agree on what the Akeleth were: deities, angels, advanced precursor aliens, or a mix. At least some of the freefolk gods, such as the Trickster Goddess and the Judge from the Underworld, siblings by birth, were suspected to have been part of the Akeleths. The samoharo had their own beliefs, but they didn't talk about them. And it was hard to keep track of what humans believed.

Moving forward, past the reliefs that depicted the events of the Dawn Age and later on, those of Queen Khary, the Silver Riders and the Montoc Dragon, Fionn stopped briefly by the engravings that depicted a young man carrying a silver horn, accompanied by a troll. It was the story of his father Fraog. Not far from there, the depiction of the Great War, between the Blood Horde and the Free Alliance, could be seen. It even included the Light Explosion. Fionn could still feel the searing of his skin, the impact of the shockwave crushing his bones and taking out all the air from his lungs. The day he became what he was now.

On the other side of the tunnel, he saw an open garden, with columns so tall that they seemed to reach the open sky. But it didn't look like the regular sky, as there were no signs of birds, clouds or rain. The inner weather seemed to be entirely artificial. Fionn couldn't but admire the whole place. Never in his life had he imagined bearing witness to the majesty that was the Ravenhall.

Between the columns, there were fruit trees and bushes, and ivies scaled up the outer wall. There were rooms upon rooms, with their white stone walls covered with books, parchments, scrolls, and tablets made from unknown materials. From their ceilings hung gyroscopes, models of solar systems, and even scale models of ships. Statues and figurines of dragons, members of the three major species and minor creatures, rested on massive tables. Those tables revealed to be painted maps of the continents of Theia, portraying different eras and kingdoms, battles and journeys. In some of the rooms were cabinets, their contents labeled in unknown cuneiform symbols. They ranged from herbs to crystals to sample objects from all the cultures that had existed on the planet, plus a few unknown ones. Most cabinets were locked under a special spell that issued a shock to the tampering hand, as Alex found out to his surprise. But that wasn't the only thing that had surprised him.

"No way! They have that here, too?" Alex exclaimed running towards an old arcade video game.

"What's that?" Fionn asked Gaby.

"Judging by his reaction, it's a copy of an old arcade game he used to play all the time. He is obsessed with finishing the game," Gaby explained, rolling her eyes.

"My mother never let me stay long enough to pass the final stages. And those bosses were hardcore," Alex recalled with fondness in his voice. "But I loved it. You have to fight your way through enemy-filled levels, choosing from four humanoid creatures with martial combat skills. She said that it was a waste of time and money."

"I can't argue with her on that," Fionn replied.

"Have you seen that?" Gaby said, pointing to a giant black stone slab standing in the middle of the garden. Its surface was covered with the same strange handwriting and images similar to those from the tunnel. The three of them got closer to the slab, examining the engravings.

"What does it say?" Gaby asked, her fingers tracing the low relief of the engraved letters. The edges were smooth with a silk-like texture and the surface was polished as if it were a mirror. Crowning the slab there was a statue of a raven descending from the skies, with the Moons as a background. For the keen observer, the library was decorated with raven motifs, appropriately since in tradition the raven was one of the preferred forms used by the Trickster Goddess.

"I will give it a try, but I haven't read ancient freefolk since I was a kid. And even then I wasn't good at it. It has a lot of Draconis mixed in, and I barely know a few words of that," Fionn replied, getting closer to the slab to read it.

"'This is our legacy, the memories of my people the Akeleth...'" Fionn leaned closer. He had never seen some of the words. "Can't understand what's next. Mentions something about their mistakes, then I think this word translates as 'birth worlds.'" Fionn knelt to read the lower lines. "Then it goes on to say: 'samoharo are mighty, freefolk are powerful, humans are indomitable.' That's funny."

"Why?" Gaby asked.

"That last line is a freefolk saying. Well, more like a warning about dealing with each species," Fionn replied. "It is usually attributed to Asherah as an explanation for the Pilgrimage. It's an event we..."

"Sam explained to me what the Pilgrimage is, and why you should do it," Gaby interrupted with a smile. "What else does it say?"

"Something about the Tempest Blades, but I can't tell if it means forged or created and finishes with 'giving the Gift.'" Fionn squinted, trying to understand the last line. "Here it just says, 'learn and hope.'"

"What are these sigils?" Alex asked. Below the writing, there were several engraved sigils of which only six could be distinguished, as the slab had sections damaged by some unknown force. From left to right there were, still preserved, a raven, a wingedlion, a dragonwolf, an orca and a hawkdove. The next one was half of a sigil, but still recognizable: an onyx falcon. The following two were the damaged ones. Given the size of the slab, there might have been more. But which ones?

"Freefolk used some of them for sigils of our tribes. Of course we use more than just those now. Originally they were sigils of the gods. The raven belongs to the Trickster Goddess, our patron god. The wingedlion represents the Guardian God and the hawkdove, well I'm not entirely sure, but it usually relates to the Seer. The Orca is the spirit of the sea. The dragonwolf is related to the wind and exploration. Finally the onyx falcon is the symbol of the Judge, god of the underworld," Fionn replied, kneeling to examine the engravings.

"But, no one really uses the onyx falcon as a sigil," Alex added. "I recall seeing some of them as totems at Ravenstone as well. The onyx falcon wasn't there."

"The onyx falcon is considered a bad omen. Usually of death," Fionn explained.

"That's a bad omen?" Alex replied. "I mean, dying is a bad thing, especially from illness or accidents, but death is a natural part of existence, isn't it? I thought the freefolk, being more connected to nature, would know that. No offense, I'm just trying to understand. There is not much known about the freefolk in the Straits."

"None taken," Fionn said, placing his hand on Alex's shoulder to reassure him. "We know that. But not everybody has the black humor that people from the Straits have with the concept of death."

"It's not necessarily black humor," Alex replied, shrugging his shoulders. "I would say that it is more like an earthly, intimate relationship. Life in the Straits is a bit harsh, with the earthquakes and the prowlers and all. Making a celebration around death, hoping that our departed are looking over us to guide us and celebrate, is how we cope."

"I can get that, but how do you explain the sugar skulls then?" Fionn looked at Alex, not satisfied with his explanation. "Or the skull cartoons and face paints."

"Those are a great tradition," Alex smiled. "And the special bread baked in shapes of little bones! You have to taste it!"

"See? That's weird."

"Guys, sorry for interrupting you cultural debate, but I think I found something interesting," Gaby said. She pointed to another set of pictograms in another nearby stone slab.

"These ones here seem to be the story behind the creation of our swords." Gaby pointed to three lines of engravings, each one with icons narrating a story.

"It seems so. I know they are called collectively the Tempest Blades. My grandfather talked about them a lot. They were created by the Akeleth through a mix of science and magick to tame the spirit of the Tempest. Here is Yaha. It was the first one created in the Dawn Age."

The icons depicted a man in front of a tree, facing a demon. Behind the man was a woman being pierced by a branch from a humongous tree covered in crystals. "According to the legend, Yaha was created to protect the Tree of Life from the First Demon by fusing the soul of a volunteer into a crystal. The crystal soul was then forged into a sword for the woman's husband. Even now I wonder how it ended up in Ywain's hands. He already had it by the time I met him," Fionn explained.

"Here is Black Fang, my sword. I know this story well, it is a tradition from Skarabear, the town where I grew up. Black Fang was the last Montoc Dragon, which died fighting the Bestial, the thing that Byron wants to bring back. The dragon's soul was transferred into his massive fang, which was later used to forge my sword," Fionn explained with pride. He then pointed at a damaged bit of the slab. There was a reference to something called Agni's Rage and Icestorm, but the writing was too damaged to be read and the names didn't ring a bell to Fionn. Finally, a pair of twin blades was depicted there, with their names engraved, but not an explanation of their origin. Fionn recognized them.

"And here are Gaby's blades, Soulkeeper and Heartguard," Fionn pointed at the image of the twin blades. "I think those are fitting names, considering who their owner is." Fionn smiled at her.

"Aww c'mon, does that pickup line really work?" Alex exclaimed with mirth in his voice.

"Shut up, Alex!" Gaby replied, raising her voice slightly.

"I find it curious that mine are part of the damaged stories." Gaby eyed Alex, her gaze conveying the unspoken message for Alex to shut up or risk a serious beating. Alex took notice of that and stepped back.

"I guess the ability of all the Blades to destroy creatures from the Pit comes from having a soul inside them," Fionn concluded.

"I find that a bit extreme," Alex said. "These weapons and the Gift work only when someone dies. I've heard that the Tempest is hard to control, but this is extreme."

"How can you protect life if you can't appreciate having it?" Gaby scolded him. "Regardless, we have food and water." Gaby pointed at the fruit trees and the fountain in the middle of the garden, which spouted clear water. "What time is it anyway? We shouldn't be wasting time."

"Judging by my watch, I don't think it will be a concern," Alex explained, giving a look at his wristwatch and then to the sky, and then looking at the shadows projected by the columns.

"What do you mean?" Gaby asked.

"How long do you reckon we have been here so far?" Alex asked back, his eyes rolling up as if he was making calculations in his head.

"An hour, maybe two," Fionn replied.

"My watch says less than two minutes. And some of the objects there must be thousands of years old and yet look brand new. There is no way those parchments could be still intact being that old and in contact with the air," Alex explained.

"That doesn't make sense," Gaby said, standing up.

"This place is magickal," Fionn interjected. "And I'm not talking about the décor. We are in the open and yet the environment feels warm enough to be comfortable."

"Then this place runs on Lucasian time," Alex stated smugly.

"On what?" Fionn asked.

"Lucasian time is a scientific term for relative times differing from the speed of the time arrow moving forward..." Alex started to ramble.

"Layman terms, please, Alex," Gaby stopped him.

"This place runs on its own time, independent of the time outside. An hour here must be roughly equivalent to a minute or less out there. If I have to guess, a day here must be more or less an hour outside," Alex explained as concisely as he could. "The Maze experiences it, too. But here it seems to not be a random event."

"Mekiri was right," Gabby said. "Ravenhall provides. Even if that means messing with the flow of time."

"That's convenient," Fionn said sarcastically. "And unnervingly familiar," he added.

"It is when you have to take a crash course in combat. But it would explain all those stories about heroes training enough to become good while the bad guys were barely doing anything," Gaby said.

"Also it explains a lot of plot holes in movies," Alex added with a shrug of his shoulders.

"Enough, let's figure out what the test is about," Fionn said with a serious, almost angry tone that surprised Alex and Gaby. They exchanged quizzical looks. He wasn't in the mood to teach anyone and it showed.

† † †

"Again!"

A loud thud could be heard echoing in the halls of the library, followed by another and another.

"No, no, no, do it again!!" Fionn yelled once more.

The training wasn't going as Fionn had expected. In fact, each attempt to teach Gaby or Alex was worse than the previous one. It wasn't the tired arms or the basic technique. Gaby had great combat technique and instincts, but wasn't moving at the needed speed; her moves were full of doubt as if she was afraid of relapsing into the Ice State. Alex was a capable fighter, albeit not as polished as Gaby. He was raw, more power than technique, a stark contrast to Ywain who had been all lightning speed, literally. The more Fionn pushed, the more frustration was starting to mix with anger and tiredness.

Fionn sighed constantly, worried that they wouldn't be ready in time. They weren't even close to learning the right fighting technique, even less to actually landing a hit on him, and he was barely using the Gift. Teaching Ywain how to fight had been easy, the kid had been always eager to learn. Izia had proven a challenge, but she always listened. But for some reason, he wasn't getting through to Alex and to a lesser extent, Gaby. His master Hikaru would be disappointed in him for failing miserably. He could hear her voice in his head, telling him the long list of things he was doing wrong, starting with his lack of patience.

"You are doing it all wrong. How the hell did you survive an incursion when you hold a sword like a baby?" Fionn exploded out of the blue at Alex. Everybody fell silent. Gaby shook her head and looked at Fionn disapprovingly. Alex threw Yaha away. It landed upright, the blade stuck in the floor. The sword did cut through anything. Alex walked towards Fionn until they were mere centimeters from each other, his left hand close to the holster where he had his collapsible bow.

"Excuse me? I had to learn how to hold a sword from a journal. But I'm much better with the bow. Wanna find out how much, old man?" Alex told Fionn, seething, despite having to look up at Fionn, who was at least a head and half taller. He wasn't intimidated.

"You can try. You won't get far before I beat some sense into you," Fionn told him, his voice low and quiet, hiding his fury behind it. He hadn't expected that reply from Alex, but then again he had documented anger management problems. And that was problematic in itself. Byron was temperamental like that and it didn't end well for anyone.

"Guys, calm down, this is not productive. And frankly, it is annoying as hell." Gaby walked right into the middle of them, pushing them both away with her arms.

"You should know better than him what I'm trying to teach you. You have actual combat training." Fionn looked at Gaby with disappointment in his eyes.

"True, but that doesn't mean I have to agree with your methods." Gaby faced him this time. Gaby was angry, and even Alex noticed it because he backed away.

"You know what? I used to admire you, but now I think you're just an asshole. I'm out of here. At least the books won't insult me," Alex said while unsticking Yaha from the floor and gathering his stuff. "I can't believe I'm stuck here with you. For a living legend you leave a lot to be desired."

"Hide behind the books, because otherwise, you will be dead meat," Fionn said, trying to move forward, but Gaby pushed him back.

"Sit on a sword you *b'ax!*" Alex yelled as he walked away, giving Fionn the finger. Electric sparks ran through Alex's arms, he was trying hard to not explode. Gaby slapped Fionn in the face so hard that his cheek sported a red outline of her hand. Fionn caressed his cheek and started to calm down.

"I... I... Gaby, I'm sorry for what I said," Fionn told her, regretful, coming back to his senses.

"Let me talk with him and fix this. But he is not wrong, you are being a lousy teacher right now," Gaby replied, walking away, following Alex into the library halls.

Fionn stood there alone, watching the sky. If training them was the test, then he was failing miserably.

"What do you want from me?" Fionn yelled in frustration.

† † †

Fionn was standing alone on one of the balconies overlooking the garden. The sky above the library was overcast, gray as if a winter storm was coming towards it. No stars could be seen. The feeling of impotence and tension, of the pressure of things to do but not enough time to do them, was growing inside him. There was no way that they would be ready for what was going to come. And he didn't have the patience to teach them. That had been his failing before, and it was now that he realized it. He skipped important parts with Ywain and Izia, even with Byron. A good fighter knew how to attack. A great fighter knew when to do it and when it was better to be patient. More importantly, a great fighter would know how to focus the emotions storming inside into tranquil fury. And controlling the Gift to the level they needed required that.

The memories of his time with Izia and Ywain flowed through his mind.

*Back then, Izia compensated her lack of power with resourcefulness. She was as clever as a fox. How many times did she trick someone to get her way? And Ywain, he just plowed through things like a hurricane. How many times did we end with bruises and cuts during our sparring sessions? The thing is, Byron had years of experience. And they were too eager to fight. Byron knew how to fight titanfighters unarmed, how to hunt down monsters. And he also had years to watch us, to study us. How long was he planning to betray us? Of course none of us were gonna be a challenge for him. We were too impatient and he wasn't.*

Fionn stood upright, his eyes opening wide in realization. Hikaru always hit him in the head when he got too impatient. He rubbed his head.

*"You always leave open your defense,"* she used to say during their training breaks. *"Because you are too hasty to attack. You need to be patient and clear your mind."*

"So that's the lesson, huh? To help them control their Gift, I need to teach them the only thing I have never mastered myself. I bet you find this hilarious," Fionn said to the sky.

While he admitted that Alex and Gaby were decent

fighters in their own right, every time he tried to calm himself by thinking that this could actually work, self-doubt appeared in his head. How could he teach them patience and calm when he himself was unable to be patient and calm? Fionn punched the wall with enough force to break his own bones, out of frustration.

"Are you ok? That wall seems like a mean foe," Gaby said behind Fionn. She was coming up the last few steps of the stairs, her leather jacket zipped up, which hugged her body tightly, showing her contours. Fionn admired the image, a welcome gift for sore eyes.

"I'm just thinking. Where is Alex?" Fionn asked while Gaby closed the gap between them, standing on his left, admiring the view from the balcony of the garden and the expansive building that was Ravenhall.

"Letting off some steam in that old arcade he found. Oddest thing I've seen here, which is already odd enough, considering the giant slab and the fruit trees," Gaby replied. She was resting on the balcony, taking in the overwhelming experience of being in such a magickal place. She breathed in deeply, filling her lungs with the moist, cold air, closing her eyes for a second and smiling. They stood there silently for a few minutes. Fionn watched her face.

"He is not taking the training well. I don't think I'm doing this right. My master would be ashamed of me," Fionn said out of the blue, his voice oddly subdued for someone like him, as he hung his head in shame.

"He doesn't like being put down. To be fair, I resent that too," Gaby replied, opening her eyes and facing Fionn with a sympathetic smile. "You need to understand something. Like you, we have baggage and sometimes it is hard to leave it behind. Take Alex for example. His family always puts him down or downright ignores him because he doesn't follow their rules. Why do you think he chose to live on another continent? Me? My father dumped me in an assassins' school the minute my mother was dead and buried, and it took me a lot not only to get away, but to recover." Gaby paused, the memories flooding her. She blinked a few times, trying to contain the budding tears in her eyes. With a wider smile, she continued. "Even Sid has issues. I bet Harland does too. And Sam. All of us have issues; the trick is learning to live with them."

"I'm sorry, I didn't want to come across as an ass. It's just..." Fionn replied with remorse showing on his face.

"I get it; you are worried that we are risking ourselves without being fully prepared. I know this fight has become personal for you. But you are not alone in this. You have to trust us," Gaby said emphatically, patting Fionn on the arm. "We are a team."

"I'm trying but it's not easy. I just keep replaying what happened last time. I wasn't alone either and it wasn't enough. And they were battle-hardened warriors," Fionn said, his hands moving to emphasize his words.

"And we are not," Gaby said, nodding her head. "We are just civilians."

"I don't want people dying again because I'm not good enough. I made a mistake before with Byron. And I haven't ever been able to beat him," Fionn said, looking dejected. "I taught him how to focus his powers, without suspecting what he would use them for later. As a warrior? He has always been better than me."

"Third time is the charm," Gaby smiled, taking his chin, lifting his face. "Look, for better or worse we are already in this, and none of us is going to back down. We might not have the experience, but we are not helpless children either. We survived an incursion and Alex barely had training back then. We can do this if you teach us how. Not just yell at us. You are a hero, to him, to me, to many. Show us why."

"You make too much sense for someone so young. Who is teaching whom?" Fionn smiled. Gaby's words eased the constant self-doubt that had been plaguing him for years.

"No offense, but making sense is not a trait of men,"

Gaby laughed. "Maybe that's your test here, learning to trust again. Do that and the teaching will come easy, I think. You just need to clear your head, relax and move forward."

"I have tried but I can't seem able to do that lately," Fionn said apologetically.

"When I have to clear my head, I dance. Would you dance with me?" Gaby smiled at him, offering her right hand and doing a curtsey.

"Here? There is no music," Fionn smiled once more.

"I can sing something," Gaby offered.

Fionn reluctantly took her hand, and she started to sing a folk song about time, love and belief. They danced as snowflakes started to fall, her sweet, soft singing guiding their steps. It was barely audible, only for Fionn to hear. It made all the anger and frustration inside him slowly evaporate, clearing his mind. Both got closer with each step. After a few minutes, Gaby finished her song and looked at Fionn. He was more relaxed now, still humming the song with a smile. He was feeling lighter.

"You really have a beautiful voice. Even the sky reacted to it by snowing," Fionn told her, looking at the falling snowflakes. The air was comfortable despite the snow, the powers of the Ravenhall in action.

"Alex is right about one thing, your pickup lines are awful." Gaby laughed sweetly and contagiously.

"You can't blame me, I'm a widower and have been iced for the better part of a century. I'm rusty," Fionn shrugged his shoulders as a sign of apology.

"I hope you are not rusty with everything, senior citizen," Gaby replied, getting closer to Fionn's face. While a tall woman, Gaby was still shorter than Fionn by almost a head, which meant she was now on the tip of her toes to reach him, even with her heeled boots. Fionn embraced her tightly, lifting her slightly until their lips were close to touching. And then, they were interrupted by a scream that echoed through the halls of the library.

"Eureka!" Alex yelled from a distance. Fionn and Gaby broke their embrace, both looking coyly at each other, their faces blushing slightly.

"We'd better check on him. I worry about his mental state." Fionn smiled, his left hand messing with the back of his head.

"I would worry about his physical state if that yell was for nothing," Gaby added with a hint of anger in her voice. Both sprinted towards the inner halls of the Ravenhall, their hands still locked. They arrived a few minutes later to the room where Alex was jumping in delight in front of the arcade cabinet.

"What happened?" Fionn asked, letting go of Gaby's hand and instinctively looking for his sword until he realized that he had left it on the balcony.

"I just managed to beat this boss," Alex replied with a huge grin on his face, almost looking like a small child.

"Really, Alex? I thought you may have found something useful," Gaby said, her face betraying a mix of anger and amusement.

"I'm trying, but I'm distracted. At first, I didn't understand its attacking pattern and then realized that it absorbed my attacks and got stronger and..." Alex's eyes opened wide as saucers, the smile disappearing from his face. "That's it!"

"Oh dear Heavens," Gaby said, cringing. "He has an idea."

"Is that bad?" Fionn asked her, confused.

"Alex having an idea is a wondrous and dangerous proposition at the same time," Gaby replied. "It can work perfectly or blow up in his face. Most of the time it's both."

"Excuse me, I have to go and check some books inside. I just hope this place truly holds all the knowledge available." Alex ran away from them and into the library.

"For what?" Gaby called after him.

"I think I found Byron's weakness," Alex replied with a wink.

††† 

Gaby and Fionn were eating the fruit that the gardens of Ravenhall offered. Most looked and tasted like regular fruit like applelimes and oranges. Others, such as a pear-shaped fruit with a rugose skin, tasted like recently baked bread. Smaller, round red fruit, whose skin felt like wax, hid a soft filling inside that tasted like cheese. The water from the fountain was clean and with some creativity from Fionn, he improvised a decent meal for him and Gaby. Alex hadn't been seen in almost a day since he disappeared into the library.

"Who would have thought that the trees in this place are basically magickal vending machines?" Gaby asked, taking a bite of an improvised cheese sandwich. "It even has full bathrooms, which I'm thankful for."

"Well, this place was built by the Trickster Goddess and she is renowned for her peculiar sense of humor. I wouldn't be surprised if the place shared that trait. After all, you can't pass a test by the Goddess if you are starving," Fionn replied, munching an applelime and looking around the place. He heard the sound of footsteps approaching quickly. Fionn turned his head around and saw Alex run towards them, his hands full of parchments and a black, obsidian cube with azure light lines running through it.

"Seems that the genius is back," Fionn pointed at Alex.

"Where have you been and why did it take you so long? Have you eaten something? Please tell me that you had a bath." Gaby bombarded Alex with questions before smacking him slightly on the head.

"Relax, Mom," Alex told her. "I was busy looking for this." He put the parchments on the floor and expanded them, holding them in place with the weight of the cube. The first set of parchments were diagrams of the dreadnought, including all of its systems. Alex then rolled a second set, which had depictions of the Bestial.

"What's that?" Fionn asked, pointing at the black cube

on the floor. Alex had grabbed a sandwich and was eating it.

"Some kind of data crystal, far more advanced than what we have at the university. Anyway, it has a digital copy of many of the books here and that made the search easy. And I'm right," Alex replied smugly, grabbing an applelime from their pile of fruit.

"About what?" Gaby asked.

"I was thinking. Fionn, you healed after you got away from him when you were falling. A few seconds after he dumped you. It means that he didn't nullify your Gift. He was just absorbing it. A subtle difference with massive implications." Alex mimicked the motion of an explosion with his hands. "This is my theory: Ywain was the one who fought him first on purpose. Byron used that fight to drain him dry. He took away Ywain's entire Gift. It explains why, according to my granddad, his father had health problems later on. Ywain never fully recovered. Byron used that excess energy to beat you all. That's why he seemed to be so unstoppable back then. But like a battery, he lost charge over the years. Now, he is recharging again. That's why you felt like your Gift stopped working. He is siphoning it."

"Are you sure?" Fionn was pondering what Alex was saying. It made sense, even if he didn't feel the energy leaving him when he was facing Byron. And Ywain had the habit of using too much energy during his fights; he was almost a living battery. Byron had used that against him. Fionn needed to keep him away from Gaby and Alex.

"Can't be one hundred percent sure but it makes sense. Otherwise, you would be dead," Alex said, still smiling. "But if I'm right, I think we have a way to beat him. If Hunt's notes were right and Byron is trying to fuse the Bestial with the dreadnought, he would have to merge with it as well to control it, right? That means that the core of the ship would become Byron's heart, giving us a bigger, easier target. Killing him would cut the head off the beast. We just need a plan. And you need to find a way to fight him without the

Gift. If you go full on against him, you will suffer the same problem as Ywain. If I'm right, even being on that ship will drain us. We need to even the odds or at least save energy for when it will be really needed."

The three of them remained silent for a few minutes. The only noise was the one coming from Alex chewing his food.

"I owe you an apology," Fionn said, breaking the silence and extending his hand to Alex. "You solved the problem in a way I would never think of and for that I thank you."

"Don't worry," Alex said, taking Fionn's hand in a handshake. "It's a matter of approaches."

"You are right," Fionn replied. "I have been trying to train you the way I was trained. But you already know how to fight and have been living with the Gift for a decade. What I need to teach you is what you can do with it, with patience and calm during a fight. Can I get a second chance?"

"Of course," Gaby said. "Right, Alex?"

"Oh, yeah, yeah," Alex said distractedly. "We still need a plan though."

"I already have one. But for it to work I need to teach you as I should have from the beginning," Fionn said.

"Let me clear my busy schedule first," Alex joked.

"First take a bath, please," Gaby told him, smacking him softly on the head again.

† † †

Alex and Gaby were sitting around a small bonfire. The garden of the Ravenhall was covered in the shadows of the artificial night, with the Long and the Round moons casting faint white light that contrasted with the yellowish hues from the fire.

"It's funny, from here the Long Moon looks like part of a ring or a puncher device," Alex mused to Gaby.

Fionn arrived with a small pouch that he had found

in the library cabinets. It had taken him a while to find it amongst the expansive rooms of the place, but the search had proved fruitful.

"What is that?" Gaby asked while Fionn took some colored powder from the pouch.

"I haven't tried this since I was a kid. But here goes." Fionn threw powder into the fire and the flames changed colors, portraying colorful yet simple images that matched Fionn's speech word by word. "This is an ancient freefolk tradition, a form of storytelling to pass the tradition on. It speaks from the heart of the storyteller, with the help of powder made from freefolk crystals and ancient macabow trees. It was created to share knowledge, to teach. So bear with me," Fionn took a seat in front of them, across the bonfire.

"I think I should have gone to the bathroom before this," Alex murmured. Gaby elbowed him and put a finger to her lips, signaling him to be quiet.

"Just look at the fire and clear your mind," Fionn said. And then he started to tell them a story. The flames rose and inside them the silhouette of a person appeared, greeting them with a hand wave.

"What is the Gift? It's the ability to draw from a deep well of inner power within our souls that allows us to perceive the world differently. I would say, with more intensity," Fionn said, as the silhouette changed into a ball of energy then transformed into a succession of shapes: a river, a forest, a mountain, different animals, ending with the head of the silhouette.

"No one truly knows where the Gift comes from or who grants it," the silhouette shrugged its shoulders. "Some believe that the gods or even the universe granted us part of their strength. Others say that maybe the Akeleth didn't disappear, but their bodiless essences merge with us at the time of our death."

The shape of a galaxy appeared in the flames,

transforming into a cloud that entered a body. "I do know how painful it is to receive it."

The silhouette fell to the ground, with the shape of a lance impaling it. "And how much the Gift messes with your head, scrambles with your mind. You keep hearing voices, seeing things that others don't see. It can drive you mad if you aren't ready."

Alex shifted in his seat and looked to Gaby. Fionn noticed how uncomfortable he seemed to be. His face turned red and he slumped in his place, trying to hide. If he had to guess, Alex still heard the voices; and given his particular manifestation of the Gift, like Ywain, he could actually see energy flows which would explain his peculiar behaviors. Fionn needed to reassure him if this was going to work.

"That's nothing to be embarrassed about, it just means that your mind is processing information at a speed your body is not used to. It takes time to get the hang of it."

The silhouette gave a thumb up to Alex, who smiled faintly.

"More important, the Gift makes you feel the life teetering at the edge of death, face to face with the Tempest, the border between the material and the spiritual world."

The silhouette was standing in front of a hurricane and on the other side there was a shape that looked like the drawing of a ghost.

"But once you get the Gift, when it is fully bonded with your soul, with the right presence of mind, you can do things that seemed impossible before. You already know how the Gift allows you to summon the wind, control electricity, command the fire or grants you rapid healing. But the Gift is more than that. It allows you to feel the heartbeat of other beings as if it was yours, to draw strength from the mountain and speed from the lightning. It can even let you see the flow of time as if it were a movie, and hear the cosmic music that the stars sing."

The silhouette first threw a fireball, and then extended

its arms and the flames flickered. Then, it stood atop of the shape of a mountain while lines representing the wind tried to make it fall. Finally, it started to run so fast that it became a blur. And while it was doing that, the faint sound of a tribal song, composed of flutes, drums and a chorus of kids speaking in the freefolk tongue about the stars could be heard.

"Now, this is the first real lesson I will teach you. Close your eyes."

Alex and Gaby did as instructed. The music increased in volume.

"Reach deep within you, feel that tiny ball of energy, the power inside you. That's your Gift's core. To attune with it you need a clear head, and to be able to calm yourself, even in the midst of a battle. You must become the eye of the Tempest. Chaos could be running amok around you, but you remain still. Grab the ball and then open your eyes."

Both Alex and Gaby's irises were glowing as they summoned the Gift. Fionn's irises were glowing as well. He smiled at his students.

"The Gift is like the wind or running water. It can be quiet and relaxing, or strong and chaotic. That's because it fluctuates with your emotions. The stronger the emotion, the stronger the output. You need to be calm. Emotions are good, but only if you are in control of them. Otherwise you won't be able to regulate how much to use, or when to use it. You won't even notice that there is a conscious version of the Gift, and an unconscious one. For example, my healing is my unconscious version, my body just does it. I rarely use the conscious one; but when I do, I focus it through Black Fang, allowing me to cut things at a distance, with the wind. That takes us to the next point."

Fionn grabbed Black Fang and unsheathed it. Its silvery blade was surrounded by a green glow.

"There is a reason our swords are called the Tempest Blades. Like us, they can dwell within the Tempest itself, and harness it as long as it is to protect others. They are living weapons, not just tools. Any being, provided that the blade allows it, can use them. But thise of us with the Gift, can synchronize with them to the point we can even control their edge. To do so, you need to learn one more thing: A tempest doesn't care about its power, it just is. You can feel fury, but it has to be a tranquil fury. Now, that ball of energy you are holding inside? Release it slowly, one breath at the time. Don't think of any other thing. Just focus on your breathing and grab your blades."

Gaby and Alex followed the instructions. Heartguard, Soulkeeper and Yaha were glowing in red, blue and golden light, respectively.

"You might not be able to do it right now, maybe not even in a few years, as you will need more practice. But if you listen carefully, you can feel the swords' souls, you can hear their faint voices speaking to you."

Fionn focused, and the flames started to react to the wind. The silhouette was sitting at the bottom of the flames, watching attentively, as Gaby and Alex's auras started to grow in size, combining with the glows emitted by their weapons. Fionn could feel goosebumps along his arms.

"You need to let go of all your myriad thoughts and just feel the Gift and control it. Be one with your blades, one with your Gift. Just let go and act, feel, don't overthink. Trust your feelings, your knowledge. Trust yourself and there will be no chain capable of tying you up. You will be invincible."

Thunder could be heard in the distance. Electric arcs were crackling around Alex's arms. Gaby, on the other hand, looked distant for a second; not noticing what was going on around her. Fionn grew worried that he had accidentally made her fall into that Ice State. But then she smiled at him with her peculiar crooked smile.

"How do you feel?" Fionn asked, smiling. He saw the energy being released by their bodies, increasing in intensity rather than flickering as usual. They were getting the hang of this, or so he hoped.

"All fuzzy inside," Alex replied, shambling from one side to another, his irises colored in a golden hue.

"I'm actually fine, relaxed even," Gaby added, smiling, her irises, in turn, colored with an intense electric blue with golden specks. "I... I think that I get how I can use the Gift to enter the Ice State without risk of losing myself."

"Good. Are we ready to truly test your Gifts?" Fionn's irises were a bright shade of grassy green, as intense as the light that Black Fang emitted from its blade.

† † †

"Shoot already!"

"But..." Alex stammered.

Alex wrinkled his brow, trying to contain the beads of sweat that ran down it. Sweat in the eyes hurt and messed with his focus. If he messed this up, it could end badly. His shoulder blades were aching. One thing experience teaches you in archery is that you don't hold an arrow on a pulled string for long periods of time. Your arms get tired, your pulse gets shakier and, contrary to popular belief, your aim doesn't necessarily improve. That's why you learn to aim and release fast, so you keep the accuracy and don't get tired. But unlike other times, Alex was not aiming at a particular spot. He was instead trying to call forth the Gift's enhanced vision. Most of the times, it came involuntarily, if it came at all, like during the fight at his school campus. The enhanced vision allowed him to follow trails of energy, detect the cores and nodes where energy – be it power or life force – accumulated. He had used it before to evade attacks and avoid being hit. But it had been involuntary, like reflexes. This time he was trying to learn to do it in an active manner. To find the energy nodes in opponents and objects around him would give him a decided edge in combat, if he learned how to use it properly.

Gaby had explained to him that certain combat techniques worked around the idea of paralyzing or even killing someone by hitting certain vital points, like nerve clusters. Those techniques were based on ancient Kuni healing teachings and the Sisters of Mercy had adapted them for their purposes. So far he had managed to do it hand to hand, using precise pokes in nerve clusters that had paralyzed the limbs of both Fionn and Gaby.

Fionn, in turn, theorized that Alex's particular version of enhanced sight could be paired with his archery skills to make him a more efficient fighter. And then, contrary to Alex objections, he decided to force him to shoot Gaby to test the theory. Of course, Gaby wouldn't be a sitting target. Her task was to avoid, deflect or catch every arrow by using her own version of enhanced sight and the basics of the Ice State. She was trying to use both in a way that didn't sink her into being an emotionless assassin. And she had found that with some practice she was on her way to doing it, with mixed results.

Yet, Alex was afraid of seriously hurting her, so he was looking for a non-vital target in case she was too slow. It was one thing to shoot at monsters, but totally different to shoot at a friend, even if it was practice. Since he'd gotten the Gift, Alex had been careful of not letting go, always keeping it in check. Otherwise the results were not pretty. When he let loose, a darker side of him appeared and the aftermath ended with the place in total disarray and a considerable bodycount, and him barely remembering a thing. That was the real reason he uses a bow instead of Yaha; the bow taught him self-control. Even with Fionn there to guide him, he wasn't feeling confident. He was starting to have serious doubts about the whole 'stop villain, save the world' thing and whether he would be able to do his part.

*What was I thinking when I offered to help?*

"Alex, seriously, shoot already. I'm not that fragile, y'know? I will catch it," Gaby told him in loud voice. "I'm getting old here."

"Just do it for Heaven's sake!" Fionn encouraged him. "I promise, it will be fine. You can do this, so can she. I believe in both of you. It's ok to have doubts, to keep yourself in check. But something I learned by fighting alongside Ywain, is that sometimes, letting go, even if it's just a bit, can be helpful. Control is not about a tight grip, it is about learning to live with what you are and what you can do, and acting accordingly. One step at a time, then move onto bigger things."

For the first time in several years, Alex let go, just a bit. He let the arrow loose.

† † †

Gaby tried to remain calm, even if Alex's reluctance was getting the best of her nerves. But the exercise had always been about patience and calm. She saw Alex letting loose the electrified arrow. She knew he had aimed for her left shoulder, but the shakiness of his tired arms sent it towards her heart. Not his fault really, and she relished the challenge.

She called upon the Gift while trying to use the basic tenets of the Ice State. And time slowed, at least for her. The arrow moved in slow motion towards her. Its movement left behind a trail of faint sound, a note imperceptible to the others. She had once read a philosophy book that said the universe moved in musical harmony. The *Music of the Celestial Spheres* was the title, and she had found it inspiring. Time and music were one for her and she even wondered if she could mix them with the help of the Gift. But right now, she had to focus on the arrow.

The only thing she had to do was sidestep it, which she did. And catch the arrow, which she did. She smiled at Alex.

"Told you."

Her irises were shifting from an unnatural icy electric blue to golden, and a wider grin illuminated her face. Easy peasy.

"You still overthink too much," Gaby said to Alex, walking towards the fountain.

"I don't know why I can't stop overthinking," Alex replied, scratching the back of his head.

"You are doing fine," Fionn replied. "Both of you have advanced so much in only a few sessions. I don't know if it will be enough, but it will have to do."

"Just fight smart. More than half a battle is winning with smarts, not with sheer power," Gaby told him. "Something I did listen to in school."

"I need a break," Alex replied, tired. He drank water as if he had been wandering the northern desert of the Straits for years.

"I think the test is over," Fionn said out of the blue, while Alex and Gaby were drinking water from the clear water of the fountain.

"Why do you say that?" Gaby asked, raising up her head and looking at Fionn.

"Because that door wasn't there a moment ago." Fionn pointed to the same door that had let them in. It was already open. Above its frame, engraved in stone that glowed green, there was a sign in the older version of the freefolk tongue, which roughly translated to 'exit.'

"Real subtle," Gaby said. "Ok, let's pick up our stuff. I doubt Mekiri, or the goddess herself, would appreciate this mess being left behind."

"Aww man! I was this close to finishing that arcade game a second time. I wanted to beat my record," Alex complained, while Fionn and Gaby started to pick up their belongings. Alex followed them and picked up his sword and bow.

"Let's go, Alex, there are people who need our help," Gaby told him, patting him on the shoulder, offering him a sympathetic smile. As stupid as the idea of being attached to an old arcade game was, she couldn't avoid finding it endearing. Even Fionn had warmed up to the idea of spending their free time watching Alex playing.

"But Gaby! Can I at least try to take the arcade game with me?" Alex pleaded fervently.

"No, but I promise you that if we survive this, I will help you get one. There must be some leftovers in a company warehouse. Now, let's go." Gaby dragged him along, following Fionn towards the door.

"So close," Alex replied with resignation, looking towards the old arcade game, which turned off by itself with a beep resembling a sad goodbye. "At least I will bring this with me." Alex stared at the black cube in his hand.

† † †

By the time they came out and into the Maze, the sun was high in the sky, shining through rain clouds. A ray of light landed on the Figaro, which seemed to be fixed already. The dents on the hull were still there, but all the breaches were sealed. The three of them walked toward the ship and noticed two figures sitting on rocks, hunched over and covered by thick blankets, playing a game of sagewar. As they got closer, they realized that the figures were Sid and Harland, with their hair grayed and sporting long, thick beards. They looked aged and infirm.

"What the hell? How long has it been?" Alex exclaimed, surprised, going over his calculations again.

"You have been away for a long time, the world has changed now. We grew old here waiting for you, almost losing hope," Sid replied with a tired voice. "Even Samantha left with an errant freefolk tribe years ago."

Gaby looked at him with suspicion. She got closer to him and ruffled his mohawk, raising a cloud of dust. She did the same with Harland's hair. Their hair was now its regular color.

"These are fake beards," Gaby pulled down Sid's fake beard. "But I'm glad you are becoming friends."

"How did you know?" Harland asked, cleaning his beard.

"Sid always says that samoharos don't go gray. And he is so vain that if he did, he would use hair dye."

"Hey, I resent that. I would never use an off-the-shelf dye. I would use magick," Sid complained. "Besides, it was a good joke. And you were away for five hours. We got bored."

"Where are Sam and the others?" Fionn asked, not amused.

"They left," Sam tried to contain her laugh, coming out from behind a crate. "Mekiri took Master Reynara with her to cure her wounds. Stealth went to call for help from the remaining tribes, in case we need them."

"Good, can you contact them?"

"Yes, why?"

"Tell them to go to Saint Lucy to alert Queen Sophia."

"Again, why?"

"We kinda have a plan. I will need those explosive mining charges that came with the ship for it to work, though," Alex said.

"You and explosive charges worry me like you have no idea," Sid mumbled.

"And one potential target is Saint Lucy," Gaby added. "We just need to find Byron first."

"Well, you are in luck, because we have a location," Sam said with a smile. "Your idea worked, geek."

"The ship started responding a few minutes ago," Harland added, activating his damaged datapad and projecting the image on the canyon wall. A map of a town on a small island located between the Emerald Island and Ionis was displayed. "If the map is correct, the Queen's holiday chalet is in Sandtown."

"That's bad," Fionn said.

"Why?" Gaby asked, turning to Fionn.

"The Queen's holiday home is where the Free Alliance charter was signed," Fionn explained.

"I think it is worse than that, Dad," Sam opened her green eyes wide. "That's where the old Ulmo capital was.

Where the Bestial was defeated the first time it was here on Theia."

"Damn," Fionn replied, clenching his fists around Black Fang's pommel.

Time was running out.

# Chapter 16

## Late to the Party

"Why is that place so important?" Sid asked, flying the Figaro at top speed. The dragon core had reenergized the original cores to the point that the ship could now easily break the sound barrier.

"Ulmo was the last great kingdom of the freefolk. They got into a war with the Asurian empire, from which Meteora is the last remaining city state," Fionn explained.

"Meteora is in the center of the desert wasteland west of the Kuni Empire. Half a planet away. How could that be?" Harland asked.

"Intercontinental weapons and dimensional portals, like the punchers," Alex said. "People back home said that Meteora had been an advanced civilization that only feared the samoharo, who protected us, and the Kuni."

"And back then, the Kingdom of Ulmo stretched from Ionis to the northern lands of Auris through the Scar," Fionn added. "Anyways, the conflict soon became kinda three-sided when the last Montoc Dragons razed Meteora's weapon facility in the city of Carpadocci, in an attempt to get rid of such powerful weapons. In turn, the Asurians summoned the Bestial as their last-ditch attempt at victory, sending it to destroy Ulmo. However, the Bestial went rogue and destroyed the Asurians first. When it arrived at Ulmo, the Bestial levelled the place and killed both freefolk and dragons. It was a massacre. Only the last surviving Montoc Dragon, Black Fang, managed to take the Bestial down, at the cost of his own life. It was a total mess that sank half the planet in chaos for centuries to come. From there, everything split into the several kingdoms and republics we know, while the freefolk went on to become mostly nomads again. They never rebuilt their kingdoms. And the dragons disappeared from Theia."

"And all of that relates to our destiny how?" Sid asked once more.

"King Castlemartell decided to build Sandtown as the place where the Free Alliance charter was signed. It even has a famous stained-glass window gallery. Each window depicts scenes from the Great War," Fionn replied.

"And it is the same place where Ulmo's old capital was, the first freefolk city," Sam added. "Which makes it the best place to summon the Bestial once more."

"I bet the King regrets building it there now," Sid remarked.

"Well, he did it on Sophia's advice. Of all his children and the Twelve Swords, she had the best spiritual attunement to the Gift. She knew that the place would attract good omens," Fionn explained. "She did the same when she ordered the rebuilding of Saint Lucy and made it her royal seat. There is a reason she is one of the most beloved leaders of the Alliance."

"I thought it was because she was a nice, really old lady that liked tea," Sid said.

"She may be old, but I can assure you, she is not nice when she is riled up. Compared to her siblings, she is the true heir of the old King."

"You speak of her fondly," Gaby said to Fionn. "How old is she, by the way?"

"She is a great friend. And she must be around my age. Except that she looks older than me. A perk of her Gift is that she ages slowly."

"Good thing for a monarch," Alex mumbled.

"What do you mean by that?" Fionn said, looking at him.

"I don't want to get political," Alex replied.

"Good, because we are here," Sid interrupted. "And you are not gonna like it one bit."

† † †

They left the Figaro on the outskirts of the remains of Sandtown. A sphere of roiling mist and clouds hung over the ruined town. And from the mass, translucent bodies and spectral forms emerged.

"Is that a portal?" Harland asked. "I thought it would be, you know..."

"A hole in the sky?" Alex asked.

"Yes, like the one in the napkins."

"Yeah... well, we live in a tridimensional world. The 3D form of a hole is actually a sphere. The ghosts, though, those are an interesting touch. I never expected that a tear in reality would release ghosts."

"That's not from the tear. The Tempest doesn't like to be disturbed," Sam said with a somber tone. "It's something that happens with massacres. That's why battlefields and murder scenes end up being haunted. It's the residual psychic energy. And if I recall the legend correctly, the initial spell to summon the Bestial needs several sacrifices..."

Fionn's blood boiled with anger. His fists clenched and released rhythmically, while he walked amidst the ruins of the previously beautiful and peaceful town and castle. They were surrounded by the corpses of the villagers and smoke from still smoldering buildings filled the air with a thick, acrimonious smoke. He knelt to pick up a charred cloth doll and his mind screamed, clamoring for vengeance. The townspeople had offered resistance but it had been for nothing. Byron's forces had proved to be overwhelming. A few yards away, Sam was using her pendant to track the energy used in the spell and was sending the information to the Figaro, while Harland and Sid were hacking into the video feed of the security cameras. Alex and Gaby only stared at the gathering of ghosts that peppered the ruins of the place.

"Is that normal?" Gaby pointed at one ghost, which for the most part was, like the rest, ignoring them.

"I guess, as long as the portal remains open, damaging the napkin of reality," Alex said. Parts of the sphere were clear though enough to reflect what was on the other side. It didn't look like the spiritual plane, not according to the books he had been reading. Stars could be seen through the portal, their faint lights signaling dying worlds. Alex looked at the curious constellations that could be seen through it. They weren't the constellations that one could see in a regular sky, but resembled the ones he had seen depicted at Ravenhall. There was floating debris from a dead planet and its moon, with a dimming star not unlike the sun. Wherever that place was, it was clear that something bad had happened.

"I have to admit that the ghosts look cool," Alex murmured, earning a disapproving glare from Gaby. "You know I like haunted houses."

"Not now, Alex."

Gaby got closer to Fionn, who was staring at the ruins of the chalet. The stained-glass windows had been viciously destroyed.

"Are you ok?" Gaby asked him. Fionn looked at her and hugged her.

"I will be." Fionn and Gaby stood there, embracing each other. Fionn inhaled the sweet smell of her hair. For a brief second, everything stopped and felt right in the universe. Alas, these moments were scarce and often interrupted.

"We got it!" Harland exclaimed, downloading the information to his datapad and then projecting it as a hologram. "It recorded everything. The attack, the summoning... No sound but..."

"There is no need to see the whole attack. Let's jump to the summoning," Fionn said. He had seen firsthand what Byron could do to a place once he let his bloodlust win. It wasn't pretty.

In the images, the flying dreadnought occupied the whole area above the chalet's front yard. Underneath it, there was a circlet, similar to the smaller one used to summon the incursion, glowing thanks to the influx of magick energy empowering the spell. A few troopers surrounded the ship. The small number was odd, considering the reported number of followers of the cult. Connected to the circlet were the five kidnapped students and professors from Ravenstone. The circlet activated and opened the portal.

"I see the Queen, shackled and bruised. Seems that she gave them quite a fight even at her old age. Hunt is next to her, badly hurt," Sam pointed out. "And my students are there, connected to the machine. That bastard! He is using them as conductors for the energy needed for the spell!"

"This is bad," Alex said, but then he realized something. "He is using an improved version of the circlet. A bigger one."

Alex pointed at the circlet, which projected a column of light into the sky. It engulfed the dreadnought and slowly opened a portal above the massive ship. From the opening, a giant pulsating mass emerged. Whatever it was, the strange matter that composed it resembled resin. It poured over the dreadnought, merging with the flying fortress. The resulting creature was an aberration of metal and something that looked like living, pulsating flesh. It had doubled in size compared to the original dreadnought, had three mouths, and there were eyes in places where there should not have been. And tentacles. Lots and lots of tentacles along with its heavy weaponry. Just by watching it, Alex's head started to hurt and Sid had to go behind some bushes to throw up. From the portal, green and lilac light flowed into several corpses, putting Byron in control of their bodies.

"Aww crap," Alex muttered, visibly nervous, shaking

and fidgeting with his hands. "That thing is bigger than we thought."

The flying fortress had the look of a humongous, deformed, blind, grey goblin shark. "Maybe this is way over our heads."

"The size doesn't matter, we stick to the plan: board the ship, blow up the core that is its heart and cut off its head, Byron, as a team," Fionn stood up tall. "Being afraid is fine, it keeps you alert. But don't let that stop you, Alex."

But the looks on their faces told him that they weren't feeling confident. Even Fionn had to admit that while the plan was simple, the risk for the six of them, not to mention the hostages, was very high and the chances of success too slim. Whatever doubts he had would have to be buried deep as it was his job to reassure his new team. Like he had done with the original Twelve Swords when they had faced overwhelming odds. He just hoped that he wasn't asking too much of them.

"According to the video, they are taking the hostages inside the ship," Sam pointed out.

"Without wanting to sound too grim, why?" Sid asked, clearing his throat. "It would have been easier to kill them here. They just erased a whole town with ease. Not even the stained-glass windows were left intact."

"He might need the students to open a second portal over its next target," Alex said. "He might be planning to increase his army. More deaths, more bodies to control."

"He doesn't need them anymore. The Bestial can do that once it touches the crystal obelisks," Sam said ruefully, looking down with sadness.

Everybody remained silent, shuffling their feet, looking for an answer. Fionn's eyes meet with Harland's and something dawned on them. Both looked at the remains of the stained-glass windows and got closer to examine them.

"The windows, weren't they created as a homage to the Twelve Swords and the end of the war?" Harland mused.

"The damage here, it is not random..."

"It's personal," Fionn concluded. "That window represented something to us, something that he could break."

"He is sending a message." Harland pounded his open palm with his fist.

"Byron has a penchant for theatrics and hates the freefolk. Good leader, poor tactical thinker," Fionn said while he returned to the hologram. He clenched his fist. "See those cameras floating around? He is planning a public execution when he gets in range of the next target city's antennas. He plans to send a message that the Alliance is nothing without the Queen, and the freefolk are filth to be disposed of."

"It makes sense. It is Sophia's royal seat," Harland said. "If he executes her there, the city will fall without opposing him. And with it, the Alliance will follow."

"We need to rescue the hostages before trying to blow up the Bestial," Sam added.

The original plan had become more complicated due to the need to rescue the hostages beforehand. It meant one thing, and Fionn wasn't happy with that. The more time they spent aboard the dreadnought, the more drained they would be, even if he had taught them how to control how much energy to use. It was too risky for his taste, despite the fact that back during the war, his team used to do exactly that, with mixed results. Gaby stared at him with a knowing look and took the decision out of his hands.

"Listen. I know what you are thinking. I'm not keen to split up, not on that ship. But there is no other option. Sam and you rescue the hostages, Alex and I will deal with the core."

"What about Byron?" Alex asked.

"He is mine. Once the hostages are off that ship with Sam, I will go and have a nice chat with him," Fionn replied, tightening his grip on Black Fang.

"Even then, if we are too close to the city, the explosion might hit it and kill thousands, including us," Sid objected.

"That defeats the whole purpose of this whole stupid plan."

"You just worry about being ready to pick us up when we call you," Alex said. "Also, I wonder... Sam, if the city is a giant magick circle, could you use it to create a magick shield to deflect the explosion, if needed? Like the one you used to deflect the bullets?"

"I guess. I have never cast a spell that big." Sam bit her lip nervously. "You'd better not play with the explosives."

"Relax, I have been known to be extremely careful with those things." Alex smiled at Sam.

"Yeah right," Sid interjected. "Tell that to my poor kitchen."

"That doesn't count. At all."

"Save that for later," Gaby told them. "We need to go. Can we catch up with them?"

"Not if we stay here talking," Sid replied, heading back to the Figaro. "Don't worry. This is a good chance to show you why my ship is the fastest on the entire planet."

In the loading bay, Harland stood behind, shuffling his feet, mumbling. Fionn let the others go into the cockpit before turning back to Harland.

"I know that look."

"I owe you an apology," Harland replied, looking down.

"For what?" Fionn was feeling befuddled.

"For taking you out of retirement and into this mess."

"Nah, don't worry." Fionn patted Harland's shoulder. "Sooner or later this mess would have found its way to my door. At least now we are still in time to do something about it. Besides, retirement is for old people."

"How old are you again?"

"Ha. I do need you to do something for me though, regardless of how this ends."

"Anything. I owe you as much."

"Promise me that you will take care of Sam, of all of them," Fionn said.

"I assure you, nothing will happen to your daughter

while I'm on watch, nor to the others. You have my word," Harland replied, extending his hand.

"That's enough for me. See you on the other side, my friend." Fionn shook hands with him. The silence between them was clear. Fionn knew he might not survive the duel against Byron.

*Well, I wanted a life full of adventures.*

# Chapter 17

## Inside the Beast

"Reports across the country talk about the devastation left by the giant creature... Bzzz, people from the city of Irisdown call it the Cloud of Death... Bzzz, withered animals and crops left in its wake... Bzzz, the Ministers say that we need to keep calm, but they are not seeing what we are seeing. Where are the emergency services? The government is losing control. Things are getting hectic down here!"

All the radio stations were talking about the same thing: a giant flying beast that left destruction in its path. No one knew where it was headed, but for those aboard the Figaro, the answer was clear.

"I could use some music right now," Sid turned off the radio. Flying at full speed, they were closing in on the Bestial, which was few a kilometers outside Saint Lucy. They could make out its terrifying form even from afar. It was bigger and uglier than expected.

"Me too," Alex said. "I think I'm gonna be sick."

"Sorry, my datapad is damaged, only video, no sound, so I can't put on my playlist," Harland told him apologetically. Silence fell upon them.

A sweet voice broke it with a song that was not that sweet, and yet was inspiring. Gaby was standing next to Sid's chair, keeping her eyes on the Bestial. She didn't notice that she sang aloud. When she finished, everybody was silent, until Sam broke the silence.

"That was awesome, Gaby!" Sam exclaimed, surprised. "Is it yours?"

"Yes, just came to my mind, just those lines," Gaby explained, blushing.

"After this, you need to finish it," Fionn told her, placing his hand on her shoulder.

"First things first, ok?" Gaby said.

"Hey, you need to see this," Harland interrupted, activating the video feed appearing on his datapad. Just as Fionn has predicted, the Bestial's onboard cameras were transmitting the events on its deck. The hostages were led to the deck of the ship. "Sid, turn on the radio again. I have the feeling that this will be on every channel."

"Of all the execution methods available, I would have never guessed walking the plank as Byron's choice," Alex said.

"Let's approach it as silently as possible," Fionn said.

Flying above the clouds to keep a certain degree of cover during the last hours of the night, the sun rising in front it, the Figaro kept tabs on the Bestial and the transmission from a prudent distance.

Byron commenced his speech, his voice filling the airwaves, booming through the cockpit speakers.

"This is the dawn of a new reign. One of stronger rulers, one that puts the non-human species under a tight grip, as it should be. Your Queen has failed you, imposing a weak alliance with those that should be under our heel. But I won't fail. I will make you stronger!"

"Nice speech," Gaby muttered under her breath.

"Told you. I fought with that asshole long enough to know his taste for melodrama. He will wait until he is almost near the city limits to execute her," Fionn replied, feeling sick. He had never realized the extent of Byron's bigotry towards the freefolk, towards his people. He wondered if the bad press they got during the war had been Byron's underhanded work. Hard to tell, but the current message was the same: He wanted a fight and Fionn would give him one. This was going to end today, one way or another.

"I guess my students will live a little bit longer, for a better show," Sam said grimly.

"We will rescue them," Fionn assured her with a hand on her shoulder. "Time to go. Sid, drop Sam and me there, on that skylight. It's the closest section to the hostages. After we rescue them, you will pick them up. I will keep Byron distracted long enough for you to drop Gaby and Alex so they can deal with the core."

"It will be tight," Gaby said. "The time window for all of that will be really small, assuming the Bestial doesn't notice us before."

"I have enacted plans with less margin for error," Fionn replied.

"Did they work?" Alex asked.

"Let's move," Fionn replied, evading the answer, which was an answer in itself.

The four of them arrived at the cargo bay, grabbing the leather straps of the cargo nets to keep their balance.

"Be careful, please," Gaby told Fionn, giving him a kiss on the left cheek. Alex groaned while Sam looked embarrassed.

"I promise I will be fine. I've been at this longer than you, you know? This is not my first rodeo." Fionn smiled.

"I know, but I still had to say it. You have fallen from the horse before," Gaby told him, trying to keep back tears.

"Avoid being turned into a brochette a third time," Alex said jokingly, earning a double slap from Gaby and Sam.

"Let's go." Fionn glanced at Alex. He was not amused by the comment.

The cargo bay hatch opened and strong winds entered, almost blowing them down. Sid had positioned the Figaro above the dreadnought's skylight to allow Fionn and Sam to rappel down.

"How are we gonna open it, Dad?"

"Alex?" Fionn yelled.

"My pleasure." Alex walked to the edge of the hatch, keeping his eyes on the skylight. He was sweating. "Although... I really don't like heights."

Alex aimed and shot an energy charged arrow, which broke the skylight glass. The Bestial barely noticed.

Fionn and Sam quickly rappelled down from the Figaro, entering the Bestial through the broken skylight. Once inside, they saw the Figaro speed away and into a cloud, disappearing from sight. The inside of the Bestial was darkened by miasma and shadows; only the light from the broken skylight gave them any inkling of how the place looked. They moved into a corridor, with a faint red light illuminating it. Fionn, consciously avoiding the use of the Gift, blinked several times until he could see properly in the dim environment. Sam was starting to cast a light spell, but Fionn stopped her.

"Save energy, don't feed the beast."

"Ok, Dad," Sam replied. Coyly she added, "I know the situation is dire and all but, is it bad that a part of me feels all giddy about sharing an adventure with you?"

Fionn was perplexed at the comment, not knowing how to properly reply. "I guess. This is not the way I pictured the whole 'bring your kid to work day.'"

"Your jokes really suck, Dad." Sam rolled her eyes. "Even worse than Alex's."

The air was humid and had a strong scent of iron and copper. The air tasted of blood. As they walked through the corridor, their eyes adjusted to the dim light, giving them a better view of the surroundings. Fionn wished they hadn't. He tried to contain the warm liquid coming up through his mouth. Sam felt dizzy and her head throbbed. The internal structure of the ship was a mix of metal and raw, pulsating flesh, with electrical arcs jumping and running across the surfaces.

But those weren't the only components of the structure. A faint moaning, barely a whisper subdued by the noise coming from the machinery, could be heard. Fionn got closer to inspect its source and his stomach churned. He breathed the moist air deeply, trying to regain a semblance of composure. It took him a few seconds to look back at the source of the moaning: a skinned man, still alive, melded with the raw flesh of the Bestial. And he wasn't the only one. Peppered all over the place, there were different bodies, in different states of melding, the skin decomposing and dripping with the black ichor that was the Bestial's blood. Sometimes it was a full body, trapped in a rictus of pain, other times just eyeballs or an earlobe or a hand clawing at the air, trying to grasp for something that would help it to get out of a living nightmare. All to no avail.

"Don't make a bad joke about the decoration, please," Sam pleaded, barely containing the disgust in her voice and the tears in her eyes.

Usually, Fionn would quip about the ironic fate of the followers of the cult. But not this time. It wasn't a laughing matter. He embraced Sam to reassure her.

"Now you know why I didn't want you to come with me on my cases," Fionn said to Sam. "Regardless of why they chose to follow Byron, no one deserves this. The best we can do for them now is to finish this quickly."

Fionn then pointed at a metal door to their right. "If I recall the blueprints Alex showed us, behind that door there is a stair that will take us to the upper deck."

Sam shuffled her feet, "There is something wrong."

"What do you mean?"

"This is too easy, Dad. We are being lured into a trap." Sam looked at him. Her eyes were teary. She was biting her lip, much like he did.

"Oh, I'm pretty sure it is." Fionn smiled at his daughter and shrugged his shoulders. "But this is where the fun begins. Be ready, munchkin."

Fionn opened the door. They climbed up the stairs quickly and soon found themselves under a medium-sized crystal canopy. It was large enough to hold a few motorized vehicles. Fionn and Sam stopped right in the middle of the room. From the shadows, dozens of troopers appeared, armed with batons, axes, swords, cleavers and a couple of rifles. The troopers surrounded them.

"A welcome party disguised as a trap! I looooove welcome parties!" Sam exclaimed, her voice dripped with sarcasm and she rolled her eyes in annoyance.

Fionn unsheathed Black Fang, while Sam grabbed a small piece of white carved wood from a holster inside her jacket. With a flourish, energy ran through it, making it grow into a full quarterstaff. It was almost as tall as she was, divided into three sections of finely carved white wood, intersected with two sections made of crystals. Fionn recognized it. It was Izia's quarterstaff, one of her few remaining belongings, which he thought had been lost.

"You had it all this time!" Fionn said. He examined the staff, which he hadn't seen in years.

"Harland found it among his father's collection. He thought we deserved to have it. I just forgot to tell you," Sam replied, sticking her tongue out playfully. Even with three generations separating them, Sam shared some mannerisms with her great-grandmother. "I will return it when we finish."

"Keep it. I'm sure she would be proud," Fionn smiled. "Are you ready, kiddo?"

"Always," Sam said, while smiling back to her father. She readied her staff in a defensive position, back to back with her dad.

"Let's give them a show then."

The air filled with tension so thick that Black Fang would have trouble cutting it. Fionn breathed and smiled the smile of a wolf, licking his lips, expectant. There was a reason you never sent a group of soldiers to attack a single, capable target in a limited space like this. No matter how much larger the force is, not all its members can occupy the same place, and the tighter it is, the more restricted their movements.

Three troopers initiated the attack with a guttural, barely human yell. Fionn tensed his muscles and jumped forwards, sword held high, cutting down while hitting them with sheer strength in the landing. No blood was spilled; instead the same black ichor that dripped from the walls flowed from their broken bodies.

"Man, that's really disgusting," Fionn said, before pressing his attack. He parried a blow from another trooper's baton and pushed back. He moved swiftly, cutting down a path for him and Sam to move through towards the exit. Sam followed him, hitting troopers with her staff, breaking helmets and probably, Fionn judged from the sound, a few skulls as well.

They got closer to the exit and were surrounded once more. This time, Sam swung her staff, knocking down a few troopers, to give space to her dad.

"We need to hurry, Sam, we have spent enough time here."

Fionn and Sam coordinated their attacks, low and high, to hit and cut as many troopers as they could. Sam pushed several backward while Fionn ducked to avoid a swing of an axe at his head. The axe got stuck in a metal column and the owner was trying to pry it free. Fionn broke his knee with a punch, and rose to hit the trooper in the chin with the heel of his right hand. Fionn ran in a circle, cutting off the legs of many troopers and then cutting the arm off the one trying to take Sam's head. She in turn jumped and kicked a few heads, her staff spinning and bludgeoning three more. The fight was messy and bodies fell all over the place. Fionn and Sam moved towards the exit. He was clearing the path, while she was keeping the following troopers at bay. She hit two troopers on their ankles, making them fall and hit the hard steel ramp of the exit. They made a sickening cracking noise.

Only the leader of the troopers remained in front of them. He unsheathed a long sword and started trading blows with Fionn, who barely moved, using only his ankles and waist to parry all the blows until the trooper hyperextended his swing, leaving himself open for a lightning strike aimed at his neck. The head remained in place. Fionn then delivered a round kick to the head, making it fall to the floor while the body dropped slowly to the floor.

"I thought that was a movie trick." Sam was surprised.

"Me too," Fionn smiled. They finally reached the open deck and the bow of the ship, where Byron was finishing his speech in front of the floating cameras he had all over the place. The Queen had her hands tied behind her back. She was dressed in combat gear and looking at her brother with a mix of anger and disappointment, without a sign of fear in her steely eyes. She may have been old, even older by regular human standards, but still had the same fearlessness that she had had as a teenager.

"...now, you will see one of your leaders fall, as all of them do when they are weak for ruling. My dear little sister, your reign is a mistake, a blunder by our weak father that I will correct. That crown should have been mine. Your city will fall as well, as proof of my power. People of the Alliance, kneel before me and your demise will be swift and mostly painless. Dare to challenge me and I will crush you under my heel."

"Dear brother," the Queen raised her voice to be heard over the wind. "You were and have always been an idiot. Father was right in disowning you." The Queen spit in Byron's face. "No one will kneel before you. You will be stopped."

"Silly little girl. Heroes don't exist anymore. I killed them, remember?" Byron gloated, while he grabbed the Queen by the neck, lifting her.

"You missed a couple," Fionn yelled at him. "You have always done things halfway."

Byron turned around. Fionn was walking towards him

at a slow pace, while Sam was trying to use the distraction to approach the rest of the hostages.

"Seems that the rat survived. I shall correct that," Byron said. He threw the Queen over a railing and signaled to his troopers to push out the rest of the hostages as well. Sam cast a spell that pushed the troopers off the ship after the hostages. Without missing a beat, she ran towards the edge, shrinking her quarterstaff and tucking it into the holster inside her jacket.

"What are you doing?" Fionn yelled at his daughter, blood leaving his face. With a twist, Sam smiled and saluted her dad.

"Taking a leap of faith, Dad. See you later!" Sam replied before jumping after the Queen and the hostages.

"Your urchin has more common sense than you. I applaud her bravery to end this thing swiftly," Byron said with disdain, readying his sword.

Fionn turned from where his daughter had jumped into the void. His eyes gleamed with green from the shining irises. His lips were tight and narrow.

"You and I need to talk," Fionn muttered, gritting his teeth. He held Black Fang in front of him. Its blade and the runes engraved on its metallic body were glowing green with intensity.

† † †

The air hit her face with fierce fury, her red hair flowing like flames. Sam was freefalling behind the Queen. *This was a stupid idea*, she thought.

This was going to be too close for her taste. She was still shaking off the draining effects that the Bestial had on her. Alex had been right; it was a good thing she had saved her energies for an emergency like this. She clicked on her left ear to activate her comm. Sam was holding her crystal pendant in a tight grip. It started to shine with violet light.

"I hope you were listening, guys, because I need your help. There has been a small change of plans," she said between gasps, as breathing had become a bit difficult at terminal speed.

"Sam! You are insane!" she heard Alex replying through the comm. "But we are tailing you!"

"You hoomans are gonna be the death of me!" Sid interjected, making Sam chuckle a little.

As she told her father, this was literally a leap of faith. Faith that her new friends would come through to help her with her improvised rescue plan. Faith that she still had enough juice to make the spell work. Faith that, at the end of the day, everything would work. Even if the ground was quickly approaching.

She put her arms to her sides, offering as little air resistance as possible, in order to catch the Queen. Sam extended her arms to catch her and with her right arm embraced her. With her left hand holding her pendant, she cast a spell that created a pentagram made of light, arcane runes rotating around it. From that pentagram, a bubble made of the same light inflated around them. They floated inside the bubble, which in turn reduced their fall just enough that they could catch their breath before the next step. Sam's hair now floated, turning from red to bright purple.

"Hold tight, Your Majesty, we still have a bumpy ride ahead of us."

"Who are you?"

"I'm Samantha Ambers-Estel. I'm Fionn's daughter." Sam smiled nervously. The Queen looked at her, her expression betraying a certain degree of acknowledgment. "Long story. Get ready, because I will need your help."

Sam cast a second spell, moving her hands in the direction she wanted to go, steering the bubble as a result. She flew on towards each of the six falling hostages, picking them up one by one with the help of the Queen, who extended her hand to grab and pull them inside the bubble. Professor Hunt was the trickiest one to catch as he was barely conscious. It took the help of everyone inside the bubble to grab him.

"Why a bubble and not a flying spell, Samantha?" Professor Ortiga asked.

"This is not the moment to debate spell selection." Sam rolled her eyes. Leave it to Ortiga to question her choices. "But I can't carry seven people by myself. At least the bubble can do that."

"And how do you propose to not hit the ground?"

"This is not an exam!" Sam yelled. "Just focus whatever energy you have left to keep this thing floating until help arrives!"

All the magi inside the bubble followed her orders, even Ortiga, who did so with apparent reluctance, and they focused the meager energies they had left to arrest the bubble's fall.

"I hope your faith works!" the Queen exclaimed, her irises glowing with a faint pink and gold glow. She was apparently sharing her Gift's energy with the spell.

"Do you hear that?" Sam smiled.

The roar that filled the air was reminiscent of a dragon of yore. Of a time when the Silver Riders crossed the skies, battling the outsider creatures. Sam had heard those roars thanks to the records kept at Ravenstone. Except that this time, the roar came from the ion engines of the Figaro, closing in, spewing plasma. Dragons might be extinct on Theia, but their spirit was alive and well in their metallic successor.

The ground was starting to look worryingly closer.

The Figaro dove after them.

Sam saw the distance closing. She closed her eyes and focused on keeping the bubble as strong as possible, just in case. This was going to hurt.

"Guys. Hurry up, please," she whispered. Her heart was thumping in her chest. Each thump closed the gap with the merciless ground. And then she heard it.

Sam heard Sid yelling something in samoharo, as he

was pushing the ship as hard as he could, trying to match the speed of the bubble, passing it and flying just in front of it. The back hatch opened and from there a black ball tied to a metal cable was shot towards the bubble. The ball opened into a net that wrapped around the bubble, towing it inside. The net and the cable had electricity running through them, the towing speed increasing. Sam saw Alex tied with a harness to the back of the hatch, pulling the cable with his bare hands, using his Gift to empower himself and in turn, to pull the bubble in faster. Once the bubble was in, Gaby, tied to another harness, pushed a big round button on the wall and closed the hatch.

"We have them!" Sam heard Alex yell in the comm, the reply was a string of curses from Sid. The Figaro roared and turned up, barely avoiding crashing into the ground by a dozen meters. Rising again and leveling, the ship finally stabilized. In the cargo bay, the bubble broke with a loud pop, dropping the Queen unceremoniously on the floor.

"No time for resting," Alex exclaimed, releasing himself from the harness. His hands were dripping with blood from handling the cable. "Take the professor to the med bay. Your Majesty, please come with us."

"Phew." Sam let her breath out in relief, examining Alex's hands. "That was quite close."

"Too close," Alex eyed the hatch. "I don't know if I would be brave enough to do the same as you."

"Don't worry, you have been doing fine so far." Sam smiled at him. "Let's go. We need to drop you off on the Bestial before we get to the city."

† † †

In the cockpit, Sid and Harland were arguing.

"What now?" Alex was fed up with the constant bickering. By the looks on their faces, Gaby and Sam shared the feeling.

"There is no way I can drop you in the same spot as Fionn and Miss 'Let's take a dive' here," Sid said to Sam. "The place will be secured and you will face more opposition now."

"He is right," Sam added with some regret.

"Then we need to find a way to get closer to the core," Alex pointed out. An idea was forming in his head.

"Oh no. I know that look," Sid exclaimed. "I don't like it."

"What? I can use my Gift to track the exact position of the core so you can leave us close."

"Then what? Dig? That thing has military grade metal plating!" Sid yelled at Alex.

"You said that this ship has special weaponry capable of cutting through that." Harland smiled at Alex. "It will work."

"You hoomans are crazy! C. R. A. Z. Y," Sid threw his hands in the air.

A cough could be heard behind them.

"Excuse me, but who are you people?" the Queen asked, still dizzy and confused.

"I will be brief for the sake of expediency. I'm Harland Rickman and we have already met Your Grace. These are friends of Fionn." Harland pointed at the rest. "And we need to stop that ship from touching the crystal obelisks in Saint Lucy or it will all be over. Right now, we need your help if we are going to save the city. We have the commander of the Solarian Knights online and he is angry."

"What can I do to help?" the Queen asked, this time more at ease.

# Chapter 18

## Showdown at Dawn

"You and I need to talk," Fionn said, with a gravelly voice. His body was battered from the fight with the troopers; bruises covered his face and arms. There was a particularly nasty gash on his left cheek that didn't stop bleeding. But he was relishing the challenge of fighting once more without having the Gift as a safety net. He had turned it off, saving as much energy as he could. And yet, if he focused, he could feel the odd sensation of it being drained. It was similar to when someone takes out a blood sample with a syringe, but applied to the whole body.

The wind blew across the deck of the Bestial, with the sun soon to rise and the lights of Saint Lucy and its three giant crystal obelisks in the background. Fionn would have enjoyed the view under different circumstances. His breathing was heavy, his shoulders pushing back despite the ache. Inside his head, he had to put away any fear or concern for Sam. He just hoped that everything had gone all right. The chatter in his comn was scrambled, thanks to the presence of the Bestial. Fionn had only understood 'hold on,' 'keep busy,' 'on our way to drop...'

He needed to keep Byron distracted. *Talk the monster to death*, he thought. With Byron, that would be easy. Or so he hoped.

"You are a glutton for punishment," Byron replied with a gleam in his eye and mirth in his tone. "What makes you think this time it will be different?"

"Just a hunch," Fionn replied, turning the blade to point the edge upwards. The muscles in his calves and the tendons in his feet tensed, ready to spring. "I will give you a better fight this time."

"You are stupider than you look. It will be a pleasure to prove you wrong," Byron paced the deck and extended his left hand with an open palm as an invitation. "I hope you are enjoying my creation. And my new sword."

Byron unsheathed his weapon. It was larger than the old one, with jagged edges and a golden hilt. In Fionn's opinion, it was a sword made to intimidate, not for an actual fight. Then again Byron liked to showboat... even if that was the case, Fionn had to be careful. Any sword in Byron's hands was a problem, due to his sheer might.

"Well... your taste in decorations needs some work. I would have gone with fewer tentacles, but that's just me. I mean," Fionn waved a hand to take in the Bestial, "it looks like something out of a horror movie. And not a good one."

"What's with you and interior design?" Byron raised an eyebrow.

"I had to pick a hobby after the war," Fionn replied with a shrug. "You know what? I missed these talks. I wonder why we stopped having them... Ah right, it was because you killed all of our friends and are trying to start the end of days." Fionn's fists wrapped around the hilt of Black Fang, making his knuckles turn white.

"Ah, that. Well, you know, eggs and omelets to bring a new world order. Par for the course. What's a couple of dead bodies among friends when something greater is going to be built? By me, of course," Byron bared his teeth and readied his sword.

"You had to say the omelet thing, didn't you? That's so cliché. But then again, you love the sound of your voice too much." Fionn shook his head. The muscles in his back tensed. "I'm so gonna enjoy beating you up."

Both Fionn and Byron eyed each other for a moment, their gazes meeting, while they remained immobile. Then, without warning, they jumped at each other with lightning speed. They clashed, blocking each other's attack, each pushing forward. Byron freed his sword and slashed, while Fionn parried the blows. He moved to Byron's left to make space between them, pointing Black Fang towards his opponent.

Byron twirled his sword with a flourish, even if his expression never changed: dead eyes and tight lips. For a second Fionn thought that for once, Byron was taking him seriously, no boasting and no laughing. With a jump, Byron closed the gap, spinning in the air, trying to land a direct hit on Fionn's neck. Fionn barely parried the attack. Instead, it earned Fionn a hard kick in the gut that took out all the air from his lungs. It sent him reeling.

Catching his breath, Fionn saw Byron advancing towards him. He attacked with a horizontal slash at Byron's neck, but he simply blocked it and spun once more, breaking Fionn's nose with his elbow.

"I wanted a better challenge. Without your abilities, you are neither a threat nor entertainment."

Fionn wiped the blood running from his nose. He pressed his lips together. It was just a matter of holding on for a few more seconds. He could hear a distant roaring in the wind. He knew that roaring. He heard a whisper in his ear.

Fionn took a deep breath and launched himself once more to hit Byron. The build-up of lactic acid made his muscles sting with pain. This time, Fionn pressed the attack, pushing Byron towards the middle of the deck. He took a few seconds to circle Byron, but instead of attacking him, Fionn slashed the cannons that guarded the deck.

"This is a bad moment for you to start redecorating my

ship," Byron quipped, betraying a hint of amusement. He then slashed at Fionn's legs.

Fionn jumped into the smoldering pieces of metal and once more flipped over Byron, landing behind him. In turn, Byron spun a third time to unleash a second slash. Fionn parried it, both blades rubbing against each other, unleashing sparks. They separated once more and looked at each other.

"I thought you were angry at me and yet, you haven't even touched me." Byron looked confused. "Many of your attacks are failing to land. Was I wrong to actually expect a challenge?"

"I'm just getting started," Fionn replied, pointing at a deep gash on Byron's shoulder. "The downside of being whatever you are, is that you didn't feel that."

Byron looked at the gash, from which tiny white worms were coming out. His only reply was to laugh.

"Ah, finally! The last person to get this close, besides you, was Ywain. Killing him was satisfying." Byron's eyes opened wide, his pupils contracting and his lips tightening into a wide grin. Foam spilled from his mouth.

A rain of slashes and stabbing thrusts followed, with Fionn barely managing to evade them and reach the center of the deck. Byron pressed the attacks and once more both blades were locked. Byron pushed forward, slightly cutting Fionn's chin.

Fionn let his feet slide a few inches backward and then moved to the right, making Byron fall by his own inertia. His blade hit the deck, getting stuck there. Fionn moved fast and tried to hit Byron's neck, but Byron instead caught Fionn's arm and broke it like a twig. Fionn kneeled, while Byron went to unstick his sword.

"Now I'm disappointed. That has to be the most worn-out move in the book. I'm wondering if you actually thought you could beat me on your own."

"Who said I was on my own, you miserable bastard?" Fionn replied through gritted teeth, resetting his broken bone. He allowed just enough of the Gift to flow into his arm to heal it, but focused on saving the rest for the end. As Alex had pointed out, Byron got stronger the more he absorbed someone's energy. Fionn had been repressing his own healing ability on purpose, to avoid feeding the monster. This was a small allowance, as he needed both arms to remain functional. And yet the healing would take some minutes. Fionn was hoping he would have enough time.

By then the howling of jet engines was clear enough for all to hear, the distinctive roar closing in. "This is a team effort." Fionn's smile grew into a wide grin, while he got ready to move. "Ywain's family sends their regards."

"What?" Byron was confused. Fionn saw the Figaro rising on the side of the Bestial and aiming its energy cannons to a spot a few meters from where they were standing. The Figaro unleashed all its power into a single focused beam that cut the metal until an explosion a few decks below rocked the whole place, sending Fionn and Byron careening away.

"You fool. You will never beat me, no matter how many tricks you have up your sleeve!"

Fionn thrust Black Fang into the metal deck to slow down. "I think we will have to agree to disagree on this one," he yelled.

† † †

The smoke cleared just enough for Gaby and Alex to descend onto the Bestial's upper deck. A small crater was visible, wide enough to show some of the core engines of the Bestial.

"Damn, a few centimeters to the left and Sid would have hit the bastard," Alex moaned.

"And Fionn with him. Leaving us with a pissed-off abomination after us. Let's stick to the plan and get this done thoroughly and right," Gaby replied with a frown on her face, not amused at the idea. Alex and Gaby tied a rope to a handrail and were starting their descent.

"Have I told you that I suck at rappelling?"

Gaby was about to reply when she opened her eyes wide and big. With all her force she pushed Alex to the deck, while drawing Soulkeeper with her right hand, barely deflecting a metal tendril that ended in a sharp point. The tendril hit a wall, and then it recoiled back to where it came. A few meters away, Madam Park recalled the wiggling tendril that returned to shape the long sleeve of the strange metallic robe she was wearing.

"What the hell?" Alex exclaimed while getting up. "Isn't she the woman that attacked Ravenstone?"

"Do you mind going on alone? I need to attend to someone," Gaby replied. Her fists were shaking and the muscles in her neck tensed, tightening her face. She never lost eye contact with the woman.

"I know that look and that euphemism. Just do me a favor, please?"

"What?" Gaby asked, her voice conveying her annoyance. Alex looked at her with pleading eyes.

"Don't lose yourself there. Remember who you are and what we practiced. You are not a heartless assassin. You are my friend."

Gaby smiled briefly at that comment. She kissed him on the forehead. "Be careful too. She might not be alone, and we have little time before we will feel the draining effects."

"I will be fine, I think," Alex replied, eyeing the drop to the core, clearing his throat. "Aww crap."

Gaby unsheathed Heartguard while covering Alex's descent from possible attack. Both women gazed at each other. Gaby twirled both swords in her hands, trying to calm her mind down. Once she was sure Alex was gone and wouldn't witness this, she stood as tall as she could and her irises started to glow with a faint, eerie blue light.

"Shall we?" Gaby asked. "Because dropping in unannounced on someone is rude."

"You are one to talk. It is always a pleasure to teach a young person some manners," Madam Park said with a dismissive nod towards a large space on the deck, far from where Fionn and Byron were fighting.

Madam Park moved fast, with a celerity that created ripples in her armor. It looked as if it was made out of woven metallic silk. Gaby stood calm, waiting for the attack. Her ponytail streamed behind her from the wind blowing across the deck.

Tendrils came her way at lightning speed, forcing Gaby to move as fast as she could. But even that wasn't enough to save her from getting scraped. Gaby tried to block the pain the small, deep cuts had caused her.

"Nice moves, child," Park replied, smiling. "One last chance to escape, as a courtesy."

"I don't think so."

"As you wish."

Park let out some air in frustration and ripples ran through her armor as she launched the tendrils once more at Gaby. They came from three different directions. At that point, Gaby decided to throw caution to the wind. This was not a time for half measures, not with the lives of Fionn and Alex at stake. If she lost, Madam Park would surely go after them, spoiling the plan. Gaby was their shield now. If she was going to win this fight, she needed to use the Gift. What she was planning to do was a gamble, but consequences be damned, it was a risk that had to be taken. Though with the training Fionn gave her, she was sure it would work. She closed her eyes for a second, drew deep from the Gift, and felt its energy fusing with the mental conditioning of the Ice State. This time, like during the practice with Fionn and Alex, felt different. It was less cold than usual, but just as focused. The rhythm it suggested was more akin to a rock song, like the one she had sung on the Figaro, than a dance.

*I ought to change its name now*, Gaby thought.

Each second of the fight stretched into minutes, the tendrils moving slower for her. Not slow enough that she didn't need to worry, but enough that she could let her mind envision what was going to happen next. The key was, as Fionn had suggested, being the calm in the eye of the storm. She could hear inside her head, clear and loud, the notes that her 'song' was creating. Every time Park tried to grab her, punch her or kick her, she was in a different spot. Her technique was a matter of fluidity, like water flowing through space in a continuous movement, one step taking her to the next without a break.

Each movement, each counterattack synched to her breath, to the song. Breathe in, dodge the attack, a twist, a pirouette, a side jump. Breathe out, a punch, a slash with her blades, a kick. Every move perfectly measured, with enough strength to hurt but not enough to get her tired.

To an outsider, it was a beautiful dance between two skillful practitioners of an ancient art. Another series of attacks by Madam Park forced Gaby to jump as high as possible, thrust by the Gift into a somersault whose descent for her seemed to appear to be in slow motion, as if time was freezing around her. It was then when Gaby noticed something. Madam Park wasn't even breaking a sweat, she was smiling even. And it dawned on her with trepidation and a self-admitted sense of excitement: Madam Park had been trained by the Sisters as well. That's why Park didn't make a boast or a challenge or a demand, she was already in the Ice State. Gaby's face must have betrayed her realization because Madam Park grinned.

"Finally, an even match with a fellow student." Park readied her armor, to attack Gaby as soon as she descended from her last pirouette.

*This is not a dance. It is a song. MY song.* Gaby just smiled. It would be the fight of her life.

††††

Alex finished his descent into the crater, hating every second of it because of the smell of rotting corpses that flooded the place. Only through that downward trip into the innards of the Bestial could he envision the true horror of what the creature was, what it had done to its previous crew. They had been absorbed alive into the fuselage and now their moans filled the air. The lower he descended, the more he lost his sense of location. The whole place made him feel nauseated. And the ringing didn't help either. The damn ringing in his ears was becoming an annoyance. No matter how much he tried to block the Gift, the danger warnings it gave him were always on.

*I know I'm surrounded by evil, dangerous things, so no need for the alert,* he thought.

Once Alex touched the last intact deck, his first instinct was to throw up. The smell was more potent here, and the miasma that floated around hit him. It took him a minute to regain his bearings enough to focus just enough of his Gift to be able to track the energy ebbs and flows from and to the core of the ship. After a moment he could see the orangish tendrils of energy. The color told him what he suspected, that the ship was alive. If it had been just mechanical, the energy would look blue for him. Soon, he felt the drain on energy in his body. It was draining him and he needed to save energy just in case.

Luckily for him, the Figaro's shot had been quite close to the core and it didn't take him long to reach the core chamber. It was a vast room, where blood dripped from the beams and a grave, pulsating sound, like that of a drum, could be heard echoing in the chamber. Alex slowly walked towards the entrance, the thumping resounding stronger with each step. What he saw left him breathless.

Three guards protected the entrance to the core. Behind them, the Bestial's core was a monstrous heart made of pulsating metal, crystals and living tissue, with a rugose quality to its external surface. It looked like lizard skin, glowing with a faint purplish light that turned green and back in a rhythmic sequence. The core was surrounded by three metal rings, arranged as if they were a gyroscope. The arrangement looked eerily familiar to Alex. It was an enlarged, more powerful version of the machine that had created the incursion at the Straits.

*So it's a gate as much as a power source*, Alex thought. *That will be a problem.*

He realized that to create a controlled explosion, he would have to place the explosives in strategic points inside the chamber instead of peppering the place with arrows. That would take time.

Alex took a deep breath, calming his mind and getting ready for the fight. This would be easier with Gaby at his side. Taking another breath, he came out of his hiding place, fired three arrows in quick succession and hit two of the guards, the third managing to evade the shot. Alex closed the gap between him and the guard. They started trading punches. Alex dodged the vicious attacks until he managed to grab the mook's head and slam it into a nearby metal column, leaving him unconscious.

"Why don't you sleep that one off..." Alex said, then he noticed the body lying in a weird position, the head turned completely around. "Or not. Yeah, sorry 'bout that. Guess I put too much force into that one."

Alex crossed the entrance into the chamber. The core and the surrounding gyroscope were suspended over a wide vent, but not far from reach thanks to a bridge that crossed the vent. The bridge was wide enough to allow three grown men to walk side by side and still have breathing space.

Alex took out most of the small explosive charges he was carrying in the pouch tied to his belt, and proceeded to install them, hoping they worked. A single one wouldn't do too much damage, but a chain of explosions timed properly would send enough energy feedback into the core to make it implode by itself. Or so his theory went. He finished setting up the explosives and allowed himself a smile. He then walked away from the bridge.

*That was easy,* Alex thought. It was then that the ringing in his ears, which he had been trying to ignore, exploded into a continuous buzzing. *Too easy.*

"Aww crap."

Alex felt a presence behind him and he turned his head to see who it was. Behind him was the same massive man who had beaten his friend Birm back at the university.

Alex felt himself being picked up from behind and thrown away toward a metal column. He braced for the impact.

# Chapter 19

# When One Thing Fails,
# Try Something Else

"I can't believe that Alex got that right," Sam muttered.

The Figaro flew at maximum speed towards the center of the city, where the three crystal obelisks, joined by a sculpted bronze belt, stood as a memorial to those that had died during the Great War. No one knew where they had come from or who made them, only that King Castlemartell had them erected on the hill overseeing the small town which had now become a bustling city. The public illumination, shining at full, delineated the shapes of the roads and parks that started at the center and ended at the round white walls that bordered the city. As Alex had pointed out, Sam could now see how the lattice of the city's roads and public spaces resembled a magick circle of power.

"He gets things right nine times out of ten," Sid maneuvered the Figaro around the Towers, looking for a place to land.

"And the tenth?" Sam asked.

"He fails miserably," Sid interjected.

"Are you ready, Your Majesty?" Harland asked, standing up from the copilot seat. "We are on a tight schedule here after the transmission of your failed execution, and we need to disembark some passengers."

"Yes. My Knights must be ready too," the Queen replied, surprisingly calm for a lady her age. This emergency crisis must have felt for her like a welcomed break from boring protocol life.

"Sam?"

"I think so," Sam replied nervously, as so much rested on her shoulders.

"You will do fine, Sam. I trust you, Fionn trusts you." Harland reassured her with a smile.

"If it helps, I believe in you too," Sid added, while he was landing the ship a few meters from the obelisks. Five armored soldiers waited for them. Harland noticed the delicate handiwork on their armor, gleaming in gold and silver, like the one worn by the Dragonking. The Solarian Knights, the personal guard of Queen Sophia, masters of the titanfight style. They were the replacement of the Twelve Swords and had been drafted from noble houses. They were unbelievably smug as well.

The cargo bay opened, extending the ramp to allow the Queen and Sam to disembark, followed by the students and professors who carried the injured Professor Hunt. A few soldiers picked up the professor, taking him to a waiting ambulance. Not soon after Sam put a foot on the ground of the plaza, her hair turned bright purple, attracting the looks of the Knights.

"This place is full of power. I can feel it in my bones," Sam said with a mix of concern and elation, kneeling to be the same height as Harland.

"That's good, kid. That means that any spell you cast will be more powerful than ever," Harland told her, his hands placed on her shoulders.

"You know what will happen if I do that," Sam replied, returning the looks of the Knights, who were being lectured by the Queen. "The uncomfortable effects of using magick at full force."

"Who cares about them?" Harland looked at the soldiers.

Sam felt uneasy. A mix of emotions and sensations crawled beneath her skin. Like an electric shock, her body was absorbing too much energy.

"Pricks!" Harland raised his voice, sure that the soldiers were listening. "Where is the rebel that drove Fionn crazy a few years ago? The one that just jumped without a parachute to rescue the Queen? You have more guts in your pinkie finger than those idiots. Be proud of who and what you are. Never back down. Besides, you look pretty in purple."

"Thank you," Sam hugged Harland.

"After tonight, they will be the ones to thank you. Do you have everything with you?"

"Yes. Now you have to go." Sam stood up. She smiled at Harland and walked towards the people gathering at the feet of the obelisks. Freefolk members of the Fire Tribe arrived through the underground roads of the city and surrounded the obelisks. The Knights looked at them with disdain and at Sam with surprise.

"What? Haven't you ever seen a combat magus?" Sam told them with renewed strength in her voice. "Time for you to learn, boys. Soon, creatures will land here trying to touch those obelisks and close a circuit through the circlets on their necks. That circuit will allow their master to summon monsters even worse than that thing that has been destroying the land. Our job is to stop that from happening. So try to keep up."

"We don't take orders from you," a Solarian Knight replied with disdain and prepotency.

"You do now!" the Queen ordered, her voice loud and clear. She was getting her combat gear on and was testing a falchion sword. "Her orders are as good as mine and shall be followed without delay or complaint, are we clear?"

The Solarian Knights seemed to be taken aback. But none dared to contradict or even argue with the Queen. Her tone of voice and the faint glow of her irises left no room for argument. They simply nodded in acquiescence. Sam wondered if she had looked so fearsome when she was younger, during the war. No wonder her dad seemed scared of her at times.

"Thank you, Your Majesty." Sam nodded to the Queen, and then she addressed her students and colleagues. "I'm gonna ask all of you for one thing, students and teachers. If you stay here, give it your all! Nothing crosses this garden without us burning it. We have power here, let's use it!"

"She takes after her father," the Queen murmured to Harland with a smile.

"Then we are in safe hands."

With a flourish of her left hand, Sam unleashed the magick spell that made a quarterstaff grow from her palm once more. The weapon hummed with the power running through it.

"That's Izia's quarterstaff," the Queen noticed, walking to Sam. "Where did you get it?"

"Family heirloom, Your Grace," Sam explained, while her hair, electrified by the magick currents running through her body, started to glow. "Here they come!"

Sam saw a cloud coming their way. Except that it wasn't a cloud. It was a multitude of flying humanoid critters, followed by a volley from the Bestial's belly cannons. Sam and the freefolk students let lose a volley of their own, full of magick spells, while the Queen and her Knights braced for impact.

† † †

The Figaro had taken off just when the first volley of attacks from the Bestial hit the city, spreading panic and fire through its quarters. Harland barely had time to fasten his seatbelt when the Figaro rocked from one of the impacts.

"They don't waste time," Sid muttered, adjusting some settings on the control console. "Let's go, we need to pick up the guys before they blow up that thing... whatda..." Sid fell silent, looking at something on his screens.

"What the hell are those?" Harland asked, seeing two giant-sized metal balls composed of several plates impact in the outskirts of the park. The plates opened and released several mutated men, similar to those Harland had witnessed at Carffadon. "Forget that, I think I already know."

"I'm more worried about that," Sid pointed at something far away. He pushed a couple of buttons and a screen in the HUD grew, showing the Bestial's slow advance towards the city, surrounded by flying critters, a mash-up of the drones that attacked the Figaro at the Maze, and insects with strange features.

"Remember the news reports."

The Bestial, in all its massive glory, cast a shadow so dark, it was unnatural. Once the shadow left a spot of ground behind, the land was withered, devoid of all life and covered by a grayish frost. It was as if it had sucked all the vital energy from the land below. Any living being unlucky enough to be caught under that shadow ended up as nothing more than dried bones glowing green. And the sensors of the Figaro reported temperatures well below what was normal for the area at this time of the year.

"Damn, if that thing closes in on the city, thousands will die. Get to the gunnery station," Sid barked at Harland. "We are going to slow it down."

"How? Towing it?"

"Let's call that Plan B. Right now I'm going with the stupid Plan A. If Fionn is right, the Bestial hates dragons, right?" Sid pulled some levers and adjusted the gyroscopes.

"Yes, but what does that have to do with us?"

"The Figaro now has a dragon core."

"We are going to bait it." Harland opened his eyes in realization. "It will slow down because we will distract it."

"Yep, just long enough for Gaby and Alex to finish their thing and get the Pits out of there. And since our automated guns were knocked out at the Maze, I need you to keep the sky clear while we do that. I can't fly the damn ship and shoot them down at the same time," Sid replied, slightly annoyed while pushing the yoke of the ship, accelerating it. "I'm gonna regret this."

"Ok, ok, no need to go ballistic."

"I handle this kind of pressure poorly."

"I have noticed."

Harland arrived at the gunnery station just when the Figaro accelerated to full speed again. He barely had time to adjust his seatbelt when Sid yelled at Harland through the screen that transmitted the internal comms.

"Signal is… bzzz bad…The Bestial is causing… bzzz too much interference…Get ready."

The AI alarm blared until Sid pushed a button and it went silent.

"I know, this is stupid and dangerous," Sid said with resignation. "You don't need to blast it into my ears."

He was talking to the ship's AI, and issued a command. "Be ready to shoot countermeasure three at my command."

The Figaro flew at full speed against the Bestial, dodging its fire while shooting down any metal sphere and flying critter aimed at the city. Sid piloted the ship to give the best aiming window to Harland while evading the constant volleys from the cannons. Barreling to the left, the Figaro dodged a renewed volley of attacks. For a ship of its size, it flew like a swift dragon. At any another time, Sid would be bragging about his baby, but at the moment he was busy trying to keep it afloat.

Sid focused on the front of the Bestial. The ship had that face he had seen in the video feed. It was a nauseating mockery, a mix of a goblin shark and a blind worm, from which tentacles wiggled, grabbing the occasional critter to consume. It acted like a brain-dead creature, moving more by pure instinct than by any conscious mind. Sid guessed that Byron, being busy with Fionn, had no current conscious control of the ship. Or at least he hoped that was the case.

"Let's see if that ugly puppy follows the shiny ball. Let's sting him a bit more," Sid muttered in the comm, getting a static damaged reply from Harland that he guessed amounted to something like 'you crazy bastard.'

Instead of slowing down, the Figaro pushed harder, as if it was on a collision course. The horizon rotated in front of Sid until the ship was upside down, with the ground above and the belly of the Bestial below his feet. Sid was flying the Figaro upside down below the Bestial, across its underbelly. The shadow started to corrode the Figaro's hull. Sid hoped that the alloys that composed the hull of the Figaro could resist long enough until they cleared the other end.

From the belly of the Bestial, more tentacles appeared trying to catch the Figaro. Sid deftly dodged them as fast as he could, barreling through the myriad of appendages. Looking up close, those things had teeth and eyes, with a cracked skin full of blisters and callouses.

"I think I'm gonna lose my breakfast," Sid exclaimed, while banking to the left to evade a particularly fat tentacle.

"You think?" Harland replied through the comms.

"Just keep shooting, we need to annoy it to grab its attention."

"Just keep us alive long enough to annoy it!"

Harland kept shooting at the tentacles that inched closer to the Figaro, clearing its path, as well as shooting at the belly of the Bestial, creating holes that regenerated slowly. Right in the middle, there was a particularly nasty looking vestigial eye, from which the darkest part of the shadow came. Sid aligned the ship so Harland had a clear shot at it. The shot was true and soon an explosion covered the belly, unleashing energy currents that shook the Bestial to its core. A few seconds later, the Figaro turned again, having reached the rear end of the Bestial. Rising towards the sky, the Figaro cleared the Bestial, which started a slow turn, followed by a growl that echoed through the entire valley.

"Wahooo!" Sid exclaimed with excitement. "We have its

attention... wait a minute, we have its attention and we blew up one of its eyes. Why am I celebrating? Damn it!"

"I was going to ask the same," Harland said through the comm. "Nice flying."

"Nice shooting," Sid replied. "Now what?" he muttered. The AI apparently got annoyed, shaking Sid from his seat. The Bestial was now focusing all its firepower and tentacles on the Figaro.

"Me and my stupid heroic ideas."

† † †

Alex felt like an impotent ragdoll. He was getting trashed by a guy twice his size and four times stronger who kept throwing him around. He hadn't been able to land a single hit on the guy and his body ached. He was surprised that his body had withstood so much punishment. His left eye was so swollen that he could barely keep it open. The heavy breathing was a sign of a broken nose and ribs.

Right now, he was managing to evade his opponent's grasp but was still receiving hits. He needed to do something; otherwise, he wouldn't be able to activate the explosives. He needed a plan but was having difficulties focusing. It was like when Fionn trained them at Ravenhall; he needed to be able to concentrate despite external factors. Fionn had suggested Alex back then to think of a person to help him block any distraction and call forth the Gift. While Fionn had mentioned that he had focused in Izia at the time, Alex was sure that his friend's focus was changing to someone else. And that train of thought took him to Gaby and then to Sam...

*Don't worry, you have been doing fine so far,* Sam had said, smiling at him. Alex focused on that memory and felt the energy inside him building up. He didn't care about the Bestial draining it. As long as he had something left in the tank, he would use it to kick this guy's ass.

Alex's irises glowed with a golden hue.

"Enough!" Alex thundered. He channeled all his anger and feelings of impotence into fury, and then converted that fury into power. Biting his bloodied lip, he caught the incoming fist with his left hand. "I'm done with you."

Alex pushed back the fist with such strength, that it sent the other guy back several meters. The guy managed to steady himself by grabbing a column and faced Alex, cracking his neck. Alex stood there, defiantly.

*Time to think this through.* Alex focused his sight once more. Through the Gift his sight was enhanced. He saw electric blue currents crackling below his rival's skin. Those currents were powering what seemed to be subdermal grafts under his opponent's skin. The man was not a hundred percent human, but some kind of cyborg. And he was using the energy he was draining from the environment to become freakishly strong. That explained so much. His aura resembled a mix of a bear and a raptor. No wonder why he fought like a wrestler: all force and no finesse.

Alex did the math. Speed wouldn't help because he was tired. A blow-for-blow match was out of the question, as he was battered enough. But he had a bow. He ran as much as his legs allowed to give himself some space, extended his bow and got ready to shoot.

"Are you coming for me or not?" Alex taunted him.

"You annoy me. And you killed my brother." The brute replied with a baritone voice.

"He speaks! So your brain is not just for ornament... Wait, that thing at my school was your brother?"

"We had the same dark father who granted us our enhancements."

"Ah!" Alex replied with a mocking smile. "So you're more like science experiments bonding than actual brothers. Gotcha. I would say sorry for killing him, but at this point of my life I'm way beyond apologizing for getting rid of monsters like him."

"I don't care about him," the brute said. "But that a

chubby weakling like you beat him and is refusing to die, embarrasses me and the legacy of our father."

"Chubby weakling?" Alex said angrily. "Now, those are fighting words!"

"I will crush you!"

The brute charged forward towards Alex, like a bull, putting all his weight into it.

Alex started by shooting fully charged arrows at his enemy. It wouldn't stop him, as he was freakishly strong. But it didn't matter; they were aimed at the grafts, to short-circuit them. The power influx to his cybernetic parts reduced during the run, allowing Alex to sidestep him.

Turning, Alex hit him with his bow at full force on the back of the head, breaking the weapon. The hit managed to cut the man's skin, leaving the short-circuited grafts exposed. It was then that his opponent decided to grab a loose girder to use as a club. The man grunted while raising the girder, his muscles twitching from the effort. Plan A had only been mildly successful.

*Ok, time for Plan B,* Alex thought while drawing his sword. The hilt felt familiar in his hand, the blade light and nimble. Alex was not exactly the best swordsman ever, but he was sure he could get by against a brute using a metal girder. Parrying, deflecting blows with precision and ease, Alex used his enemy's strength as an asset. He felt his body becoming weaker, all the power from his Gift starting to fade. But Alex held on. And started to taunt the man.

"Not so scary when you don't have the help of your cheat codes, are you? Uh, look at me, big man that can barely lift a metal bar."

Frustrated, the man made a wide swinging blow, the inertia of the movement leaving his chest fully exposed. It was the opening Alex needed. Focusing all the power he could muster, Alex swung Yaha, cutting the girder as if it was made of butter, leaving scorch marks on the edges. Without missing a beat, Alex freed his right hand and hit the man's chest above the liver with two precise strikes.

The man dropped to one knee, weakened by the nerve-blocking technique. Alex didn't waste time and hit the man with an uppercut to the chin. The punch had such potency that he could hear the bones breaking. The brute hit the floor like a sack of rocks, barely conscious. Alex's fist was crackling with electricity.

Alex spit some blood from his mouth. He sheathed Yaha and grabbed what was left of his bow. He took the cartridge out from the bow and held it with two hands. He concentrated, and an arrow formed in each hand. Putting all his remaining strength into this, Alex impaled the man with the arrows, hitting him in each shoulder. The arrows pierced the flesh and bone, even the metal below. They were stuck in the floor, crackling with electricity, keeping the man restrained.

"That is for my friend Birm," Alex let go a gratifying sigh. With a cocky smile, he put a timer close to the man's line of sight. "Enjoy the fireworks."

Alex left the chamber and stared at the way up. It would be a long way back to the upper deck. Alex smiled. He needed to hurry, push through the pain and probably face a couple of obstacles. It would be fun.

The man that had been his opponent was still pinned down, screaming, the countdown running close to an end, the ticking of the clock echoing in the chamber.

Tick Tock. Tick Tock. Tick Tock.

† † †

That had been close. And yet, despite the danger or maybe because of it, Gaby was enjoying the fight.

"You are not bad. I give you props for the landing and avoiding my attacks in the last second," Madam Park said. Under any other circumstances, Gaby would have judged that smile as fake, but this one felt sincere. When two former Sisters of Mercy faced each other, no matter if they were on opposing sides, which was a surprisingly common occurrence, they had their own rules of etiquette.

"I don't think we introduced ourselves properly, so the customary question is in order. Are you House of Light or House of Shadow? Honest answer."

"Light of course. But you already knew that. The signature styles are noticeable for the trained eye," Madam Park freed her hands from her long sleeves with a flourish. "I have heard of you, the girl that ran away after surviving the labyrinth punishment."

"I hope it wasn't through the alumni newsletter," Gaby replied, cocking her head to the side while readying her twin swords, twirling each one and then gliding into a guard stance. "Now what I truly want to know is how you went from the Sisters of Mercy to joining forces with a monstrosity like Byron?"

"Sweet, naïve child. What you see as a monstrosity I see as a ruler with the steady hand to lead us into an enlightened era. One where people will do as they are told if they want to remain safe."

"And that requires attacking a whole species, kidnapping and killing children, and summoning an eldritch abomination?"

"You have to tear down a house if you want to rebuild something better. And that includes getting rid of a few pests." Madam Park paced in front of Gaby as if she were a teacher lecturing a student, or a predator waiting to pounce on its prey.

"Even the Sisters have limits," Gaby replied, tensing her leg muscles. She was getting ready for the final assault.

"You still don't see it. Whatever you and your friends are trying to do will be pointless. Byron was awakened by like-minded people. We are many. We realize that the power granted by the Masters can be used as a tool for a better future."

"You are playing with fire. It won't end well for anyone," Gaby said. Her Gift kicked in and a myriad of possibilities exploded inside her head.

"Maybe for you, it won't." Madam Park guided the metal tendrils at lighting speed, aimed at the vital parts of Gaby's body. "But I will be merciful..."

Gaby was not there anymore as she had jumped in the nick of time to avoid the attack. With her Gift running low, she had to use the break in the conversation to muster as much energy as she could. Her leg muscles ached; signs of strain and cramps were appearing. It was high time to end the stalemate, and her twin swords, glowing red and blue, seemed to agree as they struck down one of the tendrils.

Madam Park groaned loudly in surprise when one of her tendrils returned to its place, with the tip cut off and cracks all over the place. Gaby went on the offensive and, with each blow, damaged the metal plates that formed the armored tendrils. She dodged the last attack, the tendril getting stuck in a turret. Gaby jumped onto it and ran its full length to close the gap. She made a slash aimed at Park's head.

"You are breaking etiquette, child. No killing blows to the head, only the chest and other vital points. You are not following the rules of the dance!" Madam Park complained.

"To the Pits with etiquette," Gaby replied, kicking her in the head, sending Madam Park reeling backward. Relentlessly, she pressed the attack, managing to cut off a decent chunk of the tendrils and ending with a blow that cracked the armor covering the ribcage. "You are nothing but an ice-cold bitch. You don't deserve the rules."

"Like you are one to talk. You are using the same icy tricks as me. Soon you will be like me."

"Wrong. Because I still care about people like my friends." Gaby remembered Alex's words to her. "I don't need it to beat you. It's not a dance anymore. It is a song. My song!"

Gaby was ready to press her advantage and cut deeper when an explosion rocked the Bestial's deck. Both Gaby and

Madam Park lost their footing. Madam Park looked at her damaged armor while another explosion rocked the place. She met Gaby's eyes and with alacrity got to her feet. Then, like the coward Gaby knew her to be, she turned and ran away, jumping off the deck and into the void.

*So much for loyalty*, Gaby thought, running towards the edge. Madam Park seemed determined to cut her losses. Gaby could see Madam Park's armor undergoing a transformation, shapeshifting into metallic wings nearly identical to those of a great eagle. She flew away, disappearing into the tops of the tall trees of the nearby forest.

"I need to learn that trick," Gaby whispered, trying to regain her footing. She saw Alex coming out from a nearby hatch; half of his face was swollen and was acquiring a purplish tone. He was staggering a little, but standing. When he saw Gaby, he tried to smile, but a painful grimace crossed the side of his face that hadn't been punched like a bag of meat.

"What happened to your face?" Gaby asked, softly caressing the injured side of his face. Gaby was feeling a bit guilty about leaving him alone. Even now her cuts and scratches, which Alex was looking at with attention, seemed barely a nuisance.

"Can I say now how it feels to be hit by a freight train?"

"Maybe." Gaby chuckled.

"It's time to go," Alex said with another attempt at a smile, with better success this time. He looked around. "Those explosions? They are just the start. This thing is more unstable than I thought. Let's get Fionn and us out of here."

"Get out of here now," a voice sounded in their comms.

"Fionn? Are you ok?" Gaby asked.

"Just lots of smoke in my lungs. I will be fine. Listen, you need to reach the Figaro and get the Pits out of here. I will take care of the rest," Fionn said, his voice sounding artificial and distant. They could hear him panting, trying to catch his breath.

"No. Not without you," Gaby replied with determination and hurt on her face. "We are a team, you need us."

"I have better odds than you two of surviving this. Let me finish this."

"He is right, Gaby," Alex said, his bloated face showing the pain that the decision was unleashing on him. "I don't like to leave him behind, but we need to go. The chain reaction will start soon. There have been three explosions so far. Six to go for the big badaboom."

"Promise me that you will hurry up. We will be waiting for you on the Figaro," Gaby told him, holding back the tears appearing in her eyes.

"I promise I will escape. But you need to get away from here now!" Fionn replied. "Oh boy, here he comes."

The only sound they heard afterward was that of clashing blades. Gaby was tempted to go after Fionn, but Alex stopped her.

"You know he is right," Alex said, his eyes swelling with tears as well. "And I think you would do the same if the places were reversed."

"Still, this is stupid," Gaby replied, wiping away her tears. "It's the second time he's done this."

"I don't think this time will end like before. Besides, you don't become a legend by dying," Alex told her jokingly, trying to lighten the mood.

"Actually, yes that is the way," Gaby replied, exasperated.

They ran across the Bestial's deck looking for signs of the Figaro. They found it towards the Bestial's rear, trying to evade a tentacle.

"Some help here!" Sid yelled at them through the comm.

Gaby and Alex looked at each other in agreement and ran towards the tentacle, swords in hand. With quick moves, they sliced it, allowing the Figaro to land and open its cargo bay. Both entered it quickly and closed the door behind them.

"What the Pits were you doing?" Alex asked through the internal comm.

"We were keeping the Bestial distracted, but when we got closer that thing hit us and damaged the weapons systems," Sid replied, annoyed. Apparently, the effort was taking a toll on the ship because Gaby could hear the hinges and unions groaning. Added to that, the bay was poorly lit at the moment, with the emergency lights casting a dim amber hue.

"Where is Fionn?" Harland asked them.

"Doing the stupid thing he always does," Gaby replied. Alex was silent.

Without warning, the ship shook once more, and with such strength that it sent Alex and Gaby flying and bouncing inside the cargo bay. Gaby felt the sudden change of speed and direction, which would have sent them tumbling worse than usual if she hadn't acted so quickly, grabbing a leather strap. She then grabbed Alex by the neck of his t-shirt, holding on as tight as she could.

"What the hell? Why are we accelerating?" Alex asked, feeling pushed towards the back of the ship.

"Ba'x! Tentacle just hit us!" Sid screamed in anger. "We are on a collision course with the ground and the engines are offline!"

"Aww crap," Alex muttered.

Gaby had wished they had waited for Fionn. Now she was wishing that Alex had gone on a diet.

# Chapter 20

## Famous Last Words

Fionn coughed from all the smoke that had entered his lungs. That had been quite close, even for his taste. Another explosion rocked the Bestial. He and Byron had been fighting nonstop amidst the explosions. The man... the monster had barely acknowledged them. Instead, he was full of anger and fury, judging by the ferocity of the attacks Fionn had been evading so far. He counted the explosions, six so far. According to Alex, there would be eight small ones before the ninth, the core fueled explosion.

He was running low on energy. His breathing was shallow and forced. He was under no illusions; the odds weren't in his favor.

When the dust cleared, he saw Byron coming closer. Half of his armor was torn. Beneath it, his rotting body could be seen. Whatever happened to him had put him in contact with an otherworldly intelligence that infused him with great power, but also took a toll on his withered body. Wormlike creatures moved underneath the skin of the once-powerful warrior. His veins were visible, blue due to the lack of oxygen. His mortal body was nothing more than a walking corpse, powered by a powerful spiritual connection with whatever forsaken deity he had made a deal with.

"You think this will hamper me?"

"Actually... yes," Fionn replied, gasping for air. He stood tall, the cracking of broken bones audible. Whatever energy he had to empower his Gift would have to be used wisely. "Y'know? For years I wondered why you did what you did. It gnawed on me. But then I realized that I don't care anymore. I don't even hate you. I pity you. You are just a self-entitled childish prick that is throwing a tantrum because Daddy told him no for once."

"You pity me? You call fighting to realize my vision a tantrum?" Byron replied, his voice stammering with anger.

"Yes." Fionn shrugged his shoulders. "A vicious tantrum, I give you that. But I will do what your father should have done a century ago. Kick your friggin' ass."

BOOM!

Fionn waited for Byron to come closer. On previous occasions, he had let that prick of a prince dictate the terms of their fights. Not this time. This time Fionn was going to take control of what would happen next. And then his breathing relaxed. Everything would be fine; somehow, this would end here one way or another. He just needed to stand firm. "Goddess, gimme strength to finish this," Fionn muttered, cleaning the blood from his mouth and closing his eyes. He called forth the last ounces of the Gift.

"I will kill you, you and your new friends, and I will have your heads mounted in my trophy room," Byron yelled while jumping at Fionn, who simply dodged the attack that almost cut off his head. With a streak of green light coming from his sword, Fionn made a cut on Byron's face, taking an eye.

*The past is a lesson, the present a gift, the future an opportunity,* Fionn remembered and opened his eyes, which glowed with the same intense green light of Black Fang. He let go. He didn't keep the Gift turned off anymore, instead, he unleashed all its power, overwhelming Byron and healing himself in the process. It wouldn't last long, as he knew Byron would keep draining the Gift away to power his own abilities. But Fionn only needed a couple of minutes. Maybe less if the initial shock of the sudden energy release had dazed Byron enough to give Fionn the opening he needed.

The Gift was inside him, the Tempest that empowered his sword. Energy whirled around him like a hurricane. It wasn't mindless fury trying to strike down an enemy. It was measured, each movement as simple as a sidestep, or as complex as a backhanded swing. Each blow, kick and punch that Fionn delivered hit like a meteor, sending Byron backward, putting him off balance, slicing bits and pieces of his armor, unleashing a gust of wind.

The cracks were showing, leaving the withered corpse of Byron visible.

BOOM!

Byron tried to counter the sudden onslaught, but Fionn's speed was increasing in an unexpected way. For all his bravado, Byron wasn't expecting this, nor the fact that the only strike he managed to land on Fionn's left leg healed almost instantly.

"How?" Byron replied, surprised. His body trembled with spams.

"A clever kid found the weakness in your ability to drain us. Ironic, given that he is a descendant of Ywain, the only one of us that truly frightened you. But it doesn't matter anymore. This is the end of the road for you," Fionn said with a smile. He could smell the fear on Byron's body.

"Stop talking," Byron stammered, taking a few steps back. "Stop right there."

Fionn ran and went for the left knee with a low kick, busting the kneecap with a loud crack. Next were the ribs, which received the worst of a straight swing. Black Fang's edge cut deep into the armor, slicing the ribs and the dead heart, leaving behind a gash full of worms and black ichor.

"This is for Izia!"

With a spin on his heels, Fionn used his left fist to deliver a punch to the upper back, breaking a couple of vertebrae. With a swift motion, using Black Fang as a lever, he dislocated

Byron's left arm. Fionn finished with an upward slice that cut the tight tendons of Byron's right leg and left a wide gash on his chest, from which worms spilled onto the deck, releasing a foul odor. Fionn readied his sword, which felt as heavy as a mountain in his tired arms.

"I will be back," Byron stammered, with a look in his eyes that betrayed fear. "My masters, the Golden King and the Creeping Chaos, will sort you out."

"Yeah right," Fionn dismissed him, getting ready for the last bout, holding his ground. "I'm dying to meet them."

"What are you waiting for? Or are you trying to plot an escape plan?" Byron taunted Fionn.

"I'm just waiting," Fionn replied off-handedly, dodging a swing aimed at his head, countering with a kick to the side with such strength that it blasted a plate of the armor away.

"For what?" Byron asked exasperatedly.

BOOM!

The structure of the Bestial started to bloat, the metal panels deforming as they tried to contain the multiple explosions taking place inside.

"That." Fionn smiled, glancing at the metal being deformed under their feet.

Fionn swung Black Fang, and Byron hefted his own sword to block the attack. Both blades clashed with a force that sent shockwaves all over the deck, damaging its surface and almost ripping apart a couple of hatches, leaving them hanging. Black Fang hit true and shattered the other sword as if it were made of glass, leaving both Fionn and Byron dumbfounded. Not waiting for another chance, Fionn swung Black Fang with all the strength he could muster in his tired arms and aimed at Byron's neck. Byron's head, with his eyes bulging in surprise, fell with a thud and rolled away, degrading into a blob absorbed by the ship's hull. The same happened to the rest of what was Byron's humanoid body. The Bestial shook, a shriek filling the air, as its death rattles took place. While Byron was alive, the Bestial did what it could to contain the explosion. But with its master gone, the final chain reactions engulfed the place in flames.

Fionn looked around for a way to escape and ran towards a half-burnt flag, which he ripped from its pole. Then he saw an unhinged door. With a kick, he ripped the door from the frame and jumped onto it, sliding across the surface of the, by now, curved deck and into the air.

*I have had worse ideas than air surfing,* Fionn thought. At least he knew that he would survive the fall if he arrested it long enough.

"Oh shiiiiit!" Fionn yelled as the Bestial finally exploded, sending shockwaves. Gathering his bearings, Fionn rode the shockwave on his improvised surfboard, closing fast to the ground. The initial stages of the heatwave and the light of the explosion soon engulfed him, making him disappear.

*This is gonna hurt,* Fionn thought, regretting his idea. *A lot.*

† † †

The Figaro was on a crash course, barreling through the skies with little control. Sid was doing his best to regain it, to little avail.

"With no power, and at this speed and altitude, we won't make it," Alex said, his face illuminated with the determination given only by a stupid idea with one chance in a million of working. "Sid, just give me one minute of stability and we will make it."

"You are asking for a miracle!" Sid replied, yelling through the comm. "Not this again! C'mon! Not another crash landing! I just fixed my ship!"

"No. I'm going to give us that miracle," Alex opened one of the access panels in the cargo bay. Inside, there were cables and conduits that routed the energy flow inside the ship. Taking the largest of the conduits, he closed his eyes and started to focus his mind.

"What are you doing?" Gaby asked, concern filling her voice.

"As always, something really, really stupid," Alex replied. For a brief moment, Alex just stood there, eyes closed, listening to the noises made by the ship's hull. He focused all the energy he could muster, which gave him a headache. It felt as if the surrounding electromagnetic field was water opposing his will. He pictured the electric energy inside the Figaro's core and sent his own to jumpstart it. By doing so, he felt as if an electromagnetic field expanded from his body outwards. He pushed the energy again. He was trying to resuscitate the core the same way you would restart a heart under cardiac arrest.

"Just focus, let it flow," Gaby whispered into his ear. Alex focused once more on Sam's smile.

The light was restored and the roaring of the engines could be heard outside.

"I don't know what you are doing, but keep doing it," Alex heard Sid yelling at him through the comm. He could feel how the samoharo was pulling the yoke, trying to steady the ship long enough to lessen the impact of the crash. The core sent faltering energy to the engines, just enough for Sid to slightly arrest the fall.

He closed his eyes and just let himself go. Alex felt the waves of energy around him, like water that he could push and move at will. Taking a deep breath, he opened his eyes, releasing all he had left, sending enough energy from his hands to power up the engines, burning his hands in the process due to the extreme heat released by the conduits.

It had been enough to restart the Figaro, but not enough to avoid a rough landing.

The Figaro didn't stop, still pushed forward by its momentum, and left grooves in the ground.

The lights turned off.

The Figaro finally skidded to a halt. Alex opened his eyes again and saw half the cargo bay hatch ripped apart.

The soles of his sneakers were melted and he was bleeding profusely from the nose, his body shaking in a seizure. Gaby was on the floor, unconscious, and he could barely make any sense of what Sid and Harland were yelling. Smiling, Alex fainted and fell to the ground near Gaby, exhausted.

† † †

The energy blast unleashed by the explosion of the Bestial swept across the whole valley, reaching the city. From a vantage point on the hill, most students, professors, and Knights fearfully admired the incoming blast that would soon engulf the city. Only two figures stood tall against it: the Queen and Samantha.

"I hate it when he is right," Sam mumbled. She was breathing heavily, surrounded by the dead carcasses of critters.

Sam extended her arms in front of her. She closed her eyes. A shiver ran through her body, shaking it. Samantha was leaving herself open to the full power stored inside those obelisks, the magick of a whole city. She felt her bones creaking, her muscles aching and oppression on her chest. Her heartbeat was now faster than the pace of a racehorse. She felt every cell of her body overcharging with the magick flow of energy. Her ears disappeared inside her skull and, on top of her head, were replaced by silver fox ears.

It is said that a truly powerful sorcerer gets only one True Spell. The one she could cast with a mere concept inside her head, without backlash from reality. A spell that was the reflection of her true nature. Now she was on her way to becoming the first in centuries to achieve such a goal. Samantha always dreamed of reaching that level with a flashy attack spell or even a summoning one. Never with one as simple as a protective spell.

*Funny.*

Opening her arms, she let all the energy flow through

her, as a smile formed on her lips. Her eyes locked on the energy blast that from her perspective was moving in slow motion.

The crystal obelisks resonated with the energy and from them, a humongous bubble of luminous energy spread over the city. The streets and walls of the city glowed with purple light, empowering the shield. It rapidly covered everything as a defensive shield. Tiny spheres of energy floated in the air, popping in and out of existence in seconds.

Sam felt the pressure, the heat, the kinetic energy unleashed by the explosion impacting the shield as if it were an extension of her whole being. Her knees started to buckle under the effort needed to push back, but the Queen's hand never left her shoulder.

"You can do this, young one," the Queen whispered into her ear.

She felt more changes in her body, which apparently now included a fox's tail. But she ignored that, pushing back with all her strength. Samantha's hair was now an intense, bright purple color, and her irises took on a golden hue with purple specks.

No one on that hill could take their eyes off of her. Her knees straightened up, and her arms fully extended in front of her. People on the streets marveled at the spectacle of the light emanating from the streets as the whole city acted as a massive magick sigil.

Her heart was now pumping faster than a warptrain and Sam realized one thing: She was having a heart attack. Correction, something worse. Samantha felt her heart explode inside her. Blood spilled from her mouth. The cells of her whole body started to burn. Her vision started to turn to black, while her body started to go limp. At least she had saved the city.

Then, she heard a voice. It was similar to Mekiri's, reassuring her that all would be fine. Something warm entered her body and quickly grew inside of her, lessening the aching caused by the stress, rebuilding and restarting her heart. Her body felt whole again, absorbing magick energies at a faster pace without any ill effect.

Her Gift had awakened.

With her sight still blackened but feeling reenergized, Samantha let out a scream, unleashing the whole power of the spell.

"Haaaaa!"

With an explosion of light, the blast dissipated. Saint Lucy was safe. Within seconds, the shield disappeared as well, along with the bright light that surged up from the streets. Power failures cropped up all over the city. Sam fell to her knees, spent and trying to catch her breath. The Knights had their mouths open in astonishment until the Queen, with a mere glare, made them fall in line. The freefolk approached Sam and started clapping and cheering for her. The Queen helped Sam to her feet.

Every muscle, tendon, and bone ached. Her heart was still healing itself. Breathing was hard and her vision was blurry with tiny specks of light peppering her eyes.

*So this is how it feels to get the Gift*, Sam thought. *It really sucks.*

Then she opened her eyes wide as saucers and asked the Queen

"And the Figaro? My dad? My friends?"

# Chapter 21

## Denouement

Gaby opened her eyes slowly, regaining consciousness. Her head was spinning, still dizzy after the crash. Alex was next to her unconscious, his nose bleeding, laying on the floor of the ship. The interior of the ship was a mess, but at least they were alive. She kneeled next to Alex, trying to wake him up. When he didn't respond, she started to apply resuscitation measures until he opened his eyes and gasped for air. Gaby helped Alex to sit up, his back against a wall while holding his head.

"I don't know if I'm hungry, dizzy, tired, suffering the aftermath of a seizure or all of the above," Alex said with a faint voice.

"I'm proud of you." Gaby hugged him.

"I just wish I could have done more to keep the Figaro intact." Alex looked around. "You know he is gonna be pissed off." The damage to the ship was extensive.

"Let's get out of here." Gaby helped Alex stand up and they left the ship. They saw Harland and Sid outside, bruised but otherwise fine. Sid, however, wasn't sharing the happiness of having survived.

"My ship!" Sid could be heard yelling from the remains of the cockpit.

"Why are you complaining? At least you are alive,"

Harland yelled as well.

"Well, at least they are fine," Alex muttered.

The engines hadn't suffered critical damage. Whether the Figaro would fly again or not would depend on how extensive the damage was to the rest of the systems. Harland approached them, patted Alex on the back and made a bow at Gaby, as a congratulatory sign for a job well done. They stared at the smoking remains of the Bestial, which peppered the whole area. The place was littered with the mechanical parts of the eldritch flying fortress, the organic parts decaying at a fast rate due to their exposure to reality without an anchor.

"Where is Fionn?" Harland asked with concern showing in his voice.

"You don't think he..." Gaby started to ask, her heart skipping beats. She felt her stomach sink with fear.

"Third time's the charm," Harland mumbled. He looked worried.

"I think I see him, there." Sid pointed to where the biggest smoldering crater was located. "You hoomans have poor sight."

Fionn was walking towards them with a slow gait. His body was covered with bruises and injuries, but they were healing. His face was smeared with soot and his clothes were tattered and partially burnt. But it was the grin he sported that made Gaby's heart skip a beat. The sun was in the sky, a little to the left of Fionn. He had Black Fang in his right hand and was raising his left fist into the air. Gaby ran towards him and hugged him with force. Alex walked behind her.

"Careful. I just hit the ground at high speed and my ribs are shattered," Fionn told her. "Are you ok?"

"Now we are." Gaby smiled at him. Alex rolled his eyes and groaned.

Gaby was happier than any other moment she could remember. It wasn't that surviving the whole ordeal wasn't meritorious by itself, but there was another source of happiness that would take her weeks to understand. Right now, she was just glad to be able to have all her friends with her.

††††

"Nice job." Harland extended his hand to Sid. "I'm sorry about your ship."

"It's a shame." Sid looked dejected. "Don't get me wrong, I'm happy we saved the day, but this was my life's work and I don't have the funds to rebuild it."

"What if I offer you a deal, where my foundation finances the rebuilding of the Figaro into a far superior ship?"

"I thought your foundation was strapped for cash," Sid said. "Yes, I heard you say it back at my place."

"After this, we will find ways to secure donations. We just saved the day. And if you notice, there are plenty of plates of precious alloy littering the place. I assume they can be sold for a decent price once we salvage most of them, along with the leftover tech." Harland smiled, patting Sid on his back shell.

"And what do you get in exchange?"

"I get to be your copilot, because believe it or not, I enjoyed traveling in that thing. What do you say?"

Sid took a while to reply, meditating on the offer and examining Harland.

"Yeah! It's fine. Welcome aboard," Sid replied with a strong handshake that hurt Harland's hand. "Besides, for the first time, I get to be the taller one in a partnership."

An embarrassing silence fell between them.

"You had to ruin the moment, didn't you?" Harland rolled his eyes at Sid.

"We had a moment, right?"

"Yes. And you ruined it"

"Let it go," Gaby interjected. "Just be glad that we made it out alive."

She and Fionn walked together, his arm around her shoulders. Alex walked next to her, still limping. The five of them relaxed, sitting next to the Figaro.

"Do you see that cloud of dust coming this way?" Sid asked them after a while.

"Enemies?" Harland asked.

"Nah, it seems that they are a group of vehicles. They have the Queen's crest painted on them. And Sam is there."

"Good. Because we could use a ride," Alex said, lying on his back. "And a holiday."

† † †

The night was well advanced by the time Fionn and Harland came out from the audience with the Queen. It had been a long talk and there were some decisions to make on the next course of action. The rest of the team, as Harland had described them, were staying at the castle for the night, recovering from the effort. The damaged Figaro, as well as the remains of the Bestial, were being hauled away to the Foundation's base, not far from there.

Fionn went to the check on the rest. They were lodged in the private chambers of the Queen's great-grandson, who had offered them when he arrived along with Sam and the Solarian Knights to pick them up. Prince Arthur had also sent his personal physicians to check their injuries.

Fionn found Alex snoring on a sofa, knocked out from exhaustion and pain medication. The swelling on his face was finally receding. Sid, sitting next to him, was watching the news on the Aethernet with a smile on his face. Gaby and Samantha chatted quietly on the balcony and waved at him. Sam looked different. There was an aura around her that she hadn't had before. Fionn guessed what had happened with his daughter, but there would be time later to worry about that. It wasn't as if he could do anything if she had awakened the Gift.

Fionn left the rooms and walked to the castle gardens. They were located on a plateau over a massive rock that oversaw the city, enclosed by a pink stone fence, carved with delicacy. Fionn closed his eyes for a second and breathed deeply, allowing his lungs to fill with the cold air. He opened his eyes and saw the clear night above him. The lack of energy in the great sectors of the city reduced the available power to only vital services. The lack of light pollution allowed him to see the stars without restrictions. The dim candlelight from some houses gave the whole place a quaint, familiar atmosphere. The Round Moon and the Long Moon could be seen perfectly. In fact, he could swear that the Long Moon had its own candles lit. He often wondered what mysteries were hidden on that strange celestial body that appeared at random times in the sky. He always did.

"Nice view, isn't it?" Harland said, taking Fionn out of his reverie. He was carrying a bottle of ale and two cups. He offered one to Fionn. "The Queen didn't take kindly to what happened. Especially with what happened to that stained-glass window"

"That's expected." Fionn kept his gaze on the Long Moon. "You wanted to ask me something back there. I know you."

"We won, we survived, rescued the professor and saved the day. Probably stopped the end of the world for a while and yet, you don't seem happy," Harland told him, facing Fionn and leaving his cup to the side. "Why?"

"Don't get me wrong," Fionn said, turning to Harland. "I'm delighted that this whole case is over and ended fine, that our new friends survived this mess. But the whole ordeal made me realize something."

"About?"

"The Gift and what it implies."

"I'm not following you."

"Look, I'm thankful for the Gift, for what I can do with it. I can help many people. But having it also means that I have this target on my back. It means that these cases will keep coming my way. That's partly the reason why I tried to withdraw from the world. It was already hard to conceal who I am or my actual age."

"It didn't work because I dropped it at your feet. And if the news is right, you are now a celebrity." Harland extended his hand, moving it in an arc in front of them as if envisioning a marquee. "World's first superhero."

"In part, although I think Ywain would have a better claim to that title." Fionn tried to smile. "But that's the thing. He is not here. Izia is not here."

"You have new friends, a new team: Sam, Gaby, Alex, even that pest Sid, and I would like to think that I'm included there."

"Of course you are, mate. You are my tether to sanity. And there lies the problem: This is a life not conducive to long living."

"Tell that to the Queen."

"She might be the sole exception. Look, I wouldn't like to outlive my friends again, and that's the downside," Fionn replied, his voice hiding a sense of sadness and sorrow.

"That's a fair point," Harland grabbed his cup again. "But, didn't Mekiri tell you that the difference in the journey lies in the path we take, and with whom we choose to walk it?"

"Meaning?"

"You have been given what many haven't: a second chance. Not to be secluded at that lonely house outside your hometown. Not to be taking cases here and there, and checking upon your daughter from time to time. But to actually do whatever you wanted to do after the war that you couldn't. So what you should be asking yourself right now is, what now?"

Fionn and Harland remained in silence for almost an hour, just admiring the moons, the garden, the city. The beauty of the things they just had saved.

"Can I give you a piece of advice?" Harland said, breaking the silence and looking at Fionn.

"Sure."

"I honestly think you have earned the right to rebuild your life. Izia would have approved. So I hope that whatever idea comes to your head about what to do, includes at some point the company of a certain Goldenhart, as the media is calling her." Harland smiled, pointing at the balcony of the room where Gaby and Sam were sleeping by now.

"What?"

"That's the name the media is giving to the blonde woman who fought on the deck of the Bestial alongside the legendary Greywolf," Harland explained. "You know how they like that kind of thing, giving titanfight-esque nicknames to people."

"Alex will want to get one."

"Yeah... it will be annoying."

"But I think you are right." Fionn stared at the balcony. "I would need to talk to Sam first, though."

"I know I'm right." Harland smiled. "And I don't think you should worry much about Sam. She is smarter and more mature than you give her credit for. She will understand. Now, I can't seem to catch some sleep, so do you want to join me in speculating what in the Pits is actually the Long Moon?"

"Do you have enough to drink?" Fionn asked, pouring another glass for Harland.

# Chapter 22

## New Plans

Gaby was bored out of her mind, verging on going crazy. She had been spending the last weeks on her grandparents' estate on the southwest coast of Ionis, waiting for things to calm down, resting. But so much rest was getting on her nerves.

Keeping a low profile for a few weeks was a sensible course of action, with the media frenzy and the political fallout that an event like that had caused. Not every day could you bring down a humongous floating fortress, save a major city of the Free Alliance, the head of the Alliance, and a whole species while taking down a conspiracy led by an undead prince throwing a tantrum. It was so complicated that it would be debated for months.

All of them had agreed to stay out of the public eye for a while. After all, most of them were lucky to remain private citizens, their participation just a rumor. Only a few people, like her direct family or Alex's university friends, were privy to what had really transpired. Fionn and Harland were in the spotlight, something that the latter proved to be a savvy operator in. Harland even managed to keep some of the heat off Fionn.

Alex had returned to his university alongside Sid in order to repair the Figaro and his bow. From what she had heard, Birm, Andrea, and even Quentin weren't too happy with what Alex had done to the bow. But with their help and that of Stealth, who had joined them, repairs to the Figaro moved fast. Mercia University had agreed to house as many students from Ravenstone as possible, in order to mend fences between humans and freefolk and as a courtesy to Professor Hunt and the Foundation.

Meanwhile, she and Sam had been tucked away together. Sam was still shaking off the side effects of the magick on her body, namely the tail and the ears, and coming to terms with the fact that for a few minutes she had been dead, and now had the Gift.

Between that and Ravenstone still being closed for repairs, Sam had nowhere to go. Thus, Gaby had offered her a place to stay and rest. If anyone could help Sam understand what had happened to her, it was Gaby.

At first, Sam had acted with reluctance, as it was rare that human girls wanted to interact with her. But in Gaby, Samantha had found a kindred spirit, one that listened without judging. And Gaby's family had welcomed Sam as one of their own, with no one minding her current appearance. They had invited her to the local festivals and Gaby's little cousins had taken a liking to Sam, asking her to play with them in the vast gardens. Sam had agreed and now she was spending her time playing with the tiny kids. That made Gaby smile.

But deep inside of her, Gaby still felt like something was missing. She worried that after this ordeal, she had become an adrenaline junkie. In her case this could be a problem, even if she was finding a way to replace the Ice State with something else.

Gaby was sitting on her bed, absent-mindedly listening to Alex's latest rant through the video chat. The list ranged from Sid and Harland's endless arguing about the cost of the new additions to the Figaro's systems to his latest fight with Samantha. And boy, did he dwell on the latter topic for hours.

She had found it odd that Alex had insisted on keeping in touch with Sam. At first, Gaby thought, it was for mere academic purposes. But Alex rarely touched those topics. Instead he took the time to talk with Sam about varied topics, from TV shows to music to historical debates, to get to know her better. While they didn't have much in common and their opinions differed, they seemed to have a good time chatting together. All their discussions were friendly banter, always ending in laughter. So when Alex offered to help Sam to go house hunting when she arrived at Mercia U, and she had accepted with faked reluctance, Gaby understood what was going on.

*They like each other. Romantically.*

"Just be careful, a relationship that starts from a bickering friendship doesn't always turn out well, and you know that," Gaby said, cutting to the chase and interrupting Alex. "It's obvious you like her and I think she likes you back. Just be patient, give her space. Try to be less... overwhelming. I know you mean well."

Alex remained silent for a couple of minutes, for which Gaby was thankful. He sighed and told her.

"You know I love you, right?" Alex asked, taking Gaby aback with surprise. They had similar chats when they were younger but those had been left in the past.

"Yes, Alex, I know," Gaby said, still surprised.

"Then, do me a favor and call him," Alex told her with a conviction she rarely had seen in him. "Being in that massive house of yours with all those servants must be boring for someone as kickass as you. And I think both of you need to get away for a while."

Gaby could only flash her crooked smile in reply. She ended the call and closed her laptop. She found Sam standing on the threshold of the door, resting against the frame. Sam's ears had returned to normal and the tail was gone. Only her hair remained a bright shade of purple.

"He is right, you know?"

"How much did you hear?" Gaby grimaced.

"Enough." Sam smiled. She sat next to Gaby. "Don't worry. Everything is ok between Alex and me, even if he is a bit of..."

"... an acquired taste?" Gaby finished.

"Something like that." Sam allowed herself a smile. "At least it will be good to know someone at the new place. I haven't been in a human school since middle school and I don't have fond memories of it."

"Trust me, that place is different, it's quite chill and accepting. Besides, you will have Alex and his friends to watch your back. They will welcome you with open arms. And ask you to join them in their crazy schemes. So I suggest that when in doubt, ask Andrea what to do. She is the only one with common sense there."

Both shared a laugh.

"Thanks for the advice. And going back to that..."

"What about the advice?"

"Alex is right. You should call Fionn."

"Since when is he Fionn and not Dad?" Gaby teased Sam.

"It's odd to talk with my best friend," Sam replied, eliciting a smile from Gaby. It had been years since Gaby had had a female friend. "About her fancying my adoptive father. It's a tad uncomfortable and weird."

"About that..."

"Don't worry. I will get used to it." Sam patted Gaby on the leg. "Besides, he deserves someone that makes him smile again. Just don't make me call you Mom."

Gaby looked at Sam and both laughed.

"Don't worry. It won't happen." Then Gaby sighed. "It's not just that."

"Then?"

Gaby took a deep breath and cleared her mind. She grabbed her guitar from the side of the bed and fiddled with the tuning knobs. After a long pause, she started speaking.

"When I was younger, I dreamt of being a famous rock

star. To share the music in my head with many people."

"I can relate." Sam nodded. "But there is no reason it should be a dream anymore. I have heard you sing. You would rock, no pun intended."

"Well that's the thing." Gaby smiled. "I still want to play music, but I feel like it won't be enough." Gaby's mind raced through the possibilities, with tension building on her stomach. She delayed her response for a while, still tuning the guitar. Sam looked at her.

"I think both issues are related. The question is, do you miss the adrenaline, or the company? My guess is that you are afraid of the first, and too confused about the second."

"Maybe," Gaby replied, unsure of herself, paying attention to the sounds coming from the strings. They were nearly in tune.

"You are only fooling yourself," Sam replied, taking the guitar from Gaby's hands. "And stop working those strings any more or they will break. They are in tune now!"

"What do you mean?"

"When we arrived here, you told me you had never composed a song before. You just were good at playing others. And yet, when we needed encouragement you sang that song on the Figaro. It helped us to regain focus. It was a great song."

"It was barely a song. Just a few lines."

"That's my point: You created them because you had the motivation to do it. Inspiration." Sam paused for a moment. "I think that maybe, just maybe, if you allow yourself to work on your music while having exciting adventures, you will have something to sing about. And what's more important, you will have someone to share it with."

"You are really insightful." Gaby looked at her, smiling. The sparkle in her eyes had returned and for once her mind was calm. She felt upbeat.

"Thanks. I had a good example. So... what it will be?"

Gaby looked through the bedroom window. The first

few stars of the night were appearing on the horizon. She took her guitar back and started to work on a new tune, an original one full of joy and excitement, one proper for adventure.

"Would you help me with a call?"

"It will be my pleasure," Sam replied, taking out her cell phone with one hand and extending her pinky finger to Gaby. "As long as you promise that when I get bored at uni, I will be able to join you. I need my friend."

Gaby grabbed Sam's pinky finger with her own, sealing the promise.

"Deal."

† † †

It was a clear sunny day when Gaby arrived at Carffadon. The repairs to the city were finished and the main square didn't show any sign of what had happened there. She had traveled with Sam during the first leg of the journey. Gaby had helped her get installed at Mercia U and had introduced her to Alex's friends. After that, a car from the Foundation, courtesy of Harland, had taken her to the city where she had first met him and Fionn. That Fionn had suggested it as the place for their meeting, had been an unexpected but welcome surprise, even if Harland and Alex sniggered at that.

Gaby was wearing the same blue and black leather jacket, a silky black blouse, a choker, gray jeans, and knee-high black velvet boots. After leaving her luggage at the hotel, she took her twin swords and her guitar. Her hair was loose this time, however, reaching the part of her back between the shoulder blades. She put her sunglasses on and started to walk around the town on that sunny day, sporting a big smile. For the first time in many years, she felt light and free. She opened her Gift to the world and breathed everything that surrounded her, smelling the grass and sensing the animals in the surrounding bushes. She could feel the world around her, be one with it, and feel an amount of peace and happiness she hadn't felt since she was a baby in her mother's arms. The sunlight washed away any concern or worry from her mind.

When she reached The Harris, she was nervous. Her heart thumped like a drum. She took a booth and ordered something. Sam had advised her that her dad wasn't the most punctual man in the world. He had the tendency to stop and help people or pick up stray dogs and take them to a shelter. He had even arrived late to her high school graduation. But Gaby wasn't concerned about that. Those kinds of gestures were what made Fionn himself. There would be plenty of time.

The place soon got crowded as the open mic contest began. The afternoon was falling upon the city. Mustering courage, Gaby grabbed her guitar and asked for a chance to sing. Some patrons remembered her from her previous turn at the mic so many months ago and cheered. She breathed, trying to calm her heart. It wasn't a cover song but was the one she had started writing at her house, after talking with Sam. It was her second song if she counted the one she sang in the Figaro. With a final, deep breath, she started.

It was a song about hope, about friendship, about love, about embracing the past and looking to the future. She didn't recall the lyrics; they just came up from her mouth as if they had been waiting for this moment. The whole place fell silent when she finished. Then slow claps escalated into a rapturous applause. She raised her eyes and saw him. Fionn stood there in the middle of the audience and was clapping. For her, time slowed down. She walked off the stage to greet him and both walked outside, to the small park near the river where they had stopped during the night they had met.

He was wearing cleaner versions of the same clothes he had been wearing that day. He had added a hoodie under the leather jacket. And of course, he had Black Fang with him, whose scabbard was so polished that it reflected the afternoon light illuminating the place. She stared at him with her crooked smile.

"I thought you had stood me up." Gaby punched him lightly in the arm.

"I would never do that," Fionn said, his left hand rubbing the back of his neck. He looked nervous. "I just had a slight detour... I had to put some things in order first."

"Sam warned me of that."

"I know." Fionn smiled at her. "Sorry."

"Don't be."

"That was a beautiful song, by the way. Did you compose it?"

"Thank you. And yes."

Fionn stared at her for so long that Gaby felt herself blushing.

"Why are you looking at me like that? Are you ok?"

"Yes," Fionn replied, removing a strand of hair from her face.

"So what's next? Why did you ask me to pack and come here?"

Fionn smiled at her. The light gave her an angelic halo. The image made his heart glad. It was the most beautiful thing he had seen in his life.

"There are places in this world I want to visit. You know? Things I missed. But I want to share that with you. Are you up for some adventure with me?" Fionn asked her, taking her hands in his.

Gaby looked into his green eyes. She remembered the dreams that had led her to this moment. And her crooked smile appeared on her face.

"Always."

Life is full of parallels. And second chances if you learn to see them.

# About the Author

Born in the frozen landscape of Toluca, Mexico, Ricardo dreamed of being a writer. But needing a job that could pay the rent while writing, he studied Industrial Design and later obtained a PhD in Sustainable Design, while living in the United Kingdom. There, he did a few things besides burning the midnight oil to get his degree:

- Trained in archery near Nottingham
- Found Excalibur
- Discovered whether Nessie was real or not (but won't disclose his findings)
- Worked in a comic book store to pay for his board game & toy addiction

He is back now in Toluca, living with his wife and his two dogs where he works as an academic at the local university. He has short stories featured in anthologies by Inklings Press and Rivenstone Press, and he was nominated to a Sidewise Award 2017 for the short story "Twilight of the Mesozoic Moon", co-written with his arch-nemesis, Brent A. Harris. He also won a local contest for a fantasy short story during college. But hey! That one doesn't count, does it?

You can find his rants and other work—both fiction and opinion pieces—on his own website, www.ricardovictoriau. com, and from time to time on the Altered Instinct blog, www.alteredinstinct.com.

Tempest Blades: The Withered King, his first novel, has been in the works for quite some time. He really hopes you get awed by its kickassery.

Follow him on:
Twitter: @Winged_Leo
Facebook: ricardovictoriau